The
Forever
Stone

Gloria Repp

Gloria Repp

The Forever Stone

Cover design by Tugboat Design
Cover background photo courtesy of Bill Beck
Home birth details provided courtesy of Doreen Lawton
    M.Ed., LM, CPM

"Before the Throne of God Above" Words by Charitie Lees
Bancroft. Music and alternate words by Vikki Cook.
Copyright © 1997 Sovereign Grace Worship (ASCAP).
Administration by Integrity Music.
www.SovereignGraceMusic.org. Used with permission.

Scripture quotations are from the English Standard Version.

Published by MTL Resources LLC, South Carolina
Printed in the United States of America

ISBN-13: 978-1482022339

ISBN-10: 1482022338

CHAPTER 1

Today I walked the woods path
for the first time in months.
The brook is nothing more than
a trickle and some mud . . . like me.
~Journal

The woman was following her. Madeleine stepped past a bucket of dahlias and just missed the butternut squash—*look as if you're in a hurry*—but the woman was catching up. She wore a police uniform and a helmet of sleek gray hair.

What was her name? Rondell, that was it. Frances Rondell.

The policewoman loomed beside her. "Madeleine! Wonderful to see you again." She gestured across the Roanoke Farmer's Market. "Quite a spread, isn't it? Best in Virginia."

Madeleine nodded in greeting and summoned up a smile. After all, Frances Rondell had worked with Dad at the station.

The woman was studying her, so she bent to inspect the green apples.

Please don't tell me what a good friend he was. Don't tell me you miss him too. Don't tell me I'm doing fine.

"Heard you got married," Frances said. "How's that husband of yours?"

Madeleine took a quivering breath and tried to compose her face.

"Oh, my, did something happen?"

"Brenn died. A year ago. You couldn't have known."

"I'm so sorry . . ." The woman's gaze shifted to the pyramids of gleaming apples. "I see you're checking out those Granny Smiths."

"Yes."

"I remember the cookies your dad brought to the station. He'd have that big smile of his—always told us you're the best cook in the world."

Madeleine's throat closed up.

Frances didn't seem to expect a reply. She chose a reddish-black apple and polished it on her sleeve. "These Black Gilliflowers are my favorite for pie. With plenty of cinnamon and nutmeg, mmm! Want to try a few?"

The woman kept talking as she put apples into a paper bag. "Teaching school must keep you on your toes. A little thing like you! How do you handle those kids?"

"Teens are always a challenge." How could she tell this competent woman that she hadn't renewed her contract?

"But worthwhile! The right teacher can make such a difference in a kid's life." Frances filled another bag with apples, paid the vendor, and handed Madeleine one of the bags. Her eyes softened. "Your dad would be so proud of you."

Madeleine took the bag, nodded her thanks, and backed away.

"Gotta run!" Frances threw her a hang-in-there smile, and Madeleine hurried in the opposite direction.

She bumped into a table piled with vegetables and made herself stop, trying to ignore the clamor of her thoughts.

Just look at those beets—plump little globes, weren't they? Such an appetizing dark red! And the leafy tops still crisp and green . . .

It was no use. Frances Rondell's words had opened a locked door in her mind. *Dad.* The kind of person he was. Had been.

Slowly she hoisted a clump of the beets. What . . . what would they be like, pickled with little white onions? What . . . what would Dad have thought of her husband and the business her mother ran?

She paid for the beets and trudged past glossy bell peppers, tomatoes, and summer squash. At a table of baked goods, she paused. Something for dessert, that's what she was supposed to get. Mother had invited George again, the promising young stockbroker. She chose the nearest cake and kept going.

. . . so proud of you . . .

She stepped out from under the Market's awnings and blinked in the fall sunlight.

I've got to do something.

The thought tiptoed past before she could examine it and faded while she drove home, only to begin whispering urgently as she pulled into the driveway.

Do something? What?

The kitchen was empty, but a murmur of voices came from the living room. A conference, no doubt. The cousins would be enjoying their discussion about "poor Madeleine." The pompous voice would be Uncle Ashton's.

The living room door opened and her mother swept into the room, shaking her blonde curls. "There you are. What happened?"

"Sorry. I ran into someone at the Farmer's Market." Change the subject. "See these apples?" she said. "They're supposed to be good for pies."

Wrong subject. She knew it as soon as she spoke.

Her mother looked up from pouring a diet soda. "And who's going to make a pie around here? Not you, Miss Pastry-Chef wannabe! Not for months and months."

Madeleine eased the cake out of its bag and set it on the counter. If she could just stay quiet, in a few minutes she'd be safe upstairs.

Her mother's voice rose. "Pumpkin cake? I told you to get coconut. That's what George likes. And beets? Why beets, of all things? Really, Madeleine—you've got to pull yourself together."

Pull herself together? She could hardly pull herself out of bed in the morning.

"If teaching school's too hard, try something else." Mother tasted her soda and made a face. "It wouldn't hurt you to take a little interest in my business."

Madeleine's hands went cold, and she resisted the urge to rub them together like a character out of Dickens. Instead, she warmed them at a tiny flame of rebellion. "The business of taking money from unsuspecting people?"

"You have it all wrong. They get a nice letter telling them about the information packet—"

"—and asking for $24.99."

"But they get something in return."

Madeleine stacked cans of pineapple in the cupboard. She'd seen too many of those hopeful, hand-written letters. Indignation sharpened her voice. "All they get for their money is advice on how to set up a scam like yours."

"I don't see it that way." Her mother thumped her glass down onto the counter. "My goodness, we're critical today, aren't we? It's perfectly legal. If they don't act on the information I send, it's not my fault."

A soft voice wafted from the doorway. "Sylvia, don't be too hard on her."

It was Cousin Willa, the plump, fluffy one, who thought the world of George. True, he was an improvement on Henry the Dull and Francis the Smooth, but the guy didn't have an original thought in his head.

Cousin Willa edged closer. "Madeleine dear, we think—Vera and I—that rather than join the business, it would be much more sensible for you to marry George. He's a fine young man, so very handsome, and he has excellent prospects."

Behind her, white-haired Cousin Vera was nodding, but Uncle Ashton stepped past them both.

"I can't say I agree." He threw a sharp glance at the cousins and spoke to Madeleine in his I-AM-THE-DOCTOR voice. "You're not ready for another marriage, but it's time for you to buck up. Get moving. That's what I tell my patients, and they always thank me."

He smoothed back his silver mane, as if preparing to accept yet another accolade. "I just became a partner in your mother's business, and I'll be managing it for her. I could use some assistance."

Madeleine shook her head, trying to think of a safe way to say she'd rather starve.

The benevolence leaked out of his smile. "If you can't handle your overly sensitive scruples, perhaps you should get out and find yourself a job. At least teaching was something useful."

"Useful," her mother said. "Keep that word in mind. The way you've been moping around here makes me sick. Thirty-three years old! We're going to have to—"

Madeleine's cell phone rang, and her mother gave it an irritated glance. "It's that New York aunt of yours, isn't it? Call her back. We've got to get this settled."

Madeleine's fingers tightened on the phone, but she let it ring. Next would come the wilderness lectures.

Her mother frowned. "I wish she'd stop filling your mind with tales about that monstrosity she inherited, way out there in the wilderness. It's not a suitable occupation for you."

"That's right," Cousin Willa said, with Vera nodding behind her. "We are all dreadfully concerned about you, dearie. And we're your *family*. We'd miss you terribly if you went off to bury yourself in such a wild place."

Of course Uncle Ashton had an opinion. "The next thing you know, your aunt will be taking pictures in Alaska or someplace, and you'll be left alone. With those natives, those Pineys."

Madeleine opened the bag of apples and placed them, one by one, in a fluted white dish. Black Gilliflowers. They gave off a faint fragrance, something like pears. This shiny one—Frances Rondell had polished it for her. She cradled it in both hands.

"Madeleine!" Her mother again. "That project's going to be another dead end, like working at Hillary's antique store. And all those art courses you took! Are you listening?"

"I'm listening, Mother." In a moment of clarity, she saw herself as George's wife, discussing stock averages or the latest game won by their local team, the Hokies. She'd go shopping every day and to the beauty salon once a week, and in the evenings she would stuff envelopes.

. . . so proud of you . . .

She held onto the apple and turned to face them. "No," she said. "I will not help with the business. And I will not marry George. If you'll excuse me, I'm going upstairs so I can talk to Aunt Lin."

Shocked silence met her words, but she left the kitchen with her head up. They could have another conference.

As soon as she reached her bedroom, she returned her aunt's call. "Hi, Aunt Lin."

"I'm so glad you called back. Is this a good time?"

"This is fine." She never knew when her lively aunt would phone, and talking to her was always a treat.

"My Great Adventure. The Pine Barrens house, you know?"

"Right." The best thing about the last few weeks had been her aunt's enthusiastic e-mails.

"I feel like I've inherited a castle filled with treasures. In disguise." Her aunt's laugh was rueful. "I just moved in, and I need your help more than ever. Ready for adventure?"

CHAPTER 2

Packing: take COOKBOOKS!
I don't have much room,
but I've got to remember
my small bit of courage
—and the Black Gilliflowers.
~Journal

The wipers swished back and forth across her windshield, clearing portholes in the sluicing rain.

Runn-ing a-way. Runn-ing a-way.

Madeleine gripped the steering wheel. No, she was hurrying towards a new life. She was going to share her aunt's Great Adventure and find one of her own. Did she have the courage to make it happen?

She shifted gears and sent her red Grand Am past a lumbering truck.

First, get rid of the emotional baggage—the grief and the fearful memories. Leave them behind. She had to.

Second, do a fantastic job for Aunt Lin and save every penny she earned. The time she'd spent studying art and working at the antique store would come in handy.

Third, take one of those baking courses she'd been dreaming about.

The rain became a fine mist, and veils of fog rolled down from the Virginia hills. She changed lanes to join the slower traffic, watching for tail lights ahead of her.

Had it been like this for Brenn when he'd driven off the road into the fog? Why had her husband been up on the Parkway at that time of night, anyway? No one knew, and she hadn't wanted to find out.

The trunk of a glistening white Cadillac—an older model—appeared directly in front of her. No lights. Foolhardy.

Just as she had been, to marry Brenn in the first place.

Jettison those regrets. She'd always savored that word, with its Anglo-French roots. It implied a difficult action: heart-breaking, perhaps, but needful to save your life.

The Cadillac's lights flashed red, and she slammed on her brakes.

Her car slid forward, tires squealing, ricocheted off the Cadillac's bumper, screeched along the guard rail, and stopped.

Warning lights glared on the dashboard. The engine had died.

She bent over the steering wheel, pounded it. Not this. Not now.

The Cadillac had disappeared—such a massive car wouldn't have felt much—and she was enclosed in the fog with her dread. She ran a quick internal check. Nothing hurt. She opened her door, cautiously because of the cars streaming past, gingerly because of her legs. They were shaking.

She edged around to the front of the car, her cute little red car that gave her such delight.

The bumper was mangled, of course. Fender dented. Paint badly scratched. A strip of trim scuffed into fragments.

She stepped to the guard rail, shuddered at the red streaks along its dull gray length, and turned again to her car. The big question: could she still drive it?

A car was backing along the shoulder, a white whale in the sea of fog.

Her jaw clenched. He hadn't come to help.

She scurried to her car and reached inside for her purse. He'd want insurance information and who knows what else. She should stand in front, make sure he saw the damage.

The man marched toward her, suit coat flapping, gray hair bristling. Didn't even glance at her car. "What's your problem, lady?" The snarl was worse than shouting.

His gaze raked across her, from the loose dark hair to the T-shirt and jeans she'd worn for comfort. "Little girl like you shouldn't even be driving this highway. If you were my daughter, I'd take you over my knee."

He licked his lips, and she knew his thoughts weren't the least bit fatherly.

Anger pulled her spine rigid, lifting her chin high.

He stepped closer. She pulled out her cell phone. "I can call the police. You didn't have your lights on."

His face hardened. "No witnesses," he said in a clipped voice that was very sure of itself. "And I don't intend to wait around for the Commonwealth of Virginia to send out the troops. Call a tow truck and thank your lucky stars I didn't report you."

He swung back to his car, and she watched him go with relief and hatred, wishing for something to throw at the expensively tailored back. She memorized his license plate—New York—but knew she wouldn't use it. She didn't want to wait around either, not here in the fog with predators afoot and cars racing past.

Stiffly, she climbed back inside. Please, not a tow truck. Maybe . . . maybe . . . She eased the car forward, winced at a scraping sound, and edged away from the guard rail. Something was dragging.

As soon as she was free of the rail, she got out to check. Part of the red trim hung askew. Ruined. She kicked at it, reached down, and ripped it off the car. She stared at the torn, wet, dirty piece of plastic, and her anger drained away, leaving a sickly residue of weakness.

She threw the strip over the rail, and the fog swallowed it up. She climbed into the car, drank from her water bottle, and tried to collect her thoughts.

No thoughts? Fine.

Now she drove with single-minded caution, every sense alert for the tiniest noise from her car. As the miles passed, her tension seeped away, and the scene began to replay in her mind. Thank your lucky stars, he'd said.

Such arrogance. Most likely a lawyer or a doctor.

Cousin Willa, who believed in signs and portents, would have taken his comment to heart. A warning, Madeleine! Rethink your rash decision. Turn back!

Even before this happened, she'd left late, missed an exit, and almost run out of gas.

She let the car coast. Okay, think about it. *Running-away. Buck-up. Marry-George. So-proud-of-you* . . . One thing for sure: she wasn't going back.

The fog lifted, and she set the cruise control with hands that still shook.

"Pull yourself together." She said it aloud, her voice stern and hopeful, realized that she was quoting her mother, and frowned. Jettison that too. Leave it all behind.

She steadied her hands on the wheel, consciously relaxing her shoulders.

Better pay attention: Baltimore coming up. Still a long way to "that Jersey wilderness" as her mother called it. But Aunt Lin's castle was waiting for her. She could see it now—one of those mansions filled with history and lovely old furniture and perhaps a few valuable antiques.

Dusk was beginning to settle over the trees by the time she could start looking for Tabernacle, the town her aunt had mentioned. This must be it, judging from a brightly-lit restaurant that called itself the Tabernacle Grille.

Once past Tabernacle, pine trees that were thin as flag poles crowded close to the highway with nothing but darkness behind them. Her aunt had said to turn off as soon as she passed a lake—this one? Okay. What about that sign? Pritchard's Gun Club. Not on the map.

Go past an old cranberry bog, and when the road forked . . . Where was the cranberry bog?

She slowed to a crawl. What did a cranberry bog look like?

The trees bordering the road had become impenetrable shadows, and the road itself gleamed white. Sand? This couldn't be right. She swung into a U-turn.

Should she have waited until tomorrow and made an earlier start? No, she might have lost her nerve. Besides, Aunt Lin wanted her to come right away because of a crisis with her magazine, something about a photo shoot.

Back again, same road, same trees, but darker now. No cranberry bogs. Then the highway. Chatsworth coming up. "If you get to Chatsworth," Aunt Lin said, "you've gone too far."

How was she going to start this Great Adventure if she couldn't even find the place? She pulled off the road and opened her cell phone.

Her aunt's laugh was sympathetic. "I wondered. It's easy to get lost around here." She paused. "Let's try something else. You found Tabernacle okay?"

"Yes."

"Good. Go back to Tabernacle, and at the cross road, turn left. It goes on for a ways—quite a long ways—and then you come to Whitton Road. Turn left again, and you'll see a store in an old house. That's where I'll meet you."

Go back. She could do that.

At least this road was paved, except for the potholes, but it too was lined with miles and miles of dark trees. The pavement began to deteriorate, and just as she started worrying again, she saw scattered lights. Whitton Road? Yes, and here, with a jaunty dangling sign, was the store.

She decided against waiting in the car—let's not be quite so timid—and started down the sidewalk. A pair of men came out of the store and turned the other way. The one with a paunch was talking about a new procedure for his patients.

He sounded like Uncle Ashton. Another doctor.

A large handwritten placard on the door greeted her: OPEN! COME IN. As she did so, a jingling bell announced her presence, much too loudly. She glanced at the counter to her left and ducked away from it, behind sleeping bags that were stacked like cans of corn. The stooped little man at the counter was being lectured by someone big and blond. Maybe he hadn't noticed her.

In front of her was a shelf of books and a sign with red letters running uphill saying that they were a bargain at fifty cents each. She studied the motley assortment until the bell jingled and her aunt's voice rang out.

"Timothy, hello! Have you seen my niece? Oh, there you are."

Aunt Lin, her father's much-younger sister, looked just as she remembered: elegant and bright-eyed, with ruffled dark hair. She gave Madeleine a quick hug and kept an arm around her, steering them both toward the counter. "Timothy, this is my niece, Madeleine Burke."

The little man had a kindly look in his eyes. "Good evening, ma'am." She sensed that he'd been watching her after all, and that he knew she'd wanted to stay out of sight.

The blond man, twice the size of old Timothy, leaned toward her with an affable smile. "Hi, there. I'm Kent."

Aunt Lin smiled at him. "You're both teachers," she said, "so you've got something in common. Except now he's writing a book. Would you believe it?"

The two of them laughed together with the ease of old friends.

A minute later, her aunt was bustling her out of the store. "Follow me," she said. "It's not far."

A confusing series of turns, more trees pressing close, a long rutted sandy driveway, and here at last, the blocky outlines of a house. Aunt Lin's castle.

"An historic residence," she had called it. The house was so historic that before she could move in, she had to update the heating system, replace the roof, and renovate several rooms.

Her aunt drove into a wide clearing, and Madeleine parked beside her. She eased out of the car into silence that wrapped her round, a velvet, pine-scented silence reaching all the way to the stars. She inhaled, slowly, deeply, and let the cool air boost her spirits. The Great Adventure had begun.

Aunt Lin came to stand beside her. "It's lovely out here, isn't it?" She turned toward the house. "Not quite so lovely inside. Let's get you settled."

They each took a suitcase, and Madeleine followed her aunt to the porch, which was roofed with a sketchy collection of rafters and wide-spreading tree branches.

"I hope you weren't expecting grandeur," Aunt Lin said, key in hand. "Because what we've got is dust, mold, mildew, and some rather strange-looking stuff." She had to put her shoulder to the door to open it, and a musty smell crept out of the darkness as if it had been searching for an exit.

Aunt Lin flicked on the overhead light. They stood in a foyer that led to a shadowed hall with doors opening off both sides.

"Welcome to Dumont Manor," her aunt said, sounding apologetic. "What a pretentious name for this big old leaky box! But that's what people around here call it."

She switched on an electric heater and started down the hall. "I'm still trying to dry things out." She paused at a door to their right. "I've salvaged a couple of rooms. I made these into a suite so I could have my office and darkroom together."

At a doorway farther down, she said, "This is your room." She turned on the ceiling light, stepped across the plum-colored carpet, and pulled the curtains shut. "It's not luxurious, but you can fix it up any way you want."

"It's pretty," Madeleine said. A modern desk and chair. An old-fashioned bed and matching bureau— walnut spool, American, mid-1800's—the identification came automatically. Everything was polished to a shine and nicer than she'd expected.

"We'll have to share a bathroom," Aunt Lin was saying, "but it's new, so at least we'll have plenty of hot water. Let me help with your luggage."

A few minutes later, Madeleine's suitcases were lined up next to the bureau. She set her book box on the desk beside a vase of red oak leaves mingled with pine. The arrangement was attractive, and she wanted to remark on it, but Aunt Lin was already out the door.

"Come see the kitchen," she said, heading across the hall.

Madeleine followed, hoping she wouldn't have to deal with a wood-burning stove, but to her relief, the kitchen had been remodeled with bisque-colored appliances and granite counter tops.

"You've done a great job," Madeleine said. "I'm going to love working in here."

Aunt Lin looked around the room with satisfaction. "It's coming along. How about some tea?" She filled two mugs with water and slid them into the microwave.

Madeleine sank into a chair at the table and a moment later accepted a steaming cup that smelled of cinnamon. She bent over it, hoping the fragrance would revive her.

"I like your hair in that layered cut," Aunt Lin said. "Shoulder-length is handy if you want to put it up. You're fortunate to have the Dumont hair."

Madeleine blinked. What a kind thing to say, when her hair must be hanging around her face like a string mop.

Aunt Lin gave her a thoughtful glance. "Here's some honey if you want it. The rest of the house is a disaster. We'll explore in the morning."

She paused to massage the frown lines between her eyebrows. "I'm glad you could come, for several reasons. There might be something valuable here, and I shouldn't leave it unoccupied."

Madeleine did her best to look attentive, but the tea seemed to be making her drowsy. Perhaps she'd sleep tonight.

"Your mother," Aunt Lin said. "Was she upset?"

"I'm afraid so."

"She's got those cousins and her bossy brother to console her," Aunt Lin said. "Besides, we're not so very far away."

Madeleine smothered a yawn.

"I saw that." Her aunt's smile was understanding. "Off to bed—get a good night's sleep." She added a less-than-comforting prediction. "You'll need it."

A clatter of dishes fractured Madeleine's dreams. With a groan, she rolled over to stare at the clock, and the muscles in her neck groaned too.

Still dark outside. Aunt Lin must be an early riser. She levered herself out of bed, pulled on some clothes, and caught sight of herself in the mirror. Do something about the face. Ponytail the hair.

Was it the nightmares or the midnight bout of journal therapy or that sleeping pill she'd finally taken? Whatever, her brain seemed dense and lumpy, like a sauce gone wrong.

When she stumbled into the kitchen, Aunt Lin was standing with a cup in her hand, gazing out a large mullioned window that framed the pine forest. She wore a hooded green sweatshirt, and she was glowing, as if she'd just come in from a run. "Rough night? I know about those. There's coffee, and toast if you want it."

Madeleine started to nod, but splinters jabbed at the back of her neck. She leaned against the doorframe. Coffee.

Aunt Lin waved at the coffee pot. "Help yourself. Or there's tea. I'll make it for you."

"Coffee is fine," she said, trying not to mumble.

Don't spill the coffee, she told herself. Sugar. Lots of cream. She found her way to a chair. Soon, maybe, she'd wake up.

Her aunt buttered a slice of toast and put it in front of her, along with a jar of jam. "We have peanut butter too. And juice."

Madeleine took a sip of coffee and massaged the back of her neck.

"Stiff neck?" her aunt asked.

"Yes." Madeleine told her about the accident, trying to sound matter-of-fact.

Aunt Lin's eyes narrowed. "What a fright! What a *jerk*." She put down her cup. "Men! I get so fed up with them sometimes—the whole thick-headed, overbearing tribe of them."

"Me too," Madeleine said.

"And your little car—it's all bent, isn't it? I liked that car. I hate to even think about the damage. And your neck. On top of everything, just what you needed. You've probably got whiplash."

"No doubt." Her aunt's tirade was the most satisfying thing she'd heard in a long time.

"But God kept you safe," Aunt Lin said. "See? You were supposed to come. I'm thankful."

An uncharacteristic remark from her aunt, but certainly welcome. "I'm glad to be here." Madeleine massaged her neck again.

"Are you sure your neck's all right? We've got our very own doctor with a clinic and everything. You could get him to check it."

Madeleine shook her head. She grimaced at the pain, mumbling, "No more doctors for me."

Aunt Lin gave her a sympathetic glance and began talking about her magazine.

Madeleine finished her toast and a second cup of coffee while she listened.

"It's about dogs," her aunt said, "but we target the knowledgeable, educated reader, so we run in-depth articles tied to the theme of each issue. Plus plenty of good photos to pull it together. That's my department."

Her eyes shone, and Madeleine recognized the green fire that brightened her father's eyes when he told her about the teens he worked with—his ruffians.

An ache, much too familiar, gnawed inside her.

Leave it behind, remember?

She asked, "Where's your photo shoot?"

"Upstate New York. One of those fancy-poodle breeding places. We've been trying to get an interview for months." She gave Madeleine an appraising glance. "I'll only be gone a few days. I hope you don't mind being alone. I think it's safe."

"Are you concerned about the people around here?"

"Not really." Aunt Lin shrugged. "From what Kent says, some of them are deficient, but I'm not sure what to think. This close to New York, there might be a criminal or two. I've heard tales."

"The old man at the store, is he local?"

"Timothy? I'm not sure." Aunt Lin finished her toast while she thought about it. "But he's quite the gentleman. He knew your father, from what he tells me."

Madeleine refilled her cup. She'd keep her distance from the nice old gentleman, in case he wanted to talk about Dad. "And the other man?"

"Kent moved here last fall, but he grew up in the Barrens, so he must have relatives around somewhere." She laughed. "He's definitely not deficient."

A minute later Aunt Lin was dispatching the breakfast dishes. "Now for the tour. I hope you're not allergic to mold."

Madeleine followed her through an arched doorway beside the kitchen pantry, and paused to stare. A long table in the center of the room was piled with china, glassware, vases, and candlesticks. Glass-fronted cabinets lined the walls, each one filled with sets of dishes.

"The dining room," her aunt said. "But there's no place for anyone to eat, even if they wanted to. What colors!"

The orange brocade draperies at the window had faded to a sickly brown, and the green walls reminded Madeleine of canned peas.

Aunt Lin paused beside a bevy of pink china ladies. "My cousin Henrietta had this thing about collections, and apparently she didn't know when to stop. The house is full, and there's another building, back in the trees, that's probably stuffed to the ceiling." Her voice was tolerant. "Most of this looks like junk, but you never know."

A connecting door led to the next room. "One of the parlors," Aunt Lin said. "That leaky roof caused a lot of water damage."

"I see what you mean." Madeleine eyed the peeling wallpaper, the gray-streaked green carpet, the dusty orange sofas.

Aunt Lin sneezed as she walked through the room. "Never did care for orange florals. I'm going to toss it all out."

Across the hall, a second parlor held multiple chairs, sofas, and lamps, all done in shades of blue. A royal blue carpet and draperies extended the theme.

"Our Blue Room," her aunt said, "as you can tell." She paused beside a piano. "Ruined by mice, and I'm still trying to get rid of them." She threaded her way to the back of the room. "Here's our very grand fireplace."

It was wide enough for a Yule log, and its tiled border of blue cabbage roses looked absurd.

Except for a rosewood table with graceful cabriole legs, the whole room could have come from a yard sale. "I feel like I'm standing in a used-furniture store," Madeleine said.

Disappointment tightened her shoulder blades. Aunt Lin hadn't said anything about antiques, but she'd let herself hope.

"Henrietta just lived for this house—she wanted it to become a Victorian showpiece." Aunt Lin clicked a fingernail against a blue lamp shaped like a flamingo. "All the clutter makes me crazy. Thank goodness she never got around to changing the outside. I like its simple lines."

Madeleine tried for something positive. "I'm sure there's plenty of potential here."

Potential for scrubbing and dusting! Not much of a Great Adventure. Aunt Lin had hired her for research, and she'd do a good job, but this . . .

Aunt Lin handed her a Blue Willow plate from the fireplace mantel. "Doesn't your mother collect this stuff?"

"Used to." The plate had the requisite blue pagodas and flying birds, but it lacked the traditional border. Her mother would give it a disdainful squint, the same look she'd given Madeleine when she announced her decision to work for Aunt Lin.

"You won't last! I can tell you that," Mother said. "You'll be back in a couple of weeks."

Madeleine returned the plate to the mantel. Not a chance. First thing, she was going to sign up for her baking course—that certainly had possibilities for Adventure. Someday she'd have her own shop, earn some money, and be independent.

They left the Blue Room, and her aunt paused to look up the staircase. "It's more of the same up there, plus boxes and trunks. Rooms and rooms full of stuff. I can't even think about it right now." She glanced at her watch. "Let's get some groceries."

On their way down the hall, she laid her hand on a Chippendale desk that stood outside the kitchen door. "This is one piece I'll keep."

"It's lovely," Madeleine said, tracing the shellwork on the drawers. "I wonder where your cousin got it."

Aunt Lin laughed. "Who knows? Oh, I meant to tell you, one of the local girls is coming over this afternoon to help. Bria is good at just about everything. She has a younger brother too, if you want to make use of him."

They bought a month's worth of groceries in Hammonton, the nearest large town, returned by noon, and were finishing up their lunch when someone knocked at the back door.

"Bria!" Aunt Lin said. "Come on in." She introduced Madeleine and said, "We're going to get a lot done this afternoon."

The slim, dark-haired girl gave Madeleine a shy smile and began loading the dishwasher.

Aunt Lin ate the rest of her sandwich while she called someone on her cell phone and asked how soon they could send a truck over.

"The Truck Guys are coming," she said. "Let's get ready for them."

She marched across the parlor. "These go—" The orange-flowered sofas and chairs. "And that rug, of course." She waved a hand at the draperies. "Those too. Totally depressing."

Bria had found an oak rocking chair on the other side of the room.

"What do you think, Bria?" Aunt Lin asked.

The girl tossed the worn cushion onto a sofa and sat down. "It's plenty strong," she said, rocking back and forth.

"It's yours if you can use it. Why don't you and Madeleine empty the glassware out of that bureau? I'll clear a spot on the dining room table."

They worked until a white truck rumbled past the window. The two brawny men knew their business, and an hour later, they'd emptied the room. "Good riddance," Aunt Lin said. "I wish I could do that with the whole house. Bria, I'm going to let you keep pulling down wallpaper."

She started for the door. "I still have a couple of errands to run. Madeleine, why don't you see what you can find for supper?"

Her aunt left, and Madeleine returned to the parlor, where the girl stood on a chair, scraping at wallpaper. "Do you usually stay for supper, Bria?"

"Yes, and then I clean up the kitchen afterwards."

"That'll be a big help," Madeleine said. "I'll try not to make too much of a mess." She paused. Bria was probably the one who had put the vase on her desk. "I like the bouquet you fixed for my room."

Still scraping, Bria gave her a polite smile but said nothing, and Madeleine headed for the kitchen. The girl had an aloofness about her that was hard to read.

She opened the refrigerator, stared into it, and decided to make Beef Stroganoff with the steak and sour cream they'd bought. While she sliced onions, she thought about dessert. Should she use the Black Gilliflower apples? Not today. She'd seen blueberries in the freezer—they'd do for a cobbler.

And . . . and as soon as she got started on her baking course, she'd come up with something more interesting. Tonight she'd go online and start looking around.

Supper was ready and most of the wallpaper down by the time her aunt returned. They ate a leisurely meal while Aunt Lin explained the difference between teacup and toy poodles and Bria looked as if she were somewhere else.

Madeleine had just taken the blueberry cobbler out of the oven when Aunt Lin turned her head to listen. "Someone's coming up the driveway."

A green Ford Bronco cruised past the window. "I should have known by the way he drove in. Doesn't like those bushes to scratch his shiny car." Her aunt's voice grew more animated. "Kent has come to pay us a visit."

CHAPTER 3

I'm beginning to like this old place.
Beneath the gaudy trappings, it has dignity,
like a dowager with a painted face
and fine bones.
~Journal

Kent leaned back in his chair, making it creak. "That sure was good cobbler, Lin. I stopped by at the right moment."

"Thanks to Madeleine," her aunt said. "She's the cook in this family."

"Did you tell her about my book?"

"No, I didn't. Go ahead."

He turned his blue gaze upon her. "It's my second. My first book is called *The Forest Primeval Prescription*—it's rather academic. I don't suppose you've heard of it?"

Madeleine shook her head, while mentally editing that title, and he continued. "This new one is in the planning stage, but I've already found some good material."

He adjusted the crease in his pants and rested a hand on the sheathed knife at his belt. His voice took on the cadence of a lecturing professor as he described the local museums and their links with colonial America.

"So," he said, "I came out here, rented a cabin, and started my research."

"How do you research?" Madeleine asked.

He patted his shirt pocket. "My trusty voice recorder. I've been interviewing people, getting family histories. They're all related around here. Intermarriage, with its attendant complexities, is not unusual. If I need more information, I send the kid to the library in Hammonton."

"The kid?"

"My assistant," Kent said. "I ran into him at a campground in Kentucky. There he was, cold and hungry, sleeping in his old truck. Found out he had an education of sorts and offered him a job. He comes in handy."

Aunt Lin looked thoughtful. "Remi seems like a smart young man. I wonder how his parents feel about him wandering across the country by himself."

"He doesn't have parents anymore," Kent said, "but I'd guess he's the product of one of those Hispanic-white marriages. Says he comes from an orphanage in Ohio. Reminds me of myself at that age, trying to make it on my own." His gaze fastened on Madeleine, as if to gauge her reaction to this bit of personal history.

Aunt Lin pushed her chair away from the table, and Kent glanced back at her. "I still have work to do tonight. *Beant goin'* as the Pineys say."

He stood to his feet, a big man who carried his weight well. "Okay, Lin. I'll see you tomorrow for lunch."

A lunch date with her aunt?

"That's right." Aunt Lin's voice was matter-of-fact.

"I'm looking forward to it." Kent tossed a farewell over his shoulder as he strode through the kitchen. "It's been a pleasure, Madeleine."

She picked up her dishes and added them to the pots in the sink. Something about that man was less than forthright, as if he had layers, like an onion. Where had Bria gone? Never mind, they could easily load the dishwasher.

When they were finished, her aunt said, "Let's go into the parlor and make a battle plan."

The empty room, with its blank, un-curtained window, looked cheerless in the dusk. Wallpaper still clung in patches to one wall, and the floor was littered with dusty remnants.

Aunt Lin paused in the center. "Bria can clean this up."

Madeleine ran a hand over the wall's plastered surface. "Only two layers of wallpaper—that's fortunate. Do you have any paint?"

"There's some ivory left from when they did the kitchen. You wouldn't mind?"

"Not a bit. What about brushes and things?"

"Might be some in the pantry. Or buy whatever you need at Timothy's store. I have a charge account there." Her aunt looked hopeful. "Paint could make a big difference."

They walked back through the dining room, and her aunt said, "For your research, why not start by checking through each room? Make a list of what you find."

A list? There'd be hundreds of pieces in this room alone.

"A general list," her aunt added quickly. "We're looking for anything of value, so don't bother with the junky stuff. Soon as you find a treasure"—she smiled at her own optimism—"you can start digging into its history."

"Didn't Kent say something about a library in Hammonton?" Madeleine asked. "And I brought my laptop, so I can check the Internet."

"I meant to tell you, our phone line is down for a couple of days." Her aunt looked regretful. "That's one problem with living so far out. We're supposed to be getting cable too, but it might take weeks. So I've been using my company's air card."

What? No Internet access here? What about her baking course? Okay, regroup. "I suppose the library has Internet," she said.

Her aunt nodded. "And Timothy has wireless. He wouldn't mind your using it."

She turned back to the kitchen. "I've still got to pack, and, considering that delicious meal, I suspect that you haven't had a minute to yourself. Don't work too hard, Madeleine. This house will take us a long time."

She paused as if she were consulting a mental list. "There's a TV set in my office. You'll find hiking paths close to the back door. And out in the woods, after you go past that garage, we even have some genuine ruins."

"I'll be okay, Aunt Lin."

"Good. See you in the morning."

Madeleine lifted a suitcase onto her bed and unzipped it. She'd made the obligatory phone call to her mother, and soon as she finished unpacking, she could settle down with a cookbook.

She unfolded a sweater, and the paperweight slid into view. She picked it up, her fingers curving around the glass oval. The delicate flowers would still be lovely, the colors soft, the workmanship exquisite, but . . .

Her breath caught in her throat.

She tugged open a drawer, pushed the paperweight in among her socks, and let herself be distracted by the bag of apples on top of the bureau. Frances Rondell's sympathetic face came to mind. Her mother's face, resentful and unhappy, eclipsed it.

She hung up her raincoat and paused, smoothing its wrinkles, thinking back. I had to come here, she told herself. To stay at home would have been the end of me.

Soon after Brenn and her mother had formed a partnership, she'd realized how the two of them operated.

Both were determined to get ahead, no matter how the truth might be shaded.

With Dad gone, she had started to change. Brenn talked her into marrying him, Mother's business prospered, and their ethics troubled her less and less. She became a meek little . . . mouse. Madeleine the Mouse.

"I am mired in the slough of my own acquiescence."

Where had that come from? Drama Club? She'd loved memorizing the lines for those plays, but college seemed a long time ago. She shut the closet door with a snap, angry at herself, at what she had become.

By the time she'd finished unpacking, read for a while, and written in her journal, the anger had twisted into remorse. *Why didn't I . . . How could I have let them . . . I was nothing but a . . .*

No more baggage, remember? She would brush her hair and go to bed. No more sleeping pills, either.

The house creaked as it settled its old bones to rest. The noises from Aunt Lin's room diminished. Something scuttled down the hall, and she pictured the tiny feet of a mouse.

She pulled the blankets close around her neck.

Madeleine the Mouse, push-over gal. Hunkering down to stay safe.

Mice . . . She composed an ironic mental paragraph about the advantages of mousiness and expanded it into an essay on the subtexts in Rose Fyleman's "I Think Mice are Nice." When she ran out of words, there was still too much left of the night.

The next morning after Aunt Lin left, she and Bria cleaned the parlor until it smelled of soap and wet wood. Better than mildew. Bria had carried the rocking chair out onto the porch and then returned to mop with swift, competent strokes, but she'd worked in silence.

While they ate lunch, the girl answered Madeleine's questions, but her answers were brief, as if it might be hazardous to give out more information than necessary. Yes, she had a brother. Jude. He was fourteen. They lived in the woods with their mother and grandmother, not too far away. She didn't say anything about a father.

Was she merely shy? Perhaps. But her reticence was edged with caution, as if she were a wild creature in dangerous territory.

After lunch, Madeleine said, "Let's explore. Have you seen any of those rooms upstairs?"

Bria shook her head, and curiosity gleamed in the brown eyes.

The staircase had a graceful balustrade of honey-colored wood, but the carpet looked like a matted green rag. Madeleine could hear her aunt saying, "This goes too."

They found a library of dusty books, a girlish-looking pink bedroom that might have been Cousin Henrietta's, and a modernized bathroom. At the back of the house was a locked room.

"I'll have to get the key," Madeleine said, scribbling in the margin of her notebook.

They took a quick tour of the crowded all-yellow bedroom across from the library and looked into the storage room beside it. Bria made a sound that might have been a giggle and pointed to a stuffed owl glaring at them from a plant stand. "Looks like he's guarding those trunks."

"Maybe he is," Madeleine said. "You never know about treasure."

Trunks, she wrote in her notebook. *Inventory contents.*

She glanced at her watch. "Perhaps we should check on brushes and things, so we can paint tomorrow."

"I looked in the pantry," Bria said. "There's paint, but no brushes."

"Aunt Lin told me that we could get supplies at Timothy's store. When does it close?"

"Not ever," Bria said. "He lives upstairs, and if someone bangs hard enough, he'll come down."

"Good. I'll grab my purse, and you can show me the way."

Timothy's store might have stood on its corner for a hundred years. Its walls had weathered to silver gray, and it leaned toward the street as if wearied by the weight of its dormers and the thick, dark roof.

Inside, half a dozen customers strolled past canned goods, hardware, medicines, and camping equipment stacked to the ceiling. The walls displayed everything from tools and fishing gear to paintings by local artists.

A rosy-faced old man stood talking to Timothy at the counter, but when he saw them, he tucked a package of toilet tissue under his arm and picked up a bulging plastic bag. He shuffled past with a nod, his eyes inquisitive beneath shaggy brows and a bald head. His red plaid shirt was almost as wrinkled as his face, and his jeans sagged over dusty sneakers. One of Uncle Ashton's Pineys?

After he'd gone, Madeleine asked Bria, "Who's that?"

"Dan'l Forbes. He's lived here forever."

She didn't ask anything more because Timothy was saying, "Hello, young ladies! How can I help you today?" His wizened little face was so cheerful, his brown eyes so lively, that the room seemed to brighten.

"We're going to be painting," Madeleine said. "So we need some brushes."

"Brushes we have in abundance." He limped purposefully out from behind the counter, one shoulder hunched a little higher than the other.

Bria had gone ahead of them, but Madeleine stayed beside the old man. "I have a favor to ask," she said. "My aunt mentioned that you have wireless here. Could you possibly let me use it until we get ours?"

He slowed his halting pace. "Certainly. Anytime. How's the writing business coming?"

Aunt Lin must have told him about her website that offered editing services.

"It's not. I closed it . . . a while ago."

Had her reply been too abrupt? She hurried on. "I appreciate your letting me use your space. I'm hoping to take some courses online."

"But you kept your skills, I'm sure," he said. "If I may ask a favor in turn, I know someone—the local doctor—who's looking for an editor."

She'd heard that request once too often. "I don't think I'll have time to do any more editing," she said, "and I must confess that I've developed an allergy to doctors."

He cocked his head. "Why is that?"

"Close acquaintance," she said. "My uncle's one, and I know several others."

He didn't look convinced, so she had to explain. "As far as I'm concerned, they're all highhanded and egotistic. They think they're medical deities."

A smile rearranged the wrinkles on his face, but all he said was: "Sounds like you're renovating the Manor. I'm glad to hear it."

He wasn't going to argue. She felt a twinge of remorse for what she'd said—he'd been so friendly—but she wasn't about to change her mind.

They had reached the display of painting supplies, and he asked, "Are you using latex or oil?"

"Latex," Bria said.

Timothy picked up a paint roller and handed it to Madeleine. "I'd suggest using this for the walls, and brushes for the trim. And how about one of these?" He lifted out a long pole with a paint roller attached to its end. "For those walls and the high ceiling."

The doorbell jingled and Kent's voice called, "There you are! What are you trying to sell to our newest resident?"

Smiling as if they were best of friends, he strolled toward her.

"They're painting at the Manor," Timothy said.

The bell jingled again, and Timothy glanced at the woman who marched in. "Excuse me a minute please." He limped off to meet her.

Kent took the long-handled roller from Madeleine and hefted it. "Yes, this will do," he said. "How about a step ladder? Do you have one?"

Madeleine looked around for Bria, but the girl had walked off, her pony-tail bobbing as she went. "I don't think so, but we can—"

"Oh, no, you're such a tiny thing, you've got to have a ladder." Kent smiled down at her. "Chairs can be dangerous. I'll bring one by for you."

He gave her another smile, one that might or might not have been meaningful, and hurried after Timothy. "Hey, old friend, can you sell me some ice cream real quick? Then I'll let you get on with your wheeling and dealing."

Bria reappeared, and they added brushes and a paint tray to the rollers Timothy had suggested. While they paid for their supplies, a large coffee-brown dog peered around the end of the counter. "He wants to meet you," Timothy said. "He takes a personal interest in my customers."

The dog regarded her with intelligent eyes. His rough coat suggested no particular breed, and one ear was torn, giving him a comical, lopsided look.

"He's a dear old critter," Bria said. "Just checking you out."

The phone rang and Timothy turned to answer it, but first he said, "Thank you, ladies! I hope to see you again." The dog seemed to think it was his duty to escort them to the door.

As they drove away, Madeleine commented on the dog, and Bria remarked that he took care of Timothy like a protective uncle.

It was a picturesque comparison, abstract and unexpected. She wanted to ask whether Bria was going to school anywhere, since she looked old enough for college, but the girl had fallen into one of her silences.

Her own thoughts returned to the store, weighing Kent's eagerness to "drop by." Did he think he could just come on over and they would have a cozy little visit? Surely he knew that Aunt Lin had left for New York.

The Manor's driveway came up fast, and she almost missed it but her thoughts didn't pause. She should have told him, "No thanks. I'll get a ladder of my own."

Why hadn't she? . . . Mouse!

She parked the car, gathered up their purchases, and looked at Bria's remote face. "Can you stay for supper?"

Bria shook her head. "But I'll work tomorrow morning if you want."

The wooden rocking chair on the porch caught Madeleine's eye. "Why don't we put that chair into my car, and I'll drive you?"

"I've got my bike here," Bria said. "Jude can come over for it, later."

"But he shouldn't have to carry it when I could—"

"I'm sure." Bria turned away. "Thank you, anyway." A minute later, she and her bike had disappeared into the woods.

Madeleine ate leftovers for supper, watching the pine trees fade into twilight. She'd forgotten to ask Timothy where she could get her car fixed. It drove as well as ever, but it didn't look like itself. Tomorrow, she'd go back and ask him. And she could start on some research for her course. Finally!

The sound of a car's engine jerked her gaze to the driveway. Kent. With the stepladder? She dropped her fork and hurried to the back door. If she went outside, it would be easier to send him away.

At least he wasn't alone. When the Bronco stopped, a young man wearing a red baseball cap jumped out to open up the back. Kent slid from behind the steering wheel and sent her a high voltage smile.

She closed the door behind herself and waited.

CHAPTER 4

Note to Self: don't tell Mother about Kent.
She'd consider him quite eligible
and give me no peace.
I don't plan to consider him at all.
Or anyone else, for that matter.
~Journal

Kent's companion was half his age, half his width, and equally tall. He lifted out the ladder with one hand and joined Kent on the porch.

"Oh," Kent said, "this is Remi."

Remi gave her a sunny glance. A knockout, sure to captivate any teenage girl, with that caramel-colored skin and black sparkling eyes.

"And this is your ladder," Kent said with a self-approving smile. "We'll put it inside for you." Without waiting for an answer, he reached past her to open the door.

"Which room?" he asked, already halfway down the hall. "This empty one, right?"

"That'll do." What did he mean by marching right into her house?

Remi set the ladder in one corner while Kent surveyed the parlor as if he were going to buy it. "Nice proportions," he said. "Look at that molding up there. Remarkable."

He nodded, agreeing with himself, and stepped through the connecting door to the dining room. "This is what you've found so far?" He coughed. "Dusty, isn't it? And me with a bad cold."

The room, crowded with boxes, cabinets, and the long, over-full table, seemed to shrink when the two men walked into it. Remi whistled as he bent over a pile of gilt-edged dinner plates.

"You said it, kid." Kent picked up a clear quart jar, and ran a finger over the name embossed on it: COHANSEY.

"I'm learning about South Jersey glass," he said. "It's important, historically." He sounded as if he were sharing a secret. "I'm going to have a whole chapter about it in my book."

He replaced the jar with elaborate care. "We'd better go. Remi has to put those notes of mine into the computer, and there's a stack of books for him to read."

"I can handle it." Remi's smile told her that he liked the work.

Kent coughed again. "I've still got this congestion—don't I sound terrible? It might've settled in my lungs."

Madeleine eyed him, not sure what to say. That cough didn't sound very bad.

He gave her a pitiful look. "I need to get plenty of sleep."

Remi grinned, as if remembering something pleasant. He said in a low voice, *"The innocent sleep; sleep that knits up the raveled sleeve of care."*

"Whatever." Kent was already on his way out of the room.

"Thanks for the ladder," Madeleine said, keeping her voice impersonal. "Aunt Lin will appreciate your bringing it over."

She watched them drive off. *Sleep that knits up the raveled sleeve,* huh, Remi? A quote from *Macbeth.* How did an orphanage dropout happen to be quoting Shakespeare?

She stood on the porch for a minute, listening to the soft *shussing* of wind in the pines. Maybe it was thoughtful of Kent to bring her that ladder. He reminded her of a big, friendly puppy. But still . . .

Her cell phone rang, and she answered it on the way inside. Her mother sounded cheerful today. "Hi! Anything exciting going on?"

"We've got one room all ready to paint and we found some old—"

"—Pretty tame, don't you think? I just met this gorgeous blond guy, Wayne. He's an auctioneer. Lots of fun." Her mother's laugh had that disgusting undertone. "How about you? Met anybody good looking?"

"Not really."

"Too bad. Is your aunt off on another trip?"

"Yes."

"Just as I thought. And you're stuck with the work. George is still asking about you. Don't forget, you can come home any time."

"Thanks, Mother. Bye."

So, she'd found herself another one.

The evening stretched ahead. What about taking advantage of the new kitchen? She could do something with the Gilliflower apples.

Why had it seemed important to bring them?

Because they represented her conversation with Frances Rondell, which had led to her declaration of . . . rebellion? No. Independence.

She didn't feel like making a pie, but cookies would taste good. With walnuts. The recipe came easily to mind, and it wasn't until they were cooling on a rack that she realized why.

She'd made apple-walnut cookies a hundred times for Dad. "I need some goodies for my young ruffians," he'd say. The next day he'd go off with the bag of cookies and return to tell of progress made with Pol or Jose or Shawn—whoever his current project might be.

The lumpy brown cookies smelled tantalizing, but the first bite turned to ashes in her mouth.

Would she ever get over this? She'd been improving, getting used to missing Dad, until she'd married. And then . . .

She yanked open a drawer, shook out a plastic bag. Give them away. How about some cookies for Bria's little brother? She labeled the bag and put it outside on the rocking chair.

Bria arrived early the next morning, and with her came a large black Labrador. He stood in the doorway, wagging his tail and grinning in the amiable manner of all Labs.

"And who's this?" Madeleine asked.

Bria put a hand on the dog's head. "Lockie. May he come in? He can sleep on the porch if you'd rather not."

"Sure," Madeleine said. "Is he yours?"

"Sort of." Bria sounded as if she didn't want to discuss Lockie's history. "Jude said to thank you for the cookies. He loves to eat."

"Good! I like to cook. Be sure to tell him we've got plenty of work."

They painted all morning, and while they were cleaning up, Madeleine asked, "What are you going to do this afternoon?"

The girl hesitated with that same caution. "I have some other painting to do."

Bria left after lunch, and for the next hour Madeleine scraped old paint off the small panes of the parlor window, but finally she put down her razor blade. To reward herself, she'd go check her e-mail at Timothy's store. She'd take him some of those cookies and see about finding an online course.

Timothy greeted her cheerfully from behind the counter. "Hello, Mrs. Burke. I see you brought your laptop. Come to do some work online?"

"If that's okay with you. I want to take a baking course." She handed him the bag of cookies. "In the meantime, I've been practicing, and I thought you might like a sample."

"Capital! I've got a significant sweet tooth. I'll save them for our afternoon break."

He led her through a curtained doorway to a large room that might once have been a parlor. Against one wall stood filing cabinets and a roll-topped desk. A long table took up most of the center, and at the far end was a green corduroy sofa flanked by matching overstuffed chairs.

He waved at the table. "Would that be a suitable place for you?"

"Just right." While she was setting up her laptop, he began sorting papers at the desk.

She read her messages, wrote to three friends about her "wilderness adventure," and began researching online baking schools. A course on breads would be a good place to start.

From dozens of courses, she chose one that looked promising. It had videos to watch, articles to read, even tests to take. She scribbled in her notebook. Each item she baked had to be evaluated by a proctor.

A door opened at the far end of the room, and Timothy spoke to someone. "Time for a break already? It's just as well, I've tangled these figures again."

She glanced up—an older man carrying a mug—and back to the note she was writing to herself.

Timothy stood beside her. "Mrs. Burke? I'd like you to meet a friend of mine."

The man had a trim, athletic frame and an air of coiled energy that belied his weathered face. Perhaps not so old.

"Nathan Parnell," he said. In contrast to Timothy's plaid flannel, he wore a dress shirt, pinstriped blue. His gray eyes seemed to take her measure in a single glance, but she couldn't tell whether he'd filed the data or discarded it.

"Hello," she said, closing her laptop. She'd have to come back later.

Timothy was limping over to an old mahogany sideboard. "Please, don't go. Won't you help us sample your cookies?" He gave her a twinkling smile that she couldn't resist.

"Thank you, I will."

"Would you like root beer? Or maybe some tea? I can make a pot of chai."

"Chai sounds good."

Timothy moved with the confidence of an experienced host, filling an electric kettle with water, setting out mugs, arranging the cookies on a plate. This must be their afternoon ritual.

His friend looked out of the window by Timothy's desk, tapping a finger on the mug as if he were inventing a tune for himself. The light picked out the reddish tints of his brown hair and gleamed on a thin, puckered scar that ran down one side of his face.

Not the sociable type? That was fine with her.

While they drank their tea, Timothy praised the cookies and asked why she wanted to take a cooking class. "I like to bake, anyway," she said, "but while I'm out here, a course would give me a chance to improve. It's something I've always wanted to do."

"No chance at home?"

"Not really. I was teaching, and besides . . ." Something about the kindly gaze invited her to speak with candor. "Things at home will be changing. My uncle is going to manage my mother's business, and he wanted me to help."

Timothy's smile encouraged her to go on. "The doctor-uncle?"

Uncle Ashton's speech still rankled. With a curt nod, she said, "It wasn't just that. But I'd have hated to work with him, he's so . . . arrogant. That's a doctor for you. You'd think he'd keep busy enough with his adoring patients."

Timothy bent over his mug. Was that a smile glimmering on the wrinkled face?

The man across from her had listened in silence, but now he chose another cookie from the plate and gazed at it. "Excellent cookies," he said, "apples, and walnuts, and some flavor I can't quite identify."

"Cinnamon."

"And you want to improve on this?" He had a warm, mellow voice that put her at ease.

"Not this recipe—it's an old favorite, and I've tinkered with it long enough. But the whole baking scene intrigues me, there's so much to learn."

"More than you could get from a cookbook?" Timothy asked.

"Yes, insights, professional tips, history. I can do cookies and pies, but I don't know much about baking with yeast, for example."

She wouldn't tell them her idea of becoming a pastry chef. Her mother thought it ridiculous, and Brenn had too.

But Timothy looked as if he understood dreams, and his friend eyed her thoughtfully. His gaze was somewhat diagnostic, as if he were estimating the volume of blood in her veins.

Blood? Oh, no, was he—?

"You're the doctor, aren't you?" When would she learn not to spout her opinions? "I didn't mean to be rude."

His eyes glinted with amusement. "Don't worry about it. After all, you didn't know you were speaking to a medical deity."

Even worse. He'd heard that from Timothy .

The doctor took a bite of his cookie, chewed slowly, reflectively. "I've met doctors who are exactly as you have described. But you may find that they're not all alike."

His reasonable tone was disarming. "Perhaps I should give you the benefit of the doubt," she said, the doubt lingering in her voice.

"I hope so, Mrs. Burke. Perhaps you will even change your mind."

"That's a generous response."

"It's a self-serving response, since I'm sitting here eating your cookies. And I have a project that could use your expertise."

She should have left when she had the chance. She glanced at Timothy. "Did I mention 'opportunistic'?"

He looked wise and said nothing.

The doctor nodded, as if he would agree to any shortcoming she cared to mention, but she stiffened her resolve. "I'm sure you can construct a sentence properly," she said.

"I just thought you could give me an opinion, since you're a professional."

"But I don't edit, not anymore. I don't teach English anymore, either." Nothing that would remind her of Dad and his ruffians or the stories they wrote.

The gray eyes challenged her. "You really don't want to do this. I wonder why."

Persistent, wasn't he? She'd give him something to think about.

"Here's one reason, doctor. People say, 'Tell me what you think,' but what they mean is, 'Tell me my work is good.' And if I can't say that, their feelings get hurt. If I presume to give advice, they don't listen. It all comes down to a matter of ego, and I'm done with that."

He leaned back in his chair, and his eyes still had a cool gray look but the corners of his mouth turned up.

"What do you find so amusing, Dr. Parnell?" She used his title deliberately, edged it with a trace of disrespect.

"At risk of offending you, Mrs. Burke, I was thinking that you probably had no trouble controlling your students."

"What do you mean?"

"A glance like the one you just gave me. I've seen glaciers with that blue-green color."

"I got along well with my students."

"I would work as hard as any of them."

More determined than most. She frowned at her mug, aligned it with her plate. Loosen up. Perhaps he deserved a chance.

"I think you're reading the wrong script," she said. "This is where you're supposed to give me a cold stare and walk off, clutching your papers to your manly chest."

He grinned, a quick boyish grin that transformed the scarred face. "You'll look at it?"

"Tell me why it's so important."

Timothy pulled himself to his feet, smiling, and reached for the kettle. "More tea, anyone?"

The doctor described his high-school English teacher, now a family friend and successful writer. Her latest project was to edit a collection of essays about Alaska, and she had asked him to submit a chapter for the book.

"I've done three drafts," he said, "but it's missing something. I can't disappoint her with work that's second-rate."

"Will you give me a copy?"

"Our printer just died," Timothy said. "The new one should arrive next week."

The doctor leaned forward. "If you wouldn't mind coming over to my office—it's just next door—you could read it on my laptop."

But she *would* mind, very much.

She looked a question at Timothy and he nodded, so she said, "Why not bring your laptop over here?"

"That's a good idea," Timothy said. "If you'll excuse me, I hear a customer. Our Friday afternoon rush, you know."

At least the man had enough sense not to watch her read it. He set up his laptop on the table, opened the document, and went to stand in front of the window.

She read with care, scrolling back once or twice to check what he'd said on a previous page. Length was suitable, content original. Technically, it was flawless. Depending on what the editor wanted, it might do. But it could be better.

Without looking at him, she said, "It is informative, doctor. Shaped well. Sentences properly put together. You might work on some of the passive constructions."

He left the window and sat down across from her. "Mrs. Burke."

Reluctantly she met his eyes, caught his don't-kid-me look.

"It isn't very good." His voice was as crisp as his writing. "Can it be fixed?"

Might as well find out. For Timothy's sake, she'd do her best.

"I think it can, but it will cost you."

"What do you charge?"

"I'm not talking about money. If you want to work on it, you'll see what I mean."

"I want to work on it," he said quietly.

"Remember, you're the one who said that." She took a slow breath, thinking through an approach. "How long since you left Alaska?"

"Four years."

"How long did you live there?"

"Most of my life."

"Good. Now I'd like you to go sit down on that sofa, lean back, and close your eyes. Talk about someone in Alaska who made a deep impression on you."

As he stood, he paused and gave her a look she couldn't interpret.

He started in a monotone, telling her about Denny Woods, the young Inuit who'd sold him his first dogs.

His voice warmed as he described how they became friends, went hunting, and ran their dogs together. Denny didn't have much of a problem with alcohol, just took a drink now and then. He'd prayed for Denny and had seen him start coming to their little church.

"One day—" He sounded as if the words were choking him. "One day, Denny hitched a plane ride to McGrath with a friend of his, a pilot who'd had a few at the bar. Their plane went down somewhere in the Alaska Range. We never did find it."

He stood to his feet with a jerk, but when he finally spoke, his voice was impersonal. "Is that enough of a story for you, Mrs. Burke?"

She suppressed her pity. Plenty of emotion there. If he could manage it, the writing would be good.

She waited, not answering, letting him collect himself. He went over to pour himself another mug of tea. He picked up her mug and filled it too.

Finally he sat down at the table and looked at her.

She kept her voice as detached as his. "Thank you, doctor. The reason I had you do that is because your piece has all of its necessary body parts, but it is clinically dead. No pulse."

He frowned, but she ignored him.

"And here my analogy breaks down because you can give it life. As it stands, it's merely a documentary. To be effective, it needs heart—some reality, some passion."

She glanced up. The gray eyes burned with intensity, and she continued with more assurance. "When you told me about Denny, I saw that heart. You chose well. His story fits with your topic. If you can weave it into what you've written, you'll succeed."

He was quiet for a minute. She hadn't expected a burst of gratitude, but to see the lines deepen on his face was disconcerting.

"Thank you," he said. "I'll work on it." He stood to his feet and pulled out his cell phone, presumably to check for messages. While he was doing that, she slid her laptop into its bag and left.

Timothy was waiting on a customer. Just as well, because she didn't feel like talking. That look on the doctor's face . . . It wasn't an offended ego. Pain, maybe. Pain related to something more than the death of a good friend. Why had he left Alaska?

CHAPTER 5

Looks as if mousiness is not easily shed.
I stood by while Kent,
the handsome do-gooder,
came barreling into my house.
I never used to be like this.
I need to toughen up.
~Journal

Back at the Manor, she decided to do one more thing today—work on that cluttered old library she and Bria had found.

Before long she was sorting through books, sneezing as she crammed the useless ones into boxes. Dust! She eyed the plum-colored draperies, took up a handful of velvet, and pulled. It came away in her hand with the sigh of rotted fabric. She sneezed again. These had to come down.

It was while she was standing on a box unhooking the draperies that she discovered the window seat. If she cleared off the boxes, it would make a good place to sit and look at the view.

First, get this finished. She bundled the draperies into a super-sized trash bag, vacuumed everything including the brown couch, and marked the boxes to be discarded. As she shelved the last of the books, a convention of squabbling blue jays made her look out the window. Below, the forest spread in all directions, mysterious and inviting. Aunt Lin liked to jog there, on the many paths.

In Roanoke, too, there were hiking paths. She and Dad used to . . .

Her fingernails dug into the window frame. Don't think about him. Don't think about the hikes. Don't risk it, not for a minute.

She turned away. It was almost dusk, and if she could discipline her thoughts, a walk would do her good. She could check on those Dumont ruins, run for a while, and wear herself out.

That night she slept well, for once, but she awoke at dawn to wonder about Bria—such a mysterious young woman. Would her little brother be the same? Bria had said he liked to eat. If she had pancakes waiting for him, maybe they'd get off to a good start.

By eight o'clock she was ready, and just in time. When she opened the door, the dog brushed past with easy familiarity, but Jude hung back, as if unsure of his welcome. He was thin and wiry, shorter than Bria.

"Hi, Jude," she said. "We sure can use your help today."

"Hello." He gave her an assessing look from somber black eyes.

She returned his look with equal gravity. "I'm especially glad you came because otherwise I'd have to eat all the pancakes myself."

His eyebrows shot up into a fringe of shaggy brown hair. "Pancakes?" He glanced sideways at his sister, as if to ask whether this person was for real.

A smile tugged at the corners of Bria's mouth. "She likes to cook."

The expression on his face altered, enough for Madeleine to know that she had gained points in his estimation. "C'mon," she said. "Let's eat."

Jude ate nine large pancakes. He didn't say much beyond a quiet 'thank you' each time she refilled his plate, but Bria emerged from her silence to offer a comment: "I told you he likes to eat. I think that's why he likes to cook. Someday he's going to weigh three hundred pounds."

Jude ignored the sisterly remark and put down his fork with a sigh. "Okay, show me to the work. I'm ready." Lockie, who had been sleeping at Bria's feet, rose and stretched, looking expectant.

After they finished sorting and cleaning in the library, Madeleine said, "Let's do some more exploring. I want to see what's in those old trunks."

The largest trunk, to Jude's evident disappointment, was filled with ball gowns. "I wonder who wore them," Madeleine said. "The lacework is priceless." She wrote an entry in her notebook. "Jude, please put a piece of masking tape on the lid and write a big number one on it. Let's see what's over here."

Trunk number two held more gowns, trunk number three held children's clothes, and trunk number four was filled with blankets that smelled of mothballs. By the time they started on the last trunk, Jude had wandered off to look at the stuffed owl.

"Hey, this is a great horned owl," he said. "His ear tufts are way cool! Lockie, how'd you like to meet him some dark night?" The dog thumped his tail but looked unimpressed.

Madeleine opened the fifth trunk.

Jude glanced over. "More clothes?"

"Towels. With treasures wrapped inside, no doubt." Madeleine unrolled a towel and found a wooden duck staring up at her. She held it out to Bria. "A model duck."

Bria took the duck into her hands as if it were made of crystal.

Jude crossed the room in a single bound. "That's a decoy." He squatted down to look at it. "A black duck, Bria. Kind of like we make, except it's scratched."

His sister caressed the long, rounded back. "Nice. It has simple lines and is probably quite old." She turned it over. "No signature."

Jude was digging into the trunk. "Here's another one. A merganser?"

"A red-breasted merganser," Bria said. "See the tuft of feathers? Good work on the head—dark green, as it should be, and the white neck ring is neatly done. It's weathered, but that's okay."

Madeleine studied the two of them. Bria, saying more than one sentence at a time? Where had they learned about decoys?

"Oho!" Jude lifted out a white-crested duck. "This has got to be a hooded merganser."

"I've seen pictures of those," Madeleine said. "So pretty!"

He looked back into the trunk. "Maybe there's some more." He unwrapped china dogs, boxes of costume jewelry, and a pink ceramic alligator, obviously hand-painted.

He held up the alligator, grinning. "You could do better than this, Bria."

His sister frowned at him.

"Let's put it all back," Madeleine said. "I don't think Aunt Lin is going to be interested in this stuff."

Jude looked astonished. "But the decoys!"

"I'll show her the decoys." His enthusiasm piqued her curiosity. Perhaps they were valuable. "Are you hungry? Let's get ourselves some lunch. I made applesauce, and there's plenty of ham for sandwiches."

While they ate, she thought about the decoys and Jude's remark: 'like we make.'

"So, who in your family makes decoys?" she asked him.

"We mostly work together."

Bria said nothing, but Madeleine addressed a question to her. "Is that what you were painting yesterday?"

"Yes." Jude sounded eager. "We're getting a whole bunch ready for a . . . a *consignment*." He said the word as if it were newly minted. "We're going to earn a lot of money."

So the two of them made decoys. Perhaps decoys were a valuable commodity around here. And older ones more so?

Bria put down her sandwich. "That's what he said, anyway."

"Who?"

Again it was Jude who answered. "Kent. He says he can recognize quality when he sees it." His voice grew hopeful. "You never know."

Bria gave him a warning frown and pushed her chair back from the table. "What would you like us to do this afternoon?"

"We'll clean out a couple of closets, and then I've got a baking project. Want to help?"

Jude's eyes took on a sparkle. "What're we going to bake?"

"Our supper. And my aunt likes carrot cake."

He jumped up from the table. "Can I see your recipes?"

Bria shook her head in mock despair. "He's a crazy guy. I never heard of a kid who liked to cook so much."

Jude struck a dignified pose. "Most of the great chefs are men. Someday I might have my own restaurant."

Madeleine laughed at them both and found her recipes for Jude.

"Here's one with coconut that looks good," he said. "And cream cheese icing. Do we have cream cheese?"

"I think so. Bria, you choose what to make for supper."

"No hot dogs, okay?" Jude said.

His sister gave him a look of reproof and bent over the cookbook.

Madeleine started Jude grating carrots while she set out the other ingredients. He mixed up the cake with ease and slid it into the oven, looking gratified.

He smiled to himself while he beat the cream cheese for icing, and from time to time, he dipped in a finger, which seemed to be his method of checking for consistency.

Madeleine watched him lick off his finger, thinking what an unusual child he was. No, not a child. Something in those dark eyes was older than you'd expect at fourteen.

Bria worked with her usual competence. For supper, she had decided on chicken baked with rice and green beans, and apart from a question or two, produced it by herself.

"You guys are pretty good," Madeleine said while they were cleaning up. "Where did you learn to cook?"

Jude started to answer, and Bria interrupted. "He's always liked to mess around in the kitchen."

After supper, Jude looked longingly at the cake and Madeleine knew what he was thinking. "I'm sure Aunt Lin won't care if we each have a piece," she said. "It's not for a party—it's just for us. A cook should always test his work."

They left soon afterwards, apparently unconcerned about the darkening sky. She was turning back to the house when she realized that a green Bronco was halfway up the drive.

"I will not have this." She said it aloud, her voice indignant, but deep inside, she had started to tremble. She should confront this man, tell him he was not welcome.

She should say, 'Don't you come here when my aunt is gone.'

Right, that's what she should do. She reached for her purse and jacket. As an afterthought, she snatched up her notebook.

Kent was getting out of his car when she stepped outside. The door locked behind her with a click.

He gave her a beckoning sort of smile, as if he thought she had come out to greet him. He hurried toward her, carrying a white plastic bag, and gestured at the woods. "Do those kids come over here much?"

What business was it of his? But all she said was, "Why?"

"They can be pests." He looked smug. "I wouldn't want them to become a nuisance." He moved closer, taking up too much of her space, and lowered his voice. "Their mother lets them run wild. Of course, she's a sad case, herself. You wouldn't believe—"

She opened her mouth to interrupt, to tell him to go away and never come back, but found herself stepping around him, heading for her car. "I'm sorry," she said over her shoulder. "I was just leaving."

"But—" He lifted the white bag, looking forlorn. "I brought ice cream."

She had reached the car. Inside, and safe. Not proud of herself, but safe. She started the engine and lowered the window. "Another time," she called. "When Aunt Lin gets back."

She threw him a wave, squeezed her car past his Bronco, and went on down the driveway, trying to focus her thoughts. Cold in here. Close the window. Turn on the headlights.

Would he follow her? Probably not.

Just an over-eager puppy. So why was she still trembling? And her neck had started to ache.

She rubbed at her neck and kept an eye on the rearview mirror while she thought about where to go. How about the library in Hammonton? Would it be open on a Saturday night?

Timothy would know.

She parked at one side of the store, hoping Kent wouldn't see her car if he happened to drive past. The OPEN sign was gone, and the door was locked. Not surprising for a small town.

Through the glass she could see a dim light and someone moving around. He might still be in there. Bria said he didn't mind opening up after hours. She knocked timidly, glancing at the dark street.

A voice answered, and Timothy limped over to unlock the door. She stepped quickly inside, knowing he would wonder, but she didn't care.

"Hello again," Timothy said. "Brr-rr! It's cold out there. You in a hurry? Running away from the Jersey Devil?"

He chuckled and limped ahead of her into the store, finally stopping to lean against the counter. "It's our local legend," he said. "A mystical creature that's half horse and half man. With wings. I almost forgot the wings. Some of our staunchest citizens claim to have seen it flying out of the swamps at night."

His smile eased the tension clawing at her neck.

"I'm sorry to bother you," she said, "I just wanted to find out—"

"No bother at all, Mrs. Burke."

"Please, call me Madeleine," she said. "I wanted to go to the library at Hammonton. Will it still be open?"

Such a trivial question.

He looked regretful. "Not on a Saturday evening. Do you need some books?"

"I've got plenty to read, but I thought I'd get started on my research. Tonight would have been a convenient time."

Too much explaining. And now she'd have to go back to the house, that dark house. Would Kent hang around, waiting for her?

Timothy studied her with his wise old eyes, and she had the feeling that he knew what had happened.

She should say, "Never mind. Another time," sounding brave and careless, but she couldn't manage it, not under his searching gaze.

A shrill burbling came from his office, and Timothy said, "I'm making tea. Won't you please join me?"

She hesitated. Had Kent gone by now?

"It's very good tea. Earl Grey." Timothy's brown eyes looked hopeful.

"Thank you," she said.

"Then I'll just lock up my pretties." He bent over the display case, and she looked to see what he was referring to. Beside the knives was a row of paperweights, each with a striking design captured in the glass.

"Fascinating, aren't they?" he said. "I've seen some that are incredibly complex."

All the paperweights were round, except the one with red roses, which was an egg-shaped oval, like hers.

He opened the cabinet door. "Would you like to take a closer look?"

She backed away. "Oh, no. I already have one that . . . that someone gave me."

He nodded, locked the cabinet, and moved on down the counter. She followed, pausing when he stopped to lock another sliding door. He had model ducks at this end. No, she corrected herself, decoys. One was a mallard, she could tell that much.

He straightened, slowly. "That's it for the night. Let's have our tea."

With the lamps lit, Timothy's office looked inviting, more like a well-used living room than a work space. "Let's be comfortable," he said, and when he'd filled their mugs, he led her to the sofa and chairs at the far end. She sat cross-legged on the sofa, and he lowered himself into one of the chairs with a faint grimace.

He stirred his tea, dropped in another cube of sugar, and stirred again. "I never did properly welcome you," he said. "What do you think of our pine barrens?"

"The woods around here? Different, but pretty. I sort of knew that because . . . because I'd heard about them." She hurried on. "Have you lived here all your life?"

"No. Right after high school, I ran off. Had to see the world."

"But you came back. When?"

"Only eight years ago—I'm practically a tourist."

"Tell me why? And what you've been doing since?"

Timothy paused to think, and the doctor stepped silently through the door beside them. The old man glanced up. "There's tea left, Nathan."

He lifted the mug in his hand. "Thanks, I've got plenty."

"Sit for a minute." Timothy waved at the other chair. "She's got me talking, and I'm not about to stop."

The doctor nodded at her as he put his mug on the table between them. If the writing were going well, he'd say so. They always did. But he leaned back against the thick green cushions and closed his eyes.

Timothy told her how he'd been injured while he was stationed in Alaska, had remembered his growing-up years in the Barrens, and decided it might be a good place to heal.

He nodded in affirmation. "People think it's just trees and sand, but there's something here that never quite let go of me."

None of his family was left so he'd started working at the store and ended up buying it from the ninety-year-old owner. With the help of electricity and indoor plumbing, he'd modernized it, expanded the business, and by God's grace, it had prospered.

She sipped her tea, listening. *By God's grace.* Odd that he didn't take credit for what must have been a lot of hard work.

He paused, and she refilled their mugs from the tea pot. He dropped in two cubes of sugar, saying, "Have you decided on a baking course?"

"I found one that looks perfect, except for one requirement. I'm trying to work up the courage to ask you for another favor."

He shrugged, his face inscrutable. "I'm a very busy man, as you can tell. We've already exchanged favors once this week. There might be a quota, you know."

She tilted her head. This quiet person—such a tease? "Timothy?"

"Not the glacier look, please, anything but that."

"But I didn't . . ."

"Correct. That was a melt-the-glacier look. Yes, whatever you want."

"Whatever? I didn't think you were so reckless."

"You should have seen me when I was flying my little red Super Cub."

"I can't believe that. I've heard the saying: *There are old pilots, and there are bold pilots, but there are no old, bold pilots in Alaska.*"

"You're remarkable, little lady. Tell me what I've just agreed to."

She put her mug on the table and sat forward. "For my course, I need a proctor."

"An impressive title. I think I've always wanted to be a proctor. What does one do?"

He was in rare form tonight. She glanced at the doctor, but he was asleep.

"I need someone to watch when I'm taking my tests so I don't cheat. And to evaluate what I bake—that means you'll have to eat it—and fill out a report."

He smiled. "Really?"

"They suggest that the proctor be someone in retail sales—a business person who can judge the commercial value of my work."

"Am I permitted to keep the samples?"

"Of course. You may also feed them to your dog, and I'll never know."

The doctor stirred. "Sounds like tough job," he murmured. "But you can rise to the challenge."

"Done," Timothy said. "I'll be glad to help you out. When do I start?"

"Maybe I can download some files on Monday. Then it depends how much spare time I get. There's a lot to do in that old house."

Timothy drank the last of his tea and gazed at her. "I knew Henrietta," he said. "She'd be happy to see your aunt taking such an interest in the Manor."

"Perhaps not." Madeleine pictured the truck that had driven away with most of one whole room. "We've done quite a bit of clearing out."

"Your aunt had to make a business trip this weekend, is that right?"

She nodded, ready to insist that she was doing just fine.

She'd thought the doctor was asleep again, but he opened his eyes. "You're alone in that big house?"

"I don't mind."

At least, she hadn't minded until Kent showed up. From the look on Timothy's face, he was remembering her hasty arrival.

The doctor looked at Timothy. "The dog?"

"Exactly what I was thinking."

Timothy smiled. "I have an idea, if you will permit me." He whistled a low three-note call, and a minute later Timothy's dog ambled toward them, waving his plumed tail.

"Hey you," Timothy said. "We need to have a talk."

The dog pricked up his ears and snuggled close—that was the only word for it—with his brown muzzle resting against Timothy's shoulder.

Timothy whispered something into the dog's ear, and the animal turned to look at Madeleine, as if he were sizing her up, once more.

"Put out your hand so he can sniff it," Timothy said.

She did so, and the dog's wet nose brushed her palm. He sat back on his haunches, as if he were waiting for something.

"Mission accepted," Timothy said. "Would you mind having a bodyguard for the night?"

"That's not necessary—"

"I think it is. He's the best watchdog I've ever had."

"But what about you? Won't you need him for something?"

"Not tonight. I'm going up to bed."

He pulled himself to his feet, and his slight body seemed to droop with fatigue. The doctor stood up too, saying, "Good night, Mrs. Burke."

So stiff and proper. He must be wishing he'd never mentioned that writing project. "Good night, Dr. Parnell."

Timothy gazed at her. "I don't mean to find fault, but may I point out that the doctor has a first name?"

His earnest expression made her want to laugh. "Really! And here I thought he sprang into the world with a tag attached to his big toe, saying—in all capitals— DOCTOR PARNELL."

"That's the morgue," the doctor said. A corner of his mouth quirked up.

"You're right, as almost always, doctor. My apologies." She turned to Timothy. "With a tag attached to his pink little thumb."

Timothy shook his head. "This is all my fault, I see it now. You two haven't been properly introduced."

His voice rose a notch as if he were laughing inside. "Madeleine, this is Nathan. And vice versa."

"Smoothly done," she said. "What next?"

"You're supposed to shake hands."

She wanted to put her hands behind her back, but the doctor seemed amused, giving her a look that said, 'Let's humor my friend.' He didn't move, allowing her to take the lead.

"Far be it from me to break the rules." She extended a hand, saying, "I am honored, Nathan, to make your acquaintance."

He took her hand, barely touching it, as if aware that she'd forced herself do this. "On the contrary, Madeleine, the pleasure is mine." He gave Timothy a mischievous glance. "Is this where I get to kiss the lady's hand?"

She pulled it away. "Certainly not! Think of the germs. No wonder all those people died in the Middle Ages."

No more kisses. She'd make sure of that.

But she smiled up at him—she wouldn't be rude, not again—and he smiled back.

The dog bumped against Timothy's knee, as if to mention that he'd been waiting through all this talk, and

Timothy said, "We didn't forget you, old boy. Just had to transact some important business."

She followed as Timothy limped into the store and turned toward the front, his big sneakers making an irregular *thum-thud* on the old floorboards.

She glanced at the dog beside them. "What's his name? I don't think I have any dog food."

Timothy pulled the door open. "His name is Hey-You. And he likes tuna sandwiches: no mayo, hold the pickles." He gazed at her. "I think you're going to sleep well, little lady. I saw you smile tonight for the first time. The Lord will use my companion to protect you."

CHAPTER 6

Can't wait to get started on my course.
It's going to open a door to my new life.
Independence!
~Journal

She stepped out onto the quiet sidewalk, and the dog followed. "Come, gallant protector," she said, "Let's go home."

The house stood dark, its bulk almost lost in the shadows, and she parked close to the porch. "I'm glad for your company, Sir Hey-You." She picked her way up the steps by the dim glow of the porch light, fumbling in her purse for the key.

As soon as they were inside, the dog disappeared on a tour of inspection. Her cell phone rang, startling her, but it was only Aunt Lin, saying she'd be coming back tomorrow afternoon.

By the time the dog returned, she'd made herself a peanut butter sandwich. "Tuna for you, sir?" She picked up a can of tuna, and his eyes widened. She forked half of the tuna onto a piece of bread, folded it, and set it on the floor.

Hey-You bent over the sandwich, and it vanished. He looked up at her—was that a grin?—and licked his chops with a long pink tongue.

She held out another sandwich. "More?" He took it daintily in his teeth and wolfed it down.

"Good work." She carried her snack into her bedroom, and Hey-You nosed the corners while she chose a cookbook to read. He dropped onto the rug, rested his head on his paws, and watched her, looking satisfied.

Under normal circumstances she would have been able to lose herself in a discussion of strudel pastry, but her thoughts insisted on darting back to the events of the evening. Besides, her feet were cold. Socks.

As soon as she moved, the dog sat to attention. She opened the bureau drawer, reached for her blue socks, and the paperweight rolled into her hand. The smooth cool surface warmed under her fingers.

Dad's present for her birthday, a month before he died.

She sat down with it and allowed herself to remember.

"Mountain laurel," he'd said of the star-shaped pink flowers. "The blooms look fragile. But the plants grow in rocky woods and swamps, and they're tough."

He put a hand on her shoulder. "Like you, Mollie— lovely, but tough inside."

His smile had blessed her. "Always remember, God loves you with His forever-love. I'm praying that He will keep you strong."

She quivered as if she'd been slapped, and grief whirled within her, dark and ravenous.

She closed her eyes. *I'm glad you can't see me now, Dad . . . Something's crippling me.*

After a time, she became aware of warmth that pressed against her knee. The dog gazed at her with troubled brown eyes, and she realized that she had been rocking back and forth, holding the paperweight to her cheek.

She stroked his soft muzzle and his tail thumped, and she stroked him some more. Finally she hauled herself to her feet. She slipped the paperweight inside a sock, rolled it up as if she were going to bury it, and put it back in the drawer.

She turned away, scuffed her feet into slippers, walked out of the room. What time was it? Late. She'd check that the doors were locked and get ready for bed.

The dog showed no inclination to leave. When she opened the bedroom window, he sniffed at the fresh-scented air and flopped back onto the rug as if he intended to stay.

A cold nose was nudging her hand. Sunlight filtered into the room. Ten o'clock already!

"Thanks a bunch, Hey-You," she said. "You did a great job!"

The dog wagged his tail, accepting her praise, and she sent him outside to run around while she got dressed. Breakfast was scrambled eggs with toast for her and two more sandwiches for him. She ate quickly, thinking about the day ahead.

Sunday morning. She'd already missed church, if there was one around, and anyway, she didn't feel inclined to go. Mother wasn't here to insist that it was the proper thing to do. Freedom!

She wouldn't unpack dusty bottles today. She'd take a walk with the dog, and sometime before Aunt Lin came back, she'd return him to Timothy.

Hey-You bounded ahead of her on the sandy path, detouring to investigate a mouse or chipmunk or whatever scent he picked up. She allowed herself to relax into the stillness of pine trees and sand-laced clearings.

There'd be wild blueberry bushes along here, from what Dad told her . . .

No! Pay attention to where you're going.

The path slanted down into a congregation of cedar trees, and a minute later she stood in their dignified midst. A wide, slow-moving stream flowed at her feet, sliding past the mossy roots that clung to its banks. It was a dim, enclosed place with the faint tang of cedar, a place for hopeful dreams.

The dog paused to lap at the water, crossed on a muddy plank, and disappeared into leather-leaved bushes on the other side.

The first time the path forked, she turned to the left and so did Hey-You, but at the next fork he turned right. He ran a short distance ahead and sat down.

His comical version of a come-hither look made her laugh. "Tyrant! I hope you know what you're doing."

After that, she let him lead, and she took careful note of the turns. When the sun had passed its zenith, she thought they'd better go back, but the trees were thinning ahead, and the path ended at a paved road. Whitton?

Sure enough, from here she could see the back of Timothy's store. Hey-You galloped ahead toward Timothy, who was leaning over the rail of a wide balcony. "Come on up," he called.

Hey-You raced up a staircase that slanted across one side of the building, and Timothy opened a gate at the top. "Looks like you both survived the night."

"We did. And Hey-You showed me how to get here." She patted the dog's head and turned away, saying, "I don't like to run off, but Aunt Lin will be back soon. Thanks again."

"You are most welcome," Timothy said. "Remember, he's here any time you need him."

She smiled into the warm brown eyes. "I'll remember."

Aunt Lin arrived before noon, and Madeleine help to unload her suitcase and cameras. The first thing her aunt noticed was the cake. She lifted its foil covering. "You didn't! Bless your heart, Madeleine." She tasted a smudge of icing from the foil. "It must be pretty good if you've eaten three pieces already. Mmm—it is!"

"I had some help, but I'll tell you about that," Madeleine said. "There's cold chicken and tomatoes for sandwiches."

"Wonderful."

While they were eating, her aunt asked, "Did you get outside?" At Madeleine's nod, she said, "Are you enjoying our pine woods?"

"Very much." How could she put it into words—the way these silent trees helped to smooth her splintered edges? "The other day when I took a run, I poked around in the ruins for a while," she said.

"The family's been pretty secretive about that place, but there's not much left, as you saw."

"Old stones are always interesting," Madeleine said. "Did your photo shoot go all right?"

"So far," Aunt Lin said. "We were half done when the owner suggested a different perspective, which means more research and another shoot, but it'll be worth it. I have to go back."

She took a bite of her sandwich and gazed out into the trees. "Wednesday. For who knows how long. I don't like to leave you again."

"I've got plenty to keep me busy," Madeleine said. "And Bria too. She's good. Her little brother came over, and I put him to work."

"From what I hear, that family can use the money. Did you find anything interesting upstairs?"

"Decoys. They might be antiques." Madeleine wanted to ask about Bria's family, but Aunt Lin was getting up.

"Let's go see."

On the way, her aunt stopped to look into the parlor. "What a difference!"

She paused beside the boxes in the hall. "Discards from the library? Good. I'll phone the Truck Guys." She eyed the worn green carpet. "I wonder what's underneath this old thing."

She tugged on a loose edge and it came up easily, revealing dusty planks of pine. "This goes too. Now show me the decoys."

Madeleine opened the trunk and lifted out the duck with a black-and-white head. "Jude called this a hooded merganser."

"Beautiful!" her aunt said. "I don't know about such things, but it looks valuable." Her green eyes glowed. "Your first project?"

"I'll check them out." Bria and Jude might be willing to help.

Aunt Lin gazed at the stuffed owl. "When I first met Cousin Henrietta, she was already in a nursing home, and rather strange," she said slowly. "She used to go to auctions just to talk to people, and then she ended up buying whole boxes of stuff."

On their way downstairs, Madeleine asked about the locked room.

"I noticed that," her aunt said, "and it made me laugh. Every old house has to have its mysterious locked room, doesn't it?"

"If you have a key, we could find out," Madeleine said. "Maybe she stashed boxes of jewels in the closet."

Aunt Lin smiled. "I never did find a key, so we might have to get a locksmith. It was a family joke, the way Henrietta loved jewelry, but I haven't seen a single bit."

"I'll keep my eyes open," Madeleine said, and they both laughed.

The phone in the kitchen began ringing. "They must have fixed the lines," her aunt said. "Hello? Oh, hi!" Her voice took on a lighter note. "Yes, had a good trip."

After she put the phone down, she said, "That was Kent. He wants to come over tonight with Remi, said you'd suggested an ice-cream party. What a good idea, Madeleine."

The skunk.

"Not quite accurate," she said. "Last night he arrived on my doorstep with ice cream and I decided that I needed to go do some research." She smiled, making it a trivial thing, and immediately wished she hadn't.

"I'm not surprised—he's always wanting to party." Her aunt shrugged. "I've learned not to take him too seriously. Kent is useful for local information and he's a charming date when he exerts himself, but that's about all. I said they could come for supper, if that's okay. I know you'll think of something good."

She smiled at Madeleine and yawned. "I need a shower and a quick nap. Then I'll help with the food."

Kent greeted her with his genial smile and was equally cordial to her aunt. Just as well. She had every intention of putting him in his place. Maybe he'd think twice before dropping in on her again.

She wore the same jeans and blue sweatshirt she'd had on all day, but her aunt had changed into slacks and an attractive green sweater. Remi had dressed for the occasion too. His curly black hair shone, and his open-necked white shirt showed off a chain that glittered against his tan skin.

Kent was pleasant, often humorous, and except for the occasional digression about his book, carried on an interesting conversation with her aunt. As the evening progressed, Madeleine began to wonder whether she'd misjudged him.

Along with the ice cream, he'd brought them a gift— the game of Monopoly. She expected him to be a noisy, aggressive competitor, but he played silently, took wild chances, and looked wounded when he had a setback. Aunt Lin's careful strategy put her into the lead, and she stayed there. Remi played well too, but he was kind, apologizing as he foreclosed on Madeleine's houses and giving advice that kept her from going bankrupt.

Finally Kent kicked back his chair and left the table. "I've had it," he said. "Give Madeleine my properties. Looks like she could use them."

He strolled into the dining room and returned with the Cohansey jar. "The old glass stuff fascinates me," he said. "I was right about this one. It's a genuine antique." He handed it to Remi. "What did they use it for?"

Remi put down a handful of bills from the game. "Canning fruit," he said. "Produced around 1850. Too bad the covers are missing." He turned it over. "Hand made. See the pontil mark—that little scar?"

Kent looked gratified. "You're doing your homework, kid."

Remi glowed at the careless praise, and something about the expression on his face stung Madeleine. The "kid" must have a case of hero-worship.

Kent started back to the dining room. "You've got a treasure trove, Lin, historically speaking. I'd like to make use of it for my book."

He glanced back at Remi. "Did we bring the camera?"

"Always." Remi pulled a small digital camera out of his shirt pocket.

"Here," Kent said. "Take some pictures of me holding this jar. Make sure the name shows clearly."

Kent beamed as Remi took the photos. "Now that I'm over my cold, I must say that the book is going well."

Aunt Lin was putting the game away. "How about researching some genuine New Jersey carrot cake to go along with the ice cream you brought?"

"Great idea," Kent said, and Remi looked appreciative.

While Madeleine cut the cake, Kent began telling her about a place called Batsto. "It's like a reconstructed village, with a museum," he said, and described the farm buildings and restored mansion in careful detail.

"We could go see it tomorrow," Aunt Lin said.

"They've got a pretty decent bookstore too," Remi said.

"I'd like that." Madeleine took a spoonful of ice cream. "Do they have anything about duck decoys?"

"Probably," Kent said. "And if you're interested in cemeteries, there's an old one just down the road. I've found some good leads there for my book."

Remi grinned. *"Let's talk of graves, of worms, of epitaphs . . ."*

It took her a minute, but then she had it. "Shakespeare," she said. "Richard II." Why hadn't Remi gone to college?

His eyes sparkled. "Yeah, that old guy sure could write. How come you know him?"

"I taught British Lit for a while."

Remi leaned forward to say something more, but Kent interrupted. "This is good cake, Madeleine. Homemade?"

"Yes." Should she tell him that Jude, one of those "nuisance kids" had done most of the work? No; she'd probably end by apologizing or doing something equally mousey.

Finally Kent stood up to make a graceful exit, and Remi echoed his words. "Farewell, ladies. See you tomorrow."

That night, as she wrote in her journal, Madeleine hesitated over what to say about Kent. She settled on: *Self-centered but probably harmless. Unpredictable. Do I still think he's an eager puppy? Not sure. He tries to impress.*

By morning, wind screeched around the corners of the house and rain pounded on the roof. No Batsto today, and Madeleine didn't mind. If she had any spare time, she'd rather spend it at Timothy's store, getting started on her course.

She and Aunt Lin made plans for organizing the china, glassware, and oddments still on the dining room table. They began investigating the rest of the cabinets, and the morning passed quickly.

After lunch Aunt Lin phoned the Truck Guys and came back looking disappointed. "Not until tomorrow. I asked about boxes, and they don't have any left."

Madeleine wondered aloud whether Timothy might have boxes, and her aunt said, "He probably does. He'll let you have them, I'm sure." She paused in the kitchen doorway, looking preoccupied. "My partner phoned. He's come up with another great idea, which means I've got a lot of work to do before Wednesday."

She left the kitchen, murmuring to herself, and Madeleine knew she wouldn't reappear until evening. What next? She'd finish up that cabinet, and go see Timothy. Take the laptop.

CHAPTER 7

Timothy keeps surprising me.
He looks like a little old gnome,
but he's funny and wise and kind.
I feel as if I can tell him . . . some things.
~Journal

The street was lined with cars, but Timothy's store looked empty. What was the attraction on this rainy day? He answered from a corner when she called his name, and she found him standing on a box beside a stack of canned peaches.

"Where's the big sale?" she asked. "Or the fire?"

"All those cars? Monday and Tuesday mornings are Free Clinic. Nathan and a couple of other doctors run it together."

"Free?"

"Almost. A lot of people around here don't have insurance, so the doctors arranged for them to pay what they can."

"They won't break even, will they?"

"Probably not, but it was Nathan's idea, and he's convinced the other doctors that it's important. Did you come to work on your course?"

"I did. Are you hungry yet?"

He smiled, turned back to the canned peaches, lost his balance, and almost fell off the box. Half of the cans tumbled to the floor.

"Careful!" Madeleine picked them up. "You should have a stepladder."

"I do, but someone borrowed it."

"I think I know who."

"I didn't mind. He said he needed it."

"I have a feeling he'll bring it back soon," she said. "Can I help? What did you want this display to look like?"

The old man lowered himself to the floor. "I thought a pyramid might be effective, maybe with a sign. Something about fresh-picked flavor."

"Sounds good." She began arranging the cans. "Do you have any more of these?"

"In the back."

The doorbell jingled, and a gaunt, red-haired man strolled in. His jeans were stained at the knees, and his jacket looked as if he'd been using it to wipe up an oil spill. One hand was bandaged. Had he just come from the clinic? He hunched over the display case while he waited for Timothy.

The man made a purchase, answered Timothy's question with a grunt, and ambled back out into the rain.

"Not very talkative, is he?" Madeleine said.

Timothy's smile was forbearing. "Sid's a good mechanic when he's sober."

"Does he fix cars?"

"He can fix anything on wheels. You have a car problem?"

"I guess I need a new bumper and a paint job, so I'm looking around."

Timothy was kind enough not to ask how she'd damaged her car. "I can give you Sid's number," he said. "Maybe you'll catch him on a good day."

While he wrote it down, she asked, "Do you know him very well?"

"Not especially. He comes in to buy spark plugs and always looks at those paperweights." His face softened. "Always says he's going to buy one for his little girl someday."

She took the number, although she wasn't sure she wanted to hire a man with a drinking problem, and Timothy started for the back of his store, saying, "I'll get you another case of those peaches."

While they built a larger display, he talked for a while about the store. Then, after handing her another can, he asked, "How are you doing these days, little lady?"

She placed the can with more precision than necessary. "I began a new life when I came here." She tried to sound brisk and capable. "So it's hard to tell. A new situation, new people. I'm sure it will all be fine."

Fine. The word seemed to hang like a small dark cloud just above them. He must know that Dad had been shot, and Aunt Lin had probably told him about Brenn's accident. How could she expect him to believe that everything was fine?

He looked up at her with his searching gaze. "The other night, you were running away from someone."

"An evasive tactic, you might say. It worked."

"Good for you." He bent to get more cans from the box. "Hey-You is taking a nap right now, but he sends greetings. He reported that you make an excellent tuna sandwich."

They laughed together, and he said, "Tell me what you've discovered in your new life."

She rearranged two of the cans, wondering how to answer. She wasn't going to admit to anyone, even Timothy, that her new life wasn't what she'd envisioned. "You wouldn't believe all the cartons full of stuff in that house," she finally said. "And one of the rooms is locked."

She stepped down off the box. "There. How does it look?"

"Just the way I hoped it would."

She eyed the scribbled little signs on each aisle. "Would you like me to make the sign?"

"Capital! I've got a few markers. And I've got paper too, or would you rather have poster board?"

He produced everything she suggested for a simple sign, and after she hung it in place, he beamed. "I'd buy some peaches myself if I didn't have plenty." He nodded toward the office. "I won't keep you from your work any longer. Go ahead."

Once she got online, it didn't take long. She registered for the course, paid for it, and downloaded the syllabus and videos she'd need for the first module. Plenty to keep her busy. But she had forgotten to get boxes for the Manor.

She went out to ask Timothy and caught sight of the decoys in his display case. Better learn what she could.

"Those ducks," she said. "Are they for sale?"

"Seventy-five dollars each," Timothy said. "They're made by a local woman, Paula Castell."

The name wasn't familiar, but Bria might know of her. "Would older decoys sell for more than that?"

"Usually. It depends on their condition and the artist's reputation."

She bent over the case. "That's a mallard, right? What are the other two?"

"Green winged teal—a drake and a hen." Timothy handed her the drake. "Realistic, isn't it?"

The duck was surprisingly light, and it had a personable expression in its eyes. "We came across some decoys," she said, "and they look old. I need to find out whether they're valuable."

"I just sell them," Timothy said, "but I know someone who might help you out."

"Around here?"

"Yes, indeed. Dan'l Forbes by name." Timothy glanced at his watch. "We could go visit him now, if you have time."

"What about the store?"

"All my customers? They'll come back. This will be my late lunch. You don't have to go home right away, do you?"

"No, but I meant to ask—do you have any empty boxes we could use at the Manor?"

"I do. We'll break them down and put them in your car. Follow me in case you want to visit Dan'l again."

Madeleine drove close behind Timothy's old black pickup, trying to watch for landmarks and count the turns. Before long he left the paved road, and it was all she could do to keep him in sight. His truck rocked over the rutted sand, and the only time he slowed was when he splashed into a swampy puddle that spread across the road. She drove gingerly through it, hoping she wouldn't get stuck.

Soon after, he turned again, this time into a long, sandy driveway. On either side were rain-streaked cars in stages of disrepair. One was perched on cement blocks, two were sharing their space with bushes, and two more looked like rusted blue ships afloat in the grass.

They parked beside a green car with the sweeping tail fins of the late fifties, and Timothy motioned her ahead to the cottage. She hung back as he skirted a pile of firewood and limped up the porch steps, avoiding the splintered holes in the planks.

"Hello, Dan'l?" he called. "Anybody home?"

A voice replied, indistinguishable but hearty.

Timothy opened the rusted screen door and paused to glance into a darkened room. Together they picked their way toward the lighted kitchen, past shadowy masses of furniture, a wood stove, and a rifle that leaned against the kitchen doorway.

Dan'l, wearing the same plaid shirt as the first time she'd seen him, looked up from the newspapers he'd scattered across a dented wooden table.

"Timothy! With the young Miss! This sure is an occasion. It sure is." He stood to his feet with a grunt, and looked her over with careful blue eyes. "I was just goin' to have myself another dish of tea. How about you? Sure you'd like some."

He stacked the newspapers and pulled two straight-backed chairs away from the table. "Go ahead! Sit down, both of you."

He took thick white china cups from a shelf, dropped a tea bag into each one, and filled them from the kettle on the stove. After refilling his own cup, he pushed a pink sugar bowl across the table toward them.

"Thank you kindly," Timothy said. "Might there be a spoon for the sugar?"

"Sure!" Dan'l reached across the counter to a can filled with spoons and forks. "Here's a nice clean one."

The counter also held unwashed dishes, a frying pan, a box of cornflakes, cans of baked beans, a wrench, a hammer, three screwdrivers, and a bucket of water. Nothing was particularly clean, but neither was it filthy.

Timothy spooned sugar into his cup and stirred. "How's your car been doing these days?"

"Can't complain, I guess. Got lucky and missed a deer the other night, so it don't have any new dents."

The men talked about cars while Madeleine sipped her tea and looked around. She found herself thinking critically—as her mother would—about the old man and his kitchen with its faded green wallpaper.

But most likely he'd lived here all his life, and he was a bachelor as well. Was he a lesser person because his kitchen didn't fit into middle-class notions of a sanitized life? Wasn't it more important to take note of his kindness and courtesy?

She tightened her grip on the cup as if it might be snatched away. What about her new life? Maybe she should try a different way of looking at people.

Dan'l turned his gaze upon her. "So they're doing some work on the Manor? I've heard that aunt of yours is sweeping it out with a new broom."

Madeleine smiled at the way he'd put it. "She certainly is."

"Tell him what you found," Timothy said.

"Some decoys," she said. How had Bria identified them? "Two mergansers and a black duck. They look hand-carved."

"Old?"

"I think so. They're weathered, and the paint on the black duck is scratched."

Dan'l nodded. "Probably shot over it." He leaned forward. "Were they signed? Did you see anything like a signature on the bottom?"

Bria had looked for one. "I don't think so."

"I sure would like to see them sometime. Sure would. I used to make decoys, and so did my friends. Everybody's got their own style, you know? I might recognize one of them."

"I was hoping you could tell me whether they're valuable. And something about how they're made."

He rubbed at a shaggy eyebrow. "You writing a book too? Got more people around asking questions."

She smiled, wanting to put him at ease. "Just curious. Timothy showed me a couple of the decoys in his store."

"I made some pretty good decoys in my time," Dan'l said. He looked down at the swollen joints of his hands. "Not any more. That new doctor gave me some pills, but I keep forgetting to take them. Not his fault. He's a good neighbor, I can tell you—comes over, and we swap fishing tales. He used to live in Alaska, you know that?"

"Yes," Timothy said.

"That's right. He's a friend of yours. Now what were we talking about? Decoys." He thought for a minute. "That woman, what's her name—the one who makes 'em for you?"

"Paula Castell?"

"She carves them at her house. I don't know how she manages, the way she is now." He gave Madeleine a measuring glance. "She might show you what she does."

"A fine idea," Timothy said. "Thanks for the tea, Dan'l. I'm going to have a line of customers if I don't get back soon."

He pulled himself to his feet, and Madeleine stood too.

"Bring those decoys by any time you want. I'll tell you what I think." Dan'l grinned. "I'm most always here."

"I'd like to do that," Madeleine said. She should stop trying to label the man. He was an original antique, more intriguing than anything made of wood.

On their way across the porch, she glanced at two small cabins half-hidden in the trees. Water gleamed behind them. "Is that a lake back there?"

"A cranberry bog," Timothy said. "It belongs to Dan'l. He turfed it out himself."

He turned to get into his truck. "Dan'l is right. I should have thought of Paula. She's the best person to ask about decoys. She might be interested in seeing the ones you found. For sure, her children would be."

"Her children?"

"Doesn't Bria work for your aunt?" He climbed into his truck. "I'll take you back to the main road, and then you'll know where you are."

"Thank you," Madeleine said. Bria and Jude were Paula's children? No wonder they'd looked at those decoys with such interest. She'd have to ask them a few more questions.

Overnight, the rain continued but temperatures dropped, and Madeleine thought about old Dan'l. How would he stay warm? Maybe he'd fire up that wood stove and sit close to it.

For breakfast she had made scones, her first baking project. She'd tried out two different recipes: blueberry streusel and lemon ginger. According to Aunt Lin, they were both successful. Her aunt had been encouraging when Madeleine told her about the class, but now she was positively enthusiastic.

Afterward, she took samples of the scones to the store for Timothy and showed him the online form to use for his evaluation. Once again, cars were clustered by the clinic. Had the doctor found time to work on his writing project? She wouldn't ask, even if she did see him.

Back at the Manor, she worked steadily, and the day's highlight was a visit from the Truck Guys. They loaded all the boxes of discards and took the green carpet too.

Aunt Lin smiled as they drove away. "Better and better!"

The next day, Aunt Lin left early, and Bria and Jude arrived in the afternoon. "I see you got rid of that old rug on the stairs," Bria said with a trace of a smile. She waxed the steps and Jude helped to polish them.

"Did you find any more interesting stuff upstairs?" he asked.

"I haven't looked," Madeleine said. "I wish we had a key for that room."

"What room?"

She showed him the door at the end of the hall, and he studied its old-fashioned lock. "Easy," he said. "Have you got a coat hanger? The wire kind."

By the time she found a hanger, Jude was coming out of the pantry with wire cutters and a pair of pliers. He snipped off a piece of the hangar and bent it into an L shape. "Let's see how this works."

He poked the wire into the lock, shook his head, pulled it out, snipped off a fraction of an inch, and tried again. Something clicked, and he grinned as he turned the doorknob.

This room felt different from the rest of the house. A red-checked quilt lay smooth on the narrow bed. The braided rug had not been rumpled for years. Toys on the shelves stood in precise order, furred with dust.

Jude broke the silence. "It's a kid's room." He shot a longing glance at the red model plane suspended over their heads. "Huh," he said, "a rich kid."

"Don't touch anything," Bria said.

On the top shelf, wooden blocks rose beside a fleet of tiny metal trucks. Pairs of brightly-painted Noah's Ark animals marched past the trucks. On the lower shelf, a metal coin bank shaped like a house stood next to an open box of marbles.

Jude blew the dust off the marbles. "Red ones are missing," he said. "Must have been his favorites."

Madeleine took a step backward. Grief hung in the room like the odor of something walled up, decaying, and it filled her lungs with an intolerable stench. She wanted to turn and run.

"I wonder," Jude said. "I wonder what happened to him."

But after so many years, what did it matter? Only that he was gone and would never come back.

Jude turned to an oak cabinet. "Can I open this?"

Madeleine nodded yes, but she edged toward the door. She shouldn't be breathing this air.

The cabinet held an elaborate train set, unused. Nearby, a closet was filled with clothes the size of a young boy.

They followed her out of the room, and she quickly pulled the door shut.

Think about something else. "Jude, where did you ever learn to open locks like that?"

Bria laughed, a brittle sound in the dim hallway. "You don't want to know. It does come in handy, though."

Madeleine started down the hall. Get busy and do something.

She paused beside the storage room. "Let's look at those decoys again."

Jude opened the trunk. She lifted out one of the mergansers and handed it to Bria. "Your family makes decoys, right? Can you tell me how you do it?"

Bria turned the bird over in her hands as if she were inspecting it for cracks. "All I do is paint them."

"Jude, what do you do?"

"Cut out the chunks of wood."

The two of them seemed to have an unspoken pact to say as little as possible.

Madeleine chose her words with care. "Aunt Lin wants me to learn about decoys. Do you think I could visit your workshop?"

Bria stared at the floor. Jude shifted his gaze when Madeleine glanced at him. "It's not our workshop." His words came out in a mumble.

"Whose is it?"

"Our mother's."

So that was it. Protecting their mother?

"Do you think she would let me visit, for just a few minutes?"

Jude fidgeted. "She don't like visitors."

"Doesn't," Bria said. *"Doesn't* like visitors." She handed the decoy back.

"What if I sent her a gift?" Madeleine said. She couldn't let this chance slip away. "What does she like to eat?"

The two exchanged a glance. "Fudge cake," Jude said. He looked interested, but Bria had a wooden expression on her face.

"That's it!" Madeleine filled her voice with cheer. "How about we make her a cake this afternoon, and you take it home and ask if I can come and visit tomorrow? What's a good time?"

"After school," Jude said.

"Perfect," Madeleine said. She looked at Bria. "Can you work tomorrow morning?"

"No."

"Then could you phone tonight and tell me? Do you have a phone?" Madeleine busied herself with putting the decoy back into the trunk.

"Sure we have a phone," Jude said. "What's your number?"

Madeleine tore a page out of her notebook and wrote her cell phone number on it. "Here."

Bria's dark eyes were shadowed. "We'll . . . have to see."

CHAPTER 8

Jude—he's shy but inquisitive;
self-assured and protective.
He seems to have secrets too, like Bria.
Not your average teen.
~Journal

Jude liked Madeleine's fudge cake recipe and did most of the work himself. She packed it into a box for him to tie onto his bike, Bria warned him not to try jumping over puddles, and they were gone.

Tonight she wanted to do some serious course work. Her next project was French Bread, and from reading the syllabus, she discovered that she was expected to write a paper on the reasons that it had declined in quality over the years.

The article she'd downloaded wasn't much more than an introduction. One of her cookbooks had a short section on the history of breads, but tomorrow morning she should go back to the store and see what she could find online.

She began reading about artisan breads and stopped to wonder why Bria hadn't phoned yet. The look on the girl's face, was it dread? Something was wrong in that family.

The evening dragged on. Her mother called, and then she took a shower, and finally her phone rang again. Jude's voice sounded deep and grown-up. "Mom liked the cake, a lot. She said it's okay for you to come. I'll walk over after school and get you."

"Thanks, Jude."

She felt like singing as she put down her phone. Why was this visit so important? For her research, of course. But those two—was she beginning to care about them? Perhaps.

First thing the next morning, she set off for Timothy's. She would download everything she could find about French bread and get a good start on that paper. What had Timothy thought of her scones?

Since he was busy with customers, she went right to his office. She found an article by a Cornell professor and was taking notes from it when the doctor came in.

He nodded to her, poured himself some coffee, and sat on the sofa to drink it.

Moving kind of slowly, wasn't he? Not a morning person?

She found another article to read. All of this could go into her paper. How should she organize it? She began outlining her ideas.

He got up, rinsed his cup at the sink, and came to stand beside her.

"Yes . . ." she said, finishing a sentence.

"I didn't think you were so reckless." He had a smile in his voice.

She leaned back to look up at him. "Wait a minute. That was an interrogative sort of *yes*, not 'your wish is my command.' "

"Just checking." His face sobered. "I've been afraid you'd ask about that piece I'm supposed to be writing."

"I've been careful not to."

He leaned against the table, gazing down at her. "I'm grateful for that. You made it sound easy—just weave in the story, transplant a heart."

She studied his face. Except for the scar, it was gray, the lines etched more deeply than usual. Worry? More likely just plain tired.

"You look worn out," she said. "You can't expect your brain to work without sleep. That's tough writing, doctor."

"You're not supposed to call me that."

"Nathan." She smiled at him. "Take a nap."

"Yes," he said. "Not interrogative."

He strolled back to the sofa. She finished her outline and downloaded a half-dozen more files to read at home. The next time she looked up, he was stretched out on the sofa, asleep. At least he didn't snore.

She pulled her thoughts back to the task at hand, worked until she had more than enough information, and went to find Timothy. He was in the storeroom unpacking boxes of corn flakes.

"Here she comes, the scone princess," he said.

She laughed. "I hope you didn't put that in your report. They might wonder about your objectivity."

He stacked boxes into a faded red wagon. "I put plenty in my report, but not that. My biggest challenge was deciding which variety to evaluate."

"And?"

"I did the blueberry ones. I've eaten a lot of them in my time, and those were exceptional."

"I'm glad. The next project is French bread, complete with a paper to write."

"Are you going to write it here? Our printer finally came."

"That's good news, but I have what I need for now, and I'm going back to the Manor. Your friend is asleep on your sofa, by the way."

"I'm not surprised. He was up all night with the little Shupert girl."

"I didn't think doctors made house calls anymore."

"This one does. He's the most determined man I know."

That afternoon when Jude knocked on the door, he was breathing fast, as if he'd run all the way from school.

"We could drive," she said.

The eagerness drained from his face. "No cars. Not today. She don't—doesn't—like the sound of them. She'll like you better if we walk."

He led the way with a swift, loping gait, and she concentrated on matching his pace instead of puzzling over what he'd said. A chilly breeze swept them on their way.

The forest varied with each turn of the path—countless pines, oaks with russet leaves, thickets of dark cedars. They came to a grove of charred pines that were nothing more than blackened skeletons. Some of them had a fuzz of green at the tips of their branches, and knee-high ferns grew among them.

"Forest fire," Jude said, "but the pines always come back."

She knew that. Dad had camped in the Pine Barrens. He'd told her about the pitch pines, how they survived fires.

She thrust the memory aside and answered Jude's question about hiking on the Appalachian Trail.

"I knew you were a hiker," he said, "when I saw you out here the other day." A fleeting *scritch* stopped him short. "Lots of red squirrels around." He pointed at a small pile of pinecone bracts beneath the tree. "There's his feeding station."

They paused to cross a stream, and he began walking more quickly. A few minutes later he veered onto a narrow path that led to a clearing.

Before them stood a brown bungalow with twin dormers. The house seemed to droop, perhaps because a gutter had come loose and slanted down in front of the porch.

Jude caught the direction of her gaze and muttered, "Got to fix that."

Bria met them at the door, her mouth set in a tense line. "There you are. Mother's in the living room."

Paula Castell sat upright in a fiddle-back chair, her hands folded in her lap, unmoving as a blonde porcelain doll.

After a long minute of silence, she turned her head. "Hello, hello! Come and join us." She waved gracefully at the table beside her, set with fragile-looking cups and plates. "We were just having our tea."

She sounded as if she were reciting the lines of a play. The room itself, with flower-sprigged wallpaper and Queen Anne furniture, looked like a set designed for this scene.

Madeleine perched on the edge of a wing chair, and Jude dropped into another. Bria hovered in the doorway.

Paula Castell inclined her head. "I'm so glad you could come for a visit." She seemed to be looking past Madeleine, past the walls of the house into the trees. "Are you writing a book too? It's such a great deal of work, I hear."

Madeleine tried to reach her with a smile. "I'm helping my aunt restore an old house. We found some decoys, and I was—"

"—Brianna, is the tea ready?" her mother said. "We are waiting to be served."

Jude leaped to his feet, and a minute later, Bria carried in a silver teapot. Behind her came Jude with a platter of sliced cake, the one they had baked yesterday.

Bria poured a cup of tea and handed it to her mother, but she said, "Cake first, please."

Jude slid a piece of cake onto a plate, and she took it from him with a smile. "Fudge cake! It's delicious." She gazed at a point somewhere above Madeleine's head. "A kind lady made it for us."

Jude flushed, but his voice was gentle. "Mother, this is Mrs. Burke, the lady who made it for us. She wants to know about your decoys."

Her blue eyes widened, and she laughed, a silvery sound. "Of course! Brianna, Jude, have some tea with us."

Bria poured the tea while Jude served the cake, and silence fell. Paula Castell wore a meditative look that no one seemed disposed to interrupt. Madeleine drank her tea and tried to look meditative as well, but Jude ate his cake in three bites and then started on his thumbnail. Bria studied the carpet as if she were analyzing its colors.

Paula Castell finished the last crumbs of her cake. "Now, what were we talking about?"

"Decoys," Jude said. He nodded toward the next room, which held a long table with tools, unpainted decoys, and blocks of light-colored wood. "She wants to see how we make them."

The blue eyes gazed at Madeleine as if this were a fascinating new topic. "How nice. Did you know my grandfather?" She put a hand on the worn rocking chair beside her. "This is where he sits. He's really the one you should talk to. I learned everything from him."

Jude twitched forward. "Can Bria show her a decoy?"

Bria gave her mother a vigilant look, but the woman didn't object, so she stepped into the workroom and soon returned.

"Here's a canvas back duck," she said.

"What beautiful colors!" Madeleine said. Its head was chestnut-bronze shading into a black breast, its back and sides white. Compared with the decoys from the trunk, this one glowed.

She turned to Bria's mother. "I understand that you carve these yourself, Mrs. Castell."

The woman's eyes clouded. "Please, call me Paula. I don't use that other name any more." She rose to her feet, poised and erect. "It has been very nice having you over. I hope you'll come again someday. Perhaps we'll have another cake by then."

For an instant, Madeleine couldn't move. Then she stood too, smiling into the shadowed blue eyes. "Thank you very much. I've enjoyed meeting you."

To Jude, chewing on his lip, and Bria, white-faced, she said, "Thank you for the tea." She gave them a don't-you-worry smile. "That's the prettiest decoy I've seen."

Bria followed her to the door. "I'll come over on Saturday," she said in a low voice.

"I'll be glad for your help." Madeleine took a last look at the tall blonde woman, now gazing into the workroom, and stepped outside.

"I'm sorry," she said to Jude, "but I can't find my way back without your help."

A smile eclipsed the worry on his face, making him look young again. "That's okay. I'll show you." They left the house and soon turned onto the wider trail. "We need to make you a map," he said.

"That's what I was thinking. Everything looks the same in these woods."

Jude told her a complicated story about two of his friends, how they'd wandered in circles for a whole weekend, but her thoughts kept returning to his mother.

Paula Castell . . . Abstracted? Unstable? Drugged?

No wonder they hadn't wanted her to visit.

"Sorry," Jude said. "I guess you didn't find out very much." He kicked a pinecone off the path. "Sometimes she has a bad day."

"Don't let it bother you. Maybe I can come back when she's feeling better."

Meanwhile, she'd have to research the decoys some other way.

They crossed a swampy spot in the path. "She got along okay with you," he said. "Not like some of the others."

"Do you get a lot of visitors?"

"Once in a while, because of the decoys. She sends them away. She likes Kent Sanders, though. He's supposed to be a cousin of ours. He's got this book he's working on, and he keeps talking to Mom about it."

Yes, Kent would talk your ear off about his book. So that's how he knew them.

Jude didn't say anything more until they crossed another stream. He waved a hand into the woods. "There's some ruins over there."

"I like ruins."

"We've got a whole bunch of 'em in these woods," he said, and interrupted himself to glance at his watch.

"What's the matter?"

"It's Gemma."

Bria had mentioned a grandmother. Did she live with them?

"I've got a test I'm supposed to be studying for," he said, "and I forgot to tell her where I was going."

"Better run!" Madeleine said. "I can get back from here. And thanks for showing me the way."

"Okay!" He took off at a trot.

That evening Madeleine took her laptop into the kitchen so she could refer to the recipe for a French baguette. She had watched the video, gathered her tools—except she didn't have a scale for the flour—and was ready. How hard could it be, anyway, with only four ingredients?

She chose a Bach CD from Aunt Lin's collection and began.

The kneading wasn't as easy as it looked on the video, but it was pleasant to feel the dough become supple and elastic under her hands. She set it to rise and worked on her paper until the dough had gone through its two risings and was ready to form into loaves.

She plopped it out onto the kneading board, and the phone rang.

Kent. He said that tomorrow he and Remi were going to a place called Widow Bentley's Attic and he thought she could find some useful information there. Would she like to come along?

She hesitated. "Are you sure Remi's going?"

"Wouldn't miss it. He likes talking to the widow's granddaughter."

"Okay," she said. She'd check out their website and drive her own car.

"It'll do you good to get out." He sounded like a genial doctor. "See you around ten o'clock."

Widow Bentley's Attic? She pictured Remi flirting with the widow's granddaughter and smiled to herself. That would be fun to watch.

She should have said something to Kent about the stepladder he'd borrowed from Timothy. So gallant, letting her think it was his. She would set it on the porch and make sure he took it back.

The dough was still waiting for her. She shaped it into three loaves, which gave her only a little trouble, slashed the tops as directed, and stood back to admire them. Just like the picture. Into the oven now, and she'd have fresh bread for a snack.

By the time she'd cleaned up, the kitchen was filled with the mouth-watering aroma of baking bread. The timer rang, she took the baguettes out of the oven, and immediately knew something was wrong. They had browned nicely, but they looked like . . . sticks.

She picked up one and broke it open. Crust too hard. Dense inside.

Check the recipe.

The third rise! She'd forgotten it. After Kent phoned, she hadn't gone back to the recipe. She'd just shaped the loaves and put them in to bake. And she'd also forgotten to set a bowl of water beside them in the oven.

She ate half of one anyway, dunked into cocoa, but didn't have the heart to finish it. Try again tomorrow.

The next morning she made a quick trip to the store to check out *widowbentleysattic.com*, studied a list of their books, and printed out directions for getting there.

When Kent's Bronco drew up behind the house, no one sat in the passenger's seat.

He hadn't taken her hint, had he?

"Good morning!" Kent smiled, striding toward her. "Don't you look pretty today! Like a woods elf, I think, with that brown jacket and your shiny dark hair."

"Pointy ears too?"

His smile faded, and for an instant she felt sorry for him, but then he said, "No, your ears are as cute as the rest of you."

Best to ignore this. "Where's Remi?"

"Oh," Kent looked uneasy. "He got held up. He'll join us there."

Not likely.

"The stepladder," she said.

He frowned. "What?"

"The one you borrowed from Timothy for us to use—he needs it back. It's over there." She waved at the porch behind her.

His brow cleared. "I'll come get it sometime."

"Why don't you put it into your car now? You can drop it off on your way through town. Timothy needs it."

He opened his mouth to protest, but something about the look on her face must have made him change his mind. "Whatever you say, elfin princess."

While he was getting the ladder, she slid into her car and started the engine. He stopped with the ladder halfway to the Bronco. "You don't have to drive. Why don't you ride with me?"

"That's kind of you, but I want to shop on the way back." She waved her printout. "I've got directions."

He gave her a salute before climbing into his Bronco, and she followed his sedate progress down the driveway. He remembered to stop at Timothy's store, and then they headed out to Route 532, past Chatsworth.

Widow Bentley's Attic turned out to be a restored Victorian, complete with gingerbread trim. In the parking lot, Remi was leaning against the fender of a dented black truck.

Kent grinned at him. "I thought you'd be talking to that girl."

Remi made a face. "She's not working today."

"Tough luck," Kent said. "Now, Madeleine, we'll show you around."

He stopped his elvish nonsense and became an entertaining tour guide. Each room in the building had a theme relating to the Pine Barrens, with displays on woodcraft, iron production, and glass blowing.

In the early American room, a table was set with period linens and china, along with goblets, cruets, relish dishes, and a covered cake plate, all hand-blown glass.

"This is fascinating," Madeleine said.

Kent looked smug. "Worth the trip?"

"Yes, and me without my camera."

"Not to worry," Kent said. "I'm sure Remi will take pictures of anything your heart desires."

"Sure thing." Remi took out the camera. "What do you want?"

"One or two shots of the whole table, from different angles, please, and then a few close-ups."

Remi circled the table, snapping one photo after another, while Madeleine wrote in her notebook. "Especially that relish dish," she said. "I think I've seen one like it at the Manor."

Remi bent over the dish.

A voice spoke from the shadows. "That will be close enough."

Remi straightened, his eyes wide.

A skeleton of a man shuffled toward them. His hair and face were so white, they might have been powdered. "Beware, young man." His voice cracked, as if dust lay thick on his vocal cords. "You don't want to fall into all that expensive glass." He wheezed out a laugh. "You'd spend the rest of your life paying for it."

"Yes sir, I'll be careful," Remi said.

The old man tilted forward, watching as Remi took the picture.

"Thanks," Madeleine said in a low voice. "That's plenty. Where's the bookstore?"

The man trailed after them. "He's going to keep an eye on us," Remi whispered. "Beware, don't fall into the books."

Madeleine found the books she wanted, and as soon as they were out in the parking lot, she said, "Whew! Who was that?"

For once Kent said something clever. "Must be the Widow Bentley's husband."

"Vex not his ghost," Remi said, throwing a glance at Madeleine, and she laughed with him. *Macbeth* again.

"Time for lunch," Kent said, "and I know just the place." He took them to a nearby restaurant and insisted on treating them to thick meaty sandwiches that he called "genuine New Jersey subs."

Afterwards, she thanked them both and drove back to buy milk and eggs at Timothy's store. Widow Bentley's Attic had been more fun than she expected. Had she misjudged Kent? He'd been charming and generous. Why did she always have to be so critical? Give the guy a break.

CHAPTER 9

Timothy seems to have a gift of empathy.
Wish I had it too.
I don't want to be critical—or judgmental—
of people like Dan'l or Paula Castell.
But where does compassion come from?
~Journal

Hey-You ambled across the store, waving his tail, and escorted her into Timothy's office. The table was covered with pieces of soft yellow fabric, and at the far end, behind a sewing machine, sat Timothy.

"I apologize for not getting up," he said. "Zippers give me trouble."

"I have to take a firm hand with them, myself," she said. "What's your project?"

"A bunting."

She picked up the pattern from the table. A bunting always reminded her of a miniature snowsuit, but her friends said it was the coziest thing in the world for a baby.

Timothy bent over his work, and the sewing machine whirred as he guided the fabric through it. He seemed to be concentrating, so she held back her questions.

After a minute, the machine stopped and he said, "Too bad. I'll have to rip it out again."

"You sound like me. I tried making a baguette last night, and it was terrible. I'll keep it to beat off the burglars and try again."

He leaned back, smiling. "You look as if you've had a good morning."

"I did. We went to a place called Widow Bentley's Attic. It's quite something."

"Indeed it is," he said. "You went with your aunt?" He pulled himself to his feet, gathered a handful of yellow pieces, and took them to the ironing board.

"No, she's gone again. I went with Kent and Remi."

"I'm just going to press these sleeve pieces." He pointed to a chair. "Stay a minute. Tell me what you saw."

She described the displays, and the books she'd bought, and the ghostly old man who waited on them. She hadn't planned to say anything about Kent, but Timothy might give her some insights.

"Sometimes Kent is a bit too . . . attentive," she said, "and sometimes he's irritating, but we had such a good time today, I might have to change my mind about him."

Timothy put down the yellow fleece and gazed at her.

In case he thought she had romantic notions about Kent, she added quickly, "Not that it matters. One marriage was enough for me."

Too much, she could have said. But it was her own fault. She'd let herself be pushed into it by her family—*marry a doctor, imagine that!*—and Brenn had a knack for making himself irresistible.

"No more entanglements." She straightened in the chair, picked up a pincushion. "From now on, I'm going to be independent—strong and independent, no matter what. I don't want to need anybody. Not ever again."

Two pins fell off the pincushion. She jabbed them back into place and looked up in time to see Timothy's eyes darken with concern.

But all he did was start sewing another seam. "And Remi went along today? I find him interesting."

"So do I." A safer subject. "For someone who grew up in an orphanage, he seems to have had a remarkably good education."

"Why do you say that?"

She arranged the blue pins into a circle while considering the question. "In general, he's more polished than I'd have expected. He has above-average research skills. And he's acquainted with literature—Shakespeare, at least."

"He's learning to play the guitar, too," Timothy said. "Nathan's teaching him. Did he tell you?"

Madeleine shook her head, and Timothy went on. "Remi plays at our singing time—it's good practice, he says—and I think he'd like to play during the song service at church, but he's not ready yet."

"What do you mean?"

Timothy finished pinning the sleeves onto the body section. "Besides knowing the right chords, his heart should be there too. God wants us to worship Him in spirit and in truth. Right now Remi cares nothing for God, so he can't properly lead us in worship. But he may change. God has a way of doing marvels."

He fixed his bright eyes on her. "Have you heard about our little group that meets on Sunday mornings? Upstairs." He nodded at the ceiling. "Eleven o'clock."

The unspoken invitation was there, but she'd try to get out of it, if she could. She had endured enough church services to last a lifetime. Her gaze fell on the dog. "And does Hey-You join in your worship?"

Hearing his name, the dog rose to his feet, stretched, and laid his head in Timothy's lap.

He rubbed the torn brown ear. "I'm thinking that he worships in his own way." He smiled down at the dog. "Speaking of our canine friend, would you like to have him visit for a few days?"

"Oh!" She hadn't expected such a gift. "But Aunt Lin will be back on Sunday."

"At least for tonight and tomorrow, if you wish." He braced himself on the table and stood up. "Let me send along some dog food. Is there anything else you need?"

"Milk and eggs. But first, tell me about your project."

"This?" He picked up a scrap of fleece. "Every once in a while I amuse myself by making something warm for a baby."

"Any particular baby?" She had to smile at the thought of Timothy with a baby.

"For my friend—Charlotte Martinera. She's a midwife, and many of her young mothers can't afford the luxury of fleece. She's had a busy fall, so I set myself a goal of making at least a dozen buntings before Thanksgiving."

"What a good idea," Madeleine said.

Timothy limped ahead of her into the store. "You mustn't forget your groceries."

"You wouldn't happen to have a small scale you could sell me?"

"How small?"

"Ounces, up to maybe three or four pounds. I'm supposed to weigh my flour."

"I've got an old one I used for weighing letters before we went digital."

He searched under the counter and found it. Dusty, but she could read the numbers, and it worked fine. "Perfect. How much?"

"It's used. Take it."

"I'll pay you in . . . cookies? Or would you rather have a pie?"

"I like pies, but you've got enough to do."

"What's your favorite?"

"Plain old blueberry, I've got to admit."

"Done." She glanced at the handwritten signs all around them. "And I'd be glad to make some more signs for you."

He began to protest, and she said, "It's only a fair trade for the professional protection I'm getting." She leaned down to Hey-You, and he lifted his nose to hers. "You want to come home with me today?"

His feathery tail moved slowly from side to side, and she straightened up. "Thank you again, Timothy. He's good company."

She slept well and awoke early. Today, another try for the French bread. She had made baguettes again last night, and they'd risen correctly, but they'd been too dry.

This time, the whole process seemed to go more smoothly, and the caramel-colored crust looked inviting. After she wrote out the criteria for Timothy, she and Hey-You could take a walk.

She offered him one of the failed baguettes, and he carried it in his mouth for a long time. He liked to race, she discovered, and he usually won. For almost an hour, they hiked along a stream that was the color of root beer.

Before turning back, she paused to look down the stream with its overhanging trees. Such a marvel, these so-called Barrens: serene and mysterious and lovely, with a vibrant undercurrent of life. What did they remind her of? Bach, that was it. Adagio. Oboe and violins.

She called to the dog and he followed obediently, but as they neared the Manor, he streaked ahead of her.

Jude was sitting on the porch steps with something wrapped in his jacket. Hey-You danced up to him, but the boy sent him off with a quick command. Closer now, Madeleine could see a tawny head, smeared with blood. A cat?

Jude looked up, his dark eyes worried. "I think some dog got it. Can we take it to Timothy?"

She nodded, concealing her reluctance. Take a bloody cat into the store? How did she get herself into situations like this? But she had planned to go over with the baguettes, anyway.

She collected the bread and her purse, and then opened the car door for Jude. Hey-You jumped into the back seat, panting with excitement.

As she drove, Jude told her how he'd found the cat beside a river. "I figure it swam across and collapsed," he said. "It's pretty beat-up."

They parked in front of Timothy's store, and Jude said abruptly, "I'll take the bread and Hey-You." He handed her the bundled cat.

Did he think she'd be a better spokesman? It might not matter, though. The cat looked as if it had died on the way.

Timothy's store was crowded with Saturday-morning customers, and she felt their stares as she walked in with an armful of fur wrapped in a dusty jacket. Beside her, Jude marched with his chin up as if he expected a fight, and Hey-You preceded them both, looking delighted.

Timothy glanced up from a customer and nodded toward the storeroom. Jude darted ahead to push the swinging doors open, and Bria, coming out, gave them a startled glance. Madeleine heard Timothy ask her to take over the cash register.

He was beside them a minute later. "Over here." He led them to a laundry nook, saying "Put it on the counter." He didn't seem surprised. Did Jude often pick up vagrants?

Under florescent lights, the cat looked more pitiful than ever. It was large, but so thin that its ribs showed through the spotted fur. Blood streaked its neck and back and clotted along one leg.

Jude said, "The doctor?"

"He's here somewhere," Timothy said. "I'll go see."

Jude picked pine needles out of the cat's fur and arranged its sprawled limbs into a sleeping position. He put a hand on the finely molded head and then took it away, as if he weren't sure he should do that.

He looked so anxious that she had to say something. "It's nice that you have a vet around. I'm sure he'll—"

"He's not a vet."

Timothy came back through the door, followed by Nathan Parnell. He was carrying his cell phone and looked hurried. "You've got a *what* back here?"

Of course he'd think the whole thing ludicrous.

He caught sight of her, nodded, pocketed his phone, and went to the sink. While he washed his hands, he asked, "Where'd you find it?" and Jude told him.

The doctor put a hand on the cat's chest, and after a minute, he nodded. "Still breathing, that's good." He gently parted the bloody fur on its ribs and neck, and took his time examining the torn leg.

"Another abandoned pet. This one's young, but it's in bad shape." He glanced at Jude, and she sensed his compassion for the boy. "It probably won't last through the night."

His cell phone rang. Before answering, he said, "If it lives, keep it warm. Plenty of liquids."

He spoke into the phone. "Give her some oxygen. I'm coming."

He and Timothy left, and Jude huddled over the cat's body. Should she try to discourage him? No. She could at least match the two men in their kindness.

She ran water into the sink, dampened a handful of paper towels, and started wiping blood off the cat's face. After watching for a minute, Jude did the same.

Timothy must have returned because he spoke from behind them. "I'd suggest feeding it with an eye dropper. Something warm and sweet." He reached supplies down from a cupboard. "Here's some honey and a bottle of disinfectant for those cuts. Help yourself to a box and rags."

She picked up her bag of bread from where Jude had set it on the washing machine. "This is the latest attempt," she said. "I put a check-list inside, for when you have time."

He smiled. "I'll look forward to it."

They cleaned up the cat as well as they could, and Madeleine dribbled warm water with honey into its mouth. It swallowed, and she gave it some more.

Yellow eyes blinked open. It moved its legs.

"No." Jude said. "Stay down." He put a hand on its head and the cat grew still, its thin sides heaving. Soon after, its eyes closed.

Jude spoke into one of the elegantly-pointed ears. "You cannot die," he said, sounding both dubious and hopeful. "Just sleep."

He glanced at her. "Now what?"

She'd been wondering that herself. "Put it in a box with some rags, like Timothy said. Then you can take it home with you."

He seemed to age before her eyes. "Can't."

"Why not?" But she could guess.

"My mother . . . she wouldn't . . . you saw—" He swallowed and added more firmly, "Lockie would eat it alive."

"You could make him stay away like you did with Hey-You."

He shook his head. "Lockie was my father's dog, and he doesn't obey unless he feels like it."

His unspoken hope floated between them, and she couldn't bear to puncture it. "I guess Aunt Lin won't mind. Let's take it to the Manor."

He drew a quick breath and she added, "For a few days anyway." But Jude might not have heard. He was stroking the cat's downy head, whispering into its ear, telling it the good news.

At the Manor, they put the box on the kitchen table, and Jude studied the cat as if the disheveled bundle of fur were the most fascinating thing he'd seen. "Look at that tail," he said. "What do you think happened?"

"I've never seen one like it." The tail was a mere stub, tipped with a black stripe and a white tuft. This was no ordinary house cat.

They gave it a little more to drink, and it opened its eyes.

"Look!" Jude said. "Let's try some milk with honey."

The cat accepted a dozen or so drops of milk, struggled into a sitting position, then sank back down again.

"You know what?" Jude said. "Doc didn't sound very hopeful, but I'm going to pray for this cat." He spoke with confidence. "Do you ever pray?"

She tucked the rags around it more securely. "Sometimes."

"Timothy says that a person who is a child of God can pray to His heavenly Father any time, any place."

He gave her a hesitant glance. "Are you a child of God?"

Perhaps realizing that he had asked a personal question, he hurried on, "I am. Because of Christ—the Lord Jesus Christ." He said the name as if he were announcing an eastern potentate.

He glanced out the window and the glow on his face vanished. "What's Kent coming here for?"

"I don't know."

"Smithereens!" Madeleine expected him to make some excuse about leaving, but he didn't. He waited, watching the Bronco park, his face set in lines that were much too grim for a fourteen-year-old.

Madeleine opened the back door, thinking to get rid of their visitor quickly, but Kent brushed past her into the hall. "Hey, little elf! I'm glad I caught you." He flourished an envelope. "I brought these over."

He took a stride into the kitchen and halted. "What're you doing here?"

Jude lifted his chin, his dark eyes challenging the man who towered over him. "I am helping Mrs. Burke with our cat."

"Your cat?" Kent stepped to the side of the box. "Looks half-dead to me." The cat, scrawny and bloodstained, huddled into a corner of the box.

"He's in bad shape," Madeleine said, "but he'll make it, I think. What did you want?"

Kent looked at Jude. "Mrs. Burke and I have some personal matters to discuss. You can leave now. I'll help her with the cat."

Jude stiffened at the man's rudeness, but before he could answer, Madeleine said, "No. Jude will stay."

She put a hand on the cat's chest to check its breathing. "He's better now. I think we're making progress, Jude."

"I've got photos from Widow Bentley's Attic, the ones you wanted." Kent sounded sulky. "But since you're so busy, perhaps I should come another time."

"Yes." Why had she ever thought this man was charming?

She gave him a dismissive glance. "Jude and I have to get quite a bit done before Aunt Lin comes back."

Too mousy. Why did she put up with this?

He started for the door, and she followed him out onto the porch.

(*Do you ever pray?*) Lord, please help me.

She felt the muscles of her throat move in a convulsive swallow. "Kent!"

He turned, and at the look on his face, she wanted to shrink back against the railing. But she said, "I don't like it when you drop in on me. Please phone the next time, or I will not open the door."

He shrugged. "Whatever you say, elfin princess. You're sure cute when you get mad." He laughed and marched to the car, swinging his arms.

Jude was bending over the box, feeding the cat again. He looked up with a lopsided grin. "I prayed for you. I hope you told him off."

She tried to laugh. "Sort of. But it didn't seem to faze him."

Jude nodded. "He's after you."

"Don't say that." She opened a cupboard door at random. "How would you like to do some baking before you go? Something to welcome my aunt back tomorrow?"

"Sure. Did she like our carrot cake?"

"She loved it."

The cat stirred, and he continued with the feeding. "Maybe chocolate this time?"

"Good idea," Madeleine said. "We could make a torte."

"What's that?"

"A rich chocolate cake. You cut it into thin layers and put nuts and butter-cream frosting in between."

He grinned. "Go for it!"

Dusk had fallen by the time Jude left for home with half of the torte. Madeleine fed the cat again and carried his box into her bedroom.

He'd slept off and on during the last few hours, and now he could sit up by himself. He licked at his injured leg, taking a long time at it, and when he was finished, he fixed his yellow eyes upon her.

"What do you need?" she said.

Her phone rang, and the cat stared at it, flattening his ears.

It was Jude. "My family liked that torte," he said, "especially Mom. There's something about chocolate that's good for her. She didn't lock—" His voice jiggled, breaking off in mid-sentence as if someone had punched him on the shoulder. "How's the cat doing?"

"Mostly sleeping, but he took some more milk and even groomed himself a bit."

Jude's voice was less sure now. "I'm going to church tomorrow, and I was wondering if you'd like to come with me."

Our little group that meets on Sunday mornings.

"Mrs. Burke? I didn't mean to . . . I mean, if you don't want to go, that's okay, I just thought . . ."

"Thank you for asking, Jude. I've got the cat in my room. Do you think it would be all right to leave him?" (You're stalling, Madeleine.)

"Sure. Maybe shut your door."

Now she had no excuses left.

"I could give you a ride if you want to come over here," she said.

"Thanks. Around 10:30."

Slowly she put down her phone. Just an hour to please a couple of friendly people. Couldn't she manage that? She'd take Dad's Bible.

The cat was still watching her. How about a litter box? With all that sand outside, she could fix one easily.

"There now." She put the litter box in a corner of the room and lifted the cat into it. When he had finished scratching, she carried him back to his sleeping box and moved it onto the foot of her bed. "You're doing very well, you know. I'm glad you didn't hear what the doctor said. Are you ready for some real food?"

She shredded canned chicken into a dish, mixed it with milk, and he nibbled at it. While she changed for bed, he licked his paws in a leisurely fashion and settled down to sleep. "Me too," she told him, "soon as I finish my journal."

She was ready to turn out the light when her cell phone rang.

Aunt Lin. She sounded tense. "Something has come up, or to be more exact, someone didn't show up, and I'm going to have to stay. But I should be home Monday night. How are you getting along?"

"Fine. Made some French bread. Bought books at a place called Widow Bentley's Attic."

"Good. How'd you happen to go there?"

"Kent asked me to go with him and Remi."

Her aunt laughed. "So that's why I couldn't get a straight answer out of him. He thinks he's being so clever." She paused. "What's this he tells me about a dirty old cat you picked up?"

So he'd retaliated. Of course—she'd hurt his pride.

"It's an abandoned pet," she said. "A young one, and it's not dirty any more."

"I hope not," her aunt said. "We'll talk about it when I get back. See you Monday."

After she hung up, Madeleine shook her head. "I don't know what's come over me," she said to the cat. "Telling people off. Adopting vagrant cats." She turned out the light and pulled the blankets up to her chin. "Even going to church."

During the night, she awoke to the sound of claws on cardboard. The blankets shifted as the cat stepped out of his box. He curled himself against the hump of her feet, and she smiled into the darkness. "Nathan Parnell, eat your gloomy words."

CHAPTER 10

Aunt Lin . . .
She's smart about so many things—
I wish I had her talents and her confidence.
I hope she's still glad I came.
~Journal

The upstairs room at Timothy's store was a large, white-painted rectangle with three windows, six or seven rows of folding metal chairs, and a wooden podium. It was the plainest church Madeleine had ever seen.

By the time she and Jude walked in, many of the chairs were filled. "Let's sit in the back," she whispered. Before long, a plump blonde woman sat down beside her and smiled a greeting.

Sitting around them were women she'd seen in the store, some with families, some alone. Six teenagers clustered near the front, and Timothy sat in the front row, with Remi beside him.

At the piano, Nathan Parnell played a spirited prelude. Why should she be surprised? Even a doctor could be musical, couldn't he?

A beaming man who looked as if he spent his life outdoors opened the service with prayer and announced the first hymn. It was a favorite of hers: "A Mighty Fortress is Our God." The man waved his arms with exuberance and his voice boomed.

Singing was the best part of church, she'd always thought. They sang, "O Great God," then "Immortal Invisible," and she closed her eyes to concentrate on the music and enjoy the harmony.

When the song service was over, Timothy, wearing a white shirt, limped up to the podium with his Bible open in one big hand. She had a quick memory of that hand smoothing the yellow fleece, and then he began to speak.

"I was reading in Isaiah, chapter 40," he said, "and at the end of verse 9, I found three little words that challenged me."

Pages rustled as everyone turned to the passage, although Jude had some trouble finding it and she, using her father's Bible, was slow too.

"This is a command." Timothy read it aloud: *"Behold your God."*

The old man seemed to grow taller and straighter as he spoke. "Behold your God," he repeated. "Each of us has a god. What's your God like?"

His gaze traveled across the small gathering, and if he saw Madeleine, he gave no indication. "Look at the next verse," he said. "Isaiah's God is mighty and powerful, and He cares for his people. Look at verse twenty-five: He's the Holy One."

The Holy One?

It had been a while since she'd even thought about God, never mind His holiness. He wouldn't like what she'd become, not any more than she did.

She gazed out the window at a female cardinal perched on a branch, its feathers fluffed against the cold, and let herself wonder where it had come from, how far it had flown over the millions of pine trees.

Beside her, Jude, seemed to be listening intently. What was going on inside that dark head? He was a more complex person than she'd expected, and so was his family.

Timothy was saying, "Take a look at your God this week. How well do you know Him? Is He the same as Isaiah's God?"

Madeleine closed the Bible. Mother had always insisted, "We're a Christian family." But mother's god seemed to be herself, and Brenn's god had been medical science. Aunt Lin? Hard to tell. Dad? Definitely Isaiah's God.

And Madeleine?

She wasn't sure she wanted to think about it. She shouldn't have come today.

The cardinal flicked its wings and was gone. The congregation stirred, preparing to stand for the last hymn. Not a very long sermon.

After the closing prayer, the woman beside her turned with a smile. "My name's Charlotte Martinera," she said. "I'm glad you could visit."

Madeleine smiled in return and recognized the name. Charlotte? This must be Timothy's friend, the midwife.

The woman said, "I couldn't help noticing that you sing. You must come from a singing church."

"Yes." At least, she used to, before her mother changed churches.

Madeleine introduced herself, adding, "It sounds as if this group likes to sing—and you've got a great song leader."

Charlotte smiled, showing a pair of dimples. "That's my husband, so I'm glad to hear it."

Jude leaned over. "Mrs. Martinera, tell her about SING."

"That's a good idea!" Charlotte had a deep-toned voice that added warmth to everything she said. "On Wednesday nights we get together for an hour or so, just to sing. Jude comes, and a few of the teens and a couple of the adults. We'd love for you to join us."

Madeleine avoided Jude's eager gaze. "Thank you. Maybe I will, sometime."

"Good! Seven o'clock if you can make it." Charlotte smiled a farewell, and Madeleine turned toward the door with relief.

Jude was quiet until they reached the car, and then he said, "SING is kind of fun. I like this church. Sometimes they have a potluck afterwards. They'd love your walnut torte."

"That's a nice idea," she said. "Do you want to take a look at the cat before you go home?"

"Sure!"

The cat was curled into a tawny ball, and he didn't stir when they bent over him. "He's looking better," Jude said. "Maybe he'll be a lot better by the time your aunt gets back." His eyes shone with hope. "Then she'll let him stay."

The next morning when Bria came to work, she said, "My brother gave me strict instructions to check on the cat."

The cat looked up at them, ears pricked forward. They were large ears, black-tipped with a white spot on the back of each one.

"Pretty ears." Bria put out a tentative hand, and the cat allowed himself to be stroked. He must have worked hard at grooming, because his fur was clean and smooth.

"He's eating well," Madeleine said. "I need to buy cat food and a bunch of other groceries before Aunt Lin gets back. Would you like to come along?"

"Yes." Bria's face grew more animated, and Madeleine wondered whether she had many opportunities for an outing. Perhaps she could get a little closer to the girl today.

They talked about commonplace things on the way to Hammonton, but on the way back, Bria asked, "Do you think your aunt is going to let you keep the cat?"

"I don't know," Madeleine said. "Are you sure he can't stay at your house?"

"My mother doesn't like cats and besides, there's Lockie."

"Lockie was your father's dog?"

Bria's voice grew distant. "He and Jude and the dog did everything together. He even used to read them Shakespeare."

"Lockie is an unusual name."

"One of my father's favorite characters." She gave a short, dry laugh. "Shylock. The guy says something like, *I'm a dog, beware my fangs.*"

Madeleine nodded. *The Merchant of Venice.*

"We used to make jokes about Lockie's fangs." Bria turned her face away.

Madeleine kept her eyes on the sandy road, but her heart ached for the girl. Bria's father must be dead.

"I miss my father too," she said softly.

Bria looked at her. "Did he die?"

"He was a policeman," Madeleine said, the words tangling together in her throat. "Someone shot him."

"When did it happen?"

"A couple of years ago, but I still . . ." She had to let the sentence hang unfinished.

Just keep the car on the road, she told herself, and watch for the driveway.

Bria knotted her hands together in her lap. "I wish I knew about my dad."

"He's still alive?"

"We don't know. He just disappeared. It's been three years." Her voice began to shake. "People always ask, like they probably ask you, if I miss him. Yes, I miss him a lot. Probably more than he misses me."

Bria pressed her fist against her mouth, as if she'd said too much. As soon as Madeleine parked, the girl reached for an armload of groceries and hurried inside.

The afternoon's work was uneventful, except for finding a box marked POTTERY, and by then it was time for Bria to leave. Before Madeleine could take a look, her mother phoned, so it was late in the day when she finally opened it up.

The box held gracefully curved terra-cotta vases, painted with black geometric designs. As she lifted one of them onto the dining room table, headlights gleamed through the trees.

Aunt Lin. The cat! She hurried to shut her bedroom door and went outside to greet her aunt.

After everything was carried in, Aunt Lin paused at her bedroom door to describe their latest feature idea and interrupted herself to ask, "What's that wonderful smell?"

"Chicken in the slow cooker," Madeleine said. "I thought you'd be hungry."

"I'm starved." Aunt Lin pulled off her jacket and threw it onto the bed. "But first, where's the cat?"

"In my room." Madeleine opened the door, hoping he hadn't jumped out of the box and shredded the curtains.

He peered at them from the box, blinking sleepily.

"Hmm," Aunt Lin said. "You've got it cleaned up." She studied the cat for a minute. "Looks like a bobcat mix. See the big ears with the tufts of hair? Short tail, right? The spots are typical."

She turned away. "Where'd it come from?"

"Jude found it in the woods."

"Then why doesn't he take it home?"

"We talked about that. They've got a dog, and his mother isn't well."

Her aunt nodded. "That's what I've heard. I guess it'll be okay here, especially if you keep it in your room. There's enough to clean up in this house without a cat shedding all over everything."

Her smile was tired. "Let's eat before I fall over. I love your cooking."

Madeleine sliced a baguette to go with the chicken, and they ate a quiet meal. Her aunt looked exhausted, so she didn't bother her with small talk. At least for now, it seemed that Jude could stop worrying about the cat.

She fed the cat some leftover chicken and scratched behind his ears. A vibration began deep inside him, a throbbing that swelled into a full-throated purr. A contented, comforting sound.

The next morning, as soon as they'd eaten Aunt Lin said, "Did you ever do anything with that locked room?"

She didn't want to go back in there, not ever, but since her aunt had asked, she told her what they'd found and slowly followed her up the stairs.

She watched from the doorway while her aunt walked into the room. "Look at all this," Aunt Lin said softly, turning from side to side. "It's incredible. She kept everything."

She picked up an elephant from the Noah's Ark parade. "Henrietta mentioned her boy. He died young, I gathered. But I'd no idea . . ."

After a minute, she put the elephant back onto the shelf. "Collectors would love to get their hands on these things." She opened the cabinet and gazed at the train set. "Almost new, isn't it?"

Madeleine nodded. Something was making it difficult for her to talk. She backed into the hall.

Her aunt looked thoughtful. "This explains some of Henrietta's strangeness. How sad!"

They left the room in silence, and as they passed the storage room, her aunt said, "Those decoys—I'm thinking about using your research in a magazine feature, maybe with a cover too. Timothy's got decoys for sale. Why don't you buy one and ask a lot of questions?"

"I'll do that," Madeleine said. "I learned that Paula Castell carves them."

Aunt Lin hesitated and finally said, "She might not be much help, but you could try talking to her."

Madeleine nodded. Sometime she'd tell her aunt about the visit, but not yet. "Do you know Dan'l Forbes?" she asked. "I met him the other day. He used to make decoys."

"Good for you," Aunt Lin said. "Why don't you take ours over there and see what he has to say?"

Yes, and she'd take him some cookies, too.

Dan'l greeted her politely and eyed the decoys with interest, but it was the cookies that seemed to surprise him. Of course they had to have a dish of tea, he said, and how did she know that "chocklit chip" was his favorite, and was she writing a book too?

A couple of writers had come to visit him, he said—a man from New York with shiny shoes, a woman who was terrified of snakes, and "that Kent fellow."

While they drank their tea, he told her how he'd turfed out cranberry bogs, harvested cranberries and blueberries, picked pine cones, moss, and greens for florists. She thought it all fascinating but hoped he'd soon get around to talking about the decoys.

Finally he picked up one of the mergansers, turned it over to look for a name, and talked about old Harry Shourds and his son. "I don't think either of them made this one. See how the wing tips go off to the side?"

She asked why the decoys were so light, and he explained the hollowing-out process, calling them "dugout bodies." He paused, gave her a sideways glance, and asked whether she'd been to visit Paula Castell.

"Sort of," Madeleine said. "We didn't talk much."

He nodded. "One of her bad days, prob'ly. You're lucky you saw her at all. I've heard she locks herself into her room for days at a time."

And Jude was good at unlocking doors.

Madeleine ventured to ask what had happened, and Dan'l didn't seem to know much, just that her husband had disappeared and no one, not even the police, could find him or his car.

He plucked a cookie from the stack beside his cup, studied it, and took a small, careful bite. "The whole thing took her hard, though, since her old grandpa died just a couple years back. Taught her everything about carving decoys. She's good."

"She mentioned her grandfather."

"Paul Clampton? Best I ever knew." He turned to the doorway. "Someone just drove up. That writer guy. Keeps comin' back." He heaved himself out of the chair with a sigh.

Nothing wrong with the old Piney's hearing.

"He must enjoy talking to you," she said.

"Nope. Likes my decoys. Took a bunch of pictures."

She got to her feet. "Thank you very much for the tea. I'd better finish my errands."

She wanted to ask whether the Manor's decoys were valuable, but he'd forgotten about them, and Kent would talk on and on.

"Hey, Dan'l, you in there?" Kent's voice sounded impatient.

"I'm comin', I'm comin'—just keep your shirt on." The old man trudged through the front room and held the door open for her.

"Hello!" Kent's frown vanished. "What are you doing here?"

"Visiting," she said. "And you?"

Kent glanced at Dan'l and raised his voice as if the old man were deaf. "I'm looking for Remi. Have you seen him?"

Dan'l looked toward the cabins behind his house. "Nope."

"He's not there. I checked. Has he been back today?"

Dan'l shrugged. "Not my business. Don't know what the boy does and don't care, long as he pays his rent."

Kent gave him a look of mingled impatience and contempt, but Dan'l ignored him.

The old man sauntered past them, nimbly avoiding the holes in the steps, and took an axe from inside one of the car bodies. He swung it with a practiced hand. "Guess it's time to cut me some wood."

He lifted a thick chunk off the woodpile as easily as if he had picked up a cookie, placed it on a chopping block, swung the axe high, and split the wood neatly in half.

Madeleine watched, fascinated, but Kent made an exasperated sound and stalked down the porch steps. As he raised his voice with another question, she took the opportunity to get into her car and drive off.

Why would Kent take photos of the old man's decoys? For his book?

CHAPTER 11

That locked room haunts me.
It feels like a tomb in there.
It makes me think.
I'd rather not.
~Journal

The next day, Aunt Lin had to drive to Philadelphia, but she promised to be home before suppertime. "And Kent wants to come over again, with Remi. Would supper on Friday night be okay with you?"

Madeleine shrugged. But if she was going to cook a meal, why not have someone more interesting? "Invite that doctor too, why don't you?" she said. "We might as well feed all the local bachelors at once."

Her aunt looked intrigued. "I'll do that. Kent's going to bring the photos he took at Widow Bentley's Attic."

"Remi took them for me," Madeleine said. "I'm curious to see how their glass compares with ours."

"You have the mind of a true researcher." Aunt Lin paused in the doorway. "Since this is cranberry country, do you think you'd have time to make a cranberry-something dessert?

"I'd be glad to," Madeleine said, and her aunt left with a smile.

First, buy groceries. As long as she was in Hammonton, she bought a stepladder, along with paint and poster board.

Next, a visit to Timothy's store to find out what prices he wanted on his signs.

The placard said AT LUNCH, but he opened the door with a welcoming smile. When she mentioned the prices, he said, "Let's go into the office so I can check."

As they passed the display case, she paused to take another look at the decoys.

"You need to see them up close," Timothy said, and set them on the counter.

She picked up the mallard. "What beautiful colors," she said, "especially this blue patch on the wing." The wing tips didn't go off to one side or the other, so Dan'l would approve.

She turned it over but couldn't find Bria's signature. "Aunt Lin told me to buy one," she said at last, "and I think this is it."

"Good choice," Timothy said.

In his office, he made a note of her purchase and wrote out the prices she'd asked for. From under the table came the sound of light snoring: Hey-You, curled into a shaggy hump.

"I meant to tell you," he said, "I thought your French bread met all the criteria. It tasted good too."

"I'm glad to hear that. Hey-You was the only one who liked my first try—he thought it was a stick."

"Not so easy? Even for you?"

"I need a lot of practice," she said. "Last night I tried a Challah braid. I didn't bring it because it would have failed the appearance test." She laughed, remembering. "It looked like a couple of balloons twisted together."

His smile was sympathetic. "Can you stay a minute?" He sat down at the table, which was spread with newspapers, saying, "I'm just doing a little polishing here."

After he'd moved a tube of cream out of her way, he set to work on a brass bookend that was shaped like a duck's head. "Have you been back to see Dan'l?" he asked.

She sat across from him. Maybe the doctor would wander in, and she'd tell him that Jude's cat had survived his dire prediction. "I went yesterday," she said, "and showed him the decoys we found. He's kind of roundabout with me, but I learned a few tidbits."

"He'll warm up," Timothy said. "How's the Manor project coming?"

"We're still making discoveries. Jude opened the locked room. It looks as if it hasn't been touched for a long time . . . Cousin Henrietta's boy." The sorrow in that room flicked across her. "I think she kept it as a shrine to his memory."

"She did. For years and years." Timothy's voice held a deep sadness. "Henrietta often spoke to me of her grief. She could not let go of the child."

Madeleine's throat began to ache. She knew about memories, how they could cling, how they could torment, how they could fill you with longing.

To see his face once more. To hear him laugh . . .

She bit her lip to keep it from trembling.

Timothy must have noticed. "I liked your father," he said. "A genuine, godly man. Did the two of you do things together?" He spread polishing cream on the duck's neck with a blackened cloth.

She'd never been able to talk about Dad. Perhaps now? The store was empty, and Timothy's quiet smile gave her courage.

She rested her elbows on the table and told him about the hikes they'd taken, the jokes they'd shared, the skills she'd learned from him.

"And he taught me the Bible too," she said. "I belong to Christ because of Dad."

Timothy's wrinkled face shone. "I'm glad to hear that." He put down his cloth. "Tell me, do you think your father is happy?"

She sighed. People always asked that, and then they would say—as if she needed to be convinced—that he was in a far better place.

"Of course he's happy. But I'm not. I'm miserable." Hurriedly she added, "Not that I'm angry at God. I suppose He has His reasons."

She gazed down at the smudged newspapers. What she said was mostly true. She hadn't talked to God very much since her father died, and even less since she'd married. That part of her seemed to have shriveled.

She fidgeted with the nearest sheet of newspaper and tore off a corner. She crumpled it into a ball. "I try not to think about Dad, but it doesn't help. Nothing helps. I just hurt. "

"I know." His voice was gentle. "You will hurt for the rest of your life."

She stared at him. What a terrible thing to say.

"It's what you do with the hurt that matters." Timothy picked up a clean cloth.

"What do you mean? Sublimate it?"

"You can nurse your grief, like Henrietta did, but it will cripple you. Or you can ignore it, but it will harden you. Or you can accept it."

"Accept it?" she said. "I don't have any choice. I have to accept it."

"That's resignation. Not what I meant." He polished on the duck's neck for a minute. "Remember, Sunday, when we were talking about God? Our God—your God—does marvelous things. If you can accept this from His hand, He will change how you look at it."

"So I won't hurt?"

"You won't hurt in the same way." Timothy leaned
forward. "Grief is a wall that each of us runs into, sooner
or later. The wall has a door. You can walk through the
doorway and live, or you can stay on this side of it and
wither away."

She listened, trying to ignore the turmoil inside her.
Maybe she shouldn't have talked about Dad so much.

"Here's how it looks," Timothy said. "On the front of
the door is a sign that reads: *His work is perfect.* And
when you say, 'Yes, Lord,' and walk on through, you find
another sign: *The Lord is my Rock and my Fortress and
my Deliverer.*"

She could see the doorway in her mind. "So how do I
. . . ?"

"Talk to God about your hurt," Timothy said.
"Remember, He's your loving Father. Tell Him that you
choose to accept this grief from His hand."

Timothy grew still, looking away. "It's hard. But not
as hard as trying to deal with it by yourself."

So he'd been there.

After a moment he looked back at her, his brown
eyes steadfast. "Read Psalm 18, the first couple of verses.
It helps me."

She tried to say, '*I want what you have,*' but her jaw
locked, her lips stiffened, her words froze.

Timothy seemed to understand. He flourished his
cloth over the duck's head with finality and pulled
himself to his feet. "I'd better get to work. Let's put your
decoy into a bag."

As he wrapped the decoy in tissue paper, he said,
"I'll tell you a quick story. I knew someone who lost his
family in an accident. He left his job, moved to the other
side of the country, and buried himself in good works. He
became a hard and bitter man. But one day he walked
through that doorway, and it changed his life."

Timothy handed the bag to her, and she followed as he limped to the front of the store. He took down the AT LUNCH sign and pulled the door open. "You want to be strong, little lady? This is your first step."

Strong? How did *giving up* equal *strong*?

The weight of grief pressed down upon her, painful as a sharp-edged block of steel.

Hey-You was wagging his tail and Timothy was saying, "About those decoys—remember to check with Paula Castell."

She managed a coherent answer. "I went last week but didn't get very far."

"Her children like you," he said. "She'll talk eventually."

His gaze was affectionate. "Come see me again," he said, and all she could do was nod.

By the time she reached the Manor, the weight had settled so deeply into her chest that she could hardly breathe.

Groceries. She started inside with two small bags, stopped on the porch to fish out her key, and a scratching sound made her glance overhead.

The cat dropped from the tree onto the railing and arched his back into a stretch, looking proud of himself. He must have found her open window.

She stroked his head, wishing she could pick him up and cry into the soft fur, but she had long since run out of tears.

He trailed after her into the kitchen. She should feed him. And she had groceries to put away, meals to plan. Bria and Jude were coming to work.

Not now . . . the weight . . .

She dragged herself up the stairs and along the hall to the boy's room. She leaned against the doorframe. How many times had his mother stood here, thinking about her child and aching to have him back?

Her own grief was crushing the air from her lungs. She dropped onto the bed and buried her face in her hands. "Lord, You did it. You took him away." The words trembled in her mind, laden with pain.

"Lord, help?" Silence pooled around her, a waiting, compassionate silence.

She took a ragged breath. "Okay, I accept this from Your hand," she whispered. "But I don't understand why You did it. I don't understand how it's perfect. I don't understand any of this . . . and that's all right."

She lingered in the silence, letting it enfold her.

The weight slipped off, the pain eased, and she understood one thing: He had heard.

Slowly, with a sense of wonder, she got to her feet and found that she could breathe more freely.

She left the room, closing the door behind her, and the cat's inquiring face peered at her from the top of the staircase. "I'm coming," she said.

He stopped, one ear flickering, and looked down the steps. She heard it too, someone knocking. Bria?

She ran downstairs with the cat bounding ahead of her. By the time she reached the hall, he was crouched on the Chippendale desk, looking like one of his wild ancestors. She gave him a pat on her way.

She pulled the door open, ready to smile at the whole world. "Hi, Bria! I'm glad to see you!"

Bria gave her a curious glance, but she smiled back. "What needs to be done?"

"A lot! Can you believe I've still got groceries in the car? I bought us a stepladder too."

After everything was put away, she showed Bria the pottery vases she had found, and the girl examined them with interest. "These were painted by hand," she said. "I think the artist signed them."

She put a finger on a scrawl that seemed part of the design. Sure enough, it reappeared in the same place on each vase.

"All artists should sign their work." Madeleine hesitated. "Why doesn't your mother sign hers?"

Bria shrugged. "Doesn't care." She traced the curved lip of the vase. "But I do."

"You sign the decoys? I looked for your signature but didn't see it."

Bria looked embarrassed. "I just paint a swirling sort of B on the wings."

"Good for you," Madeleine said. "Your work is excellent, and your name should be on it."

"Thank you," Bria said. "What should we do with this pottery?"

Madeleine surveyed the dining room. "Let's pack all of this stuff into boxes and then we can clear off the table."

Jude soon arrived, carrying a sheet of paper. "I made you a map, Mrs. Burke."

"Mollie," she said. "That's my name from now on. We don't have to be formal."

"Mollie?"

"It's what my father called me." She could say his name more comfortably now.

"My dad used to call me Peanut," Jude said. "Here, take a look at this."

He spread out the map on the kitchen table and showed her the trails he'd marked. Then he wanted to see the cat. They found him on her windowsill, staring into the bushes.

Madeleine said, "Guess who went out that window and met me on the porch today?"

Jude stroked the thick fur, looking triumphant. "You're getting stronger, boy!"

With Jude's help, the packing went quickly. As he taped another box closed, he asked, "I was wondering, can you come to SING? It's tonight."

She didn't feel like socializing. Besides, she'd planned to give the Challah braid another try.

He picked up a stack of plates and gave her an appealing glance.

"I guess I could," she said. "If you're there, I'll know at least one person."

He grinned. "You know Timothy," he said. "And Remi, and Mr. and Mrs. Martinera. That's a lot more than one."

While they finished up, she remembered her decoy project and said to Bria, "My aunt wants me to research those decoys we found, for her magazine."

They were both eyeing her. "I bought the mallard drake from Timothy's store," she said. "It's beautiful."

Conscious that she was chattering, circling around to get to her question, she said, "Timothy told me your mother is the best authority on decoys. Do you think she'd mind another visit?"

Bria and Jude exchanged a glance. Jude studied his sneakers.

"She's sick right now," Bria said. "Maybe next week."

Aunt Lin arrived in time for supper, as promised, and asked about her day.

"I bought a decoy and plenty of groceries," Madeleine said. "We can have a turkey on Friday, and there'll be leftovers for sandwiches this weekend. I'll make cranberry tarts for the supper. How's that sound?"

"Wonderful." Aunt Lin picked up her fork. "And look at this roast beef!"

While they finished dessert, she told her aunt about SING.

"Good for you," she said. "Your father was musical. Didn't he lead the singing in your church?"

"Yes," Madeleine said. "And he was always singing around the house. Did he do that when you were growing up?"

"Definitely. I was a lot younger, but I used to follow him around, trying to copy him. I sounded awful, but he didn't seem to mind."

Madeleine smiled. That sounded like him.

"I'm glad to see you smiling again," her aunt said. "What are you going to wear?"

"I don't know." Did it matter?

"Jeans are good on you. And how about that long-sleeved green top? It brings out the green in your eyes."

Madeleine wanted to laugh. "The Dumont green, is that it?"

"Of course." Her aunt's eyes softened. "That Dumont blood is a gift, you know. The Dumont women are tough—and you are too, whether you realize it or not. Have some fun for a change. I'll see you in the morning."

CHAPTER 12

Why are Jude and Bria
protecting their mother?
She's a talented person,
judging from the decoys.
But she's distraught about something.
Her husband?
~Journal

As Madeleine walked up the steps into Timothy's store, the Martineras joined her. Charlotte welcomed her to SING and introduced Howard, her husband, who hurried ahead into the office. He took down the long table, rotated the sofa, and set up folding chairs and an electronic keyboard.

"Sit with me," Charlotte said. "I hope I can stay. I have a client who's due to go into labor any moment. Oops, I'll be right back. Forgot to pass out the song sheets."

Madeleine wanted to ask about Charlotte's midwifery, but half-a-dozen adults had arrived, including a pregnant woman who sat near Charlotte to talk.

Remi walked in with his guitar, sent her a dazzling smile, and pulled out a chair facing the group. Three girls clustered around him, and he kept them laughing as he tuned his guitar.

Jude arrived soon afterwards and introduced her to his teenaged friends, dark-haired Pumper and Fritz, who told her they wanted to start a band. They eyed Remi's guitar longingly.

Timothy smiled at her and sat up near the front.

Nathan Parnell came in while Howard was welcoming everyone. He sat at the keyboard, looked the group over, and gave her a nod, which seemed to be his chosen method of communication.

Howard started them off with "I Sing the Mighty Power of God," and they sang praise songs, hymns, and choruses with equal enthusiasm. Madeleine knew most of the songs, thanks to her father, and today she enjoyed them all.

Howard asked for favorites, and then he chose the last song: "As the Deer." Madeleine leaned back and sang with her eyes closed. *He alone*—was her heart's desire. *He alone*—had set her free today.

Was this what they called joy? Thank You, Lord.

After Timothy finished with prayer, most of the adults left, but the teens stayed, drinking lemonade and eating chocolate chip cookies that tasted as if they'd come from a box.

Jude, carrying a handful of cookies, grinned at her. "Mollie, wasn't that great?"

She smiled at him and at Remi, who had joined them. "It was fun, just like you told me."

Remi elbowed Jude. "How come you get to call her Mollie?"

Jude looked smug. "She said so. Her nickname."

"Just for my friends," she said to Remi. "Like you. Don't tell your boss."

He grinned, and Pumper and Fritz came up to talk to them.

Maybe she could leave now. She had planned to sit in the back, but here she was in the middle of everybody. No point hanging around any longer. Were these cookies stale, or was she getting picky?

The doctor appeared at her side, carrying his lemonade and cookies. He looked more rested, the gray eyes clear. He nudged one of the cookies on his plate. "Yours are better."

"Thank you, doctor."

"I have a name, remember?"

"Right again. Does it ever bore you?"

He eyed her. "My name?"

"Being right all the time."

He grinned, looking as young as one of the teens. "I will not be vexed by you—it's Mollie, isn't it?—as long as there's a chance for real cookies. I hope you caught the embedded request."

She had to smile at that. He'd picked up on her nickname already. She should stop needling him.

One of the boys called him over to their group, and the Martinera sisters sidled up to her. Bonnie, tall and blonde, looked studious. Her sister, Connie, with frizzled brown hair, wasn't much taller than Madeleine, and had already said at least a million words this evening.

Bonnie smiled at her. "I like the way you sing alto, Mrs. Burke. Would you teach me?"

"I'd be glad to," she said. "Let's sit together next time."

Connie had been talking to a girl behind her, but she swung back, saying, "Did you ask her?"

Bonnie shook her head.

Connie put on a pleading face. "Can you swim, Mrs. Burke?"

"Yes."

"And paddle a canoe?"

She nodded without enthusiasm. What was this about?

"Hoo-rah!" Connie turned pink. "Hey Doc! Doc! Come over here."

He looked up from the boys gathered around him.

"Not so loud," Bonnie said. "You always sound so rude. Can't you grow up, just for once?"

"Sorry." Connie didn't look a bit sorry. "Here he comes."

He was there a minute later, and Connie said, "I found her! She can swim and paddle!"

Madeleine looked at him with a shrug.

He grinned. "Well now, do you paddle when you swim?'

"Not usually."

"Actually, it's not a requirement. Are you wondering what they're talking about?"

"I certainly am."

"I often do, too. But this time I think they're referring to a canoe trip I was planning." He glanced at the two girls. "With the guys."

Connie's voice rose. "You promised! You promised!".

He smiled at Madeleine. "Which I may regret."

To Connie he said, "There's one more important detail."

"What?"

"Did you ask whether she wants to come?"

Two pairs of blue eyes fastened on her. "Do you?"

A canoe trip? She hadn't been on one for years.

"When is it?"

"A week from Saturday," he said. "We think."

They looked at her and she said, "I'll have to see." Hedging, wasn't she?

"Hoo-rah!" Connie said. "Now Doc has to keep his promise." She grabbed Madeleine in a hug, then turned and hugged her sister.

The doctor stepped back. Didn't he want a hug too?

"What's this promise?" she asked.

Bonnie said, "He takes the guys canoeing, and he never takes us. He told us we had to find a lady who's good at canoeing and can swim too."

"I'm no expert," Madeleine said.

Connie was bouncing up and down. "You'll be great. Better than Mom. She hates the water."

The doctor said, "All right, girls. Let's wait until next week. If everything works out, we'll make some firm plans at SING."

They nodded, and Connie grabbed her sister's arm, taking her off to discuss something vital with one of the other girls.

Madeleine looked at him. "Thank you for giving me a bit of breathing space."

"Only for the moment. Don't let them pressure you."

"Dad and I did some canoeing. I kind of miss it."

He glanced at the girls, now huddled on the sofa. "This won't be a peaceful trip, not with those two along. I've got to admit I made that rule so I wouldn't have to deal with them. Especially the rattle-brained one."

She gave him a teasing smile. "I'd have thought you could deal with anything."

His smile had an edge to it. "They're all yours."

"I'm used to teens," she said. "As far as the trip is concerned, let me think about it."

Did she want to get involved in something like this again? With him? Maybe. Maybe not.

The question followed her home, but it wandered off as she was getting ready for bed. Her father's Bible caught her eye, and she remembered Timothy saying she should read—what? A psalm. Was it the eighteenth? She sat down to find the passage.

I love you, O Lord, my strength.
The Lord is my rock and my fortress and my
deliverer, my God, my rock, in whom I take refuge.

It sounded like the sign on the inside of Timothy's doorway.

Both verses were underlined. Had her father walked through that doorway too? The word *rock* was circled, with an arrow pointing to a note in the margin: Ps. 73:26

She turned to it, knowing what she'd find:

My flesh and my heart may fail,
but God is the strength of my heart
and my portion forever.

He had underlined the word *strength*, and in the margin he'd written: *See Ps. 18:2. Means ROCK.*

She'd always liked rocks. When they went hiking, her father would tease her about bringing home the mountain, piece by piece. Somewhere she still had the chunk of granite she'd carried back from Mill Mountain.

"The Lord is my rock." She said it aloud, and the cat stopped washing his face to gaze at her. She glanced back at the psalm. "And my fortress and my deliverer."

God would show her what to do, even about a little thing like a canoe trip. And about . . . the fearful things too. Perhaps He would make them disappear—*poof!*

She opened the window to let the night air cool her face, and while she finished getting ready for bed, the two verses cycled through her mind. "Thanks, Dad," she whispered.

The next morning, Aunt Lin stepped out of her office to say that she'd invited Dr. Parnell for tomorrow's supper and he'd agreed. Meanwhile, she'd be working in her darkroom for most of the day.

Madeleine packed up more of the dining room clutter, and, wanting to match her aunt's efficiency, started on Timothy's signs and put the turkey into the fridge to thaw. Later, during her run in the woods, she plotted the rest of tomorrow's menu.

That evening she finished her first draft of the paper on French bread—she'd print it out the next time she went to Timothy's—and read about the historical background of Challah. Now all she had to do tomorrow was cook.

On Friday, except for a short walk, she spent most of her time in the kitchen. Aunt Lin was still working, but she said she didn't mind music, so Madeleine put on a Mozart CD and filled the room with trumpets.

She'd begin with the Challah, to make sure it didn't bomb again. This one looked better, so she brushed on an egg-white glaze and sprinkled it with sesame seeds. In the afternoon, when Jude came to help, she rolled out the pastry for tarts and let him make the cranberry filling. Next, she'd put the turkey into the oven and check her list.

She was finishing up when the phone rang. A minute later, Aunt Lin came out of her bedroom. "That was Dr. Parnell. He's got an emergency, so he can't come. He apologized. Said he hoped I'd invite him another time."

Her aunt gave her a sidelong glance. "Too bad, isn't it? I'd have loved to see him and Kent interact."

Disappointment flickered, but only for an instant. She hadn't expected him to show up. Such a busy person.

Kent and Remi arrived just after the turkey had popped its timer, and the kitchen smelled deliciously of roasting meat. The dining room still looked cluttered, but the long table was clear. She should have put candles or flowers at one end, not that these two would notice. Well, Remi might.

The boy ate swiftly, as if he hadn't seen food for a week, and after emptying his plate for the second time, he sat with his head tipped back, examining the chandelier over their heads.

Aunt Lin and Kent were talking about the eastern pine looper worm, discussing whether it caused more damage than a forest fire. Apparently Kent had spent a couple of summers fighting fires at Yellowstone and considered himself an expert. Remi, from the look on his face, had heard it all before.

Madeleine leaned toward him and said in a low voice, "You read Shakespeare? I'm curious about that."

He grinned. "My senior year in high school, we had this English teacher who made us watch the BBC videos. A couple of them were cool. Our drama club put on *Macbeth*. I guess it kind of rubbed off on me."

She started to say that she knew how he felt, but Kent asked him a question, and the conversation turned to the recent fires in the Barrens, continuing amiably enough until she served dessert.

Remi ate his cranberry tart with evident pleasure and accepted another. "So you made these little pies?"

"Jude did the filling."

"That dark-haired kid?"

"He's fourteen, older than he looks," she said. "His interest in cooking is unusual, but he's good at it."

Kent interrupted himself to say, "Not surprising. He has to do all the cooking at home."

"Why is that?"

"There's a lot you don't know about that bunch, my dear."

Madeleine sent him a look. The glacier one.

Her aunt caught it. "Don't be upset, Mollie. You have such a soft heart, giving them food and all, but they're—"

"Losers," Kent said.

He licked the whipped cream off his fork, looking as if he enjoyed the sound of that condemning word. "The father disappeared, probably took off with one of his students. The mother lives in an alcoholic daze. The grandmother has lost half her marbles, and the kids run wild. They should be put in a foster home."

"Not Bria!" Aunt Lin exclaimed. "She's at least twenty. And Jude is quite capable of taking care of himself."

Kent drew his knife out of its sheath and studied its shining length. "That boy," he said, "is a menace."

"Hey," Remi said, "I asked if there were any girls my age around here, and you said no. What about this Bria?"

"Not that one," Kent said. A flush colored his cheeks. "She's got claws. Wouldn't trust her for a minute. Another loser."

Remi fingered the band of white coral at his neck and shot him a glance that said, 'Maybe for you, old man.'

Madeleine put down her fork. "You're wrong about Jude. And especially about Bria. She's hardworking and talented."

To Remi she said, "Her father was a Shakespeare buff. He named his dog Shylock."

Remi raised an eyebrow. "Mmm. Got her phone number?"

She turned back to Kent, anger simmering. "How can you talk about your cousins like that?"

"Distant cousins." His eyes had narrowed to slits. "Very distant cousins. I do what I can for them, but there comes a point . . ."

He sheathed his knife, giving her a dark glance, and she knew that for once she'd succeeded in breaching his affable façade. "Stay away from that trash," he muttered. "They're nothing but trouble."

He glanced at Remi. "You too, kid."

"Let's get rid of these dishes," Aunt Lin said quickly, "and Kent can show us the photos from Widow Bentley's Attic."

Madeleine helped to clear the table, reminding herself that Remi had taken those photos for her and she'd better pay attention.

Yes, the glassware was beautiful. And yes, the decanter and sugar bowl looked like ones they'd found here, but it was hard to concentrate. Remi had brought double prints, so she'd look at her set later.

What was the matter with her? Was she being overly protective of Jude and Bria? She rubbed at the gooseflesh on her arms. Or was it Kent? Something about him?

Remi was saying that Widow Bentley's Attic had the most authentic display of Jersey glass, unless you went to the museum down in Millville.

"A museum? We should go there," Aunt Lin said, and asked him for directions.

They played Monopoly again, as doubles this time. Madeleine tried to be a good partner for Remi, tried to be clever and enthusiastic, but they lost. He murmured encouragement to her, and she liked him for that.

Would they be leaving soon?

Yes, Kent was standing up.

He put on his jacket, said the usual charming farewells, and started into the hall. He sprang back into the kitchen, cursing under his breath.

Madeleine looked past him. The cat was crouched on the desk, eyes glaring yellow, ears laid back. He bared his teeth and hissed.

Remi chuckled. "Kent looks like he's seen a ghost." He stepped into the hall and she said, "Careful . . ." but Remi was smart enough to move slowly with his hand outstretched.

He spoke in a soothing voice. "Are you the new kitty? I think you're a very handsome guy."

Madeleine followed him. "It's okay," she said to the cat. "It's okay." The fire went out of the cat's eyes, and his ears swiveled forward.

Remi looked back at Madeleine and gave her a conspirator's grin. *"Hence, horrible shadow. Unreal mockery, hence!* Do you think perhaps it's Banquo's ghost?"

"Enough clowning!" Madeleine said.

She glanced at Kent's furious face and moved to stroke the cat's head. "I'm sorry," she said to no one in particular. "I'll get him out of the way."

After their guests left, Madeleine thought Aunt Lin might say something about the cat, but her aunt strolled back into the dining room. "All this *stuff* is asphyxiating my brain cells. I could hardly stand to eat in here tonight. Keep clearing it out and we'll think of what to do next."

She yawned. "But not tonight."

Madeleine agreed and headed for her bedroom, wondering why she was so tired. She found the cat curled up on her bed, and had to smile at the memory of Remi's intervention. Banquo's ghost indeed!

Her smile faded at another memory: Kent's malicious words. The things he'd said about that family were insulting. Way out of line, even if he thought they were true.

She snapped the curtains shut. First chance she got, she was going back to visit Paula Castell, no matter what Kent said. She had a lot to learn about decoys, for one thing. But . . . Paula an alcoholic? Dan'l didn't seem to think so.

Later, as she drifted off to sleep, a question slid into her mind, stealthily, as if it had crept out from under the piled-up events of the evening.

Why was Kent so judgmental when he spoke of his cousins? Was he merely intolerant? Or was there another, deeper reason?

CHAPTER 13

Baking bread—nothing more satisfactory.
Especially breads with history:
the baguette, the Challah.
I don't need an ivory tower.
Put me in a bakery, and I'll stay forever.
~Journal

Saturday, Aunt Lin said, they would take a day off from Manor work, so Madeleine made plans. Timothy was first on her list. She'd take him the signs and the Challah braid—and some of the leftover turkey and a couple of those tarts.

Maybe she'd have a chance to talk to him about Kent, get his thoughts, and silence the questions inside her. Better take her laptop, too. She could print out her paper and start revising it.

Timothy was pleased with the signs, and even more so with the bread and the tarts. After she helped him to hang the signs, they went into his office. He made tea and opened a jar of blueberry jam for the Challah while she looked over his sewing project, spread out on the table. They sampled the Challah, discussed its texture, and he made notes as they ate.

"You'd never know," she said, "but I came to work."

"You put me to shame," he said. "Domestically speaking, I'm behind. Ripping out zippers takes a lot of time." The store bell jingled. "And so do customers."

He left, and she set up her laptop. First she'd do some research and then print out that paper.

She was reading about the Jewish traditions for Challah when the doctor strolled in with a handful of papers.

He put them on the table, saying, "There you are!"

"Here I am." She gave him an appraising glance. Jeans and a blue denim shirt. Eyes bright, but face worn. Maybe he'd been up all night with that emergency.

"I phoned the Manor and no one answered," he said. "Do you have a cell phone?"

She had to smile at his indirect approach. "Is this another embedded request?"

"You don't miss a thing, do you?"

After they'd exchanged numbers, he said, "I wanted to tell you that I'm sorry I couldn't make it last night."

"All that good food going to waste?" She regretted the words as soon as they left her mouth.

He gave her a wary look. "I wanted to be there."

Timothy spoke from behind them. "She brought me leftovers. If you're especially helpful, I might share."

"I'll change the oil in your truck—how's that sound?"

"This is turkey with stuffing, and cranberry tarts. Surely you could fix the windshield wipers too? They make a grinding noise."

"It's a deal."

Timothy sat down behind the sewing machine, and the doctor went to get himself some tea. "What's this?" He'd found the rest of the Challah braid.

Timothy said, "Ho-hum. Another item for me to proctor. Only delicious. We've already dissected it, so you may help yourself. There's jam too."

"Doesn't need jam," the doctor said through a mouthful, bringing a piece back to the table. As he pulled up a chair, his cell phone rang. He glanced at it. "I'm on call today."

He spoke into the phone, asking whether someone was still breathing and had they called an ambulance. Then he picked up his papers. "See you later," he said, and helped himself to another piece of Challah on the way out.

It had been thoughtful of him to apologize to her. Was he always so hungry?

Timothy began pinning pieces together, pink fleece this time. "So how did your dinner party go last night?"

She told him about Kent's criticism of the Castells and his slighting remarks about the local people, expecting Timothy to say how ignorant Kent was, or how shortsighted.

Timothy sewed a seam and then gave her a thoughtful look. "I see a new peace in your eyes, little lady, and I think you've walked through the doorway we talked about. Am I correct?"

She nodded, and his quiet smile came as a gift. "Not to say it will be easy," he said, "but you'll find that you're not as crippled by your grief. You'll be more free to do what God's planned for you."

God's plan? Something to think about, later. What about Kent?

Timothy picked up a long zipper, stared at it, and dropped it onto the table. "My nemesis. I've wasted more time on these things."

He glanced over to the clock on his desk. "There's a tour bus coming by in few minutes, so I won't get any more done today."

An idea had taken shape as he spoke. "How about we have a sew-in?" she said. "Tomorrow's Sunday—maybe late afternoon and evening?"

His face brightened. "Like a barn-raising?"

"Almost. If we work together on those buntings, it'll go a lot faster."

"Especially if you do the zippers."

"I'll bring supper in a slow cooker."

He started to protest, but she said, "Something easy," and they settled on a time and a menu: chili and cornbread. He'd provide the drinks and paper plates.

On her way back to the Manor, she planned the food in more detail. Bring Tabasco in case he liked his chili hot. Not too many onions, and hold the green peppers this time. Cornbread would be quick and easy.

Maybe she'd try out her next project, a Sally Lunn cake. It was a rich, yeasted cake, studded with currants and dusted with powdered sugar. Timothy would like that.

She scribbled out a list as she drove. Why hadn't he given her an opinion about Kent? Perhaps, respecting her strong-and-independent wishes, he wasn't going to tell her what to think.

Sunday morning at church, the first thing she noticed was the midwife's absence. Charlotte's client must be having her baby this morning, or maybe it had happened last night. Madeleine smiled to herself. After working at the birth center in Roanoke, she would never forget the excitement of being part of a birth.

The same small group had gathered, and Timothy spoke again from Isaiah chapter 40. He started reading at verse 12: *Who has measured the waters in the hollow of his hand?* and ended at verse 18: *To whom, then, will you compare God?*

"What's your God like?" Timothy asked. "Is He like the idols these people made, something that will rot in a few years?"

He put his Bible down on the podium. "I asked you the same thing last week. Have you thought about it?"

He went on to speak of God's everlasting love, and sadness tugged at Madeleine. This sounded like Dad. He'd say, "My forever-God has forever-love."

Jude was nodding agreement.

Timothy smiled at them all. "This is my God," he said. "The mighty Ruler of the universe who loves me, even me. And nothing will change His love."

Rock-solid love. *The Lord my Rock* took on a new meaning.

That afternoon, when she carried in the slow cooker, Timothy was already sewing. He pulled himself to his feet. "Do you need help with that?"

"Find me a place to plug it in, that's all."

She went back to her car for the cornbread and cake. Would the doctor wander in? Yesterday, he'd looked as if he ought to take a good long nap and then go fishing, or whatever he did to relax.

"Smells good," Timothy said. "I need to put our drinks in the fridge. I brought along some birch beer for you to try—it's made from birch roots. I'll be right back."

While he was gone, the bulletin board over his desk caught her eye, and she paused to read the green banner that stretched across the top. *Remember his marvelous works that he hath done; his wonders, and the judgments of his mouth. ~ Psalm 105:5*

A good verse. Like the song, "Marvelous Works, Marvelous God." She began humming it as she studied his thumbtacked collection of postcards and photographs. Timothy must have a lot of friends.

One photo caught her eye: Nathan Parnell beside a sturdy-looking blonde who was laughing at the camera. She held a small blonde girl in her arms. The caption gave their names: Susan and Susie.

The humming died in her throat. She knew he'd been married and had a child, but no one ever said where they were, just as no one ever asked her about Brenn.

Slowly she moved to the end of the table, gazing at the scattered shapes of blue fleece. She wasn't going to wonder about Susan—why should it matter? She was going to get busy and pin these pieces together and enjoy Timothy's company.

He returned a moment later, and she sat down at the sewing machine to do battle with a zipper.

They had worked for at least an hour before the doctor came in, carrying his laptop. "Such diligence inspires me," he said.

She looked up from the machine. "This is a sewing party. Don't tell me you sew too."

"I sew up people, all the time. Last night it was a boy with a six-inch cut in his leg."

She snipped her thread. "And I don't suppose you can rip it out and start over again, can you?"

"Unlike writing." He set up his laptop halfway down the table, next to her chair. "I've ripped this chapter apart, a couple of times. Can't seem to get it right."

"What's your deadline?"

"Have to mail it by Wednesday. I can't believe I'm not done yet."

She wasn't going to write it for him. It was his project, and, competent as he was, it might be good for him to struggle a bit.

She picked up another pair of front sections, basted in the zipper, and began to stitch it into place. By the time she finished, Nathan was typing, but slowly.

She showed the zipper to Timothy. "How's this look?"

"Capital! I can hem those sleeve and mitten sections. Would you like to check the one we finished and trim the seams?"

"Here's the machine," she said, and took the bunting to her chair.

Nathan spoke to his computer screen. "I wonder if it might be better to phone the editor and say it's not coming together. She's probably got more submissions than she can use."

"Don't," she said, surprising herself. "You have to write about this—it's important." She turned the bunting inside out while she thought. "It's worth fighting for. Too many people think of Alaska as a wild, beautiful place where you can grow dreams as big as cabbages."

He leaned back in his chair, listening with a quizzical look on his face.

"They need to know about the Inuit people, that the much-celebrated, stalwart native has his problems too." She shook out the bunting. "Furthermore, you have an authentic voice. You've got a wealth of firsthand knowledge. Don't let it go to waste."

Had she convinced him? Why was he having so much trouble with this?

He looked back at the screen, frowning, so she said, "Let me see your first paragraph."

He slid the laptop toward her.

She did a running commentary, which sometimes helped her students. "Good opening anecdote—Denny's family. What next? Yes, the data on alcohol-related deaths. Suicides. Young male Alaska Natives. And the focus groups."

"That's where I start bogging down," he said.

She studied him, wondering whether he had a peculiar species of writer's block. "The solution is right there in your subconscious. Do you need a nap?"

"I took one this afternoon."

"No excuses, then."

"Yes, ma'am."

The expression on his face was so piteous, she couldn't help laughing. "You're not supposed to call me that. Here, this is how you do it."

Since he was left-handed, it took only an impulsive moment to pick up his hand and put it on the mouse. "Position cursor . . ."

She kept her hand on his and guided the mouse to the beginning of the next paragraph. "Engage brain."

She removed her hand. "Now type: *What I want to say here is . . .*"

The corners of his mouth turned up. She watched as he typed, paused, and finished the sentence with IMPOSSIBLE TO ARTICULATE.

"How's that?" he said.

"Now you're being obstructive."

"Do you give such personal attention to all your students?"

"Only those with special needs."

He grinned. "Show me again—what's that I do with the mouse?"

So he'd felt it too, that leap of connection. A mistake on her part.

She reached for the pinking shears and spoke in her teacher's-voice. "Some people will try anything to get out of work. You promised to work hard."

"I stand rebuked." His eyes were unrepentant. "But can't you give me a suggestion for this part?"

She moved the laptop closer and looked again at what he'd written. "How did the focus groups work?"

He told her, and she asked, "Was Denny involved? Were you?"

"Yes, he was a group leader, and I was one of the attending doctors."

"Perfect. Put that in—it'll fit right there—and it should help."

He typed for a while, and she finished her trimming.

"How's this?" he said.

She read it. "Just right. You get a gold star." She read further. "Culturally-based interventions . . . this is interesting. And Denny's ideas . . . what he did. Nice quote here about the elders' council . . . tribal council . . . advocacy. It flows well."

She paused. "Here, about the group discussions, you already told us that."

"I'll take it out."

"Now," she said, "all we have left is the ending. It's going to be sad, but it will clinch your point."

She began reading again. "Good approach, the two men talking in the bar. About Denny, he'd just been in there for a quick drink. But where's the rest?"

"Mollie . . ."

The way he said her name, it was almost a groan.

"Denny's plane crash?"

He nodded.

She leaned back and gazed at him. "It's more than that. Can you tell me?"

He was silent for too long, didn't look at her. What boundary had she trespassed?

Finally he spoke in a frayed voice. "My wife and my little girl. Killed in a plane crash." His shoulders hunched. "It just hit me again. Four years ago. I thought I'd gotten past it. Sorry."

She knew how that felt. His pain crept into her heart, swelled her own grief. After a minute, she said, "A friend told me, 'You will hurt for the rest of your life.' " She had to steady her voice. "It's true."

"You've been listening to Timothy." He turned his head to look at her, the gray eyes sympathetic. "Your husband?"

"My father."

"I thought something about you had changed."

Yes it had, but she wasn't ready to talk about it.

"Here." She leaned over and used his mouse to scroll back up through the document. "We don't have to make it a sad ending. See what this elder said? Why not move it to the end and reinforce it with a forward looking statement. Make it hopeful."

He pulled himself upright in the chair. "Good idea," he said. "That should work." He glanced down to the end of the table, where Timothy had been working quietly, almost invisible. "Anybody hungry? Let's eat."

It wasn't true, the saying that misery loves company. To know he was hurting didn't make her feel better. It made her hurt for him, and it suggested that Susan was still very much alive.

Nathan was cheerful—in a determined fashion—while they ate, and she put on her best smile for them. Timothy was in rare form once again and had them both laughing.

He liked the chili, praised the cornbread, and did a hilarious in-depth evaluation of the Sally Lunn cake before he let her cut it. She thanked him for the birch beer and declared that it was her new favorite.

Finally she could leave.

She had told Aunt Lin she'd be going to the sew-in, and when she returned, she expected a dozen questions—Mother's style—but her aunt only smiled, thanked her for the piece of cake she'd brought, and went back to work in her office.

On Monday, her aunt left for another trip to New York, saying that she and her partner were going to interview someone to manage their marketing. She would stay overnight at her condo and drive back Wednesday evening. Bria and Jude came to help at the Manor, and the day went quickly.

Tuesday morning, she studied for the test that marked the end of this module and made a blueberry pie for Timothy. She took it over after lunch, intending to stay and work on her course.

Kent intercepted her at the store, asked who the pie was for, and said, "I want to take you out for supper tonight. It's a great place, famous for good food. How's that sound?"

"Thanks, but I've got a project to finish."

Why did she have to make excuses? Couldn't she just say 'No'?

"You could at least give me a smile." His voice hardened. "You never smile at me." He shot her a dark look and marched out of the store.

She put the pie down and hung onto the counter, conscious of a trembling in her bones. The look on his face . . . why did this man frighten her?

If Dad were here, he'd take it seriously. "Listen to your gut," he had told her, again and again. "Your intuition will give you a sense of danger that you'd better not ignore."

Timothy came out of his office, talking on the portable phone, went to check a display, and answered someone's question. After he'd hung up, he looked at the pie and smiled his thanks. "That looks downright delectable."

She eased her grip on the counter. "I'm going to take the test," she said. "Want to watch?"

He gave her a thumbs-up. "Leave it on my desk. I'll send it in today."

His office seemed a quiet haven, and a cup of strong coffee settled her. She printed out the test, finished it, and began downloading videos for the next module. The printer started up again, on its own it seemed, but a few moments later, Nathan came in and gathered up the sheets.

He brought them to her. "It's done. Want to read it one last time?"

"I certainly would."

He'd made a dozen improvements, and the ending fit well. The editor-friend should be delighted.

She handed them back, smiling up at him. "This is excellent. Are you happy with it?"

"I'm happy when you look at me like that."

She bent her head. Don't start—*please, don't.*

He gazed down at her for a minute. "Thank you, Mollie," he said, and put a hand under her chin.

She flinched, and he pulled his hand back.

Shouldn't have done that . . . his hand was so gentle.

"What is it?" His voice was gentle too.

She shook her head, turning it away. She could never tell him.

"Well," he said, his voice brisk, "I'll get this in the mail first thing tomorrow."

She nodded, wanting only for him to go, and he did.

She packed up her laptop, washed out her mug, and left the office. The red-haired man she'd seen the other day staggered past the counter, on his way outside. He was mumbling to himself with his head hanging low.

She paused, diverted. This must be Sid. Just as well she hadn't called him about her car. "Poor guy," she said to Timothy. "He's upset about something."

Timothy knit his brows. "He is. He asked whether I'd seen his girl around. But he's also had too much to drink. I never know when to take him seriously."

She left the store with Timothy's words swirling through her mind. They curdled into a warning she wished she could post:

Don't take me seriously, Nathan. Don't think about me. Don't care about me. You can't imagine the risk.

CHAPTER 14

I hate to even think about this,
but I get the shivers
whenever Kent is around.
What's my intuition trying to tell me?
~Journal

The next day when Bria and Jude came over, Jude
worked diligently until they'd finished. Then he asked, "Is
there any cooking to do?"

He sounded as if it would be a privilege, and she took
him up on his offer. They made the cinnamon-walnut
muffins he suggested, plus a chicken-and-rice casserole,
tripling the recipe so there'd be enough to stock the
freezer.

As she filled several small casserole dishes, Jude
watched her with eager attention. Was he hungry?

"If you'd like a snack," she said, "there's cookies in
the pantry. Help yourself. And get a drink of milk too."

"Yum!" He came out of the pantry eating a cookie,
and one of his pockets bulged.

When the casseroles had baked, he bent over them
with such intensity that she could guess what he was
thinking.

"Why don't you take one of these home with you,"
she said. "And some of your muffins. Tell your mother
she needs to taste them because you're going to be a
famous chef someday."

He grinned, and something about him relaxed.
"Thank you."

Bria looked up from her work at the sink, and a glance passed between them that Madeleine couldn't decode.

"Mother's feeling better," Bria said. "Would you like to come over tomorrow?"

"I'd like that," she said. At last.

The two of them certainly had a secret, or, considering the look on Jude's face today, a whole string of secrets. Would they ever trust her enough to confide?

That evening at SING, Charlotte smiled a welcome. "I can't tell you how thrilled my girls are about the canoe trip. They've been talking about it all week."

Madeleine picked up the stack of song sheets, thinking that she really should go on that trip. Maybe she wouldn't have to interact with the doctor, except in a superficial way.

She asked Charlotte about the client whose baby had been born on Sunday and told her about her friend Arlene, who was a doula and had taught her to help at births.

Howard looked as if he wanted to start the singing, so she finished passing out the song sheets and sat among the teens with Bonnie. The girl had a good ear, and soon she could join Madeleine in the alto parts. Nathan was there at the keyboard, and Remi played his guitar, as before

To keep her mind off Nathan, she watched Remi. If Remi wasn't a believer, what did he think about these songs? Some, he didn't play at all, like "Before the Throne." He shook his head and handed the guitar to Nathan. Others, like "Your Mercy Flows," he played with a thoughtful look on his face.

On the last song, Bonnie picked up the harmony right away, and they smiled at each other as they sang.

Afterward, she gathered up the song sheets, returned them to their cupboard, and paged through one of the song books she found there.

"Mollie?"

Her shoulders tensed at the sound of his voice. She'd been careful to avoid eye contact with him. He was probably offended at the way she'd reacted, and she couldn't blame him.

She put the book back and turned. Get it over with.

"About yesterday," he said. "Do I owe you an apology?" His tone was polite, almost formal.

She looked up at him. His eyes were dark as granite, and wary, as if he weren't sure what to expect from this conversation. She wasn't sure either, and she kept her voice equally polite. "I don't think so," she said.

"Still friends?"

That was safe. "Friends."

"I wanted to make sure. Have you decided about the canoe trip?"

"I'll come."

His eyes grew bright. "You could recant, but the noise from the Martinera girls would be deafening. Before I finalize the plans, let's talk. Any suggestions?"

"Just to warn you, the girls want their own canoe."

He frowned. "What do you think?"

"They probably won't last the trip in the same canoe," she said. "They'll self-destruct and then we can rearrange them. Remi wants me to go with him, but later on, you can put one of them with him, and one with me."

"Good plan," he said. "Jude asked for some pointers on steering, so I'll share a canoe with him. Pumper and Fritz work well together; I don't want to split them up."

"What about food?"

"Everyone brings his own lunch." He paused. "Do you have any stale cookies lying around?"

He was being cautious with her. If he thought he had to tiptoe, it was her fault. Maybe she could make up for that.

She gave him a teasing smile. "I see we've got Choco-Creams tonight. How about All-Chips?"

"Your cookies."

"What kind?" Good thing she'd brought her recipes.

He grinned. "Cheesecake petits-fours are not necessary. Chocolate chip? With nuts?"

"Yes."

"The best kind." Whether he was referring to her answer or the cookies, she couldn't tell. He added, "I'm bringing the drinks. You seem to like birch beer."

"Please. And lots of water?"

He gathered the teens and outlined the plans for Saturday. They'd meet at the store, and Howard Martinera would take them and the canoes to the drop-off point. Then he'd return to pick them up around four o'clock.

Nathan's voice wasn't half as loud as Howard's, but they listened.

"Bring your own lunch and a change of clothes," he said. "Pack everything in plastic, unless you like soggy sandwiches. We'll leave at seven-thirty."

Connie groaned. "On a Saturday morning?" She looked at Madeleine. "Do we have to?"

"We sure do," she said. "That's the prettiest time. Girls, I want to talk to you after this."

She told them to dress in layers, since it would be cooler in the morning. They should wear plenty of sunscreen and bring bug repellent. "And," she said, "make sure you don't complain about anything when the guys are around, or they'll never let us come again. Let's show them we're just as tough as they are."

They both hugged her and went off grinning.

Nathan caught her eye and grinned too.

The next day at lunch, her aunt suggested that they take a research visit to the glass museum in Millville—

perhaps tomorrow?—and set off with Kent, who wanted to show her the Pygmy Forest.

Madeleine tried to organize her thoughts for the visit with Paula Castell. Jude would be here in a few minutes, but first, she wanted to check on something.

She studied the four decoys lined up on her bureau. Each one had personality, but the mallard drake was the best, perhaps because of the calm, friendly look in its eyes. Was that expression characteristic of Bria's work?

She held the mallard under the lamp. Where had Bria hidden her initial? She found it on a wing: just a line and a squiggle to form a loose B. The letter blended perfectly into the gray and brown feathers.

She looked over the list of questions, slipped Jude's map into her notebook, and was ready when he knocked on the back door. What had he been up to? His face was powdered with dirt, and his jeans had brown kneecaps, as if he'd been digging.

As they walked, she took out the map and tried to match it with their route. Jude added comments and explanations. He put a finger on the map, leaving a smudge. "There's a really cool place over here. I'm making a den for the cat, in case your aunt won't let him stay."

"I wish I could tell you for sure." She described how the cat had almost attacked Kent, and Remi's joking response.

Jude grinned as he listened. *"Hence, horrible shadow,"* he said slowly. "Where'd Remi get that?"

"It's from a play written by Shakespeare."

"Which one?"

"Macbeth. There's this ghost, see, of someone who's been murdered—"

"Macbeth." Jude's face had a remembering look. "My dad read that to me. He taught Shakespeare in school."

"He was a school teacher?"

"Yeah . . . Macbeth." He seemed to be listening to the word, testing the way it sounded.

They paused to jump over a stream, and he said, "I like that. Can we name the cat Macbeth?"

"But he was a murderer!"

"Doesn't matter. Dad would like it. Call him Mac for short."

When they reached the Castells' house, Jude didn't look as worried as he had the last time. "Mother's having a pretty good day," he said.

Maybe she could get a useful interview. Even more important, maybe she could pick up on Kent's reasons for disliking this family.

The flower-sprigged living room was empty, but the workroom was not. Bria raised a disproving eyebrow at the sight of Jude's dirty face and jeans.

"I know—I know," he said. "I'll get a shower." He hurried off, and Bria motioned for Madeleine to come in.

Paula Castell didn't look up from where she sat on a stool, her long blue skirt falling around her in graceful folds. Madeleine opened her notebook and moved silently to stand behind her. Paula's knife flashed in confident strokes, shaping the upper part of a duck's head.

Bria slid onto her stool and bent over the decoy she'd been painting. This one had a chocolate brown head and back.

Madeleine took careful notes as Paula picked up a thin-bladed saw to work on the neck of her duck.

After another few minutes, Paula put down the saw. "Hello," she said. She smiled, although the smile didn't touch the blue shadows in her eyes. "I'm glad you came back."

Paula spoke as if Madeleine had visited only the day before, but at least her gaze was focused. "Do you have questions?"

She had to find out about the eyes. Each one of the finished decoys had the same look.

"What gives a decoy the expression in its eyes?" she asked.

"My grandfather taught me about that," Paula said. "I like to give mine a deep eye groove—deeper than he did on his."

She scooped out the eye area with her knife, giving shape to the duck's cheeks, and held the decoy so Madeleine could see what she'd done. "When Bria paints, she has her own way of using light and dark to get the expression she wants."

"And Jude? What does he do?"

"He's our cut man." Paula gestured toward a square table in the corner that held tools. Curls of wood littered the table and the floor. Her brow puckered. "He's not very tidy, but he does an acceptable job."

Paula began smoothing the duck's neck with a small rasp, and a tapping sound came from over their heads.

"Oh!" Bria sounded as if she'd been awakened.

"It's okay." Jude, his dark hair slicked-down wet, spoke from the doorway. "I'll get her dishes."

He touched Madeleine's notebook. "Want to meet my grandmother?"

Bria looked up again. "Do you think . . . ?"

"Just for a minute. Gemma will like her."

He took her upstairs to a large bedroom at the front of the house. In the alcove formed by a dormer window, a small, white-haired woman sat with one foot propped on a stool. A knobby brown cane leaned against the wall. That would explain the thumping sound.

The old lady put down her knitting as Jude bent to kiss her cheek, and her black eyes glinted with affection.

"This is Mollie." Jude pulled out chairs and motioned for her to sit down. "She's the one who sent the cookies and your rocking chair."

His grandmother lifted a tiny wrinkled face to study Madeleine. "My thanks, indeed." She spoke in a clear voice that was distinctly British.

Jude said, "Why don't you tell Gemma about the stuff you've discovered?"

"Certainly." Madeleine described the glassware, the china, the candlesticks, and the odd furniture, and the old lady seemed happy to listen.

"We found some duck decoys upstairs," Madeleine said. "That's why I'm here. Timothy, over at the store, told me about the ones Paula makes, and I wanted to watch her work."

"How do you find Timothy?" Gemma asked.

"An unusual person," she said. "He's been kind to me."

Gemma nodded. "He was my first friend when we moved here."

"He took me to visit Dan'l Forbes so I could ask him about decoys."

"Huh."

So that's where Jude had picked up his favorite expression. Come to think of it, they had the same black eyes, except that hers were more shrewd.

"I know that Dan'l," Gemma said.

Madeleine said, "Dan'l thought I was writing a book, like Kent Sanders. Do you like having an author for a cousin?"

"No cousin of mine," Gemma said. "Kent Sanders is a snake." She gave a short, decisive nod and picked up her knitting.

Jude collected her dishes. "We can't stay," he said. "Have a good nap, Gemma. I'll bring you some tea later on."

"Thank you." The busy hands paused, and Gemma gave Madeleine a sharp glance. "Come back," she said, and resumed her work.

On their way down the stairs, Jude was grinning. "She likes you. I knew she would. Otherwise she wouldn't have said a word. You should see how she behaves when Kent tries to get her to talk." He chuckled. "Disgraceful. He tries to charm her, and she hates that."

Paula was still at work, but Bria had finished, and Madeleine stopped to admire the new pintail decoy.

"Will Timothy be selling it for you?" she asked.

Paula looked up. "Maybe," she said. "Our decoys are being sold in other stores too. Kent says they're a good product and he's helping us. He's my—"

She looked at Jude. "What did he call it?"

"Distribution manager," Jude said, biting his thumbnail.

Madeleine closed her notebook, sensing that it was time to leave. She had picked up some details for her research, but nothing to account for Kent's attitude.

"Thank you again," she said.

"You're welcome," Paula said, already immersed in her work.

Jude walked with her out onto the porch. "Can you find your way back okay?"

"I think so, thanks to your map."

She could tell that he had something more to ask. "Do you have time," he said, "to come see the den I'm making for Macbeth?"

"I'd like that. How about late tomorrow afternoon?" She and Aunt Lin should be back by then.

He grinned. "Four o'clock? Wear hiking boots if you have them. I'll come get you."

Now that they had a cable connection, Madeleine spent the evening downloading information about the museum and looking at the next module for her course. Rolls. She chose Vienna rolls from the list and researched different types of leavening for the required paper. A short one this time.

The next morning dawned gray, with sullen clouds hanging low, and something about the wind muttering through the pines made her feel unsettled. Or maybe it was the thought of going to Millville and looking at all that glass.

Normally, she wouldn't mind. But old Jersey glass reminded her of Kent because of the way he carried on and on about his book. Please, let's not clutter this day with Kent.

The glass museum was more extensive than anything she'd imagined. Room after room displayed collections: Early American Glass; Nineteenth Century Art Glass; Cut Glass; Art Nouveau Glass, and more.

Aunt Lin's main interest was the New Jersey gallery, so she took photos and Madeleine made notes. A very old, green, flat-sided bottle seemed familiar, and an aquamarine vase looked identical to one in the dining room. Henrietta's hoarding may have resulted in some genuine antiques.

Finally Aunt Lin said, "I've seen enough glass for a while. How about lunch? One of my favorite restaurants is down Route 49, not too far from here."

The Mullica Place looked as if it had once been a mansion, and its antique furnishings complemented the expensive menu. When they'd finished their apple cobbler, Aunt Lin put down her fork with a sigh. "Just as good as I remembered. Now I'm ready to shop."

The gift shop had the same refined atmosphere as the restaurant, with polished wood shelves that displayed books, pottery, and hand-blown glass. "Beautiful colors," Aunt Lin said. "I'd love to get some of these for props— the magazine cover, you know—but look at the prices!"

"We have plenty of candlesticks and bottles," Madeleine said. "And dozens of vases. Maybe they would give the effect you want."

"You're right."

They paused in front of a sign: WOODCRAFT— SOUTH JERSEY ARTISTS. Among the wooden toys and candle holders was a trio of duck decoys.

"Decoys?" Aunt Lin picked up a mallard hen. "Look at the detail on those feathers." She turned it over. "And it's signed."

The blocky initials, PC, were burned into the wood. The price was $215.00.

Her aunt shrugged. "I don't know who PC is, but he's expensive."

"Probably because it's signed," Madeleine said. "And it's worn. Must be old." She picked up each of the other decoys. "Neither of these are signed, and they're only $100. I can see why."

They were neatly painted, but they didn't have the meticulous detail of the PC decoy.

Aunt Lin held onto the mallard hen. "Let me think about our Americana cover. Colors. Hmm." She half-closed her eyes. "We've got four, but five would be better. How about this hen? Her colors will fit, and she'll make a pair with the drake."

"She's definitely the best," Madeleine said. "But at that price?"

Her aunt laughed. "She's a necessity. I'll put this bit of pottery back." She glanced at her watch. "Let's go."

As they drove north, her aunt was silent, probably thinking her endless magazine thoughts, and Madeleine took another look at their new decoy. Who had carved it? Who had shot over it? Who had sold it into the careless hands of a dealer?

They swept up the highway, past small houses, strip malls, and billboards, and finally entered the green solitude of the pines.

By the time they reached the Manor, it was early afternoon. "I think I'll try a conference call," Aunt Lin said, and disappeared into her office.

Madeleine set the new decoy on the kitchen table and studied it. What would Dan'l think of this? She'd take him some cookies, and maybe he could tell her something about PC.

At the sight of her, Dan'l's rosy face wrinkled with pleasure. He started to thank her for the cookies, but halted, staring at the decoy.

He took it into his hands. "Nice work," he murmured, and turned it over. "By golly, I thought it looked familiar! I've got a PC too."

He lifted a shoebox down from the cupboard and took out a decoy, a pintail duck, wrapped in tissue paper.

Wordless for once, he set it beside the mallard hen and sank into a chair. He turned them both over and compared the signatures. "Signed the same," he muttered. "Sure looks the same."

The color drained out of his face. "But see—this one of yours got more detail on the feathers. It's not the same kind of duck, I know, but . . ."

Madeleine studied the mallard. Compared to Dan'l's PC, was there something different about the eye?

She was about to mention it when he said, "Not my business, not at all." He lurched to his feet, wrapped up his decoy, and put the box into the cupboard. "Just remembered," he said, "I gotta go into town." He spoke a little too quickly, and his eyes flickered away from hers.

Why were his hands shaking?

Out of pity, she said that she had to leave too. He didn't walk her to the door this time, but he did say, as she left the kitchen, "Thank you, ma'am, for the cookies."

Never mind. She couldn't have stayed much longer or she'd have been late for Jude. But Dan'l had never acted this way before.

Aunt Lin was still in her office when she returned. Good. No more decoy talk. She'd hurry into old clothes and go to meet Jude. A hike and Jude's friendly chatter—that's what she needed.

Judging from the condition of his jeans, Jude had already been hard at work. A trowel jutted from his back pocket, and he carried an armful of pine logs. He started away from the Manor at a fast lope, soon turning off onto a different path.

The landscape was nothing new—pine trees and sand, invisible singing birds, but she felt her disquiet easing toward serenity.

The pines mingled with oaks and gave way to a stand of wide-set pines with low, gnarled branches. Jude hopped across a stream and glanced back at her with a smile. They'd left the path, but he seemed to know where he was going.

He headed into a grove of towering cedars, so thickly grown that their branches shuttered the light and chilled the air. "Cedar swamp," he said. Moss floated like emerald rafts on the dark water, and a chickadee called from the shadows, singing that he was glad to be here.

Jude's grin told her that he was glad too. He circled around the swampy pools.

"You know where we are?" he asked.

"Not at all."

"Middle of nowhere, the best place for explorations."
His eyes sparkled. "You'd be amazed at the secrets in
these woods."

When they reached a small clearing, he paused with
an air of having arrived at his destination. "I like this
place," he said. "I come here to think." He walked toward
a slope-sided depression, a mere dip in the sandy ground.
Beside it stood a tree with yellow leaves that she didn't
recognize.

"Cellar hole," Jude said. He gestured at the tree.
"Walnut. They must have planted it by their house."

An uneven series of flat stones, half-hidden by grass,
stretched toward the hole. Someone's front walk.

She gazed down the walk. What hopeful wife had
watched her man set this into place? Had she lived to see
the tree grow tall, to gather walnuts for a cake?

Jude pulled out his trowel and trotted toward a cluster
of pines at the far edge of the clearing. He dropped the
logs beside a teepee of branches built at the base of a
rotting pine stump, and motioned her forward.

She knelt to look inside. He'd dug a hole, broad and
deep, and carpeted it with pine needles.

"Pretty snug," she said.

"Yeah. I hope we won't have to bring him here, but if
we do, he'll like it. I just have to finish the entrance."

After he'd arranged the rest of the logs in front of the
den, he sat back on his heels. "I've got to tell you
something," he said in a troubled voice.

Great, he'd dropped out of school or robbed a bank or
something.

He swiped at his face, leaving a dusty streak.
"There's a girl," he said, and her worry faded. Girl trouble
was easier to handle.

He reddened, as if he guessed her thoughts. "Not that
kind of girl," he said. "Stringy red hair. Skinny. She ran
away from home."

He got to his feet. "This needs a door, kind of hidden."

He paced back and forth beside the cellar hole. "There used to be bricks here, but I never meddle with ruins. Some idiot stole them, I guess."

Madeleine trailed after him. What about the girl?

They had reached the far side of the clearing when he said, "She's hiding out in the woods—scared of getting caught. She was hungry, so I took her some food."

The extra cookies? The chicken casserole?

He picked up a pair of knobby branches. "These'll work." Back at the den, he used them to form an inverted V and secured them with the logs.

"How old is she?" Madeleine asked. "Is she hurt?"

"Lots older than me. She sleeps all the time, like she's real tired."

Before she could ask any more, he got to his feet. "You don't have to do anything. Maybe she'll get well and go back home. I wasn't even supposed to tell you. Just pray."

He'd confided in her, but shouldn't she report this? Why had the girl run away? Shouldn't she find out?

"All right." She wouldn't interfere, not for now.

He pocketed his trowel with an air of finality and gave an ineffectual brush to the sand on his jeans. "Got to get home," he said. "Or Gemma will give me another talk about responsibility and stuff."

On the way back, he asked about a ride for tomorrow's canoe trip, but he didn't say anything more about the girl.

The cat was waiting for her on the porch, and she picked him up for a snuggle as she went inside. Aunt Lin had put a frozen casserole into the oven and set out fruit for a salad, so supper was well on its way.

Madeleine washed her hands, found a knife, and started cutting up an apple. "How did your phone conference turn out?" she asked.

"I'll have to go back on Monday. That deadline is breathing down our necks, and we've got too much at stake."

During supper, Madeleine tried to listen as her aunt talked about problems with the current issue, but the mental cupboard where she'd stashed Jude's secret seemed to have a door that kept swinging open. And what about Dan'l and the PC decoy? Who was PC, anyway? She should have asked him.

She made cookies for the canoe trip—chocolate chip with nuts—and turtle muffins, but it was hard to forget the look she'd seen on Dan'l's face.

By the time she finished, she was tired enough for bed. "Write in your journal," she told herself. "And pray for Jude and that girl, as you promised. Stop thinking about decoys."

She was drifting into sleep when the cat leaped onto the foot of her bed and begin grooming himself. By now, she knew the routine. First his legs, one after the other, then his back, his chest, his face. On and on and on.

Finally she sat up. "Macbeth! Can't you do your laundry some other time?"

She stroked the long silken back, and a drowsy question circled again through her mind. Who was PC?

Now the answer came: Paul Clampton. The grandfather who taught Paula all she knew.

Madeleine turned on the lamp, slid out of bed, and carried the gift-shop decoy into the light. The expression in its eyes—familiar? The eye groove—deeper? It was hard to tell without Dan'l's PC in front of her.

She studied the wings. There it was: Bria's signature.

She turned the decoy over. The initials burned into the base, and the base itself, were soiled, as if it had been handled many times. The paint was scratched too, but such things could be counterfeited. Slowly she put it back onto the bureau and returned to bed.

Mac watched her, still licking a paw.

She turned out the light and gazed into the darkness. Who would falsify a signature like that? Who else but Paula's distribution manager?

A cheap, shady operation . . . something her mother and Brenn would think was just fine.

Coldness touched her, the same chill that used to scrabble down her back when Brenn put a hand on her arm.

Brenn . . . fear . . . Kent.

"Lord," she whispered. "Be my Rock and my Fortress. I'm . . . I'm afraid."

She piled the pillows around her, pulled the blankets close. No more thoughts about the decoys or Kent.

Think about tomorrow's canoe trip. Think about the canoe gliding weightless beneath her. Think about the water sliding, sliding, sliding past.

CHAPTER 15

Dad used to take his ruffians on canoe trips.
"When your life is out of control," he'd say,
"it feels good to rule something,
even a frail bit of metal."
. . . Maybe this trip will calm me too.
~Journal

The next morning, while Madeleine was loading her backpack with food, Aunt Lin returned from a run through the fog-hung trees. "Canoeing at dawn, are we?" she remarked. "Not a bad idea—it won't be as crowded."

"That's what Nathan said." Madeleine slipped cookies into a side pocket, muffins into another.

"You look like a teenager yourself, with your hair pulled into a ponytail like that."

"I just don't want it hanging in my face while I'm trying to paddle," Madeleine said. But she did feel younger this morning.

By the time she neared Timothy's store, the fog had thinned enough for her to distinguish the Martinera's van and trailer. Three men were doing something with the canoes—Nathan, tall and slender; Remi, mid-sized; Howard, square-built. A huddle of teens waited on the sidewalk.

As she stepped out of the car, Connie shrieked, "Here she is!"

Were we just a little excited this morning?

Nathan glanced over with a smile of welcome. He must be glad, already, that he was canoeing with Jude.

"C'mon folks," Howard said. "Let's get on the road."

He and Remi climbed into the front seats of the van, and the teens filled the back two benches. The front bench was open, so she sat there, and Nathan slid in beside her.

They hadn't driven more than a couple of blocks when Connie said, "I'm starved."

Madeleine looked back at her. "No breakfast?"

"Not much. Did you bring anything to eat, Mrs. Burke?"

"Connie!" exclaimed her sister's outraged voice.

"Mom said she's such a good cook and stuff, I didn't think it would hurt to ask."

"Muffins?" Madeleine said. "That's all I'm willing to donate right now."

"Hoo-rah!" Connie said. "What kind? Can I have two?"

Madeleine handed the bag to Nathan, on the aisle. "First it goes to the pilots, up front."

After Howard and Remi had helped themselves, she leaned over to put the bag into Connie's hands. "You may pass these around and serve yourself last. Jude made the cinnamon-walnut ones."

Under cover of the resulting noise, she turned back to Nathan, saying, "That may hold them for a while."

He grinned. "Don't we get any?"

"Didn't you eat breakfast either?"

"Hardly."

"I'd thought you'd fry yourself half-a-dozen eggs and a couple of sausages, the big, greasy kind. Top it off with pancakes and toast."

He cocked his head. "You're a morning person, aren't you?"

"No, but I'm starving. Even fried eggs sound good. Would you like a muffin? Or a hard-boiled egg?"

"You have your own stash? My happy day. Yes, please, to both. What kind of muffin is this?"

"Turtle."

"For extra protein?"

"For superior energy. To appease your scientific mind, I will mention that the chocolate and pecans synergize with the caramel in the center, providing powerful antioxidants and minerals."

"Superior indeed! And your muffins are named for those fast-moving turtles?"

She elbowed him. "From the candies that look like turtles. They freeze nicely, so I'm sure you have them in Alaska. The candies, I mean."

"Mmm," he said. A minute later he asked, "These eggs. What happened to them?"

"Do you like deviled eggs?"

"Mmm-hmm."

"Then you'll like these. I deviled the yolks and put the halves back together."

"Mmm." Even with his mouth full, he wore that mischievous look on his face. "What's in the thermos?"

She lowered her voice. "Is your name Connie? Chai tea. And yes, I'll share. You must have driven your teachers wild, starting with kindergarten. How far is it to the river?"

"At least two muffins farther."

"So kind of you to lighten my pack."

Mist hung over the water, and it was still cool enough for a jacket. The sun's pale lemon disc rose higher, glinting on the frosty gunwales of their canoes and turning the maples to scarlet.

While they waited for the others, she and Remi paddled back and forth, learning each other's cadence and paddling style. She had asked to sit in the bow, letting him steer, so she could keep an eye on Bonnie and Connie.

From the noise they were making, she might have to intervene sooner than she'd thought.

Finally all the canoes were in the water. Pumper and Fritz were allowed to go on ahead, as long as they stayed within shouting distance. She and Remi paddled behind the two girls, and Nathan and Jude came last.

Remi proved to be a good steersman, and they talked quietly as they passed banks that were thick with cedar and maple trees.

This was the Mullica River, he told her, and they'd put in just below Atsion. After scouting the river, he and Doc had come up with the plan to paddle as far as Pleasant Mills, which would take most of the day.

The river gleamed in the sunlight, and she said, "Look at the color of this water! Like tea."

"They call it cedar water," he said. "Doc told me the water is naturally high in iron, and it picks up dye from the roots of mosses and cedars."

"And how about this weather—for October!" The fog had burned off, and she was already glad she'd worn her sunglasses. She glanced ahead. Connie was wearing hers too, "pink, with sparklies," as she'd put it. Bonnie had stopped paddling to pull her hair into a ponytail, and their canoe turned in circles.

Remi must have been watching. "They're lucky the river's slow here, or they'd be in the bushes." He yawned. "Going to be a warm day, isn't it? Did you get some drinks from Doc? I'm thirsty already."

"Water. It's under my pack."

They let the canoe drift while she took off her jacket and he reached for the water. "Got them," he said. "Here's one for you."

For the next few hours they followed the river's gentle curves past sandy banks and bushes. After a while the bushes were replaced by hummocks of grass, and they entered a grassy marsh.

By now, Pumper and Fritz had paddled far ahead, and Doc and Jude were out of sight behind them. The girls' canoe moved more and more slowly, but finally it crossed the marsh.

The sun was warm enough that she took advantage of the slow pace to shed another layer—the long-sleeved shirt—and rub sunscreen onto her arms and face.

Soon the banks grew crowded, with trees and bushes hanging low over the water, and the river bent into sharper turns. Remi shook his head. "Connie shouldn't be steering," he said. "She can't handle the turns."

After the next turn, the girls' canoe headed for the bank and their voices rose in disagreement as they tried to keep out of the bushes.

"How deep's the water here?" Madeleine asked.

"Four or five feet. Sandy bottom."

"That's what I thought, but it's hard to see."

The girls' canoe turned lazily in the current. Bonnie pushed it away from the bank as Connie stood up, squealing, to reach across the gunwale for something, and the canoe tipped.

A minute later, it was upside down and both girls were splashing in the water.

Madeleine dropped her sunglasses onto her pack. "I'll get them. Beach this one, okay, and come help me?"

She slipped into the water—cold but not unbearable. Bonnie seemed to be staying afloat, but Connie was screaming, bobbing under, and coming up to scream again.

"Hey!" Madeleine called. "It's not that deep. Put your feet down."

Connie was still sobbing when Madeleine grabbed for her, saying, "Stand on your feet!"

Connie looked surprised as her feet touched bottom, but she clutched at Madeleine's arm. "My sunglasses! I lost them! They were brand new."

"I'll look for them," Madeleine said. "See that little beach? You and Bonnie wait for me there."

First she had to get their canoe. She fought hanging brambles to pull it out of the bushes and slide it toward Remi, who waded out to meet her.

Now for the sunglasses. She searched along the bank—more brambles—then waded away from the bank, looking into the murky water. There, a glimmer of pink! She ducked underwater, groped along the sandy bottom, and a minute later had them in her hand.

Connie, watching, sent up a cheer. Madeleine shook the water out of her eyes and waded down to where the girls stood.

Doc and Jude, having beached their canoe, were walking toward her, and Jude wore a broad grin. No doubt Jude had made some choice comments about the girls.

She handed the glasses to Connie.

"Mrs. Burke . . ." Connie's plain little face squinched up, and she began to cry. "I'm so sorry."

Madeleine put an arm around her. "Your glasses are safe, and you didn't drown."

"But I don't want you to be angry or anything. You had to jump in the water, and it was all my fault."

"Don't you worry." Madeleine gave her a reassuring smile. She wiped the tears from Connie's cheeks and pulled her close. "Us girls have to stick together, right?"

Connie nodded, sniffling, and put on her glasses.

"Now you're lookin' cool!" Madeleine said. "Got your clothes? Better go change."

"Where?"

"In the bushes on top of that bank. They'll make a nice screen."

The girls left, and Jude came up to her, but he'd lost his grin. "What happened to you?"

She looked down at herself. Blood streaked her arms, and come to think of it, they were stinging.

"Guess I ran into the brambles."

Nathan stepped closer, but she couldn't read his eyes behind the sunglasses. "Jude, get me the first aid kit, would you?" he said. "Then you and Remi take a canoe and find us a lunch spot. Give a shout to Pumper and Fritz."

"I'm fine—I'll just wash it off," she said.

"I don't trust river water," he said. "Let me put something on those scratches."

She shrugged in agreement, and he grinned. "You were wonderful with those girls. Jude had some suggestions that weren't nearly as kind as what you did."

"That's because he's never had a pair of pink sunglasses. With sparklies."

"I'm sure you're right."

He took her arm and dabbed it with antiseptic. A light, skilful touch. He started on her other arm and paused at the scar. "What happened here?"

At first she'd hated that scar because of its jagged edges, but she'd almost forgotten about it. "I fell."

"How come?"

"Someone."

He bent over her scratches, finished up the cleaning. "Someone?"

Clouds seemed to block the sun, casting shadows across them.

He covered the scar with his hand, and his voice deepened. "Mollie?"

She looked away. "My . . . husband." She almost choked on the word. "Brenn."

He kept his hand there, a gentle pressure, and then Remi and Jude came back with Pumper and Fritz behind them.

"Get into some dry clothes," he said to her. "I'll set things up for lunch." He sounded preoccupied, as if he had something on his mind besides lunch.

As she changed, she tried not to think about the things he hadn't said and hoped he wouldn't ask any more questions.

They ate lunch on a sandy spit, and the girls were subdued, as if they thought they'd caused trouble. They huddled close to her, took off their sneakers when she did, sat cross-legged like she did, and the boys sprawled across from them.

After everyone had eaten, Madeleine handed round the cookies, and they ate in contented silence. The sun felt good on her bare feet, but her ponytail was dripping down her neck, so she took off the band and shook out her hair. Might as well look like a wet sheep dog instead of a river rat.

She flipped her hair forward, finger-combed the wet strands, flipped it back, and caught a glimpse of Nathan's face.

What was the meaning of that intent gaze? He looked different today, wearing jeans and a T-shirt like the guys, but his shirt had eagles on it instead of race cars. And his arms were solid with muscles.

She dug a toe into the sand. Brenn had been Mr. Muscles personified, careful to work out at the gym, careful about what he ate.

After a while, the guys began to discuss river ratings, and then the talk veered to baseball. Nathan leaned back against a hillock with an arm over his eyes.

Connie turned to her, started on the inevitable subject—boys—and Bonnie joined in. They described their best and worst dates. Madeleine asked about the ideal guy, and Connie said, "I'm looking for someone big, with muscles."

"And curly hair, she's told me that a hundred times," Bonnie said. "I'd rather have someone with brains."

Connie wiggled her toes and smiled at Madeleine. "What kinda guy do you like?"

Bonnie elbowed her. "She's already married."

Madeleine leaned across to ask Fritz if he had a favorite river, but Connie persisted. "So tell us about him, Mrs. Burke."

"He died." She spread out her hands. The summer's tan had erased the wide white band. "See, no rings." She smiled at Connie. "And I'm not looking."

"No fair!" Bonnie's eyes held more than idle curiosity. "But . . . if you were looking?"

Even the guys were listening, so she'd give them their money's worth.

She tilted her head back, half-closing her eyes. "Short, really short—I don't want anyone towering over me. And skinny. No hair. No teeth."

The girls laughed aloud, the guys shifted and grinned.

Connie said, "Hey, talk real."

Madeleine brushed the hair out of her eyes. "If you really want to know, I don't care about muscles or brains as much as I care about heart."

Bonnie said, "What do you mean? Someone who's crazy about you?"

"That's always nice," Madeleine said, and Connie giggled. "But I'm thinking about godliness."

Fritz looked up. "Like, he goes to church a lot?"

"More than that." She paused. "It's like God is the biggest thing in his life, takes up all of his heart. There's probably a verse in the Bible about it. Next time you catch Doc awake, ask him."

Without moving, Nathan said, "In Matthew. The Bible says a godly man loves the Lord God with all his heart and soul and mind."

"Wow!" Jude sat upright. "That's impossible."

Nathan sat up too, smiling at him. "You got it. Christ is the One who makes it happen. He changes our hearts so we can love God like that."

Remi had been fidgeting with the ties on his backpack and now he stood to his feet, eyeing the canoes.

Madeleine put on her sneakers, and the girls did too.

"Time to shove off," Nathan said. "I want to make a change. Bonnie and Mrs. Burke will switch places."

Remi must have known this would happen, but he marched off toward the girls' canoe with a dark face.

Madeleine followed him, and before anyone came near, she said, "Thanks, Remi, for not making a fuss. You're one of our leaders, you know, and sometimes a leader can't do what he wants."

"Those girls kind of spook me," he said.

"I understand. Do you have any sisters?"

A shadow crossed his face. "Used to. Sort of."

"You could pretend you're Bonnie's big brother. She wants to learn."

His smile returned. "Thanks, Mollie. I'll try."

With all the canoes moving at the same rate, the rest of the trip went more quickly.

The river spread out into another marsh, but Pumper and Fritz found the right channel, and soon they were through it and paddling near cedar trees. They floated under a bridge, then past a changing landscape of grass, bushes, pines, and dense forest.

One patch of forest had burned down to the river, leaving a black expanse of stumps. Connie said, "Daddy told us there's been too many forest fires lately. It's awful what fire does to the woods."

Kent would have delivered a lengthy rebuttal to that statement, but Madeleine didn't bring it up. No need to disturb this peaceful trip.

Nathan must have phoned ahead because Howard was there to meet them. The men loaded the canoes, and the teens piled into the van.

Howard stopped her and Nathan to ask how the girls had done, and Nathan said they'd had only one small mishap. He glanced at her. "Mollie rescued them."

"I appreciate that—thanks a million," Howard said. He hurried toward the van, and they followed. The two girls were sitting on the front bench, leaning forward to talk to Remi. Only the rear seat, half-filled with supplies, was open.

Nathan smiled as he sat down beside her. "I haven't had a chance to talk to you for hours." He put an arm along the back of the seat, lightly touching her shoulders.

Just a friendly gesture, she told herself. Relax.

"How did Jude do with his lessons?" she asked.

"Very well. He and Remi are becoming experts."

She turned to look at him. "I have to take it back."

"What?"

"The aspersions I cast upon your personal valor. Regarding those two girls."

He shook his head. "You're good with them."

They talked about the canoe trip for a few minutes, but finally he said, "I'm curious about that scar on your arm."

She tensed. At least she was wearing her jacket and he couldn't see it now.

He took her hand, as if for encouragement, and kept talking. "Why didn't they get someone to stitch it up properly?"

"Brenn put on a bandage. He said it would be okay."

"What about your mother?"

"She wouldn't think of disagreeing with him. The doctor always knows best."

"He was a doctor?"

"Hemopathology. See articles on bone marrow by Dr. Brendon T. Burke. If it matters."

She leaned back against the seat, closing her eyes, but her voice shook, and a tremor rose inside her. "Please, Nathan, talk to me about . . . about . . . Alaska? Tell me about your igloo."

"It was an excellent igloo," he said, "white and cold, with a marvelous skylight, and a white picket fence that the whole village envied."

The trembling eased as he spoke, and she didn't mind when his arm curved around her shoulders.

The teens had started arguing about something, and finally Howard roared, "C'mon folks! Let's sing!" He began with "Shout to the Lord," and everyone joined in.

Nathan sang in a low, warm voice, and after a while she could sing too.

The next morning on their way to church, Madeleine asked Jude about the girl he'd mentioned. "Don't stop praying," he said.

"How did you happen to find her?"

"I was over near Apple Pie Hill. I'd followed some coon tracks to a stream and saw footprints in the mud, so I got curious. It's just summer cabins around there."

She drove slowly, wanting to hear more.

"Then here she comes, limping down to the water like some wounded animal, fills a thermos, and drags herself back the way she came."

"You followed her?" Madeleine parked in front of Timothy's store.

"Yeah. I'm getting better at tracking. Found out she's sleeping on the deck of one of those cabins." He opened the car door. "That's about all."

For his message, Timothy spoke of God's wisdom, and at the end he challenged the small congregation to begin reading the book of Ephesians. "Let God show you who He is and give you His wisdom."

Madeleine put away her notebook. Maybe she'd do that. She certainly needed wisdom. About Jude's girl. And Kent . . . and the decoys. What was going on with them, anyway?

While they sang the closing hymn, she prayed for wisdom, and during the last verse, decided to talk to Timothy about the PC decoy. Maybe she had jumped to a conclusion.

They had planned another sew-in for the evening, but she didn't want to wait that long. On her way out, she asked Timothy, "Will you be home this afternoon?"

"Sitting out on my deck," he said, "soaking up some rays. Want to talk? I'll send Hey-You over around 1:30."

She thought he was joking, but not long after they'd eaten lunch, Aunt Lin called to her. "That dog of Timothy's is sitting on the back porch. Do you have any idea why?"

Madeleine laughed. "I was planning to go see Timothy this afternoon, and he said he'd send the dog over, but I can't believe . . ."

"Believe it," her aunt said. "I've heard about that dog. He is so smart I'd like to have him on my staff."

As she stepped out of the door, Hey-You greeted Madeleine with extravagant tail-wavings. He gulped down her offering of a tuna sandwich and bounded into the woods.

Timothy was sitting on his balcony with a steaming mug and a book. He picked up a thermos and gestured toward the chair beside him. "Pour yourself some cocoa," he said. "Sit down and cover up with that blanket. It's chilly today."

She settled herself under the blanket. How to begin?

"What's on your mind, little lady?"

"It's about Paula's decoys. You get them direct from her and sell them for seventy-five dollars, right?"

"Right. I pay her sixty-five."

"Apparently Kent is handling the rest of their distribution. Bria says he gives them seventy-five for each one he sells."

Timothy shrugged. "He's not running a business."

"I understand." She took a sip of cocoa. "What if he was selling the decoys for more than two hundred dollars and not telling her about it?"

"He couldn't get that much. She's not well known."

"What if he was faking Paul Clampton's initials on the bottom and selling them as antiques?"

Timothy thought about it, knitting his brows. "Paul Clampton is still a big name in South Jersey. Are the decoys identical?"

"Almost. Bria uses a hidden signature."

"Scoundrel! He'll never get away with it. Not for long, anyway." He frowned. "The trouble is, when he gets caught, it'll be the Clampton name that's dragged through the mud."

She hadn't thought of that. "What do you think I should do?" Hurriedly, she amended her words. "I mean, what could be done? I really don't want to get involved."

Timothy turned his head to give her a considering look.

She gazed out at the trees, and the silence between them lengthened.

Maybe he would let her off the hook, change the subject, as he did when he knew she was uncomfortable.

Good, he'd started talking about Jude, how he'd come back from the canoe trip with questions about loving God.

She smiled. "Jude's growing, isn't he?"

Timothy's smile agreed with her. "He found the passage in Matthew that speaks of the first commandment. Now we're discussing the second. Do you know that one?"

Of course she did. "Love your neighbor as yourself."

So he hadn't been letting her off—he'd been sharpening the hook.

His voice was gentle. "Kind of sounds like a matter of obedience, doesn't it? Getting involved."

She dug her fingers into the blanket.

He picked up his book. "As a literary person, you might be interested in this." He turned some pages, stopped, and began to read aloud: *"There is no safe investment. To love at all is to be vulnerable. Love anything, and your heart will certainly be wrung and possibly be broken."*

He paused, as if waiting for her to say something.

She frowned. "That's a rather broad statement."

"The author explains, *If you want to make sure of keeping it intact, you must give your heart to no one, not even to an animal . . . lock it up safe in the casket . . . of your selfishness. But in that casket—safe, dark, motionless, airless—it will change. It will not be broken; it will become unbreakable, impenetrable, irredeemable."*

Piercing words. Don't think about them.

She drank the last of her cocoa, and said nothing.

After a minute, Timothy said, "It may be that God plans to use you on the Castells' behalf, little lady. Why not ask Kent about the decoys? Perhaps he can explain it as something besides plain skullduggery. Perhaps you can persuade him to stop."

"What makes you think he'll listen to me?"

He leaned back in his chair and regarded her through half-closed eyes. "We all know he thinks highly of you. And your aunt."

"It's sickening," she said. "I wish he'd go away and leave us in peace."

"Perhaps he will, after this is over." He gestured with the book. "That passage was just an opinion from C.S. Lewis. It's more important to ask yourself: 'What does my God think about the situation?' "

She nodded, but only to show that she'd heard.

This was too much. She didn't have to do everything he said.

Fear inched down her spine, chilling each bone it passed. She hadn't asked to be part of this, and she wasn't going to . . . she couldn't . . . tangle with Kent.

She pushed the blanket off her knees and stood up. "I'd better get back and check on our food for tonight. Thank you for the cocoa."

"You're very welcome." Timothy stood too, pulling his jacket close. "Be careful, whatever you do." He whistled for the dog. "Here's your trusty guide to take you home."

"I know the way," she said, and immediately tried to temper her ungracious reply with a smile.

But the air seemed to have grown colder and more biting. Even after she'd reached the sheltering trees, wind tossed the upper branches of the pine trees, sending them askew. She huddled deep into her jacket.

"Lord," she said aloud, "This whole thing scares me, and I don't know why, but I've got to stay out of it. Why can't someone else talk to Kent?"

CHAPTER 16

Every time I turn around,
someone has a problem.
Me too! And I've got enough to deal with.
Maybe old Dan'l has the right idea.
Is it any of my business?
~Journal

That evening, Timothy was congenial as they worked
on the new green buntings. He made her laugh, praised
her chicken soup and the crusty rolls, and told her how
much he'd enjoyed the pie. They discussed the history of
Vienna rolls, and he informed her that in New England
they were called bulkie rolls.

He didn't mention Kent's name or refer to the
decoys. No doubt he was praying for her—an
uncomfortable thought.

While she sewed, words trundled through her mind
on an endless loop: *Love your neighbor . . . Love anything
and . . . use you . . . persuade him . . .*

Nathan came over from his office with paperwork
and stayed for supper. His steel-blue sweater made his
eyes a softer gray, and it seemed that he looked at her
differently tonight, but perhaps she was imagining it.

The men talked about flying. They'd both owned
planes in Alaska, and both had stories to tell. Then they
talked about ruins. She described the old Dumont ruins
and the place Jude had showed her. Timothy laughed,
saying he should get her a reference book if she liked
ruins so well.

She had to defend herself. "There's *tongues in trees, books in the running brooks, sermons in stones.*" One of Shakespeare's gems.

Nathan looked at her. *"And good in everything."*

"How'd you know that line?"

He shrugged. "Must have heard it somewhere."

He talked for a while about the ruined mines he'd seen in Alaska, and then Timothy said he was kind of tired tonight. If they would excuse him, he'd go on up to bed.

She had one more hood to finish, so she said, "We'll pick up things here. Sleep well."

Nathan worked on his papers while she sewed the hood into place and topstitched the neck seam. She stacked the remnants beside the sewing machine and gave him a smile, ready to leave.

He came to her side of the table and put a hand on her arm. "Time to say good night?" He drew her towards him, and she went. His touch was gentle. Maybe it would be all right.

His face was warm against hers. "Mollie . . ." He kissed her forehead, her cheek, her chin. His lips found her mouth.

Nausea struck like a blow.

She jerked away. Her breath came in panting gasps. Her pulse pounded in her ears: *danger-danger-danger*. She clawed at him and he was saying, "What? What is it?"

She shook her head, whimpering, shivering. Cold. Cold. Too cold to breathe.

His arm went around her and his voice came low and soothing. "It's okay, Mollie. You're safe here. Breathe slowly. Breathe with me."

She huddled against him, felt the rise and fall of his chest. She could do that.

"Good girl. As if you were singing. Take a big breath, expand your diaphragm. Again . . . Again . . ."

She breathed with careful attention, letting him hold her.

"Mollie, what did I do?"

The fear lingered, freezing her voice, and she couldn't speak. She moved his hand to the scar on her arm.

"Brenn?"

She nodded.

"He hurt you?"

She shivered. "He . . . liked . . ."

She rested her cheek against the warm sweater, just for a minute, and he stroked her arm. He didn't seem to mind that she'd treated him as if he were loathsome.

He stood quietly while she searched for words. "Sorry," she mumbled. "I . . . I didn't mean for this to happen."

What must he be thinking? One of those loonies that doctors run into from time to time. Stay away from this girl.

Shame flared, scorching her face, giving her strength to push away from him, and he let her go.

She stepped to the table, bracing herself against it. Please don't let the trembling start again, not here, not in front of him. Lord my Rock, I need You.

She put away the scissors and the pin cushion, slid the rolls into their bag, and unplugged the slow cooker. No more talk. Just leave.

He watched, silent.

But now he was moving to intercept her.

Lord, help! I've got to get out of here without making a fool of myself again.

He took the slow cooker from her hands and set it on the table.

She risked a glance at him. Soft gray eyes, troubled.

"Don't go just yet," he said. "Dear heart . . ."

The tenderness in his voice gave her pause, and so did the old-fashioned endearment, an echo of Wyatt's famous poem, Shakespeare's sonnets. He had no idea how it would sway her resolve.

He slowly reached for her hand, and she allowed him to take it.

"Let's sit down," he said.

She stiffened, and he must have sensed her fear. "I won't . . ." he said in a broken voice. "I won't hurt you. Come, pray with me."

He led her to the sofa, and she sat beside him, cautiously, thinking that it had been a long time since she'd prayed with anyone. He linked his arm with hers, warming her hand in his, and it was all right.

Shakespeare's hopeful words floated past:

Wilt thou kneel with me?

Do, then, dear heart;

for heaven shall hear our prayers.

Nathan bowed his head. "Father . . ." It was the voice of a son reaching out his hand to be grasped. "Father, we are in need tonight."

He paused. "Pour your mercy upon us. You have a plan for Mollie in all of this. Hold her close." He paused again. "Show us what to do. Please, I ask in Jesus' name."

He didn't move to get up, and after a minute she leaned her head against the solid warmth of his shoulder. "Thank you," she whispered.

You have a plan for Mollie, he'd said. Her thoughts leaped back to Timothy's words: *It may be that God plans to use you . . . .*

She shook her head, and Nathan's hand clasped hers more tightly.

Your plan, Lord?

Was she supposed to do something about Kent?

What if she froze? What if it all came to nothing?

But how could she refuse to obey her forever-God with His forever-love? He knew her fears.

She squeezed her eyes shut. *Lord, about Kent. Show me? I'll do whatever You want.*

Slowly she opened her eyes. Nathan, still unmoving, sat with his head bowed over hers. Such a kind person.

She looked up at him. "I should leave now."

"You've been thinking?"

"Something you said." She leaned forward. "It's late, and you have Clinic tomorrow."

She could see the reluctance on his face, but he let her go.

She scribbled a note for Timothy—*I will obey. Pray for me.*—and pinned it onto his pin cushion.

She wanted to sleep in the next morning, just a little, but Aunt Lin was up early, taking a shower and bustling around, as if she were eager to get back to New York.

The wind had increased. "Listen to that!" her aunt said. "The way it tears at this house is downright eerie. They're saying it might snow."

Her aunt left soon after, in spite of the forecast. They had briefly discussed what Madeleine could do while she was gone. The dining room. The parlor. Inventory the Blue Room. Plenty of reasons to stay inside and mind her own business.

She had discovered three dead mice in the Blue Room traps when Bria knocked on the back door.

Jude had come too. "No school today," he said with a grin. "Teachers doing stuff."

"Perfect. I've got some mice for you to dispose of."

He emptied and reset the traps, using a piece of walnut as bait, and she wondered whether he would say anything about the girl.

He glanced up. "I went to see her this morning. She don't—doesn't—look too good. She's got a sore leg. Do you have any extra food?"

"Take all the food you want. But what about her leg?"

"She cut it. I don't know how. It's swelling up."

"Jude, she needs help. She can't keep doing this."

Worry darkened his eyes. "I know. She won't go home. Says she'd rather die."

Madeleine gazed across the room, crowded with sofas and chairs. The rug under her feet was thick and warm and dry. That girl was sleeping in the cold. It might snow.

But this wasn't her house. The girl wasn't her responsibility.

"Where is this place?" she asked.

"Not very far."

The girl was hungry. *Love your neighbor as . . .*

"Come on," she said. "Help me pack up some stuff. We're going over there."

She hurried down the hall with Jude scrambling to keep up with her. "Bria," she called, "can you get me a first aid kit?"

"Sure." Bria stepped out of the dining room. "For the girl? From what Jude says, she's going to be upset."

"She'll get over it." Madeleine started heating water in the microwave. "Jude, find some chicken in the fridge and make her a sandwich. With cheese. I'll need a thermos too."

When the box was ready, she glanced at Bria. "Do you want to come?"

Bria looked grateful, but she said, "Maybe I'd better stay here and keep working."

"Okay. Listen for the phone."

Once they were in the car, Jude gave her directions, taking back roads she hadn't seen before. Finally he pointed out a driveway.

"Let's bring just the thermos to start with," Madeleine said, glancing through the trees at the gleaming logs of a two-story home. Some cabin! It looked deserted.

At the back, a deck extended toward the trees, and a second-story balcony formed a roof above it. They tiptoed up the steps until Jude paused. In the corner lay a pile of blankets.

As they went closer, the blankets stirred, and a voice muttered.

Jude bent down. "Hey," he said in a low voice.

A hand pushed back the blankets, revealing a girl's pallid face and closed eyes. "Go away," she said.

Jude looked at Madeleine, and she said softly, "We brought you something good to drink."

The eyes opened, cinnamon-brown eyes that stared at her suspiciously. "Who's she?"

Jude dropped to his knees. "A friend. Come on. You need to drink some cocoa."

"Cocoa?" The girl pulled herself up onto an elbow, and red hair fell across her face. Stringy, as Jude had said.

She took the cup from him and emptied it in short gulps. "I told you don't bring no one," she mumbled. She gave a little *uhh* of pain. "If it weren't for this leg, I'd be gone by now."

Madeleine knelt on the deck beside her. "May I look at it?"

"Nah. Just a cut," the girl said, but her voice was faint. "Lemme sleep." She dropped the cup and sagged back into the blankets.

Madeleine shook her head. "Jude, she's sick. She's just going to get worse. And it might snow tonight."

A plan, half-formed in her mind, took on the hard edges of certainty. "I want to take her back to the Manor."

"But she'll fight us. She's all muscle." He looked as if he'd already had experience with those muscles.

Madeleine got to her feet, smiling. "Do you mean to tell me that one skinny girl is stronger than the two of us? Stay here. I'll bring the car closer."

On her way, she phoned the Manor, and on the fifth ring, Bria answered. Madeleine gave her quick instructions. "Hi, could you vacuum that sofa in the Blue Room and get some sheets and blankets on it?"

"You're bringing her here?"

"Yes. See you in a little bit."

The girl lay just as Madeleine had left her, and Jude still looked worried. "She's going to be mad. She'll kick and scream."

But, as Madeleine suspected, the girl no longer had the strength to kick and scream. She half-opened her eyes and moaned as they pulled her to her feet and helped her walk to the car.

"Back seat," Madeleine said. "I don't think she can sit up."

The girl slumped into a corner, and they loaded the duffle bag and blankets in beside her. Jude sat there too, in case she fell over, and Madeleine drove with care.

Bria met them outside and helped them get the girl inside to the sofa. Madeleine took off the heavy parka. She was, as Jude said, very thin. An older teen.

"Does she have any other clothes?" Bria was eying the girl's muddy jeans and sweater.

Jude said, "There's a duffle bag with stuff, but no nightgowns or anything like that."

Madeleine smiled to herself. A girl like this wouldn't be caught dead in a nightgown. "I've got something she can use. Thanks a lot for helping."

Bria sized up the situation right away. "C'mon Jude. We've got work to do.

The girl was still apathetic, her eyes half-closed. Madeleine washed her face and arms, stripped off the dirty clothes, and put her into a pair of warm pajamas. Around her neck hung a pendant on a greasy leather cord, and when she tried to take it off, the girl grabbed for it, so she left it there.

The cut on the girl's leg was almost three inches long, deep, and obviously infected. She bathed it carefully before spreading it with antibiotic ointment and covering it with a loose bandage.

The girl accepted a mug of thick soup and swallowed the aspirin Madeleine gave her. Then she burrowed into the blankets until her head was out of sight.

Back in the kitchen, Madeleine made sandwiches for their lunch, still thinking about the girl. Would a cut like that heal on its own?

After they'd eaten, she looked in on the girl again. Now that her face was clean, you could see the freckles across her nose and the pallor of her skin—a pretty face. Her parents must be frantic.

She stopped in at the dining room to help Bria and Jude pack boxes, but soon she caught herself staring out the window, wondering what to do.

Timothy. He'd know.

He answered the phone right away, and she told him what she knew about the girl and how she'd brought her to the Manor.

"Your aunt is away?"

"She won't mind—at least, I hope not. The cut seems to be infected. Jude said she acts like she's afraid to go home."

"She's a teenager?"

"Around seventeen."

"Sounds like a runaway." He paused. "The Lord has probably sent her to you for His good reasons. Let's see . . . that cut. Why don't you talk to Nathan?"

Perfectly logical, but she didn't want to ask Nathan for anything. He had put up with enough from her.

"Thanks, Timothy. Just wanted to get your opinion."

The girl was leaning against the pillows, drinking more soup under Bria's watchful eye. She ate some toast but didn't say anything besides, "Got any peanut butter?" Then she curled into the blankets and went back to sleep.

That was a good sign, wasn't it?

Madeleine worked with Bria and Jude for the rest of the afternoon, and the two of them left after an early supper, carrying a plate of food for Paula and Gemma.

The girl seemed to be sleeping peacefully, so Madeleine read an essay on leavening agents until her eyelids drooped.

That evening Mac stayed outside, and when he returned, his fur was powdered with snow. She watched him licking one paw after another and thought about the girl. She'd have been much too cold, trying to sleep on that deck.

Timothy had suggested reading the book of Ephesians, so she opened her Bible to the first chapter. Just a few verses, he'd said, but the marvelous flow of words, phrase upon sumptuous phrase, kept her reading. *Redemption through his blood . . . the riches of his grace . . . the mystery of his will.*

His will. His plan. His reasons for sending the girl . . . here.

"Lord," she whispered, "please help her to get well fast."

Because she didn't want to be responsible? She ignored the cynical question, scribbled a few words in her journal, and tried to sleep.

Around midnight, she heard the girl's voice and went to check on her. She was tossing back and forth, so Madeleine turned on a low lamp.

The girl cried out.

Madeleine knelt and put an arm around her. "Hey, it's okay! I'm your friend." She said the comforting words over and over while the girl huddled against her and sobbed.

After a while she quieted, and Madeleine gave her juice and more aspirin. Her cheeks were flaming. The cut looked worse, streaked with red.

She changed the bandage and sighed in defeat. She'd have to phone Nathan.

CHAPTER 17

It's so late and I'm so tired,
and I don't want to ask him for anything.
But what about the girl?
~Journal

Madeleine glanced at her watch. 5:00 A.M. Still too early to phone anyone. She sat up, stiff from sleeping on the floor by the sofa, and shrugged off her blankets.

The girl was asleep, but breathing rapidly.

She turned on a lamp at the back of the room and once again bathed the girl's face and arms with cool water. The girl turned away, moaning. It had been only an hour since the last aspirin.

5:24. Madeleine sank back down beside the sofa. What was making her feel queasy, giving her chills? It wasn't about the girl. More like . . . something she'd promised to do.

Kent. She really didn't want to talk to him.

She leaned her head against the cushioned velvet. "Lord, I can't handle any more of that man," she whispered. "Please! Don't make me talk to him—I'll do anything else."

The girl stirred, muttering, and Madeleine put a hand on the thin arm. Burning hot.

Now she had this girl to deal with, and Nathan. After what happened, she was going to feel awkward with him, and for sure, he'd want to keep his distance.

She looked at her watch. 5:32. Did he get up this early? She went back to her bedroom, made the bed, and tidied the desk. Finally she picked up her phone.

He answered on the first ring.

"I'm sorry to bother you," she said.

"Mollie! Are you all right?"

"I've got a teenager here. With a fever and a cut on her leg—it looks infected."

"At the Manor?"

"Yes."

"I'm near there. Ten minutes."

Better change quickly—jeans, and the cranberry shirt, to give herself cheer. While she brushed her hair, she made a resolution. She would be calm and controlled with him, not the clinging wreck she'd been on Sunday night. Forget Sunday night.

Coffee. She'd seen him drink it. It was so early, they'd both want some.

She set the coffee to perk and folded her blankets into a pile beside the sofa. Before the coffee had finished, a red Jeep was churning up the driveway through the slush.

A minute later, he stood at the door with a brown messenger bag slung over his shoulder. He gave her a searching look, but that was all. He was trying to forget too.

"The girl's back here," she said, and led him into the Blue Room.

He knelt beside the sofa and studied the girl's face for a minute. He took her temperature, checked her pulse, and listened to her chest.

"Has she been starving herself?"

Madeleine told him how Jude had found her, and he nodded.

He eyed the cut on her leg, and set about cleaning and bandaging it. "How'd she do this?"

"We don't know."

"What's her name?"

"We don't know."

He frowned, looking up at her. "Why is that?"

"She's hardly said a word since she got here."

The girl stirred and cried out, as if the sound of his voice had roused her. Madeleine knelt and put a hand on her arm as she had so many times during the night. The girl reached for her and quieted.

"I'm going to give her an antibiotic and leave some pills. Make sure she takes them all." He was preparing a needle as he spoke. "But what she needs is lots of liquids—whatever she wants to drink—and some good nursing care."

"I can do that," Madeleine said.

He smiled for the first time. "I'm sure you can."

She watched as he packed up his bag. He was unshaven, and he had that gray look to his face. Had he been out already this morning?

They walked side by side down the hall. Quite civil, they both were. Nothing at all had happened Sunday night.

"There's coffee. Would you like some?"

"I think so." He followed her into the kitchen. "Black, please." He dropped into a chair at the table and closed his eyes. "Sorry, I'm not very presentable." He scrubbed at the reddish bristles on his chin. "Been up all night."

She turned to look at him. "What happened?"

"Sick child. High fever. I would've put her in the hospital, but they don't have insurance." He stared out at the dark trees. "When you called, I thought it was the mother."

"Let me make you some breakfast, Nathan."

A tired smile. "I know your idea of breakfast—fried eggs and sausages and pancakes and toast." He propped his head on one hand. "Scrambled eggs would be fine. I think I'll take a nap if you don't mind."

He pillowed his head in his arms, and the tense line of his shoulders eased.

She let him sleep for as long as possible. She checked on the girl, rummaged through the pantry to find homemade jam, sliced plenty of bread for toast, and set out the eggs. He slept.

What time did the clinic open? Early, that's all she knew.

She poured herself a cup of coffee, arranged the table with sugar and cream and napkins, added knives, forks, and spoons. He didn't stir.

Might as well scramble the eggs.

She put his plate of eggs on the table and stayed there, looking down at him. Reddish-brown hair with ends that curled. A slender tanned neck.

She touched his shoulder, lightly. Nothing personal.

His head came up, his arm went round her waist, and he drew her close. He leaned his head against her. "Mollie."

Warmth stirred, flowed into her cold bones. She put out a hand, and his hair under her fingers was thick and springy. Chestnut, that was the color. She slid her hand down the side of his face, smoothing the lines, the puckered scar, the stubble of his beard, and all she wanted to do was hold him in her arms.

Not for her. Not now, not ever.

"Your eggs," she said, stepping back. "Would you like toast?"

He sat up with a faint smile. "I would like . . ." He let the sentence hang, and she turned away. "Toast would be excellent," he said, "I'm probably late already."

He ate rapidly and took another piece of toast with him. "Great toast," he said. "That's a good color on you. Wake the girl up every few hours, and give her plenty to drink and a little to eat. Soon as I get a chance, I'll stop by."

After his Jeep disappeared into the trees, she returned to the girl. Still sleeping. She spread her blankets beside the sofa and snuggled into them. A smile escaped. Almost calm and controlled.

The next thing she knew, Bria was at the door.

She told her what the doctor had said, and Bria smiled. "My brother will be so glad."

A thump from the Blue Room startled them, but when they got there, the girl was picking herself up off the floor. She held onto the back of a chair. "I'm okay, I'm okay," she said. "Where's the restroom?"

Madeleine let her stagger alone to the bathroom, since that was the way she wanted it. Meanwhile, she'd get a snack ready.

The girl ate and drank without saying anything, and then went back to sleep. Madeleine and Bria cleared the rest of the boxes out of the dining room, and when Jude came, he helped them move all but two of the cabinets into the parlor.

They stopped for a rest, and Madeleine, trying not to wonder about the girl, studied the changed face of the dining room. The green walls were patchy, as if someone had pulled down most of the wallpaper and painted over whatever was left.

"This room could use a coat of paint. We'd have to do some prep work, but it might make a big difference."

"I agree," Bria said. "When I stay in here for too long, I begin to feel seasick."

"Let's start with a good cleaning. I'll ask Aunt Lin about paint."

They were still working when the phone rang. She picked it up, rehearsing an explanation about the girl for her aunt, but it was Kent.

He seemed in good spirits—just wanted to say hello.

He must have recovered from his tantrum.

And, he said, he'd called to tell her about a wonderful place he'd found to eat, over in Tabernacle.

He apologized for such short notice, but they were having an Earlybird Special, tonight only—their Pine Barrens Beef Filet. "They put crabmeat on it," he said, "and hollandaise sauce. It's a package deal, with their signature blueberry pie for dessert."

His voice softened. "I didn't mean to make you mad the other day. Will you go with me?"

"Tabernacle?" Her mind raced. She could ask him about the decoys. Was the Lord opening this door?

If she insisted on driving her own car, it should be safe enough.

"It's a nice restaurant," he said. "Please come?"

"I think so," she said. "But I'd like to drive my car. I could meet you there."

"Whatever you wish, elfin princess." He made it sound like a gift. "Tell you what: I'll come over, and you can follow me." They agreed on five o'clock.

A snake, Gemma had said. Be careful, Timothy had warned. Yes.

After Bria and Jude left, Madeleine took the girl some juice and another sandwich, but she was lying with her back to the room, still sleeping. She had refused to talk to anyone, even Jude.

Time to get dressed. Where was the cat?

She leaned out her window, pushing aside the juniper branches to look at the dainty cat-tracks that disappeared into the trees. "Wish you were here, Mac," she said. "I should take you along for protection, but you wouldn't like the car. I should have invited Hey-You to this dinner party."

She gave herself a mental scolding. The Lord knew about tonight. She could trust Him, whatever happened.

While she dressed, she reminded herself that she'd be driving her own car and they'd be in a restaurant full of people. No need to worry about the girl, either. She'd probably sleep the whole time.

Kent drove in precisely at five, looking handsome in his leather jacket and brimming with charm. He helped her brush the snow off her car and returned to his Bronco. "Follow me," he called. "I'll wait if you get stuck in traffic."

Not likely around here, but it was a considerate thought. She pushed in the clutch, turned the key, and the engine raced but didn't start. She tried again. How about some gas? No, that didn't help.

Kent was sitting in his car, exhaust billowing into the air, waiting. She tried once more. What could be the matter? She *had* to have a car, especially tonight.

Kent was out of his Bronco now, walking over to her. "Car problem?"

"I can't imagine—it just had a tune-up. Could you check?"

"Sorry! I only know where the gas tank is." He shrugged, lifting his hands palms up, giving her a sympathetic smile. "Look. Why don't you just hop into my car? It's probably safer, anyway, with snow on the roads. We've got reservations and I wouldn't want someone else to get our table."

He stood patiently in the twilight, his manner helpful and concerned.

Maybe she could talk to him here. She put on a smile. "I wanted to ask you about something."

"Sure, when you look at me like that, I might even tell you the truth." He laughed, as if it were a tremendous joke. "But let's talk over supper. You know what they say, *Don't rile a hungry man.*"

It was too late to back out, especially if she wanted to change his mind.

"Okay," she said, hoping it would be. "I guess I'll have to phone someone about my car."

His Bronco was pleasantly warm, and the paved road, when they reached it, was clear of snow. Kent made small talk, and she began to relax in the cushioned seat. He turned on the radio, but after a few minutes of listening to business news, punched it off. "Not the right ambience," he said, giving her a smile.

Ambience? Whatever he had in mind, it was going to suffer a drastic change when she confronted him about those decoys. Should she? If the Lord wanted her to do it, He'd give her an opening. Wouldn't He?

The Tabernacle Grille looked familiar, and she remembered seeing its gabled roof when she'd first driven past. Inside, wooden beams and the abundance of wide windows, lamps, and hanging plants gave it an upscale-rustic look. Kent took her to a table beside a planter strung with tiny lights.

"That special does look good," she said, after studying the menu.

"You're so pretty when you smile," he said.

And at other times, she was an old hag, right?

But she smiled again. Keep the *ambience* happy.

The beef was excellent, topped with crabmeat, as he'd said, and the hollandaise sauce was freshly made. He ordered grilled asparagus for them both.

She ate slowly as he expounded on the benefits of forest fires.

"This area is unique in regards to fires," he added. "There are only three kinds of pines that send out sprouts after a fire, and two of them are right here—the pitch pine and the short leaf pine. Almost every woody species around here has the ability to sprout again after fire."

She ate another piece of asparagus and wished that this evening were over. "No wonder there's so many pines, if the fires don't kill them."

"Exactly." He smiled as if she'd made a remark of startling brilliance. "What we have here is a biological inertia: the cycles of fires and sprouting over the years has resulted in a preponderance of species that are highly flammable and yet will rejuvenate themselves quickly."

He talked on and on, about his college days at UCLA and his work with the Forestry Department, and he spoke at length on the advantages of prescribed burning.

Not once did he mention the Castells or anything she could construe as an opening for her to talk about the decoys.

Maybe the Lord didn't want her to ask.

But she had a growing sense that He did. Maybe He wasn't going to make it easy.

She waited until they had eaten mountainous pieces of the famous blueberry pie—sparked with lemon zest, like hers—and were drinking their coffee. He looked relaxed and good humored.

"Tell me," she said, "about the decoys you're selling for Paula Castell."

His smile didn't change. "She told you about that, did she? Poor thing. I sell a few of them for her." He glanced at the slender blonde arriving at the next table.

"I saw one of Paula's decoys the other day," she said. "At a store down near Millville. It looked a lot older, and it was being sold as an antique. Very expensive."

Now she had his full attention. Say it. "Someone had burned the initials PC on the base."

"Really?" he said, in a how-'bout-that tone of voice.

She watched his eyes. "I learned that it's considered valuable because PC was well-known in South Jersey, about forty years ago."

"Oh?" Kent took a drink of his coffee, and wiped a droplet of sweat from the side of his face. "But how do you know the one you saw was Paula's? She doesn't sign her work."

"Hers have a rather distinctive eye groove. Dan'l has a genuine PC, and I noticed a few other small differences."

She didn't give him a chance to object. "The decoy in that store was selling for an inflated price, compared to the ones in Timothy's store. What do you know about that?"

"Okay, Madeleine, don't sit there looking like an outraged mother hen. You know how it is. If a decoy looks old, it'll sell for more. And if they assume that it's Clampton's, I can't help it. They have the same initials."

She gazed steadily at him, and he shrugged. "Just wanted to make a little extra money for Paula. She's family, after all. And PC was her teacher as well as her grandfather, so, artistically speaking, they're his work."

She'd let that go. "And how much does dear Paula get out of this scheme?"

He smiled, the blue eyes opaque. "I give her seventy-five for each one."

Did he expect her to pat him on the back?

"Aren't you getting a rather huge margin of profit?"

"Perhaps. But it's not easy to process those things. And if I didn't do some creative marketing, they'd have practically no income. At least this way she gets a little something, I get a decent profit, and we're all happy."

Exactly what Brenn would have said. She took a drink of coffee, but it had turned bitter.

He leaned forward, putting his hand over hers. "I think a lot of you, Madeleine. I'm sure you don't mean to be a busybody. Stay out of this."

She pulled her hand away. "But it's wrong! Paula would die if she knew how you're using her grandfather's name. You've made a little money on the deal. Why not stop now before someone gets hurt?"

He chuckled. "You're threatening me?"

"I'm just asking you, for her sake. Her decoys are good enough that you could sell them for a hundred dollars and still make a profit."

"Peanuts," he said. "Not worth driving around to all those little stores. And I don't know what made you decide to figure all this out, but you're too pretty to get involved with complicated business matters." He gave her a look. "Don't rock the boat, my silly little elf. I want you to forget all about it."

He pushed his chair back and glanced again at the blonde. "Finished with your coffee?"

"Not quite." She lifted her cup, pretending to savor the last few drops. She didn't want to put it down. Didn't want to leave. Didn't want to go out into the dark with him.

His smile, the look in his eyes. She knew that look.

This wasn't turning out the way she had hoped. The way she had prayed.

Slowly she lowered the cup to its saucer. *Lord, protect me.*

Kent had taken his eyes off the blonde. He was watching her, and she couldn't summon up the bold, confident manner that she needed.

He stepped to her side of the table and bent low, murmuring in her ear, "C'mon, princess. Have you ever been up to Apple Pie Hill? You should see it by moonlight, with snow on the pines."

He put a hand under her elbow and levered her to her feet.

She moved away from his touch, energized by fear. "I don't want to see Apple Pie Hill right now. I want you to take me home. Or would you rather I made a scene and insisted on calling a taxi?"

He produced a grin. "Hey, relax. I'll take you home if that's what you want. Apple Pie Hill can wait."

He drove back the way they'd come and was as pleasant as ever, telling her about the redwoods he'd seen in the Marin Headlands near San Francisco, but tension spiraled through his voice.

She made herself small and kept still, looking out the window.

Somber woods slid past, and the cold expanse seemed to shrink the space inside the car. What was she doing here, enclosed with this man?

He began to drive more quickly. She knew what was building up inside him and tried to distract his attention. She told him about their research on Jersey glass and asked his advice; she told him about the pieces of Manor glass that might be antiques and asked whether he thought it was likely. Beneath her chatter, she prayed little wordless pleas for help.

He answered briefly, whipping around the turns, and she slid from side to side, straining against the seat belt.

Breathe, she told herself. Think.

At last he turned into the driveway and careened up it. She inched her hand toward the seat clasp, released it as he began to slow. He braked, unsnapped his seat belt, and reached for her.

But she was out of the car, stumbling across the snow, grabbing for her key. As usual, Mac waited on the railing.

She slipped.

He was beside her in an instant. "You want to go inside, sweetheart?" His voice thickened. "Sure thing. We'll go inside."

She elbowed him, broke away from his grasp.

Up the steps, to the door, no time for a key.

But—Mac?

She snatched up the cat, turned to face him, and the cat growled a deadly threat.

Kent swore under his breath. "Shoot that beast! It's a menace."

"Look who's talking!" she said. "You'd better leave. Right away."

She took out her key.

"Hey, you're so beautiful, I lost my head. I just wanted a little kiss. You can't hold that against a guy."

He stepped toward her while she was unlocking the door, and Mac growled again.

He paused.

She backed over the threshold, shut the door, and turned the deadbolt. She waited, leaning against it, until she heard him drive off.

Then she began to shake. She made herself breathe slowly, deeply. "Lord, my Rock, my Deliverer. Thank you for mercies."

CHAPTER 18

Madeleine took another deep breath and turned from the door. He was gone.

Now, she had to check on the girl. Mac pranced down the hall ahead of her, nudged the door of the Blue Room open with his nose, and jumped lightly onto the sofa.

"There you are." The girl's voice was raspy, and only the top of her head showed above the blanket. "I've been waiting for you."

Which of them was she referring to? Not that it mattered.

The girl's face appeared. She blinked, stretched, and sat up to put an arm around the cat. She looked more alert, and the flush was gone from her cheeks.

"Hungry?" Madeleine asked.

"Yes, a little. Do you have any ham?"

"I think so. Would you like a sandwich?"

The girl yawned, stroking Mac's neck. "Yeah. Maybe a couple. And some cocoa." After a pause, she added, "Please?"

Madeleine smiled. "I'll see what I can find."

Her phone rang while she was in the kitchen. It was Aunt Lin, full of news about how well everything was coming together for once. "And how's our restoration project doing?" she asked.

Madeleine told her about the idea of painting the dining room. "Wonderful," her aunt said. "Let's keep it simple. You can get more ivory paint from Timothy. And see what you think about a wallpaper border, up by the ceiling." She yawned. "I hope you aren't working too hard."

"No, but I found out that Kent's been cheating Paula by running his own little profit-making venture."

Surely her aunt would be indignant.

"What does Kent have to say about it?"

"He thinks it is fine and claims that he's entitled to his profit and at least she's getting something."

Aunt Lin yawned again. "These family feuds! I'd keep out of it—you'll save yourself a lot of grief. Have to run. Hope to get home by the weekend. Bye!"

Madeleine hung up, frowning. How could her aunt be so unconcerned? Perhaps because she didn't know the real Kent. Did anyone?

Her phone rang again. Nathan. She leaned back against the counter.

"Mollie! I couldn't get away, and now it's late, but I've been thinking about you. How's the girl?"

Should she tell him about her dinner-date with Kent? Not over the phone.

"Mollie?"

"She seems better. She even asked me for a ham sandwich—I'm making it now. The cut isn't nearly as swollen, and she's taken a real liking to the cat. We haven't done much talking, though."

Why was she babbling like this?

"Good. Did you ever find out her name?"

"Not yet."

"I'll check back. You sound tired—get some sleep if you can."

Later, she would tell him. She put the sandwich and cocoa onto a tray, added cookies, and carried it down the hall with the cat twining around her ankles.

The girl was still sitting in her cocoon of blankets, and Mac leaped up to join her.

"Thanks." The girl reached for a sandwich and pulled out a strip of ham. She dangled it over Mac's nose, and he snapped it up. "Thought you'd like that," she said. "You're the biggest hunk of fur I've ever seen. Want some more?"

She fed him most of the ham from her sandwich while she drank the cocoa. Then she leaned back against the sofa, her hair glinting on the blue velvet. "What kind of place is this anyway? Is it yours? How come this room is so full of stuff?"

Question after question rolled out of her pert little mouth, and Madeleine could tell that she had already explored the Manor. After a while she said, "I've been wondering about you too. What's your name?"

The girl bristled. "You just want to know that so you can tell the cops."

"I'm not going to do that, but I can't keep calling you, 'Girl.' "

A hint of a smile curved her lips. "Okay, my name is Tara."

"A beautiful name," Madeleine said. "Well, Tara, don't you think your parents are worried about you?"

The young face turned to stone. "I have no parents."

"But you have a cat, don't you?"

Tara wrapped herself in the blankets and pulled Mac close. "No cat. Not anymore." Her voice was dispassionate, almost cold. "He got . . . murdered."

Her gaze fastened on the carpet. What was she remembering?

"Tara." Madeleine lowered her voice to a whisper. "Tara?"

But the girl didn't answer, so she took the dishes back to the kitchen. When she returned, Tara was under the blanket, and only the tip of Mac's ear was visible.

"Good night, Tara." Madeleine turned out the lamp and trudged toward her bedroom. She hadn't been much help, had she?

Sometime in the night, a storm pulled her out of a dream about Kent, and she didn't mind. Lightning and thunder were better than listening to him say, "What did you decide, Madeleine? Will I have to punish you?"

He'd spoken with Brenn's voice.

Don't think about that. Was it going to rain more heavily? Better get up and shut the window. Where was Mac? Probably with Tara, but it wouldn't hurt to make sure.

Mac had slipped out of the blankets to curl at the end of the sofa, and Tara seemed to be sleeping soundly. Good for them. If only she could roll back into bed and sleep like that.

Thunder exploded overhead as she returned to the hall. She'd go upstairs to the library and watch the storm and forget the dream.

She dropped onto the window seat. Trees rolled to the horizon like a dark sea, and zigzags of fire snaked downward, sizzled, and disappeared. She gazed at the flat expanse and found herself longing for mountains.

When she was a little girl, she'd told herself stories about the mountains around Roanoke. Those tree-covered humps belonged to invisible Rocklings, creatures who were both good and wise. They kept their pantries of food and drink inside the gumdrop-shaped hills. They built their castles in the taller mountains, great fortresses of rock where festivals took place.

But here she had no kindly Rocklings, no stores of delicacies, no castles. Only sand and trees and one dilemma after another.

She tucked her legs beneath her. Think it through. Kent's decoy dealings were a scam, like the slippery shading of truth that Mother applied to her business ventures. Brenn had followed the same mindset, both in his practice and in his personal life.

Don't rock the boat, Kent said.

Don't you breathe a word, Brenn had said.

She had recognized the look on Kent's face. Something more than lust. Something ruthless, fanatic.

If she did anything, Kent would know who had scuttled his glittering barge. And he would find her. Next time she wouldn't have a cat for a shield.

Brenn had found her. She'd gone to visit Arlene overnight—that was the story. But in the middle of supper, he'd arrived. "Dr. Burke, how nice to see you," Arlene's elderly mother had said. "Madeleine, dear, your husband wants you to come home."

She had paid for it that night, and she'd never left again. She had learned not to fight back, to take herself off to a safe distance and watch. That woman couldn't be her. It had to be someone else.

Remembering made the horror creep beneath her ribs.

She shivered and crossed her arms around herself. If only Dad were here! But she knew what he'd say: "Look to your forever-God. He's your High Tower."

She pictured a tower rising above the trees, a fortress built of sturdy Virginia rock. Inside, she'd find all she needed: strength, wisdom, love. And He would keep her safe.

Why hadn't He kept her safe from Brenn?

You have a plan for Mollie, in all of this.

Maybe she would never know the whole plan.

"Lord, I am afraid." She squared her shoulders. "But I am going to sink that boat."

Breathe deeply, as Nathan had taught her. Breathe again.

"Lord, I'm praying Dad's prayer, right now. Never let me forget that You are the One who makes me strong."

She got up from the window seat, stiff with cold, and found her way down the stairs to her room. In the bureau drawer, she felt for the sock with a bulge and drew out her paperweight. The pink flowers glistened inside, lovely as ever.

She curled both hands around it, letting the ache flow through her, and after a minute, she set it on the bedside table. She would always grieve for him, but the pain had become a quiet stream, drawing her close to the God he'd loved.

Next morning, her first thoughts went to her car. It was getting old, but she took good care of it. What on earth could be wrong? And who could she get to fix it? She'd ask Bria.

She found that Tara was sitting up, scratching at her hair, and the girl agreed to join her in the kitchen for scrambled eggs and toast.

They were finishing up when Bria arrived. She smiled at Tara. "Hi! I'm glad to see you're up. Isn't Mollie a good cook?"

Tara eyed Madeleine. "That's your name?"

"That's what my friends call me." The sight of her car through the window jogged her memory. "Bria, is there anyone in town who works on cars?"

Bria frowned. "I don't know."

"What's wrong with it?" Tara asked.

"Last night, it wouldn't start."

Tara finished her cocoa. "I like to fix cars. Got your keys?"

It wouldn't start for Tara, either, but she looked interested and popped open the hood. "It's been running good before this?"

"Yes. And I just had it tuned up for the winter."

"Okay. Get in and try it again."

Tara stared into the engine compartment, muttering to herself. She told Madeleine when to turn the key and crank the engine, and when to stop. Then she looked around the edge of the hood. "You got a screwdriver?"

Madeleine showed her the tool kit in the trunk and Tara made a satisfied sound. She bent over the engine. "Let's check this—crank it again. Aha! No spark!" A minute later, she said, "No wonder. Look."

In the midst of the hoses and belts that ran in and out of mysterious blackened objects was something cup-shaped.

"Your distributor cap," Tara said, twirling the screwdriver. "Your rotor's gone, see?"

Madeleine didn't see, but she understood what the girl had said. "Gone? How could it be gone?"

Tara pushed the hair out of her eyes. "They don't just fall off by themselves, I can tell you that. You leave your car unlocked?"

"Out here, I thought it would be all right."

"Uh-huh. Someone lifted your rotor." Tara wiped her hands on her jeans. "When you got that tune-up, did they give you back the parts they changed?"

"They always do. In the trunk, I think."

Tara dug through the spark plugs and belts, and Madeleine drummed her fingers on the hood. Someone *stole* it?

"Your lucky day!" Tara held up a piece of dark brown plastic that was shaped like a stubby T. "This'll take only a minute. There. Get in and crank it."

The engine fired with a throaty roar, but Madeleine wasn't as glad as she thought she'd be. She turned it off and slowly got out of the car. Who would steal her rotor?

"Thanks, Tara," she said, and as they walked inside, she asked, "Where did you learn how to do that?"

"My uncle," she said. "Calls himself Marrick the Miracle Man. He can fix anything on wheels. That bumper of yours—he could take care of it too. I'm going to get me a shower and a nap."

While Tara slept, Madeleine talked to Bria about the dining room, and Bria said, "I'll start cleaning those walls. When Tara wakes up, she can help me with the windows."

"Now that I have a car that runs again, I can get some patching compound and paint," Madeleine said.

She went to her bedroom for her purse, and after a moment's thought, picked up Paula's two decoys. She'd show them to Dan'l: Exhibits A and B. Maybe Pineys had a backwoods system of justice and he could suggest what to do about Kent.

Dan'l was sitting on his porch when she arrived, and she held out the decoys.

"Could you give me your opinion?" she asked. "Don't you think these both look like Paula Castell's work? They even have the same eye groove."

He didn't reach for them as she expected, but she kept talking. "See, this one that looks so old—it has PC burned into it."

She glanced toward the door. "Could I take another look at that decoy of yours?"

"Uh, it's all packed up," the old man said. "I don't bring it out no more."

Why the sudden change?

His gaze slid away from hers.

So he knew, or suspected, the scam. And Kent must have already talked to him.

"But wouldn't you agree that these two were probably made by the same person?"

He stood to his feet. "I don't agree to nothing at all. Stay out of trouble."

She put the decoys back into their box and smiled at him. "Let me know if you change your mind."

The more she thought about it, the angrier she became, and as she turned onto Whitton Road, she was still seething. That big blond ox, that good-for-nothing womanizer, that *snake*. He must have threatened the old man.

At the store, she started by asking Timothy about wallpaper borders and ended up telling him what had happened last night with Kent. As she spoke, he looked more and more concerned. "I had no idea it would turn out like that," he said. "I hope I didn't give you bad advice."

"Don't you blame yourself," she said. "You told me to pray about it, I did, and I went. Now I want to stop him."

The worry faded from Timothy's eyes, and she told him about Dan'l's reaction. "Kent has pressured that old man," she exclaimed.

"Probably didn't take much. Dan'l never has exerted himself for other people. His motto is, *Look after number one.*"

The bell jingled, announcing another customer. Nathan. He crossed the floor with his long stride. "How's the sick girl today?"

"Much better," she said. "Ate a good breakfast. Then she went outside and replaced the rotor someone stole from my car."

Both men looked mystified, and she gave them the few details she knew. She glanced at Timothy. "That's why I couldn't drive myself last night."

"Does our girl wonder have a name?" Nathan asked.

"Tara. Said her uncle's name is Marrick. But she's afraid I'll tell the police, and she says she has no parents."

"Sid Marrick comes in here," Timothy said. "You remember—tall, red hair?"

That was Tara's uncle?

Nathan glanced at Timothy. "What were you two looking so serious about?"

Her shoulder blades knitted themselves taut. Did she have to tell him, this soon? She wasn't ready.

Timothy said, "You should tell him. Use my office."

She preceded Nathan to the office, but as they stepped inside, he took her elbow and guided her down to the end of the room.

He moved his hand to her shoulder, hesitantly, as if he thought she might pull away. "I wanted so much to come back yesterday."

She hurried past the distraction. "I found out something," she said. "It could get me into trouble."

"I might have to rescue you."

"You might, at that." She looked up at him. "I went out to supper with Kent on Tuesday night." The gray eyes sharpened, and she said quickly, "I suspected that he was running a scam with Paula's decoys, and I had to ask him about it. I didn't want to talk at the Manor."

He seemed to understand her reasoning, and something in her shoulders relaxed. She told him about Kent's warning, how she'd prayed and come to a decision, and how it seemed that Dan'l had been threatened.

His face grew thoughtful. "The problem is, it'll be hard to pin the guy down. He's smooth, and we're not talking about a large sum of money."

"Timothy said Paula's reputation will be damaged."

"And he's counting on that, of course." He frowned. "How did he treat you?"

She'd left out that part. "All right until we drove back."

"He made a pass at you?"

"He was furious because I wouldn't go with him to some Apple Pie place." How could she describe it? "He seemed to turn into a monster."

She shuddered at the memory. "I ran for the house, and Mac was waiting on the porch so I grabbed him up and he scared Kent off."

Nathan's eyes had gone dark. He put both hands on her shoulders.

"But Nathan," she said, "here's something I just realized. Even when he was angry, when I knew what was going to happen, I could still think. I didn't freeze up."

"That's important, isn't it?" He searched her face, as if he wished he could see inside her head.

"It's a start. If he ever touched me, I don't know what I'd do."

"He never will, if I can help it." His mouth set in a grim line. "I have a friend who's a police detective. I'll talk to him."

He drew her a little closer. "I'm going to Philadelphia for a couple of days. Have to give a speech."

Her stomach fluttered, but she kept her voice calm. "What's it about?"

"Alcohol use in the Alaska Native community."

"Sounds familiar."

"I'll use the research from my chapter, and a few of the better lines. Speechifying is easier for me than writing."

He didn't say any more, or that he'd miss her, or even when he'd get back, but that was fine. A little distance might give perspective, for both of them.

She left the store with a smile that seemed to be lipsticked on, as if it belonged to a clown. Too much emotion lately. She was supposed to be working on strong-and-independent. Remember that.

In the afternoon, Tara helped her patch holes in the dining room, watched as Madeleine started on supper, and then chose a cake—German Chocolate—for them to make together.

She must have decided that she could trust Madeleine, because she began to talk about herself. Her parents had died several years ago and she'd been sent to live with her father's twin brother, Sid, and his wife. The man owned a junkyard, was a genius at fixing cars, and spent his spare time rebuilding one for himself.

Madeleine put the cake into the oven and did dishes while Tara chopped nuts for the frosting.

Tara worked for a minute then looked up. "Things got to where I knew I had to get out of there." Fear crossed her face. "I knew I had an aunt down here somewhere—my mother's sister—so I figured I'd just hike down the Batona Trail and find her."

She chopped another few nuts and paused to stare at the knife in her hand. "So stupid of me to cut my leg like that. I've used my hatchet a hundred times. I still can't figure out how it slipped."

. . . *for a reason* . . .

"I think God sent you here, Tara."

The girl looked away. "My aunt's name is Minna Sooy. Do you know where she lives?"

"I've only been here a couple of weeks. Timothy, the man who owns the store, might know."

Tara glanced at the clock. "First thing tomorrow, I'm going to phone him."

She flipped her hair back and stood tall. "Do you think, if I clean up good and talk nice, she'll let me stay with her?"

"I'd think so." Madeleine glanced at the clock too. Was it so late? SING would be starting soon.

"I'm going out tonight," she said. "A bunch of us—teens and kids and everyone—get together to sing. Would you like to come?"

"Nah. I don't feel very social right now. Can we frost the cake when you get back? Where's Mac?"

Maybe she was expecting too much, too soon. "Mac's probably outside," Madeleine said. "He likes to prowl around, and then he comes back to wait for me on the porch. I'll see you later."

With Nathan gone, Remi did his best on the guitar, and Howard's voice was loud enough, but SING seemed to drag.

Afterwards, over cookies that tasted like cardboard, she asked Charlotte about her clients. Charlotte laughed, saying that the last delivery had been a butter birth, with only six hours of labor. Madeleine smiled to herself. That's what Arlene would have called it too.

She told Charlotte how her interest in birthing had started at a friend's home birth, with Arlene as the doula. During the birth, she had helped Arlene as well as she could, and after that, Arlene let her assist from time to time.

She didn't mention that when Brenn found out, he'd given her that cold look and said, "Birth and death belong in the hospital." After he died—not in the hospital, come to think of it—she'd started assisting Arlene again.

Something about the birth process was more satisfying than anything she'd ever experienced.

Charlotte's eyes gleamed. "I know what you mean," she said, taking a drink of her lemonade. "We get quite a few home births around here. Folks don't have insurance. The last doc we had was a druggie and made mistakes. Now we've got people who'd rather shoot a doctor than ask him for anything."

She smiled. "Dr. Parnell is my backup. What a difference! He's so good with births."

And he was good with injured cats, runaway girls, and panic-stricken women.

Madeleine drank down the rest of her lemonade. Time to get back and see how Tara was doing. Maybe she'd open up a little more while they frosted that cake.

CHAPTER 19

Tara has been here longer than I expected.
I hope she can find her aunt—
Aunt Lin might not be very pleased
with this situation.
~Journal

Next morning, Tara phoned Timothy to ask about her aunt. When she hung up the phone, she had the staring look on her face again. "Gone away. No one knows where." Under her breath she added, "Probably dead too."

Tara helped when Bria and Jude came to work, but the dull, hopeless expression in her eyes did not change.

After they left, Madeleine sent her back to the sofa for a nap. As for her, she was going to put barbequed chicken into the slow cooker and research Schnecken, the German cinnamon rolls. What was Nathan doing this afternoon?

She and Tara ate supper together on Madeleine's bed, and Tara fed Mac bits of her chicken while she looked around the room. Her gaze rested on Madeleine's paperweight. "I love that, with the calico flowers inside." She picked it up and turned it over. "What's on the back? PS7326?"

Madeleine smiled. "That refers to a verse in the Bible. My dad put it there."

"Why?"

"To remind me that God will make me strong."

"How come?"

"Because He loves me."

"You kidding?"

"I'm not. The Bible talks a lot about God and His love. Forever-love, I call it." She wanted to explain that she didn't deserve God's love, but Tara had dropped the paperweight onto the bed and turned away.

"Pink calico is my favorite," the girl said. "You're lucky. I wish I had a forever stone." She started feeding the rest of her chicken to Mac.

Madeleine watched her, praying for wisdom. What wheels were turning inside that pretty little head? Was even one of her thoughts drifting toward God?

When Tara's plate was empty, she curled into the pillows and stared at the ceiling. After a long moment, she said, "I can't go home. She'll kill me."

"Who?"

"Dixie. My aunt. I don't mind so much when she hits me, but I hate it when she gets drunk."

Her eyes narrowed. "Sometimes I feel sorry for Sid. I get scared too, when she pulls out that little pistol of hers. Even after she shot my cat, I guess I would have stuck it out for a while longer, but . . ."

She stroked Mac's tawny back until he began to purr. "But that one night . . ."

Her voice quavered as she described how Sid had been drinking with his buddies and afterward had come into the kitchen and grabbed her. She squirmed away, but Dixie had seen it and she had been furious.

Tara pushed a hand through her hair. "Blamed me for it. She hit me with that pistol of hers—said she'd kill me if I told anyone. And now I've told you."

"But she doesn't know," Madeleine said. "She's not God."

"She's the devil." Tara pulled the cat into her arms, and he stayed there. She scratched between his ears. "I pray to God sometimes. I know He's busy, and I've done a lot of bad stuff. Wish I could buy a truckload of that forever-love."

"You don't have to buy it."

"Uh-huh." She bent her head. "I've got to make some plans. That night I was sure He told me to run away. But now I don't know what to do."

Madeleine watched her, at a loss, and finally said, "God knows what you need."

"Sure, but that doesn't put beer in my glass."

"He wouldn't tell you to run away and then forget about you."

The girl's eyes fastened on her with a mixture of cunning and hope. "Maybe He wants you to help me."

"He loves you, Tara."

"That's a hoot. After all the stuff He's dished out to me—"

"It says so in the Bible."

"Mom read the Bible a lot when she was sick, but I've heard it's just a bunch of stories."

"Sounds like your mom didn't think so."

Tara stretched, yawning. "The big question is: can I hang out here for a while?"

She threw a glance at Madeleine, jumped off the bed, and started out the door.

"I'll talk to my aunt," Madeleine said, following her down the hall. "Don't worry about it tonight. Get some sleep and get strong."

"Yes," Tara said. "I've been feeling like a wimp, and I don't like that."

Madeleine watched as she slid under the blankets with the cat. "You know what, Tara? My forever-God can be your God too."

The girl slid deeper into the blankets. "Hey, how 'bout the way this Mac purrs? He runs smooth as a Jaguar."

Madeleine put a gentle hand on the girl's shoulder. "Good night. We've got plenty to do tomorrow."

She'd go to bed early herself. Trust God to work in Tara's heart.

She dragged herself back to the bedroom. Just tired, probably.

Was her phone ringing?

His voice had the warmth of sunlight. "Mollie, I'm standing here thinking about you."

Happiness bubbled up into a laugh. "Where in the world are you standing?"

"A used bookstore. They've got a whole section on British literature and another one on cooking. I've got to bring you here." He paused. "If you'd like."

"I love those stores, especially the crowded old dusty ones."

"Have you ever heard of M.F.K. Fisher?"

"Yes! *How to Cook a Wolf.* That's one of her books. No one writes like she does."

"Just wondering. How are you? How's Tara?"

She couldn't admit how much the sound of his voice had brightened her world, but she told him what she'd learned from Tara, and he told her about his speech and the conference. Finally he said that the store was closing, so he'd better go.

The next morning they all worked on the dining room, giving it fresh paint and a frieze of stenciled pinecones created by Bria.

While they were eating a late lunch, Aunt Lin phoned to say that she was on her way back, and would it be okay for Kent and Remi to come over for supper that night.

Not okay, but Madeleine didn't want to say anything over the phone. "If you'd like."

"Good." Her aunt seemed to be in a rush. "We'll talk when I get there. See you soon."

Aunt Lin admired the new appearance of the dining room and thanked both girls for their help. She didn't seem particularly upset about Tara. She asked, privately, for as much information as Madeleine could give, and agreed that the girl could stay for a few more days.

The dining room looked presentable, supper turned out well, and Kent spent most of the meal talking about his book and related subjects.

Just get through the night without making a scene, Madeleine told herself. No point in signaling her intentions.

What, by the way, were her intentions? It was all very well to talk about scuttling boats.

She cut up the cake and served it, still thinking. She'd grab the first chance that came along, but it was hard to wait.

Remi seemed subdued this evening and didn't say much, even when Madeleine tried to draw him into conversation.

Tara had disappeared as soon as the Bronco showed up in the driveway. If she'd been at the table, she would have fired up the conversation, and considering how pretty she was, Remi might have been more alert. But perhaps it was just as well.

"Madeleine, are you off in dreamland again?" Kent put a proprietary hand on her shoulder and she jerked away, almost knocking over her glass.

She stood to her feet and picked up the water pitcher, wishing she could dump it over him. Instead, she took it into the kitchen, refilled it, and returned.

He said, "I asked about the runaway girl you've been harboring. Does she have a name?"

"I imagine she does. Would anyone like more ice cream? I'll get the coffee." How had he found out?

"Coffee for me, please," her aunt said. "Let's see, you told me her name. Tara, isn't it? What's her last name?"

He'd find out eventually, and it probably wasn't important. She took her time bringing in the coffee pot and filling Aunt Lin's cup. "I'm not sure. Her uncle's name is Marrick."

Kent held out his cup and she filled it too, watching the frown gather on his face. "Where from?"

"Some place up near Mt. Misery, I think."

"What's the uncle's first name?"

What was he after?

"Why? Do you know any Marricks?"

"Depends," he said. "There's plenty of them around, common as maggots on a dead rabbit."

He fussed with his coffee, adding a spoonful of ice water, tasting it again, and his frown deepened. Finally he said, "That whole Marrick tribe is a bunch of trouble."

"So you do know them," she said.

"Went to school with some of their kids." His lip curled. "One problem after another." His voice sharpened. "That girl's going to cause trouble, I can tell you. Runaway kid! Send her back as soon as you can."

Remi straightened in his chair, watching Kent. He didn't say anything, but his eyes glittered black fire. He picked up a teaspoon and twirled it in his fingers.

Madeleine poured herself some coffee she didn't want. "I have no right to send her back. And I wouldn't if I could. She's afraid for her life."

Kent grunted. "Of course she is. That's what they all say. I'm tired of these kids who run off because they can't watch their favorite TV show."

He rested a hand on the knife on his belt. "The trouble with you, Madeleine, is that you want to adopt every stray that comes along. First it's that pathetic family. Then it's that wildcat, and now it's this girl."

Remi held the spoon lightly between the forefinger of each hand and slowly bent it in half.

She let her contempt show in her voice. "We're not talking about animals here. This is a person, a human being, with feelings and hopes and fears just like we have. A needy human being."

"If she's a Marrick, she's trouble," he said. "Get rid of her. So, are we going to play Monopoly or not?"

Aunt Lin spoke up. "We're not. I have a headache coming on, and I think you're part of it, Kent."

"Now that's a shame." He put on his genial air. "We'll get out of your hair. Thank you, ladies, for another fine meal." He strode into the kitchen.

Remi paused beside Madeleine. "If you need some help fixing up this house, leave a message at Timothy's, okay? I can do just about anything, and I work for peanuts."

"Good!" Madeleine smiled at him, but he wouldn't meet her gaze. "We serve super deluxe peanuts here. We could use some muscle, I'm sure. I'll tell my aunt."

That brought a faint smile. "Thanks, Mollie."

After they'd gone, she found the spoon he'd held. He had bent it back almost straight, except for a bump in the shaft. What was going on with Remi?

Aunt Lin moved quietly around the kitchen, putting things away. Finally she looked up. "What is it, Mollie? Did something happen with Kent while I was gone?"

Her aunt could read faces, too well.

"I wasn't exactly thrilled to see him tonight." Madeleine leaned against the counter. It was time for Aunt Lin to know.

"He took me out for supper." She explained her reasons and the problem with her car. She tried to keep her voice level, but her words gathered momentum. "He wanted to kiss me and . . . to . . . come inside, and he would have, if it weren't for Mac, and the way he looked, I think he would have assaulted me."

There, she'd said it.

Her aunt's face turned white. "Mollie! I'm so sorry! It must have been terrible for you." Her eyes flashed green fire. "I've never been sure about him. Thank God He kept you safe. Did you tell anyone? Are you doing okay?"

Madeleine nodded. "Timothy. And Nathan Parnell."

"Both are good men. I'm glad for that." Aunt Lin stood still for a minute, closed her eyes, and then put a hand to her forehead. "I hope this isn't a migraine. I've got to lie down. Do you mind?"

"Not a bit," Madeleine said. "It's all over." At least for now.

Her aunt started to nod but grimaced instead. "Thank you. I'm glad you're here."

After her aunt left, Madeleine looked down the darkened hall to the Blue Room. She hadn't given Tara any supper. Was she still awake?

Tara's face looked pale in the lamp light. "Are they gone?"

"Yes, there's no need to be afraid." She'd probably heard what Kent said. His voice had been loud enough.

She had Tara eat supper in the kitchen while she cleaned up, and they talked for a while, but Tara went back to her sofa right away. No confidences tonight. Maybe tomorrow, if they did some baking together.

She turned toward her bedroom. Just as well. She was too tired to be a good listener. She took a long shower, read six verses in Ephesians, and wrote in her journal.

When she put her Bible down, she realized that the paperweight was missing from the bedside table.

Had Mac knocked it off? Whenever she found a pen on the floor, she knew he'd been playing "Roll-it-off." She'd have to look for the paperweight. Tomorrow.

The next morning, Aunt Lin didn't appear until almost noon. Her headache must have been a bad one. Bria and Jude weren't coming today, so Madeleine and Tara did laundry, vacuumed, and started on the Blue Room. They opened the draperies and gave it a thorough dusting.

Madeleine had just finished with the piano when Aunt Lin spoke from the doorway. "You two are working hard." She was holding a piece of dry toast. "Had to get up for a while."

She walked farther into the room. "I've been wondering what we could do with all this." She waved her toast at the lamp shaped like a flamingo. "Get rid of things like that, for sure."

Tara patted the bird's ceramic head. "Never saw a blue one before. Dixie loves this kind of stuff."

Aunt Lin took a last bite of her toast. "And who is Dixie?"

"My aunt." Tara's gaze shifted out the window. "Mr. Kennedy! Who told him I was here?"

A blue station wagon was winding its way toward them. Aunt Lin rubbed at her forehead and moved slowly into the hall.

The man at the door was gray-haired and built like a football player past his prime. He nodded at Aunt Lin. "Good morning, ma'am. Name's Kennedy, from Social Services. Fine old house you've got. Glad to hear you're fixing it up."

"Thank you."

"Now the reason I came out . . . let me see." He pulled a ragged notebook from his jacket and thumbed its pages. "Miz Dumont. We got a call you're concealing a juvenile runaway. Is that correct?"

Aunt Lin's back stiffened. She took him into the kitchen, and he sat purposefully at the table. Madeleine listened with growing dismay as he asked polite questions and took notes.

He glanced up from his notebook, and his gaze fastened on the doorway. "Hello there, Sally."

"That's not my name, I *told* you." Tara stepped into the room, her eyes blazing. "And you can't make me go back."

"It's the law," he said in a monotone.

His unconcern loosened Madeleine's tongue. "Mr. Kennedy, this juvenile has been hit. I've taught school, and I know what the law says about child abuse."

He wrote in his notebook. "Any visible bruises?"

With an effort, she kept her voice cold. "You know as well as I do that an adult can damage a child without leaving visible bruises."

He wrote again. "We'll have to look into this. Ol' Dixie must be losing it."

"And what about the pistol that woman has? She's threatened the girl with it."

"Can you prove any of the alleged abuse with the gun?"

Tara folded her arms. "She hit me with it and said she'd kill me."

"Hmm." He wrote again. "Any witnesses? Would your uncle be willing to swear?"

Tara shook her head. "You know Sid."

Aunt Lin's voice was crisp. "How did you find out the girl was here?"

"A phone call, Miz Dumont. From a concerned citizen, I believe he called himself. The Marricks want you back, Sally. They promise it'll be okay."

"Sure, sure, sure."

He looked down at his notebook again. "They're claiming a theft. Said you stole a silver pendant of your aunt's."

"She's lying!" Tara's voice rose to a shriek. "It's mine! *She* stole it from *me*." A hand went to her throat, and Madeleine remembered the leather cord with something hanging from it.

The man shrugged. "Calm down, girl. Guess you'll have to work that out with her. Better pack your bags."

"Wait a minute!" Madeleine said. "You're going to take her back there? I want your name and the phone number of your agency. This is insufferable."

The man shrugged. "We'll keep an eye on it, like I said, ma'am." He handed her a business card and gave one to Tara. "You call me the next time Dixie lays a hand on you."

Tara put the card into the pocket of her jeans and turned away. Once again she wore the staring look on her face.

As soon as Tara returned with her duffle bag, the man stood. He nodded at Aunt Lin, and they walked out the door.

Madeleine followed. This could not be happening. How could she let her go—just let her go?

"Tara," she called, "where do you live? I'll come see you."

But Tara put her nose in the air, clamping her lips shut. She stalked behind the social worker, and she didn't look back.

CHAPTER 20

Tara's situation is more complicated
than I thought.
She needs to understand God's love for her,
but right now she's not interested.
~Journal

After Tara had gone, Aunt Lin took her headache
back to bed, and the house sank into an exhausted
stillness, as if a tornado had passed through.

Madeleine leaned against the kitchen doorway. Make
the Schnecken, that's what she was going to do. And
cinnamon-walnut bread. And cookies. Baking might keep
her sane.

She thought of phoning Jude to let him know about
Tara, but it seemed a cruel way for him to find out. She'd
tell him tomorrow, on the way to church.

She put on a Bach CD, one of the slow mournful
ones that did the weeping for her. Then she hauled out the
ingredients she'd need, and the bowls, measuring cups,
and pans. Good thing the Schnecken recipe was
complicated enough that she'd have to focus on it.

Don't think, just work.

She kneaded the Schnecken dough more vigorously
than required, set it to rise, made the topping and spooned
it into a muffin pan. Now back to the dough. She was
rolling it out and trying to decide about raisins in the
filling when Nathan phoned.

"Do you like raisins?" she asked.

"Yes. I mean, usually, but not in porridge. Why?"

"Just needed a vote."

He paused, but only for an instant. "Could you use some zucchini? Or are you too busy? And would you mind if I dropped by?"

"Yes, no, and at your own risk. I'm baking."

"Would you rather—"

"—There's no one I'd rather see."

She hadn't meant to say that. Never mind, she didn't care. She picked up the box of raisins and ripped it open. Somewhere, that girl was staring off into space while someone hit her.

Get the Schnecken baking.

Nathan came sooner than she'd thought, and he didn't seem to notice that dishes were strewn across the table, cookie sheets sat askew over the sink, and flour dappled the counter, the floor, and most of her apron.

He carried a brown paper bag and a zucchini that looked a yard long.

"A gift from someone's garden?" she asked

"More like a castoff."

"Okay, just put it somewhere."

She went back to mixing dough for raisin bread. The timer for the Schnecken rang. "Would you mind checking those?"

"Smells good. What're they supposed to look like?"

"Snails. Golden brown ones."

"Then your snails are done. Want me to take them out?"

"Please."

Her throat cramped tight. She'd planned to make them with Tara.

He took out the muffin pan, looked at her, and put it on the wire rack.

"Good." She dropped a cookie sheet over the muffin pan, flipped the two of them upside down, and set them back onto the rack.

She jiggled the muffin pan. "In a minute you can lift off this pan, if you don't mind. Scrape up any of the nuts and syrup that fell away. Try one when they're cool. Get yourself something to drink. Milk's in the fridge."

"Sure." His voice was reflective. "Always wanted to taste a snail. Thank you." He stood for a minute, watching her.

She knew she sounded brusque, but she turned away, threw a handful of flour onto the kneading board, and yanked the bread dough out of the bowl.

She rounded it up, pounded it down, turned it over, and began to knead it. Too soft. She sprinkled it with flour and kneaded some more, pressing in hard with the heels of her hands, folded it over, and began again.

Her thoughts kindled. She'd been the one who told Tara that God loved her. How could He let this happen?

She folded the dough, turned it. Walnuts fell out. She snatched them up, punched them back in. Press, fold, turn.

Lord, I'm so . . . angry. Please talk to me about this.

Still too soft. She dropped a handful of flour onto the dough, and kneaded some more.

You keep doing things I don't understand.

Press, fold, turn. She pinched the dough. Better. She leaned on it, hard. Fold, turn. Another walnut dropped out. She smacked it back into the dough. Almost elastic now—keep kneading.

Turn it. Mash it down and start again.

The kitchen was quiet except for Bach's "Largo" sobbing in the background.

She glanced over her shoulder.

He was leaning against the sink, eating one of the Schnecken, still watching her.

"Don't you think," he said, "that by now it's sorry?"

Her hands stilled. She bent over the mound of dough. "Nathan . . ."

He came to her, his footsteps unhurried. "What happened?"

"They took her away. Tara."

"That poor kid. You were doing so well with her. Where to?"

"Back to where they treat her like dirt." She flattened the dough, slowly now, folded it in, turned and kneaded it again.

"Why?"

"Kent." She flipped it over. "He filed a complaint."

She gave the dough another pat, shaped it into a large round, and dropped it into a bowl.

"I'm going to find out where she lives, and I'm going to go see her. Some day that man will get a taste of justice."

And she hadn't done a thing to hurry it along. Not yet.

She covered the bowl with a cloth. "It has to rise. How nice of you to bring the zucchini."

"Do you treat all your breads that way?"

She tried to smile. Failed. "Only when I lose my temper." She sank into a chair at the table, and put her face in her hands. "How juvenile! I'm sorry, Nathan."

He brought her one of the Schnecken, along with a dishtowel.

She looked up at him. "What's this for?"

"For you to eat. The raisins are good. Why do you call them snails?"

"That's what *Schnecken* means in German."

He swirled a finger through the empty pan and licked off the syrup. "They're even better than sticky buns. Would you like some milk?"

"Yes, please. And the towel?"

"To wipe your face and hands. Or I could do it for you."

She smiled then, and scrubbed the flour off her face. "I'm sure you'd do a good job. When did you get back?"

"Last night. The zucchini was on my doorstep with a note, like an abandoned child."

She had to take a look at it. "They don't know about zucchini bread." She thumped the rind. "Hard as leather. I might need a machete for this one."

"I brought you something else." He handed her the brown paper bag.

"A book? From that store?"

She slid it out. *The Art of Eating*. "M.F.K. Fisher? Nathan! How wonderful!"

A grin crept across his face and he looked like a boy quite pleased with himself.

She skimmed the contents list. "Five gastronomical works!" She paged through it. "Here's the one I read: *How to Cook a Wolf*."

"I hope you took it to heart," he said. "Might come in handy."

What did that mean? Quickly she said, "Fisher wrote it during World War II. It's about making do with wartime shortages. I love these chapter titles: How to Catch the Wolf; How Not to Boil an Egg; How to Keep Alive; How to Rise Up Like New Bread."

She stopped to take a bite of Schnecken. "You don't read this straight through, like a novel. It's a book to be dipped into at odd moments, and savored."

"Savored, yes," he said, looking at her, and something in his smile made her face grow warm.

Fortunately he kept talking. "Want to come for a ride? One of my patients lives up near Chatsworth, and I think she'd like to meet you."

"Okay." She glanced at the bowl of dough.

He followed her gaze. "How long does that have to stay incarcerated?"

"A couple of hours, or until I let it out. Wait—I'm so dusty, let me change—I'll be quick."

He opened the door of his Jeep for her, and she had a moment to wonder at herself. Driving off alone with him, without a flicker of anxiety?

Now he was telling her about Mrs. Bozarth and how she'd had a stroke a few weeks ago.

"What kind?"

"Left CVA, not severe."

She'd heard enough medical conversations to know that the woman would be partially paralyzed on her right side. "How's she doing with therapy?"

"Very well. She's determined to make a full recovery and that makes a difference."

"And you're going to see her because . . . ?"

He glanced sideways. "She could use some encouragement—her son isn't around much. She has a leg ulcer, and I want to keep an eye on it."

Mrs. Bozarth must be a remarkable person, or he wouldn't go to such trouble. A white-haired, sweet-faced saint, no doubt. She could use a dose of that herself.

Nathan knocked lightly at the door of a yellow clapboard house, walked inside, and called a greeting. The small room off the hall had wide windows, a pair of comfortable-looking blue chairs, and walls lined with books.

His patient lay on a hospital bed near a window. Black curly hair. Sparkling black eyes.

244

When she saw him, she slowly lifted a hand, and a lopsided smile crossed her face. "Doc-tor. I-am-so-glad."

"Evelyn," he said. "You're looking well."

She couldn't be more than fifty. Even half-paralyzed, she radiated energy.

He introduced Madeleine, said that she was a teacher too, and pulled both chairs close to the bed. After he'd put on gloves and checked her blood pressure and pulse, he took Evelyn Bozarth's right hand in his own. "Squeeze," he said.

She did, and he smiled. "Now both hands." She gave him the other hand and he nodded. "Not bad at all. You're working hard. Let's see how that sore is doing."

He inspected the bandage on her shin. "I'm going to change this," he said.

His hands were deft, and while he worked, he asked about her daughter in Michigan and her son's new job in Atlantic City. Her speech was slurred, but her answers reflected a wise mother's concern, and she watched Madeleine with the keen gaze of a teacher.

Finally he stripped off his gloves. "Tea time," he said, and went off to the kitchen.

The woman looked at her, and one side of her mouth pulled up in a smile. "Mol-lee," she said. "God-sent-you-to-day." She paused. "Christ. He-was-wound-ed-for . . ." She looked anxious, as if she couldn't remember the rest.

"He was wounded for our transgressions," Madeleine said. "Is that the one?"

"Yes. Trans . . . Trans-gre-ssions." Her face glowed. "I-love-the-way . . . He-loves-me."

How could she say that, lying there with her life in ruins?

"Yes," Madeleine said.

The woman seemed to read her thoughts. She reached out a bony hand, and Madeleine took it. "Do-not-forget," Evelyn Bozarth said. "He-loves."

Tara! She'd been so wrapped up in worrying about Tara, she'd forgotten that God loved the girl too. Immensely. More than she ever could.

She bowed her head. "I do forget. Thank you."

Slowly Evelyn Bozarth raised her other hand, moved it across the blankets as if it were a robotic accessory, and dropped it down to cover Madeleine's. "Pray." She smiled again. "Tell. What-school?"

Madeleine shook her head. "Back in Virginia. What was your school?"

"Sandy-Bank. Gone."

Nathan returned with a tea pot and cup. "Looks like they're taking better care of you."

"Yes."

"Are you getting some good baths now?"

"Yes. Like-a-spa. You-cleaned-their-clock."

He smiled. "Sometimes they need a little push."

Evelyn Bozarth looked at him with affection, then at Madeleine. "He-takes . . . ex-tra-or-din-ar-y-care."

He pulled her walker close to the bed. "Can you walk for me today?"

"Yes."

And she did, slowly, but with a precision that made him nod. "Excellent. You're not shuffling as much."

She slumped over the walker, tired now, and he helped her back into bed.

"Don't push yourself too hard." He patted her hand.

She smiled her lopsided smile. "Yes-doc-tor."

"I'll try to get over on Monday," he said.

At the doorway, Madeleine paused to give her a little wave. The woman on the bed raised a hand, slowly. "Mol-lee. Come-back."

For most of the way back to the Manor, Nathan drove without speaking.

Finally he said, "One of my favorite people. She taught physics and chemistry, and now each word is a struggle." He sighed. "She's only forty-eight. Ten years older than I am. Makes me think."

"Makes me ashamed," Madeleine said. "There I was, angry at God and doubting His love. So upset about Tara."

"His love is the only thing you can depend on," he said quietly. "I'm learning that."

She looked out of the window, still ashamed. If only she could learn that too, learn it once and for all, and never forget.

"Mollie, how long is it since you've cried?"

She closed her eyes, and then opened them slowly. "Not since the first week I was married."

He didn't ask any more questions. He looked straight ahead and told her about going to see the Liberty Bell, but his hands tightened on the steering wheel.

He cared.

Like he cared for Evelyn Bozarth? How kind he'd been with that poor woman, how gentle!

As he was with her. Maybe he was just being a good doctor. Kind, compassionate, and thorough. His question, for example. A clinical inquiry?

The thought nagged at her for the rest of the evening, while she and Aunt Lin talked, while she baked the walnut bread, and while she mixed up a bowl of cookie dough. Chocolate chip, with nuts.

Perhaps his interest was just sort of . . . professional. Except for the time he'd kissed her. She had managed to squelch that, hadn't she?

It shouldn't matter, anyway. A romantic attachment didn't fit with independence, and that's where she was headed.

Finally she had to leave the kitchen and pray over it. *"Do-not-forget,"* Evelyn Bozarth had said. *"He-loves."*

Thank you, Lord my Rock. Make me strong. I've got to let go of everything else.

She went back to finish the cookies, and a prayer sang through her mind. *You alone are my heart's desire, and I long to worship You.*

Sunday morning, Howard took charge, since Timothy was away for the weekend. He gave an encouraging message, everyone sang heartily, and Jude stood beside her the whole time with a brooding look on his face. She had told him about the social worker coming to get Tara, and he blamed himself.

"She kept telling me not to say anything," he said. "That's why."

"If it weren't for you, Tara would be dead now, from blood poisoning or hypothermia."

She wasn't sure that he'd been convinced.

On the way back from church, they discussed where Tara's branch of the Marrick family might live, and Jude said, "Why don't we ask Gemma? She's been hoping you'd come back."

"I'll do it," Madeleine said. "How about this afternoon?"

In the kitchen, Aunt Lin was having a spirited phone conversation with someone, probably her partner, and waved at Madeleine when she walked in. While they ate lunch, she explained what they'd been discussing and

Madeleine tried to follow the complicated threads of business politics, but Tara's face kept reappearing in her mind.

Tara, ill. Tara, withdrawn. Tara, indignant. And at the last, Tara, haughty in defeat.

Her aunt finished another chapter in what seemed like an endless story, and Madeleine said, "I want to find out where Tara lives."

"Going to visit her?"

"Yes," Madeleine said. "It's the right thing for me to do. By the way, what's your plan for the Blue Room?"

The diversion succeeded. "Let's go see," her aunt said. "Bring a roll of masking tape."

The lavishly appointed room seemed drab without Tara, but it certainly wasn't empty.

"I'll mark the things to get rid of." Aunt Lin smacked a piece of tape onto each discard. "This chair, and this one too. The piano goes. And these lamps! Both of these chairs. Keep the willow ware if you think we should, but get all that stuff off the wall."

She paused beside a brass table lamp. "This would look good on your desk."

"I'd like it," Madeleine said. "And this floor lamp would work for the library. I'll put it by the couch." She tapped the metal shade of a goose-necked lamp. "Jude's grandmother likes to knit. She could use this. I'm going to see her later this afternoon."

"She's welcome to it. You're full of good deeds today, aren't you?" Aunt Lin began to laugh. "I forgot to tell you. Your mother phoned and gave me instructions to find you a man. How can I tell her you're going to spend the afternoon with a kid and his grandmother?"

Madeleine tried to match her light-hearted tone. "We both know what we think of Mom's instructions, don't we? Besides, she's busy these days with a new boyfriend."

Her aunt raised a sympathetic eyebrow and tore off another piece of masking tape.

Jude arrived in the late afternoon as planned, and Madeleine met him with a smile, glad to be outside again. Thin sunlight filtered through the branches to warm her face, and Jude, carrying the gooseneck lamp, scanned the trees at the edge of the path.

"What have you discovered lately?" she asked.

"Green cullet."

"Sounds like a fish. Wait, that's mullet."

He dug into his pocket and pulled out a rounded piece of dark green glass, large as a man's thumb. "From one of those old glass furnaces. I like to look at it." He rolled it in his palm, and it glowed like an emerald.

"Oh!" he exclaimed. "And over by the Batona Trail I found a convertible full of pine needles. Someone stripped everything off it and left the body to rust."

After a moment's thought, he added, "Probably stolen."

He swung the lamp as he walked. "Gemma will love this," he said, and started whistling under his breath.

"I like your grandmother."

"I'm glad you went up to see her. She gets lonely, especially since she broke her ankle. She likes visitors."

"All except Kent? She doesn't seem to think much of him."

"Huh," he said. "None of us do, except my mother. But Mom doesn't live in the real world."

"I noticed that Bria disappears when Kent is around. She doesn't like him either?"

He squinted up into the trees, and after a while, he answered. "She hates him. He backed her into a corner and tried to kiss her."

"I hope she slapped him good."

"Yeah, she kneed him. He hasn't bothered her since."

Madeleine couldn't think of anything to say. Gemma was right.

A smile blossomed over Gemma's face when she saw them.

"Look what we brought you." Jude set the lamp down beside her, plugged it in, adjusted the height, and turned it on. The light fell across the knitting in her lap, and her smile widened.

"Did this come from the Manor, then? Thank you very much," she said in her soft English voice.

Jude moved his chair close to hers. "Gemma, we want to ask you something."

Her fond gaze rested on him. "I thought you might."

"There's a family called Marrick. Do you know where they live?"

"What's the father's name?"

"Sid. Sid Marrick."

"Huh," she said. "I never did care much for those Marrick boys. Hung around in school with Kent—three of a kind. The old Sandy Bank School. Why do you ask?"

Madeleine leaned forward. "I made friends with Tara Marrick and I'd like to go visit her. She's having a difficult time."

"No wonder," Gemma said. "Tara? I've never heard of her."

"What about Sally?"

"Now Sally, that would be Sam's girl. Sam was the worst of the lot."

"So you know where they live?"

"I was coming to that. Up Mt. Misery way. Ask at the gas station in Four Mile. Mr. Bontray, he'll know. Jude, you be careful if you go near there."

"I will," he said. "Would you like some tea?"

"That would be lovely. And perhaps a few of those biscuits too."

While they drank their tea, Gemma inquired about the Manor, and Madeleine described their progress in the Blue Room. Jude asked whether she could give them both a ride to church next week, and they left Gemma to her nap.

Jude walked out onto the porch with Madeleine. "What are you going to do about Tara?"

"I'd like to go see her tomorrow morning."

"I can come to work after school," he said. "Tell me everything that happens."

That evening, she searched again for her paperweight, but it didn't seem to be anywhere on the floor.

She meant to pray about the decoy scam and the Castell family, but she fell asleep wondering what Tara's Aunt Dixie looked like.

CHAPTER 21

I'm not sure what to think
about this visit to Tara's,
except that I need to go.
Her aunt and uncle sound
worse than peculiar.
I'm trying not to dislike them, sight unseen.
~Journal

He said there'd be a name on a sign, somewhere along Salty Spung Road. She'd had to detour because of a forest fire, and the officer had given her directions. She could only hope that he knew which Marrick was Sid.

The sign turned out to be a rusted iron post with a crossbar made of wood and a name painted in red: MARRICK'S MIRACLE SHOP. Trees grew to the edge of the narrow driveway, sheltering piles of car doors, fenders, and bumpers.

The driveway led to a house dwarfed by a ramshackle barn that towered behind it. Both seemed deserted, and after she parked and turned off her engine, the silence closed in. If anything moved here, it would be only the crawling vines and the creeping rust.

She picked her way around a sprawl of engine parts and hesitated before walking up the steps to the door-less screened porch.

"Mollie!" A red-haired streak rushed down the steps and pulled her into a bear hug. "Oops!" Tara let her go. "I think I crushed whatever was in that bag."

"Just your cookies," Madeleine said, handing them to her,

"For me!" The girl's eyes were puffy, but a smile lit her face. An instant later, it vanished. "You'd better meet my uncle."

A tall, gaunt figure ambled down the steps, blinking in the sunlight.

"Uncle Sid," Tara said. "Mollie brought us cookies."

The man scratched at the tuft of red whiskers on his chin, nodding, and she recognized him from Timothy's store.

He peered into her face. "I thank you," he said, "for lookin' after our Sally."

He spoke with care, as if finding and retrieving words from his brain was a risky business, but his blue eyes examined her appreciatively.

"We enjoyed having her," Madeleine said, as if Tara's presence had been a pre-arranged social occasion.

"Hey, let's go for a walk in the woods," Tara said. "Can we, Uncle Sid, just for a few minutes?"

He considered. "You be careful." He gazed at the smoky pallor of the sky, and sniffed the air. "That fire is still movin'. And . . ." He paused to drag out a new thought. "Make sure you get back before . . ."

"We will." Tara was hopping from one foot to the other. "You can hold the cookies. C'mon, Mollie."

She darted into the trees as if she'd been let out of a cage, and Madeleine hurried to keep up. She hadn't locked her car. Would it be safe? Or would the Miracle Man dismember it just for the fun of putting it back together again?

"Got to hurry," Tara said over her shoulder. "I'm grounded. But I want to show you something."

She turned off the path, pushing through waist-high bushes, and Madeleine stayed close behind.

"Over there," Tara said.

"That?" All she could see was a huge brush pile.

"I piled a whole lot of branches over it for camouflage."

Tara ducked under a tree limb, dropped to her hands and knees to crawl forward, and Madeleine did the same. She found herself in a tiny brush-lined cave that was roofed with wood scraps. It ended at the rusted body of a truck with flattened tires.

Still crouching, Tara grinned at her. "Like it? My hideout. Right in my own backyard. Got the boards from Sid's pile behind the garage, but he won't mind. We've got to hurry," she said again. "I need to ask you a favor."

She crawled to the truck body, reached underneath it, and pulled out a black metal box with dented corners.

"This is my hideaway box," she said. "Sid comes home with all kinds of junk and this was just what I needed. I . . . um . . . acquired it from him."

She crouched over the front of the box and opened it, shielding the contents with her body.

A second later she clicked the door of the box shut, and she slid it back underneath the truck before turning. In her palm lay the pendant she'd worn around her neck.

"This is mine," Tara said, her voice grown fierce. "And I'm not going to let her steal it from me again." She gave Madeleine a pleading look. "Can you keep it for me?"

"If you're sure you want me to."

Why was it so important?

Tara slipped the metal disc into the outside pocket of Madeleine's purse and zipped it shut. "There, it's safe now. It belonged to my mother. And it—oh! C'mon, or she'll catch me."

She crawled outside and plunged into the woods again, and after only a few minutes they reached the clearing. Uncle Sid stood in the sunlight where they'd left him, eating a cookie and gazing at Madeleine's car. "Need a bumper," he said. "I kin fix you up. Paint job too."

He shifted his gaze to a black pickup barreling down the driveway, and both he and Tara seemed to stiffen.

A grizzly-sized woman stepped from the truck. Her jacket, pants, and boots were black leather, and a knotted brown plait hung down her back. "Sally! What're you doing outside? You're grounded, remember?"

"Hi, Aunt Dixie." Tara's voice had changed timbre. It was lighter, more childlike. "Mollie just stopped by to say hello."

The implication was clear: she's just leaving.

Madeleine arranged a smile on her face.

The woman gestured toward the house and Tara scampered back inside. "Sid, it's cold out here," she said in a caressing voice. "And you without your jacket."

"I'm okay, Dixie. She brought cookies."

The woman's gaze skimmed across her, and the black eyes were disdainful.

She put a muscular hand on her husband's shoulder and turned him toward the house. "I will make you plenty of cookies." She linked her arm with his.

He went willingly enough, but they had gone only a few steps before his head rotated on the thin neck. "Come see us any—" His words squeezed off in mid-sentence.

As she opened her car door, Tara's shout came from the porch. "Bye, Mollie. Thanks for coming!"

How much would Tara have to pay for that cheerful expression of defiance? She did a careful three-point turn to get out of the small clearing and prayed for a chance to come back.

She had kept her cell phone off during the visit, and now it blinked at her with voice mail. Nathan's mellow voice said, "Do you have time to go visit Mrs. Bozarth with me this afternoon? I'll be with patients, so leave a message."

She told his voice mail that yes, any time in late afternoon would be fine, and stopped on the way back to the Manor to buy groceries.

Aunt Lin helped her to carry them in. "I've called the Truck Guys about the Blue Room," she said. "I can't wait to see what it looks like without the clutter."

The men arrived by the time lunch was over, and they cleared the room under Aunt Lin's watchful eye. The blue sofa went too, and Madeleine thought about the nights Tara had spent on it. What could be done about her?

Afterwards, Madeleine joined her aunt in the doorway, and Bria came to stand beside them. "That fireplace," Aunt Lin said. "I could tear off those blue tiles with my bare hands. Another of Henrietta's fantasies, and all wrong for this house."

Bria tilted her head. "I wonder what the original fireplace looked like."

"That's a good question," Aunt Lin said. "Let's see if we can find out. I hope Jude's coming today."

As soon as Jude arrived, he pitched into the work. Madeleine walked past while he was wiping down the fireplace. "What happened at Tara's?" he asked.

"I think I'd run away too. That aunt of hers is terrifying.

"Tara said she's big and strong."

"Understatement. Twice my size and all muscle."

Jude grinned. "What about the uncle?"

"He's different. Sort of quirky and passive. He seemed almost normal until the aunt showed up."

Jude asked how Tara was doing, and she told him what she'd observed but didn't say anything about the hideout or the pendant.

"What about the fire?" he asked. "Our teacher told us there's a bad one up that way."

"She's right. I got directions and drove around it."

"Our teacher said that a store in Tabernacle blew up, too, so she gave us a lesson on how explosives work. Might come in handy."

Madeleine said she hoped not, and he went to get a bucket of fresh water.

A short time later, while she was putting supper into the oven, she thought about the pendant and wondered what it would look like, cleaned up. She could try silver polish.

It was small, the size of a silver dollar, and it bore a raised motif that was lost in the tarnish. As she worked, the image of a tree with twining, interlaced branches appeared. Jude stepped through the doorway, coughing. "Bria's raising a dust cloud in there. I need a drink."

She moved aside as he filled his glass at the sink, drank it down, and filled it again. "What's that?"

"Something of Tara's." She ran water over the pendant and held it up. The tree gleamed, and its interwoven roots and branches spread into a circular border.

He set down his glass, staring.

"What's the matter, Jude?"

"Where'd you get that?"

"From Tara. She asked me to keep it for her."

"It's not hers." He spoke as if the words strangled him. "It's . . . it's my dad's."

Madeleine looked from his ashen face to the object in her hand. "Are you sure? Maybe it just looks like his."

He picked up the leather cord that dangled from the pendant. "My dad wore this all the time. He liked Celtic stuff."

He touched the frayed ends of a knot. "This is where it broke, a long time ago. We were wrestling." He prodded the second knot with a thumbnail. "Then it broke again. He was going to get a chain for it. He put it in his binocular case for safe keeping."

His voice cracked, but he went on. "I don't know where that girl got it, but—"

"Jude! You coming back?"

He jumped. "Don't let my sister see it, or it'll make her crazy, like Mom." He hurried from the kitchen.

She dried off the pendant and tucked it into the top drawer of her bureau with a sigh. Which of them was telling the truth?

Her aunt had worked in her dark room for most of the afternoon, but she came out to pay Bria and Jude before they left.

"You'll have the house to yourself," Madeleine said to her. "Supper's in the oven. I'm going with Nathan Parnell to visit one of his patients."

"Take your time," her aunt said, "I've got a project in hand. Why not invite him for supper?"

Why not?

She'd hardly finished changing when his Jeep drove up to the back door. She slipped a loaf of walnut bread into a bag and went out to meet him.

"I'm glad you could come on such short notice," he said, opening the car door. "Evelyn liked you, and it's good for her to have company." He frowned. "That ulcer on her leg. Sometimes it's easier to dress it myself."

Evelyn Bozarth began to glow as soon as they walked in. "Doc-tor-and-teach-er."

"How are you today?" Madeleine asked.

"Lov-ing Christ." Her crooked smile was incandescent.

"Me too." Madeleine put the loaf of bread into her lap. "Brought you something."

Nathan said, "Wait till you smell this."

He opened the bag. "Evelyn, I saw her make this bread, and believe me, it's going to be tender. Or whatever the term is for dough that's been beaten up."

The woman shook her head. "Knea-ded. Glut-en-stretch-es."

She bent her head over the loaf and smiled. "Cinn-a-mon. Ver-y good." She patted Madeleine's knee. "Thank-you."

Nathan checked her over, changed the bandage on her leg, and watched her walk. "You're doing well," he said. "How about trying a cane next week?"

"Good news!" She smiled. "Grad-u-a-tion."

She leaned back against the pillows while he went to make her tea.

"So you taught at Sandy Bank?" Madeleine said.

Evelyn Bozarth nodded, looking expectant.

"Someone told me that Sid and Sam Marrick went there," Madeleine said. "Did you know them at all?"

"Bad kids." Her eyes snapped.

Madeleine hesitated. Was she upsetting the woman? Maybe she shouldn't ask any more questions about them. Next time.

Evelyn Bozarth leaned forward, stretching a hand toward Madeleine. "Doc-tor," she said quietly. "Re-mark . . . re-mark-able man."

"Yes."

The woman's voice shook, just a little. "Take-care-of-him. For-me." The black eyes softened. "Our se-cret."

Pain twisted deep inside her, but Madeleine smiled. "I'll do my best," she said. "And . . . and I'll pray that the Lord keeps making you stronger."

He returned with tea and a slice of the walnut bread, buttered and cut into four neat squares. Remarkable man, yes.

It was time to leave, and Madeleine bent to give the woman a hug. She whispered, "You are such a blessing to me, Evelyn. I'll remember our secret."

Evelyn Bozarth's smile followed them all the way to the door.

After they left her subdivision, he said, "I want to take you somewhere, but I'm almost afraid to ask."

"What is this fearsome place?"

"Apple Pie Hill."

She eyed him. Was the kindly doctor suggesting a therapeutic trip? "You probably don't have the same agenda. What's the big attraction there?"

He turned off the highway. "You'll see."

At the moment, what she saw was the usual road-lined-with-pines, but the trees were burnished with more than sunlight. He wanted to spend time with her.

"How was your visit to Tara's?" he asked.

She described the aunt and the uncle, and told him about the pendant.

He slowed for a puddle. "Jude is a smart kid. He wouldn't be mistaken about it belonging to his father. Strange, though."

"Something else I find strange is Kent's attitude toward Tara and her family. He and Remi came over for supper on Friday night."

He looked at her, a question in his eyes.

"He invited himself, before Aunt Lin found out. He won't be coming back."

But she still hadn't done anything about his scam.

"Anyway," she said, "he made a speech saying I should send Tara away, and so forth."

"I wonder if that's what Remi found so offensive," Nathan said. "He mentioned that Kent's been shooting off his mouth. He might be changing his mind about his hero."

They turned onto a sand road with more trees. If it were up to her, they'd never run out of roads and trees.

"Did you have a chance to talk to your detective friend?" she asked. Maybe he could rock Kent's boat.

"We don't have much of a case."

"Why not?"

"We have to prove that fraud was intended. He said we should try threatening Kent with legal action."

"That's better than what I did. I just asked him to be nice and stop it."

"That was a good place to start. He's going to wish he had."

They crossed another swampy patch. "At least," Nathan said, "I hope we can protect Paula Castell's name. We can't even prove that he added the initials without her knowledge."

"What can we do?"

"I'm going to talk to Kent. Probably Wednesday morning—that's the first time I'm free." He turned to look at her. "I want to punch him for the way he treated you, Mollie. When we talk, I need to be rational. Will you pray for me?"

"Yes, I will."

The road climbed a small hill, ending at a soaring metal fire tower, orange and white. Beyond it was nothing but trees.

"Here we are," he said.

She laughed, gazing at the bony structure. "Can we climb it?"

He glanced across the clearing. "I bring the teens here to pick up trash, and last trip, the steps needed some work. Looks like someone fixed them." He smiled. "Just in time."

The wind tugged at her hair as soon as she stepped from the car. Let it blow. This might be fun.

She scurried up the metal steps and paused at the third landing. Already the view was impressive. They climbed up one more level and went on to the next, where the scaffolding felt rickety.

She glanced at the level above them. "Is that a room up there?"

"Locked," he said. "This is far enough." He leaned on the rail and she did too.

Trees spread before them, looking like a rumpled coverlet stitched with jade greens and moss greens and shadowy blue-greens, stretching far into the distance.

"Beautiful!" she said. The wind was brisk enough to cut through her sweater and send her hair streaming. She crossed her arms, trying not to shiver.

He glanced sideways. "Cold?"

"I should have brought a jacket."

"In Alaska, we have a custom—a wonderful old tradition—for keeping warm."

He had that mischievous lift to his eyebrow.

"I'm suspicious already."

"You'll see."

He unzipped his jacket, took his arm out of one sleeve, and spread the free half of it across her shoulders. "Hmm. For the best effect, you need to move a little . . ." He snuggled her against him. "And you don't want that arm of yours to get cramped, so could you . . . ?"

She hesitated, then slipped her arm along his back and leaned into the warmth of his sweater.

He grinned, pulling the jacket around them. "Hold onto it, that's right. See, you just fit."

"Scheming varlet!" Her face was barely an inch from his. "I don't think it's an old Alaskan custom at all."

She could feel him laughing. "Are you warmer now?"

"Yes."

"A varlet with your good interests at heart. Have mercy."

She shook her head, resisting the impulse to lay it on his shoulder. His torso was lean and solid. His hand rested lightly on her waist, and she was aware of it.

This was fine, right? Breathe. Slow and deep.

He noticed. "You okay?"

"I am happy."

He bent, touched his cheek to hers. "So am I."

They stood in silence, gazing across the trees. A tiny open space, perhaps a cranberry bog, sparkled in the light. Lovely, but . . . so flat.

He said, "What are you thinking?"

"I was wondering how they do without mountains."

He smiled. "When I'm homesick, I come here to look at the mountains."

"Show me."

He turned to the south, taking her with him. "See those skyscrapers on the horizon? Not really Atlantic City. They're mountain peaks. Kohisaat, Gurney, Sunrise Mountain."

She gestured past him to the west, at the misted outline of another city. "And those?"

"Mt. Silverthrone and Cedar Point. Sometimes you can see Beartooth."

"Show me Denali."

"You know Denali?"

"The most beautiful mountain I've ever seen."

"On a crisp day like this, look west of Mt. Silverthrone, and there it is, the tallest one."

She closed her eyes and could see the mountain thrusting into the sky with its white buttressed shoulders.

"When were you there?" he asked.

"College. I had a friend who lived near Anchorage. She took me on the tour to Denali, and I'll never forget it."

"Neither will I. Denny and I climbed it once. Susan was upset. She thought it was too dangerous."

She knew he'd talk about her, sooner or later.

"Did she worry about your flying?"

"Not usually. She liked to come with me whenever she could. Not so much after Susie was born."

"What did she do while you were away?"

"She had a ministry with the women in our village. They'd get together and sew and trade recipes. She taught them basic hygiene. They loved her. I think it was because she was always laughing."

His hand at her waist moved, restless. "I'm sorry. Maybe you don't like me talking about her."

"I don't mind," she said quietly. "Susan and Susie are part of you."

But the sunlit trees had dimmed. Of course he'd go back to Alaska. Beartooth and Silverthrone and Denali rose before her, somber shadows. Let him return to his mountains and his memories of Susan.

She straightened. Every day, she was getting stronger. Yes, she was, and she was going to hang onto her hard-won independence.

The wind freshened, murmuring around the tower, and he said, "We'd better go down. Sometime I'll wrap you up in my parka, and we'll come watch the sun set."

Not likely. But the wind made off with her thoughts and blew the scent of pine into her face, and by the time she'd scrambled down the steps, she could smile again.

He backed the Jeep and turned it down the hill. "Your aunt is going to be wondering what happened to you."

"She suggested that you might want to eat supper with us."

He glanced at her. "Do you suggest it also?"

"If you don't mind roast beef and sweet potatoes."

"What's for dessert?"

"Greedy varlet! I'll serve you ice cubes with a mint sprig, and charge you double."

He grinned. "There I go again. I might even lose my rank as varlet."

Come to think of it, what were they going to have for dessert? Something from the freezer. A pie would be done if she put it in the oven first thing.

"What do you think about pie?"

"R-squared or R-round?"

"My aunt is going to enjoy talking with you tonight. I might not be able to keep up. The round kind."

He said he liked pie, any kind, and the meal came together without serious delay. Her aunt showed him around the house, knowing that she'd rather be left alone to cook, and when it was ready, they ate at the kitchen table.

As she'd thought, Aunt Lin drew him into conversation, and before long they were discussing cameras, the merits of black-and-white photography, and favorite places to hike.

They didn't exclude her, but someone had to see to the food, and she didn't mind. He described his photographs of glaciers, glancing at her and making her laugh.

After he'd gone, her aunt gazed at her with a smile. "I like that man, very much. I'm happy for you."

"I don't know him very well," Madeleine said, and fortunately, her cell phone rang.

Mother sounded more upset than usual. "Madeleine, I'm so glad I could get ahold of you. I saw a TV special about the Pine Barrens, and they said criminals come there and bury bodies. Sounds like the Mafia, if you ask me."

"I haven't seen a single Mafia."

"You never know! I'm going to send your father's pistol. Then at least you can protect yourself."

"Please! I don't want a gun," Madeleine said. "I never could shoot straight, remember? And I don't have a permit. You wouldn't want me to get arrested, would you?"

"I suppose not. Tell me—have you met any interesting men or anything?"

She could have scripted the rest of the conversation from memory, but finally she could hang up. She flexed her shoulders to stretch out the knots. Why not take a nice hot shower?

The next morning, she made zucchini bread with pineapple, walnuts, and raisins along with the usual spices, and Aunt Lin declared it a success.

"Six loaves!" her aunt said. "Better get them into the freezer before I eat any more."

By the time she'd wrapped up the breads, Aunt Lin had walked into the Blue Room and was frowning at the fireplace. "That monstrosity! How long before we can tear it down?"

"Remi's looking for a job. He said to leave a message with Timothy."

"I'll phone this afternoon," her aunt said. "Let's work on our own projects until he gets here."

Good, she could do something more with that paper on leavening.

Mid-afternoon, Nathan phoned, with voices sounding in the background.

"Mollie."

"Yes."

"Thank you, I was hoping for that."

She smiled at the phone. Either he was having a very good day or everything had gone wrong. "You may explain."

"Charlotte's in the hospital with acute pancreatitis. And one of her clients has gone into labor. The family doesn't have insurance, so it looks like I'm going to be delivering that baby."

"At home?"

"If I don't do it, they won't have any medical support at all. I called because Charlotte said you might help."

"As long as you remember I'm not trained."

"I'll take that as somewhere between the interrogative and the unconditional *yes*. She told me about your experience. I'll give you the details when I pick you up."

"What time?"

"Around six? I've got a couple of things to tie up here."

"Whenever. I'll be ready."

CHAPTER 22

Evelyn Bozarth—so wise and loving.
I'd like to go back on my own
and talk to her some more.
We could be friends.
~Journal

Madeleine told Aunt Lin why she'd be gone for the evening, and her aunt looked amused. "You two have the most interesting dates. I won't wait up."

She wore her comfortable jeans and a short-sleeved shirt because they'd probably keep the room warm. At least it was a cool night. After she'd clipped her hair away from her face, she packed a gift basket with walnut bread and a jar of honey and tried to remember everything Arlene had taught her.

He was there by six-thirty. "I'm glad you could come," he said. "I'm not sure what to expect."

She laughed. "You've only done this a few hundred times before, right?"

"More than you'd think."

"Was it different, practicing medicine in Alaska?"

He smiled. "Everything's different there. When I got back from medical school, I realized that some of my brand-new education wasn't very useful, especially in the bush. So I decided to hang out with the older doctors and nurses."

"What about home births?"

"One of the midwives let me follow her around."

"I've only seen a couple of midwives in action, but . . . wow!"

He nodded. "This one was astonishing. Since then, I've worked with other midwives, and I've nothing but respect for them." He swung his Jeep onto a narrow road. "Tonight we may run into a problem. This couple has a strong aversion to doctors."

He glanced at her. "You may stand up and cheer."

"Not me." She tried for a teasing voice. "I have to work with you tonight."

"I'd hoped for something more positive," he said. "Anyway, Charlotte thought it might make a difference if you were there."

"She told me a little about the previous doctor."

"I guess he had some personal problems, an addiction. And he made an inaccurate diagnosis when this couple's daughter was sick. They almost lost her."

"What else can you tell me about them?"

"Logan and Greta Moore. Greta's other two births were relatively simple. The children will be with a neighbor. Charlotte's an excellent midwife, so I'm sure they'll have a birth kit."

Lights shone from all the windows in the Moore's home. Nathan parked in front, picked up his medical bag, and gave her an encouraging smile. "Here goes."

A black-haired man stepped out onto the porch and stood with feet planted wide, hands on his hips. Stained jeans and a ragged T-shirt didn't bother Madeleine as much as the enmity on his face.

Logan Moore scanned them with fierce black eyes, and held the door open without a word, Nathan put a protective hand on her arm, and they stepped past him.

The front room wasn't deep, but it was wide. To her right was a straight-backed chair and a wood stove that radiated warmth. To her left, flanked by two overstuffed chairs, stood a daybed. It looked homemade, with a wooden base and built-in drawers under the mattress.

The woman, Greta, must have been in the middle of a contraction because she was leaning onto a chair with one hand, and holding her back with the other, moaning.

Her husband glanced at Nathan and kicked the straight-backed chair into the corner behind the stove. "That's for you. Charlotte said you had to come, but you'd better stay put."

Madeleine stared. He wasn't going to let Nathan do anything? That meant she had to . . .

Nathan's calm expression didn't change. He sat in the chair and put his bag on the floor.

Logan stood unmoving in front of him. Did he think the doctor would try to escape?

She set her basket beside Nathan's bag and gave him a sideways glance. His eyes held hers with a smile. "Looks like you're on your own," he said quietly.

Thanks a lot. How was she going to manage without a midwife?

First, wash hands.

Greta straightened up, a blonde, solid-looking woman in an over-sized T-shirt that might have been her husband's.

She looked at Madeleine, sighed, and began to walk back and forth, keeping her hands on her back. "I need Charlotte," she said. "My back hurts so bad."

Madeleine went to her, put a hand on her shoulder and started rubbing her back. Where was the birth kit? How could she disarm this husband?

She glanced at him. Still standing over Nathan like a watchdog.

"Logan," she said, "I really like that piece." She nodded toward the daybed. "Did you build it?"

He turned, and she smiled at him.

"Yeah."

Greta spoke in short little bursts. "Built it for me. Our couch. Charlotte likes it. Said it's good for birthing. He set it up like she told us."

Logan's eyes softened as she spoke. He looked at his wife with love blazing across his face, and Madeleine had to turn away.

Greta was grabbing for the chair again. She let out a gasp and clutched at her back. Madeleine put both hands, one stacked on the other, at the base of Greta's spine, and Greta leaned back against her. "Oh, that feels good."

Madeleine braced her feet so that Greta could lean back as hard as she needed to, and when Greta began to breathe more easily, she shifted her hands.

"No!" Greta cried. Her face was flushed and sweating. "Not yet! Don't move. It's helping."

Where was Logan? He'd stepped up beside them, looking anxious. Put him to work.

She kept her hands in place as she spoke to him. "Your wife needs a cool, wet cloth. Can you bring us one? And a glass of water?"

He threw a dark glance at Nathan, disappeared into the next room, and returned almost immediately. She thanked him with a smile and wiped Greta's face.

Greta drank, but afterwards, she shook her head. "This baby. Thought it would be easy. Never . . . had . . . pain. Like this."

She pressed back against Madeleine's hands, moaning, and Madeleine braced herself again, marveling at the woman's strength and feeling an echo of her pain. She held her hands steady, murmured to Greta, and tried to think what else she could do.

As the long contraction ended, she sent a questioning look to Nathan.

272

"I think the baby's posterior," he said in a low voice. "Why don't we try—"

He rose to his feet, and Logan stepped in front of him. "You stay right there."

Nathan shrugged. "Mollie," he said, "see if they have an old sheet."

She glanced at Logan. "Where's your birth kit?"

"In here," he said, opening one of the drawers under the bed. It held a tiny green knitted hat, small flannel blankets, towels, and several worn sheets.

She moved to reach for a sheet.

"Don't!" Greta cried. "Don't move your hand."

Stay calm, as calm as Nathan, she told herself.

"Logan," she said, "we need you."

He was beside her in an instant.

"See how I've got my hands?" she said. "Put yours like that, and let her push against you when she has contractions. That'll be a big help."

And it would keep him busy for a while.

She picked up the sheet and took it to Nathan. "Are you permitted to advise?" she said in an undertone.

His smile gave her courage. "You'll need a long strip," he said, "about two feet wide."

"Do you have any scissors?"

"In my bag." He handed them to her and watched as she snipped the hem and tore the sheet.

"Now what?"

"Drape the strip over Greta's back—right at hip level—nice and smooth. Bring the ends around to the front and cross them under her belly. You'll stand in front of her."

She tried to picture what he was describing, and nodded.

"Then," he said, "we wait for the next contraction."

Logan still had his hands in place, but he'd watched every move they made, she was sure of it.

Madeleine went back, saying, "We're going to help that baby, Greta."

As she put the sheet into place, she glanced at Nathan and he nodded. He leaned forward. "Next contraction, you pull the ends in opposite directions, out to the side." He gestured, using both arms in a pulling motion. "You'll have to brace your feet."

Greta let out a gasp, and Madeleine began to pull. "Oh, yes," Greta said.

She kept pulling, and Greta said, "Harder, oh, yes, good. Good. More. "

At first, it seemed an easy thing to do, but her arms began to tire, and the contraction went on forever. At last it was over, and Greta clung to her in silence.

Logan began to rub his wife's back, looking a trifle less agonized.

After a minute, Madeleine said, "Logan, we need you again. You're a lot stronger than I am." She handed him an end of the strip. "Here. At the next one, you pull this."

They pulled through the next contraction, and Greta seemed more comfortable. As it eased, Madeleine smiled at Logan, and he gave her a small grin in return.

Another contraction came and went, and he said, "How long do we do this?"

"As long as it helps her."

In just a few minutes Greta began to moan again, and Madeleine picked up her end of the sheet. "Here we go."

But this time, at the end of the contraction, Greta said, "Oh!" She cradled her belly and leaned forward with a puzzled look on her face. "Oh . . . better." She sat on the bed and reached for the water glass.

Madeleine glanced at Nathan. "Seems like the baby's turned," he said, smiling.

A wave of giddy relief swept through her, and she smiled back. "Another old Alaskan custom?"

He grinned. "Mexican. They use a rebozo."

She shook her head at him and went back to wiping Greta's face.

Greta let out a low groaning breath. She flung her arms around Madeleine's waist and buried her head in her chest.

Something new. Madeleine bent her head over Greta's and held onto her.

Logan had seen what happened. He stepped closer, looking worried again. "I thought it was almost over."

"She's doing great, but we've still got some work ahead of us. Could you warm up the hat and those little blankets?"

He took them from the drawer and paused beside her. "In the oven?"

"Yes, but wrap them in foil, okay? Don't let them get hot."

Greta was trembling now, perspiring heavily. She gripped Madeleine's waist and began to rock, pulling Madeleine back and forth, and she crooned. "Come on, baby, I want to see you. Come on, I want to hold you. Come, my baby, my very own."

Madeleine's jaw clenched as she listened, and sorrow grated through her, so jarring that she almost let go. Never, never would she sing that song.

No babies for her. A woman who panicked at a mere kiss would not—could not—marry again. She strengthened her grip and swayed with Greta, crooning a nameless little dirge of her own.

Could she accept this from her forever-God? This too?

She closed her eyes and breathed with Greta, leaning into her embrace. Back and forth. Back and forth.

Yes, You are my Lord, my Rock. This too.

They swayed and rocked and sang, and finally Greta let her head drop against Madeleine, smiling an inward-focused smile.

Madeleine brushed back the clinging strands of blonde hair, wiped Greta's damp face, and whispered encouragement. She held out the glass for her to drink.

Another contraction. Logan was fidgeting beside them, but Madeleine closed her eyes, fastened her mind on Greta, sharing her pain.

The contractions came faster and faster, more and more intense. In between, Madeleine leaned away, trying to stretch out her back, but Greta clung to her.

Would this last all night?

Greta lurched to her feet. "Bathroom."

Madeleine stayed near until they reached the bathroom door, and then she waited outside.

A minute later she heard a low grunt. Greta emerged from the bathroom, turned toward the bed and stopped, grabbing Madeleine's shoulders with both hands. She dug in her fingers, pulled Madeleine's head to her chest, and bellowed.

Madeleine recognized that sound—Greta was starting to push. She held onto her and tried to keep her balance.

As soon as the contraction was over, Greta dropped to her knees beside the bed and Logan moved close. Madeleine kept her hands on Greta while she looked up at him. "The baby's coming," she said quietly. "We need the doctor now."

"I hate doctors."

"So do I. But this is a good man."

Greta lifted her head. "Logan." She spoke between her teeth. "Let him come." She gasped. "Let him come."

Nathan was sitting forward, alert.

Logan gave him a narrow-eyed glance, nodded, and Nathan headed for the sink.

Greta crouched back onto her heels, and a low sound, a growl, rose from deep within her. She bent over the bed again, the damp T-shirt clinging to her thighs.

Madeleine wiped Greta's face once more. Hurry up, Doc! How long does it take to wash your hands?

At last Nathan was there beside her, pulling on gloves, kneeling behind Greta.

Logan bent over his wife, murmuring to her. Madeleine rubbed Greta's back with long steady strokes, and gave her another sip of water.

Greta began to push again, groaning, and Nathan soothed her in a low voice. "The baby's coming fast, Greta. Don't force it . . . don't force it. Listen to your body."

Greta took a deep breath and roared, a sound of intense effort and power and triumph.

"Mollie, would you look for the head?" Nathan's voice was so calm, he might have been asking her to check the time.

She found a mirror in his bag and used it, bending down low. "Yes! It's right there."

He cupped his hand beneath the emerging head of sleek black hair and spread his fingers wide. A few minutes later, the baby was sliding into his hands, and he smiled.

"Reach down and take your baby, Greta," he said.

Madeleine steadied her as Greta sat back on her heels and drew the baby close. Logan knelt beside her, his arms around them both, and Madeleine moved away.

After a minute Logan said, "What is it?"

Madeleine had an impulse to say, "A baby," but she held still.

Greta smiled, tears glistening. "A boy. Our little boy."

"Mollie?" Nathan looked at her, still smiling, as if he knew she'd forgotten where she was. "Blankets?"

She took them from the oven and draped one across the baby, and then snuggled the knitted hat down over his damp little head. With another blanket, she wiped the baby's nose and mouth and dried off his body.

He made a thin, mewling sound, and Nathan watched him with a thoughtful gaze.

"Stethoscope?" Madeleine asked. She eyed Nathan's gloved hands, smeared with blood and mucus. "Want to change gloves?" He nodded, his eyes still on the baby as he stripped off the soiled gloves and put on fresh ones.

Finally Greta moved to stand up, and they helped her onto the bed, where she sat against the pillows, cooing to the baby. He sneezed, and everyone smiled.

Nathan spoke quietly. "I think his breathing is a little slow. Let's check him out." He spread a blanket on the bed in front of Greta. "Could I look at him for a minute?"

She nodded, put the baby down upon it, and leaned forward to watch.

The baby lay curled up, his arms tight to his chest, making weak, snuffing noises, and when Nathan gently moved an arm out to the side, he didn't respond.

Nathan listened to the baby's heart and lungs, his face impassive. "Hey, little guy, how about some help?"

He puffed air into the tiny mouth, and the baby made a small gasp. Nathan did it again, and the baby seemed to take a larger breath on his own.

Once more, Nathan listened to the baby's lungs. "Mollie, get the bottle of rubbing alcohol from my bag and open it."

He picked up the miniature hand, letting it curve around his gloved finger. "Lungs are still a bit wet," he said to her in a low voice. "Let's do this."

He tipped the baby up, and in one swift motion dripped the alcohol down the little back. The baby arched his body, gasped, and let out a yell of protest. He cried loudly, indignantly, and Nathan handed him back to Greta, looking satisfied. "Here you are, Mom, he'll be fine now."

"Thank you," she said, and even Logan smiled.

The baby's cries pulled Madeleine back to reality. They'd need something to eat. The bread she'd brought? And the honey. How about scrambled eggs?

She made tea for Greta with a bag of herbs that Charlotte had left, and by the time she was ready to serve the eggs and toast, Nathan had finished taking care of Greta. The baby was eagerly working on his first meal.

Logan ate enough for two men, stopped often to touch his wife's shoulder or to stroke his son's head, and talked with Nathan about kayaking the Skit Branch as if they were old fishing buddies.

Greta was silent, beaming, focused on her baby, but she ate everything Mollie brought to her. After she'd eaten, she wanted a shower, so Logan took the baby into his arms, crooning to him, and Madeleine stayed near Greta in case she needed anything.

After that, Madeleine tidied the kitchen, and Nathan checked Greta and the baby one last time. Finally he zipped up his bag, ready to leave. Logan walked with them to the door. "You're right about this one," he said to Madeleine. "We thank you both."

It must be almost midnight. If she could just get to the car, she could sit and do nothing. Nathan took her arm on their way down the porch steps. He came with her to the passenger door of the Jeep and gently helped her inside.

After he'd started the engine, he said, "Logan told me about a place around here. I'd like to show you."

"Now?"

"Definitely now."

A few miles later, he turned onto a road of hard-packed sand. They jolted across ruts and potholes, and soon, except for the bright swath of their headlights, she could see no lights.

He glanced at her, perhaps wondering at her silence. "You up for a walk?"

"Good idea. I'm still sizzling from that birth. Must be the adrenaline rush. I'd forgotten the marvel of it."

He nodded. "Every time, I come away thinking it's the most amazing thing I've ever seen."

Amazing, yes. And she would never do more than watch. She could examine that fact more coolly now. Besides the intimacy question, marriage implied dependence and a mutual sort of vulnerability. Not for her. Not ever again.

The road tunneled on through the trees, curved, and curved again, bringing them into a broad, open space that seemed to be all sand and knee-high grasses punctuated with the occasional silhouette of a tree. One tree, especially tall, stood with out-flung limbs and patchy white bark that glistened in the headlights.

She leaned forward to look at it, and Nathan said, "Sycamore."

He slowed his Jeep to crawl along the perimeter of a muddy hole, and after that the road narrowed, leading through more trees to a wooden bridge.

"Oh, good! A river," she said. "Can we look at it?"

He parked near the bridge, and soon she was leaning over the rail, listening to the silky whisper of water.

"The Batsto," he said. "Come, there's more."

Her eyes had adjusted enough to see the dips in the road, and soon she caught sight of tumbled stones. "What's this?" She laughed. "You found some ruins."

He took her hand. "Just for you."

The ruins lay quiet before them, nothing more than a rectangle of rough stone blocks, and he played his flashlight across the ragged walls. Some of the stones, frosted with concrete, rose in stair-steps to shoulder height; others, fallen remnants, had been stitched together with vines. Here and there, young cedars raised their darkened spires.

He turned off his flashlight, and she gazed along the silvered contours of wall and stone until they melted into the shadows. She glanced overhead. "And we have stars." The clearing was roofed with a sky so brilliant that it glittered. "I suppose you have stars in Alaska."

"Same ones. The Bear, the Big Dipper, the Milky Way." His voice had a smile in it. "Only bigger."

"Of course. You're beginning to sound like a Texan."

He bent toward her and she said hurriedly, "What's this place called?"

"Not sure. Logan said the meadows we drove through have the remains of Hampton Furnace. It dates back to the 1800's, when they produced iron. This used to be a cranberry warehouse."

"*Sermons in stones,*" she said. "I wonder about the sermons here." She propped herself against a low wall. "Maybe I like ruins because they remind me that only God is forever."

He picked up a handful of stone bits from the crumbling top of the wall. "And ruins imitate life, with its beginnings and endings." He let the stones dribble through his fingers, dusted his hands off, and reclaimed hers. "Births and deaths." His voice warmed. "Tonight you went in and set to work like a pro."

"Like I knew what I was doing? I prayed a lot, I can tell you."

"You handled Logan better than I would have. When he's not stressed out, he's quite a guy."

"Did you see his face? Such a mixture of love and worry while he was trying to protect his Greta."

"From the big bad doctor."

She laughed. "You were a model of restraint."

"You did well with Greta. That was a beautiful sight, the two of you working together."

"She did all the work."

"Yes, as far as delivering the baby was concerned."

He paused, and she pulled a dried tendril of vine from among the stones. "I guess I did some laboring of my own."

"I thought so."

She would never tell him what she'd been thinking. Lighten it up. She nudged him. "You saw a lot from your little chair in the corner, didn't you?"

"I certainly did."

She smiled to herself, thinking dreamily about the black-haired baby with Greta's blue eyes, and suddenly a man was leaning over her, too close, with his hand lifted to her face.

She cringed, ducking away, knowing sickly that she couldn't escape.

Nathan's voice said, "Mollie. I wouldn't . . ."

She blinked. "I . . . I forgot. That it was you."

How could he put up with this?

He didn't seem offended. "Remember me," he said, sliding his arm around her, but her lungs squeezed shut.

Not a threat, she told herself. No danger here. Breathe.

She leaned back against him, deliberately, to prove to herself that she could, and his long fingers traced the curve of her cheek. "I was proud of you tonight," he whispered.

He stroked her hair, smoothed back the loosened strands, and his hand lingered on the clip. "May I?"

She nodded.

He slipped off the clip and her hair fell around her face, and he brushed his fingers through it, light as a passing breeze.

"You know what color your hair is?"

"Kind of black?"

"Sable. Named for a small Arctic animal—black fur with rich brown highlights."

"Sable fur coats? I've heard of those. Poor little critters are probably extinct."

"And there's Sable Mountain in Denali's park," he said. "I'd like to show you that, someday."

The someday speech. She'd been afraid he'd get around to it.

His hand paused on the nape of her neck and a longing crept through her. If she turned toward him now, he would take her into his arms. She'd be warm and protected and he'd . . .

The longing froze.

There in his arms, she'd have to tell him: 'I cannot do this. Let's just be friends.'

He must have sensed her disquiet because he dropped his hand. "Well." The tone of his voice, doggedly cheerful, made her ache. He handed her the clip. "I promised you a walk, didn't I?" he said. "Let's find out what's up here."

He had a way of tucking his arm through hers that kept her close but not imprisoned. They circled the ruins, then walked along the curving road with wind rustling through the trees and leaves scuttling across their feet until they reached another bridge.

This must be a different river, but the starlight had followed them, gleaming on the water below and clothing the bushes with mystery.

She leaned over the railing to gaze at the rushing stream. "Would you want to take canoes along here?"

"The teens?"

She nodded, and he said, "Kayaks might work better. Dry as it's been, we'd have to portage the canoes."

"I can hear Connie now: 'You mean we've got to *carry* it?' "

He laughed. "This might be a great place for a hike, it's so wild. I'll have to ask Logan."

"A hike would be fun."

"I'll get a map. Want to check it out with me on Saturday?"

She yawned. "No decisions after midnight. Make that a conditional *yes*."

"Good," he said. "This is far enough."

He took her hand into his while they walked back, and she remembered how that hand had caught and cradled Greta's baby.

Had he caught his own little girl when she was born? An unforgettable experience. Perhaps he wouldn't mind if she asked.

"Were you there at Susie's birth?"

They passed a half-dozen pine trees before he answered. At last he said, "Susan wanted a hospital birth. She had some problems, and they wouldn't let me near her."

"But you had delivered babies yourself."

"In that hospital, I was just the father. No status at all."

He fell silent, but it wasn't the quiet companionship of the past few minutes. He must be thinking about his baby girl, and he was probably hurting. Maybe she shouldn't have brought it up?

Silently she answered her own question. No. She wasn't going to tiptoe around the subject of Susan, and neither should he, even if they were just friends. She yawned again. Let it rest, for tonight.

CHAPTER 23

Too much, too late. To bed.
~Journal

The next morning, Aunt Lin asked about the birth while they were eating a late breakfast, and Madeleine gave her a sketchy overview. But her aunt probed for details as if she were fascinated by the whole process, and she had a wistfulness about her that Madeleine recognized.

Aunt Lin might never marry, might never have children, but she loved babies. This creative, hard-working businesswoman was more complex than she'd thought.

Five minutes later, Aunt Lin's focus had swung back to the Manor and the Blue Room. She said she had hired Remi to start work this afternoon and asked Madeleine to look for wallpaper samples. Timothy would have some.

Madeleine was paging through the wallpaper books in Timothy's storeroom when she heard Nathan's voice. He and Timothy must be standing at the counter.

Had Nathan talked to Kent yet? She had remembered to pray for him.

Timothy's voice became more distinct. "I think she's back in the storeroom. Mollie?"

"I'm still here," she called.

Nathan pushed through the swinging doors, carrying a folded rectangle of paper, his eyes laughing.

She asked about his meeting with Kent, and the gray eyes chilled.

"He resented my interfering, as he put it, but he agreed to stop the forgery and give her a larger percentage."

He covered her hand with his. "I knew you were praying."

"You didn't punch him?"

"Not yet. Look at this."

He spread a topographic map over the washing machine. "Here's Hampton Road, where we drove last night, and the grassy area with the ruins of Hampton Furnace. We missed them, but Logan said there's hardly anything there. See this? It's the Batsto River. The map doesn't show the bridge, but here's the other one we walked to, the Skit Branch."

She bent over the map, tracing their route with a finger-tip. "So the ruins from that cranberry warehouse are in here somewhere."

"Still okay for Saturday?"

She smiled. "Sounds fine."

"And Friday evening, I'd like to take you to a concert. Local style."

"Vocal local yokels?"

"Not quite. Mostly instrumental. Do you like guitar?"

"Love it."

They agreed that he'd pick her up at six o'clock, and he said, "I dropped in to see the new baby. They named him Jared, and he's doing well."

"Does he still look like his dad, with all that black hair?"

"Very much so."

He bent close, as if he would put an arm around her, but Timothy rattled through the doors with his wagon, heading for the shelves. She asked whether she could borrow the wallpaper books and said goodbye to them both.

Over lunch, she and Aunt Lin discussed decorating ideas, and her aunt wrote out a list of projects for Remi and Jude, since she'd be working in her office all afternoon.

Remi arrived before Jude, and Madeleine showed him the Blue Room. He seemed ill at ease, and even when they stood by the fire place, he gave it only a cursory glance.

He snatched the baseball cap from his head and tossed it onto a chair.

"Mollie?" He shoved his hands into his pockets, rocking back and forth on his sneakers. "I've got to tell you about something."

He lowered his gaze to the floor. "Your car."

What about her car? "It's doing fine, thank you," she said. "I might even get it painted at the Marrick Miracle Shop."

He shook his head. "The other night. When it didn't start." He ran a hand through his hair and muttered, "My fault."

"What do you mean?"

"I'm such an idiot."

"You didn't—?"

"No, but I might as well have."

"What?"

He stared at his feet. "I was changing the sparkplugs on Kent's Bronco, and he hung around, watching me. Asked a bunch of questions. Like did I know any tricks to keep a car from starting."

His words came out in a rush. "I thought I was being so smart. I showed him how—just take out the rotor."

She gripped the back of a chair, feeling betrayed. "You didn't wonder why he was asking?"

"I had no idea, Mollie. But he's always talking about you. I should have known." He shot her a worried glance. "I hate myself."

"It made trouble," she said slowly, "but the Lord kept me safe."

His eyes glittered. "That man is not what he seems to be."

"You found that out too?"

He turned his head. "Someone's at the door."

The knocking became a drum-beat. Jude.

She let him in, and Jude followed her back to the Blue Room, saying, "Whose truck is that outside?"

"Mine," Remi said, "except for the dents."

"Way cool. With all-terrain tires."

"They've come in handy. So you're working this job too?"

"I sure am," Jude said. "What are we doing, Mollie?"

It took Jude and Remi the rest of the afternoon to cover the furniture and move the plates, glass, and china figurines from the fireplace shelves to the floor. She would catalogue each item, and tomorrow they'd start dismantling the elaborate structure around the fireplace.

Near evening, Aunt Lin came out to the kitchen for a snack and looked at what they'd done, nodding with approval. She retreated to her office, saying she would probably work late.

Since tonight was SING, Madeleine ate a quick supper, showered, and changed. Now she could relax and enjoy some good fellowship.

Nathan arrived late. Even though he sat at the keyboard as usual, he played with his eyes half-closed, and afterwards, while she was talking with the teens, he stood off by himself, looking through songbooks.

Finally everyone left. The chairs had been folded away and the table set back into place. Nathan didn't seem to be feeling sociable, so she might as well leave.

Timothy yawned. "Kind of tired tonight." He yawned again. "If you don't mind, I'll let the two of you finish up. I'm off to bed." The *thum-thud* of his sneakers faded into the darkened store.

Nathan put down a songbook and turned to her. "Mollie." He let out a groaning breath. "I have some bad news."

She leaned back against the sideboard, alarmed by his gaunt face.

"Evelyn Bozarth—she died this afternoon."

Something inside her broke. She had to cross her arms over her chest to keep the pieces together.

Not Evelyn. Not the woman who loved her Christ so dearly, who'd been doing so well, the woman who could have been a friend.

He lifted a hand, let it drop. "Another stroke. Massive. She died while she was taking a nap."

"But I thought she was getting better!" Madeleine said. "I was going to go back and talk to her. And . . . and we had a secret."

He moved slowly to the table without answering, sank into a chair, and knotted his hands.

She sat beside him, but he didn't seem to notice. He looked despairing, more so than you'd expect for a doctor.

"Evelyn's blood pressure was fine the last time I checked." He bent his head. "And it was fine when they took it this morning. The reports all indicated progress."

His voice flattened. "I missed something. She seemed more tired than usual. I should have picked up on it."

"What could you have done? Even if she were in the hospital?"

"Changed her medication. Hired more nurses. Something."

Madeleine thought about his kindness to the woman, and a memory flared: the smile on Evelyn's face as they left.

"She knew, Nathan. She and I spoke together and . . . and I think she was saying good-bye."

He dropped his head into his hands, and after a long silence, he whispered, "I should have been there for her."

She studied him. Was this something beyond Evelyn's death, something deeper?

"Nathan," she said softly, "is this about Evelyn or about Susan?"

A shudder rippled through him. "I should have talked to the pilot. I should have seen how the plane was loaded. Careless. I should have been thinking about her and Susie, instead of that old woman."

"You're punishing yourself."

"I deserve it. I should have . . . I tried to pull them out of the plane, but it was burning . . . and I was burning, and they wouldn't let me go back, but I should have done something."

Her chest constricted with dread. Lord, help me! He's so wrong.

"Does God hold this against you?" she asked.

"Don't know." After a minute he said, "I guess not."

"Even if you had sinned, what would God do about it?"

No answer.

She put out her hand, rested it on the table between them. "Evelyn reminded me: *He was wounded for our transgressions.*"

His hand moved toward hers, then slowly drew back, clenching into a fist.

"Whatever happened," she said, "can't you forgive yourself? Isn't Christ's blood enough?"

"It's risky to fly at forty below." His voice turned cold. "She insisted. I shouldn't have given in. What kind of leadership is that?"

"Nathan, let it go." His pain was spreading into her, icy as her own fears.

She waited, but he didn't move or speak.

She wanted to shake him or hold him in her arms or call Timothy to come and talk sense into his friend.

But none of those would help. She stood to her feet, looking at the bowed head. She reached down to touch his hair and stopped. Not now. This was between him and his God.

Would he destroy himself?

She lifted her chin. Not while she still had the breath to pray.

Take care of him for me. Evelyn was with her dear Christ now. Could Evelyn beg mercy for the man she had so admired?

She turned to leave, and song-words marched into the room.

Before the throne of God above
I have a strong and perfect plea . . .

The song continued as she drove through the darkened streets and into the darker forest.

A great high Priest whose Name is Love,
Who ever lives and pleads for me.

Christ's pleading would be better than anything Evelyn could say on Nathan's behalf. Better than all her own dried-up tears.

She dropped her purse onto her bed, and picked up a blanket and her Bible. Where was a place to pray, a place set apart? The library. That little brown couch.

From the library windows, she could see only blackness.

When Satan tempts me to despair
And tells me of the guilt within . . .

Tonight the Evil One would be seeking someone to devour. Nathan had such potential for ministry. Was he going to be smothered by his self-imposed guilt? More reason to pray.

She turned on the lamp and huddled in its circle of light. She had prayed all the way home, and she would pray again, but first, Ephesians.

She began again at chapter one, lingered over the verses about God's grace and His will, and paused at *the immeasurable greatness of his power toward us.*

"That's what we need tonight, Lord. Your power."

She read farther, through chapter two with its reminder of God's rich mercy. In chapter three, she came upon Paul's prayer for his dear ones: *to be strengthened with power through his Spirit..*

"I want this, Lord. For Nathan, and for me."

She fell to her knees beside the couch. "O Lord my Rock. Deliver him from his guilt. Deliver me too, from my fears, for the sake of your great forever-love."

She prayed until the cold air creeping past the windows made her pull the blanket close, she prayed until her voice grew hoarse, and then she prayed some more.

She awoke to find a warm, soft body curled beside her. "Mac, did you come to rescue me?" She got to her feet, stiff and cramped. Outside, light glowed at the horizon.

The great unchangeable I AM,
The King of glory and of grace.

"Thank you, my God, for your grace this night. For what You did. For what You are going to do."

She slept late, and so did Aunt Lin, but while they ate breakfast, her aunt eyed her with concern. "Another bad night?"

"Not the usual," Madeleine said. "I was—I'm burdened for Nathan. If you think of it, could you pray for him?"

Her aunt looked pensive. "Sometimes I wish I were back on praying terms with God." She got up to pour herself another cup of coffee and sat down again.

After a minute, she said, "These Schnecken are wonderful. I hate to eat the last one."

Madeleine gazed at the crumbs on her plate. She hadn't done anything with her course for days. Too much excitement. Was that the real reason?

She carried her dishes to the sink. She wasn't going to give up on it. She'd get back to her paper on leavening, right way. And she really should make some plans for the future.

By the time the kitchen was cleaned up, Aunt Lin had switched into her full-forward mode, which gave Madeleine the feeling of being caught up in a brisk wind.

"I'm leaving again tomorrow," her aunt said, "but first I'd like to check out our Lemon Room upstairs."

They looked through the yellow bedroom, discovered an armoire full of old-fashioned hats, and talked. Aunt Lin asked about her course and suggested that she might consider going to a school in New York for more training.

Madeleine smoothed a black satin bonnet, thinking about it. She'd heard there were good schools in New York. School might lead toward the new life she'd wanted. She should be invigorated.

But even while she considered the possibilities, her resolution began to shrink, and she felt as if she were staring at the ruins of an underdone cake.

"I guess I'm not sure of anything right now," she said.

"I know what you mean. My life with the magazine is absorbing." Aunt Lin said, "but at the end of the day, if I can think at all, I wonder where I'm going."

She put the hats away and closed the armoire. "I've got to make this old house pay for itself, somehow. I wonder if I should sell it."

That afternoon, Remi and Jude worked at prying off the fireplace shelves, and Madeleine decided to take another look for her paperweight.

She vacuumed every inch of her room and shook out the sheets and blankets on her bed. Nothing.

It wouldn't be in a drawer, would it? She did a quick check, and the pendant gleamed at her from among her socks. A lovely thing, in spite of the cord. How had it ended up at Tara's house? And where had Jude's father gone, that he would leave it behind?

She went back to the Blue Room and picked up her notebook. She hadn't heard from Nathan all day. Because of last night?

She would see him tomorrow for the concert. She didn't want to wait until then, but maybe she'd have to. One thing for sure, she wasn't going to phone him.

The next morning she was working in the Blue Room, still making lists, when her aunt came to say goodbye.

"Have a good time," Madeleine said.

Her aunt's face grew animated. "Our new marketing guy, Vance. He asked me out for lunch. I should be back by Wednesday—I'll phone."

She stopped halfway out the door. "Ask yourself what we could do with this dear old white elephant. What about a museum? You and I could spend our declining years dusting the artifacts."

After she left, Madeleine picked up a blue china shepherdess, stared at it, and put it back down. This dear old white elephant seemed stuffy today. She'd work until noon and then take time off for good behavior.

She had eaten lunch and was starting to revise a cookie recipe when the phone rang. Tara's voice sounded higher than usual, raised against a din of voices. "Mollie! Hey, I wanted to tell you, my aunt goes shopping on Saturday mornings. Can you come see me tomorrow? We could have elevenses."

What about the hike with Nathan?

"I'll have to—"

"—Great!" Tara said quickly. "I'm calling from school. Gotta run. See ya."

Nathan might not mind if they started their hike later. If they hiked at all. Why hadn't he phoned?

If she did some grocery shopping—really, she needed to—she could stop by and see Timothy. She could tell him about visiting Tara. He might want her to make another sign. Nathan might happen to walk in.

Maybe she shouldn't have said so much, shouldn't have been so direct, shouldn't have left. One look at his face, and she'd know.

CHAPTER 24

It's one thing to make room in your heart
for a young girl.
It's quite another to give your heart
to a man.
Then you become dependent.
Trusting. Vulnerable.
Wrung-and-broken? Not for me.
~Journal

Timothy was talking to a customer while two others stood by, but Hey-You gave her a welcoming sniff. He followed her as she walked up and down the aisles, studying Timothy's displays. How about a new sign for the bookshelf? And one for the homemade jams? Something whimsical.

Bria went past, heading for Timothy's office, and Madeleine followed. Timothy had hired Bria to do his accounts—a smart move, Madeleine thought, as she watched her down behind a new computer.

Jude was washing windows at the far end of the room. He stopped long enough to say, "I asked one of the teachers if she knew my dad and she said they did a special page about him in the yearbook a couple of years ago. She's going to find me a copy."

He squirted window cleaner onto a pane and wiped it off. "Mom's upset—Kent said he's not going to sell our decoys anymore."

"Why not?" The guy couldn't bear to give them a decent cut, could he?

"Said he's too busy."

Madeleine dropped into a chair. These two had a right to know the truth. "There's another side to that story," she said, and told them about Kent's scam.

Jude turned to stare, and streams of cleaner ran down the pane. He lifted the bottle of cleaner as if it were a club. "And he already has so much money he can eat at a fancy restaurant whenever he wants."

"My grandfather's initials?" Bria looked as if she were frozen in a nightmare. "The same as Mom's."

"Doc spoke to him," Madeleine said, "and he agreed to stop. He even promised to give your mother a better percentage. But apparently he's changed his mind."

Jude started again on the window, scrubbing at it in small, jerky circles.

"So he took the easy way out," Bria said in a tight voice. She bent over the desk. "I've got work to do."

Jude didn't look around, but the back of his neck was red.

Madeleine said quietly, "I'm going to see Tara tomorrow. Maybe I can find out a few things."

Jude half-turned. "Ask where she got the pendant." He wiped his nose on his sleeve. "Tell her it's important."

"I will," Madeleine said, and decided it was time to leave. Another important thing—seeing Nathan—hadn't happened. She wasn't going to hang around, waiting.

As she was parking at the Manor, he phoned. "Hello," he said. "Wanted to . . . had a question. Did you . . . do you still have time to go to that concert tonight?"

"Yes, I do."

Why wouldn't she go? Hadn't she said she would?

"Okay." He hung up.

Was he still struggling? Angry at what she'd said? Didn't want to go and hoping she'd cancel first?

She shrugged off more questions and carried the groceries inside.

She had asked Charlotte what one wore to a Pine Barrens concert and had decided on a blue peasant skirt and white blouse. For once, she would put up her hair. Their first real date.

After the night she'd spent praying, surely God would set her free from her fears, at least as far as Nathan was concerned. This could be a happy evening.

He arrived precisely on time. She opened the door, and he gave her an inscrutable glance, saying nothing beyond hello-how-are-you. She replied with words equally mundane, turned, and went to the kitchen for her purse and jacket.

He walked into the kitchen with her and paused beside the table. He was freshly shaved, and he wore dark khakis and the sweater she liked.

He cleared his throat. "It has been dry lately, hasn't it?"

"Yes, it has." His face didn't give her a clue as to what he was thinking. The doctor's-face.

"I appreciate your taking the time to go with me tonight. I hope it isn't an inconvenience."

Why so formal?

"It is not an inconvenience."

He glanced out the window and back. "Your hairdo is becoming."

"Thank you. I like your sweater." It was the steel blue one, and it set off his eyes, which at the moment were guarded and cool. Who was he to speak of glaciers?

He glanced at his watch. "We'd better go."

He helped her on with her jacket, managing to do it at arm's length without touching her. He opened the car door with his usual courtesy, drove at a moderate speed, and for a stretch of interminable minutes made small talk about the local culture. The many talented artists. The group of businessmen promoting this event. Piney Power.

They were following a broad, slow-moving river that reminded her of the Mullica and their canoe trip. He was a different man tonight.

She checked her cell phone for messages and turned it off.

Was he angry? And if so, why? Asking him would probably make it worse. So much for a pleasant evening of music and maybe a bit of romance.

She rearranged the contents of her purse. Put the lip gloss in the outer pocket. Much more handy. Not that she'd need it tonight.

She resisted the impulse to pat at the pins in her hair.

Enough of this. She was going to ask him. If he was the type of man—like Brenn—who was given to cold, silent angers, she'd better find out now. And she would tell him good-bye.

"Nathan," she said, "would you please stop this car and say something real? Or else take me home."

He glanced at her, slowed the car, executed a swift U-turn, and drove back the way they'd come.

Her hands began to shake, but she twisted them together, and they kept still.

This was the end. She was not going to put up with someone who behaved like Brenn. Not in any way. She'd promised herself.

A sand road branched off to the right. He turned down it, and they bumped across its ruts in silence. Minutes later he parked on a bluff overlooking the river. His face was ashen in the twilight, and the scar looked like a scrap of pale ribbon. He stared ahead, his shoulders stern.

"I have to ask you something," he said.

Every muscle in her body clenched.

"After what happened Wednesday night, are you angry with me?"

"No." The word rode on a cresting wave of relief,

He looked out the side window. "You said some things that are true. Used to be true. You asked some hard questions. I wouldn't blame you if you . . . do you despise me?"

"Not for a minute, Nathan." That was it. He was ashamed.

The color returned to his face. "Sometimes," he said in a low voice, "*no* is better than *yes*."

He came around to open her door, waited while she unsnapped her seat belt, and in one swift motion, slipped his arms around her and picked her up.

"Nathan!"

He paused, smiling. "Kind of nice, having you this close. I don't want you to get sand in your good shoes."

He walked along the river bank, carrying her as easily as he did his medical bag, set her down on a log, and sat beside her. He put an arm around her waist and took her hand. "What did you want to talk about?"

Discard prepared speech. Laugh? Cry? At least try to sound rational.

"I missed you, these two days."

"You left, and I thought you had given up on me. With good cause."

"I went home to pray."

"It was an incredible night. God has been so patient with me, so loving. He's changing me so I can let go of that."

Thank you, Lord.

She looked up at him. "I was afraid I'd gone too far, that you were angry."

"I wasn't angry."

Might as well ask him about that now. "What are you like when you're angry?"

He dropped her hand, leaned forward to pick up a twig, and threw it into the river. "You've seen me broken, Mollie. Now you want me to admit that I get angry?"

"Everyone does, sometime."

"Okay." He threw in another twig. "I tend to flare up, say things I shouldn't, slam doors. What about you?"

"Much the same, only I talk more. As you've already seen, to my regret."

"That's better than the silent treatment. Are we still taking our hike tomorrow?"

"Tara phoned." Would he understand that this was another chance to reach out to the girl?

He smiled. "She wants to come too?"

"Sorry. She invited me—begged me—to come to a tea party tomorrow morning. Would you mind if we did a half-day hike?"

"That's fine. She needs to spend time with you. Of course, I do too, but I've got plans."

He leaned closer, and a mosquito hummed between them. She waved it off. "They always come after me. Do you think the concert is over?"

"Only partway. Want to try it?"

He picked her up again, and she laughed this time as he carried her across the sand and put her into the Jeep.

The concert hall, she decided, must also serve as a packing house, considering the fields of bushes that surrounded it and the stacks of boxes inside. The audience talked quietly among themselves, facing a portable stage built of dark timbers.

"Intermission," Nathan whispered as they sat on folding metal chairs. "We got here just in time."

The crowd began to clap and cheer, and the musician walked up onto the stage.

He wore stiff new jeans and a plaid shirt, he held a baby in his arms, and his black eyes were sparkling.

Logan? What was he doing here?

He acknowledged the applause by lifting the baby over his head. "I would like to introduce my son, Jared."

Nathan smiled at her. He'd known.

"This next song, 'Cedar Streams,' is dedicated to my son."

Thunderous applause.

Logan handed the baby down to Greta and picked up a lute.

The melody flowed past, cool as the Mullica. It rippled into pools, leaped into arpeggios, and turned back upon itself, braiding in another tune, again, and once again, finally ending with a flourish of riffles.

Another song sprang to life in a stately tune that glided through a rich progression of chords and counterpoint.

Nathan squeezed her hand. He'd recognized it too—Bach's "E minor Suite for Lute." So Logan played classical as well?

Too soon, he put down the lute and picked up his guitar. Bluegrass, blues, backwoods ballads, he played them all, and finished with a haunting melody of his own. The last notes faded into silence, and Madeleine sighed.

The crowd clapped and yelled and surged toward the stage.

Nathan said, "He told me to come up and talk, but maybe we'll just slip out. Unless you'd like a hot dog? They're only a dollar."

She didn't shudder visibly, she was sure of it, but he said, "In that case, let's go."

As they walked to his Jeep, she said, "We have pineapple zucchini bread, if you feel like a snack."

"My zucchini reinvented?"

"I hope it tastes better than the last time you saw it."

His eyes crinkled at the corners. "I will do a careful analysis and give you my report."

The drive back didn't seem to take long, and even after they'd reached the Manor, the melodies she'd heard rippled through her mind. She sliced the bread and poured their milk, conscious of his gaze upon her, and something about it suggested that the evening wasn't over yet.

"This looks good," he said, "especially with the pineapple. Why don't we take it upstairs to that library your aunt showed me?"

She smiled. "The stars will be out."

The stars were brilliant above the dark forest, and they sat facing each other on the window seat as they ate and talked.

He set his empty plate aside. "Looks like you've got some old books here."

She joined him at the shelves, curious to see what he'd take down. He chose *Tracks of North American Mammals,* paged through it, and set it back on the shelf.

He turned and put his hands on her shoulders. "I was dreading this evening," he said. "But you have made it a celebration."

He drew her into his arms, and she went to him with gladness. This time would be different.

Once more he kissed her face, but slowly, lingering along the way. Her forehead, her eyebrows, the lobe of her ear. Her chin.

His lips touched hers.

She choked. Nausea grabbed at her throat and panic thudded through her veins and her heart was going to explode and she had to fight. Fight him off. She beat at his chest—make him go away.

"Mollie!"

She was drifting, drifting off to her safe place. From there she could watch what happened and nothing would ever hurt again.

Gentle hands on her shoulders. A warm voice. "Mollie, breathe."

Was it safe? She tried a quick, short breath.

"Big breaths, big and deep, remember?"

She breathed, trembling with the effort. Breathing was good. Stay here, breathe and stay safe.

"Mollie, open your eyes."

She whimpered, but she left the safe place and risked it.

"Look at me," he said. "Look at my eyes."

Gray eyes. Kind gray eyes.

"Who is this, Mollie?"

She closed her eyes.

"Mollie. Open your eyes. Such beautiful eyes—fire and ice."

She had to open them. This wasn't Brenn.

"Look at me," he said again. "Say my name."

She forced her lips to move. "Nathan." She held onto him, still shaking. "Nathan."

Not again, Lord! I thought You had delivered me.

After a minute he said, "Better?"

She nodded into his shoulder.

"I hate this for you, Mollie."

And she hated it for him. He shouldn't have to deal with the results of her foolish choice. She had to make him see that.

She brushed back a stray wisp of hair. He had a life of ministry ahead, and he didn't need someone like her to slow him down.

She would tell him, but first . . . She reached up to touch his face, one last time—the weathered skin, the smile creases, the eyes she loved to watch. Her fingers paused on the burn scar. He was free of guilt now, and he should be free of her.

Lord my Rock, make me strong for this moment.

She took a step backwards and firmed her voice. "It's no use, Nathan. I'm damaged goods. Let me go."

His eyes were shining. Hadn't he heard? He was moving to her side.

He picked up her hand, turned it over, and wrapped it with his own. "I would rather say this with moonlight and roses, but you need to know it now."

His gaze rested upon her, luminous and solemn. "I love you, Madeleine Dumont."

She took a quick, nervous breath, and filed away the precious words to think about later—not now, because her resolve was crumbling.

He'd used her maiden name, as if she were still that other person. A whole woman. He didn't realize that she'd always be broken, the wife of Brenn.

He didn't need to know what Brenn had done, but he had to understand that she wasn't worth his time.

She started to shake her head, and he said, "Come and sit down. I've got something to tell you."

On the couch she sat a careful distance away, but he moved himself close, as if he didn't want a single inch between them. "When I went to Philly, I talked to someone about your case—"

"—My case?"

"Yes, I described—"

"—You described the patient's symptoms to your colleague and the two of you decided on a course of therapy and . . . and now you're going to—"

"—Mollie! This isn't your fault. You need help."

"How do you know it's not my fault? He said I provoked him."

"He lied."

"I can be very provoking. You don't know me."

"Yes I do," he said. "Connie's pink sunglasses. I watched, and I saw your heart."

"But that was before . . ."

"You're still who you are, Mollie. And whether I get to kiss you or not is beside the point."

"Is it?"

Her hair, secured only by pins, had started to come down, and he looped a strand of it behind her ear. "My friend said that with patience—"

"—Right, be kind to the poor addled girl, and patient. You're good at that already. I won't have you hanging around for the next couple of months or years being kind. Hoping that maybe the next time you try to kiss me I won't fall apart. I told you, I'm tarnished."

"Mollie," he said, "I love you."

She had to stop him. She couldn't let him delude himself.

She put out a hand blindly, encountered his knee, and snatched it back. "Listen to me. You've had enough heartache already. You need a nice sturdy girl with no hang-ups. Take one of those back to Alaska and get on with your life."

Surprise flickered across his face. "What makes you think I'm going back to Alaska?"

"I know it. The Lord has a ministry for you there. I'll get over my little problem eventually, or maybe I won't. That's in the Lord's hands. But I will manage just fine."

"You'll be fine without me?" His voice went ragged. "Is it true?"

Pain welled up from the hollows of her bones. *Don't ask me that.*

She turned, intending to say something kind and pacifying, but misery drove her to clutch his arm. "Don't you understand? He'll always be there, between us. What he did has changed me, and I don't know how to change back, and every time we . . . I can never . . ." She bowed her head. "You deserve a whole woman."

Silence. She tried to breathe.

After a moment he said, "I understand what you're telling me. If necessary, I can live with that. But I love you, Mollie. There is a future for us. Don't send me away."

She closed her eyes. *Don't waste your time.* That's what she should say, right now.

As if she had spoken aloud, he said, "This is worth fighting for. Someone told me that once and encouraged me to fight."

He took the pins out of her hair, one by one, and buried his face in the tangle. "I won't kiss you again until you're ready. Not until you come to me and ask."

He paused, his voice rimmed with steel. "But we will fight this together, and the Lord will show us how, and we will win."

She didn't deserve this man: so loving, so determined.

Tears filled her eyes and overflowed in a warm, trickling stream, and his arms encircled her, as if to hold her safe and ward off all her fears.

CHAPTER 25

I don't know what to do about him—
I can't trust my foolish heart.
But there's Tara, and her need is clear.
Tell me what to say to her, Lord.
~Journal

Elevenses. Tea in the middle of the morning was a British tradition, wasn't it? The girl must have read about it somewhere.

Madeleine turned into the driveway, and her hopes rose. The brown truck was gone. Perhaps this time they could sit and talk without having to make a wild dash through the woods.

Tara appeared behind the sagging screens of the porch but didn't come any farther. Grounded again? She waved vigorously, and as Madeleine waved back, heading for the porch, she tripped over something in the weeds. It looked like the frame of a car, long and low with four humps, solid enough that she wished she'd noticed it.

Tara grabbed her for another hug. "I'm not allowed to go one foot out of the house," she said. "I'm so glad you came." She leaned back and laughed. "I've crunched the cookies again, haven't I? Is that what you brought?"

"I didn't know how many you got to eat from the last batch."

"Right. Uncle Sid thought they were for him. That got Dixie plinkin' mad, I can tell you. She tried to make some herself, but they turned out like rocks. C'mon."

She took Madeleine's arm and guided her through a cluttered front room to the kitchen. Aunt Dixie must like yellow. Her kitchen had yellow walls, yellow cupboards, and a yellow-painted floor—a dingy yellow, mottled with fly specks and food stains. Even the trash can was yellow.

Tara pulled out a yellow plastic chair. "Sit down, and I'll make tea and we'll do our elevenses proper."

She gave Madeleine a worried glance. "I have tuna sandwiches instead of those cookie-biscuits. Do you mind?"

"Not at all," Madeleine said. "Much more interesting."

Tara set the kettle to boil and took a covered plate from the cupboard. "Here we are, safe and sound. Tell me how Mac is doing. And Jude, and everybody."

Before Madeleine could answer, she held up a hand. "Wait! I need to explain something. About my name." She sighed. "My mother named me Salome Tara—she liked pretty names—but my dad called me Sally. These people do too, but in my heart, I'm Tara."

Madeleine smiled. "I understand." So the girl hadn't been lying about her name. What about the pendant?

Tara arranged Madeleine's cookies and the sandwiches on plates, sat down across from Madeleine, and said gravely, "You may ask the blessing."

After Madeleine finished, Tara unwrapped her sandwich, saying, "I hate to tell you, but Uncle Sid is out in the woods somewhere, drunk as a coon."

She frowned. "He's, um, different when he's drunk. If he comes in while you're here, don't let him get you into an argument. Just smile—he likes you—and agree with him. Then he'll go away."

Madeleine nodded. Perhaps they wouldn't get their quiet talk after all. She took a bite of her sandwich. "This is tasty," she said. "What's in with the tuna?"

"Pickle relish. And peppermint. I grow it in a pot next to my hideout. How's Mac doing?"

Madeleine told her everything she could think of about the cat. Then, since they might not have much time, she told her what Jude had said about the pendant.

Tara's eyes flashed. "But it's mine! My dad gave it to my mother, and she loved it—she wore it all the time. After she died, I went looking for, it but Dixie said she was going to keep it. For luck."

"For luck?"

"Because of the tree." Tara sniffed. "She doesn't even know what it means. I looked it up on the computer at school. It's a Celtic symbol for harmony in the universe."

She chewed on the last of her sandwich. "Dixie kept it hidden because something about it spooked Uncle Sid, and when I left, I took it. It's mine."

What would Jude think of all this?

"Does your aunt know you took it?" Madeleine asked.

"She hit me a couple times, but I wouldn't admit it, so she can't be sure. I think she's forgotten. Can we have cookies now? Would you care for tea, my lady?"

"I'd be delighted."

A door slammed, somewhere behind the kitchen, and the light went out of Tara's eyes. A minute later, her uncle stood in the doorway.

"Smile," she said in a low voice.

He held onto the doorjamb. "Hello, hello! It's the pretty girl again. Did you bring cookies?"

Madeleine smiled. "I did. Would you like one?"

"Not now. Thought you'd come back so I could fix your car."

He reached into his jacket. "Got something here." His red-rimmed eyes blinked with concentration as he pulled out an old soup can.

He brought it close to his face, looked inside for a minute, then stepped forward and banged it onto the table.

Madeleine eyed it. The can was badly burned and its label almost gone. What made it so remarkable?

He nudged out its contents. Black ash skittered toward her, and a clump of partly-burned wooden matches fell onto the table. They were held together by charred strands of wire.

He scratched at the whiskers on his chin and stared at her. "You ever seen anything like this?"

"No."

"You know where this here tin comes from?"

"No."

"I do. And I'm going to make me some money off it. Sally, girl, we're goin' to be ridin' high and easy."

Tara chewed on her lip.

His voice picked up a threat. "What'd you say to that, girl?"

"Sure, Uncle Sid."

His words glided on, as if oiled by the alcohol. "You don't believe me, do you? I'll show you."

He swayed, put out a hand, and lowered himself into a chair, bending so close that Madeleine could smell the liquor on his breath.

"You know Kent Sanders," he said. "Don't you?"

She shrugged.

"Sure you do. These days, he hangs around with all the grand folks down by Tabernacle."

He poked the can with a blackened finger. "You're going to take this and give it to Sanders. Tell him it's a present from his ol' buddy."

She leaned away. "I don't see him very often."

Tara sent her a worried glance.

The man frowned. "You're telling me you don't want to get your pretty hands dirty—like me—is that it?"

He rubbed his hands together, and a shower of ash drifted onto the table. "Here." He reached into the trash, pulled out a cracker box, and dropped the can inside. "There. All set."

Madeleine didn't move toward it.

He pushed it closer. "Do as I say, woman! Take it."

Tara made a small, agitated movement, and Madeleine picked up the box.

Her uncle levered himself upright.

Good, he was going to leave now.

He looked down at her. "Don't you think you've been visiting long enough? Sally has work to do. And you have a job to do for me."

Madeleine exchanged a regretful glance with Tara and got to her feet, but her thoughts had untangled themselves.

Sid and the pendant—the sight of it spooked him? His brother was Tara's father? And he got it from *where*? Sid knew something about that pendant, and if he weren't so drunk, she could get him to tell her. Next time.

She had to tilt her head back to stare into the man's eyes, but she felt six feet tall.

"Mr. Marrick." She addressed him in the firm, courteous voice she used with her students. "If you want me to do this job, then you will answer some questions for me when I come back. Remember that."

Anger sparked in his eyes, soon replaced by uncertainty. "A pretty woman with spunk—now I like that." He swayed toward her.

She gave him a warning look. "Agreed?"

"Guess so." His eyes agreed too.

"Goodbye then," she said. "Tara, I'll see you later."

The way to the front door was clear, and she left before he could decide to come after her. Getting out into the sunlight gave her such a feeling of release that she understood why Tara escaped to her hideout whenever she could.

She stepped across the iron frame, marched to her car, and locked herself inside, conscious that he was watching her from the porch. Rather than backing down the driveway, she turned her car around, swerving to avoid the engine parts, and finally left the house behind.

A minute later she'd reached Salty Spung Road, and as her nerves began to uncoil, she reviewed what she'd learned. Tara seemed to feel that she had as much right to the pendant as the Castells. How could it be the same one?

What about Kent and Sid? An unlikely pair? Perhaps not.

She glanced at the cracker box beside her. Dirty thing. What could she do with it?

No ideas, right now. But she had promised, and somehow, she'd get it to Kent.

It was past noon by the time she arrived at the Manor. She changed into the cranberry shirt Nathan liked, and while she was finishing up the deviled eggs, he phoned to say that he'd be there in a minute.

She met him at the door, and he took her into his arms as if they'd been parted for weeks. "Mmm," he said into her hair. "Will you wear it down today?"

She laughed. "That's easy." They walked arm in arm to the kitchen and she said, "Do you want to eat now or pack a lunch?"

"Both."

"I thought so. Here, you're good with knives." She handed him a knife and had him slice the bread and left-over roast beef.

"Grapes? Cookies?" she said. "Anything else?"

"Do you have any of those specialty hard-boiled eggs?"

"Done." This was going to be a happy day, she could tell already. An invigorating hike with good conversation. And she could share her worries about Tara.

By daylight, the Hampton area looked disheveled and weedy, with the furnace ruins invisible, but the tall sycamore still stood on guard, and she gave it an affectionate glance as they passed.

They parked in the same place as before, and Nathan, map in hand, walked back along the way they'd come until he found a sandy track that branched off into the woods. "Logan said we might want to look at this one too—it follows the Batsto for a while. Even has an underwater bridge. I'd like to see that sometime."

They passed the warehouse ruins and the bridge over the Skit, and continued along another sandy road, bronzed with pine needles, that grew soft under her feet.

Whenever the road forked, he consulted the map, and she was glad he'd brought it, because after a while all the roads looked the same. The landscape varied—widely-spaced pines set in dappled sand; ragged, skeletal pines; slim, close-growing pines—but always pines. The forest had its usual effect on her, and she began to hum a tune under her breath.

He picked up a fallen branch and tossed it out of their way. "How was Tara this morning?"

"Not very happy when I was asked to leave."

"Her aunt?"

"Uncle." She reached into his backpack for a bottle of water. "Besides being drunk, he was rather agitated."

She described the scene with the soup can, and he looked thoughtful. "So you're going to give it to Kent?"

"Not a chance. Their little tiff has nothing to do with me. I'll get it to him somehow, but that's all I agreed to do."

"How about Remi?"

Remi would be at church tomorrow. He could take it off her hands. "That's a good fix," she said.

The pines on their right were mixed with oaks and thick underbrush, and once in a while she caught a glimpse of the river. Swamp maples grew along its banks, alight with red leaves.

Clouds hung low, but it was warm enough that she rolled up the sleeves of her shirt. Good thing she'd left her jacket in the car.

"What's this?" She veered onto a faint trail leading off to their right. "I'd like to see more of the river."

Nathan followed her. "Could be a deer path, from what Logan said."

They had to push through barbed vines and brittle, leafless bushes, but they ended up beside a deep pool that looked like a fisherman's dream. The river, swirling past, caught the light in topaz ripples. "Worth it," she said, smiling up at him.

On their way back through the brush, he took her arm. "Those scratches are almost gone, I'm glad to see."

"Excellent medical care," she said. "And I heal quickly."

"You won't have any scars."

"I hope not." It wasn't hard to guess what he was thinking.

She brushed the twigs out of her hair and thought, Let's not spoil this day by talking about Brenn.

"So," she said, "where in Alaska did you grow up?"

He told her how his parents had homesteaded a piece of land that bordered Denali National Park. They'd hauled in supplies by dogsled or Super Cub, and his father had taught him to track everything from wolverine to moose, and he'd loved it all.

She smiled to herself as she listened.

"What is it?"

"I was just picturing you as this little boy trudging to school through the snow—five feet deep, uphill both ways—with your slate under your arm."

"Hey, it wasn't that long ago."

"Just kidding. What books did you have at home?"

"We traded back and forth, and there was a library in town. But the ones I remember best were the Bible, a one-volume Shakespeare, and *The Wilderness Homestead*."

Shakespeare? That would account for a few things.

A few minutes later, he said slowly, "I didn't go to a real school until I was a teenager and we had moved to town."

"Your mother taught you?"

"Until she left. After a while my dad decided I should have a more civilized life. I hated it at first."

"That's when you met your Inuit friend, Denny?" "And Timothy. An important person in my life." She nodded. "What was it about the raisins and porridge?"

"My dad always cooked up a big pot of oatmeal. With just the two of us, it lasted for a week. He'd put in raisins, and they got big and bloated and I'd pick them out and feed them to our pet raccoon."

The look on his face made her laugh.

As the road meandered on, he asked what her father had been like, and she told him about Dad's ruffians and the hikes they'd taken, the canoe trips together.

They arrived at another clearing, and she followed his gaze off to one side.

"Railroad tracks?" she asked.

He grinned. "Right where they're supposed to be." They followed a well-trodden path beside the tracks, which were clogged with grass, obviously unused, and she said, "The teens will like this, won't they?"

"I think so. We should run into the river again, up here."

A train trestle, with planks secured lengthwise between the rails, came into sight. "Another bridge?" she said. "I'm loving this place."

Up close, the trestle was bigger than she'd thought, built of massive, creosote-blackened timbers and huge iron spikes.

They walked out across it to look at the river, gleaming as it curved away into the pines. She was wishing she'd brought her camera when the trees bent before a gust of wind and rain began to fall, spattering the boards.

"C'mon," he said, turning back. "Let's see what's underneath this."

A steep, cindered slope took them down to the river's edge, and they ducked into a space beneath the trestle. The beams slanted above them, looking strong enough to gird a skyscraper, and the rain fell in quick, wind-driven bursts.

"Good idea," she said. "Snug and dry enough, and we can still watch the river."

He leaned against one of the uprights and put an arm around her. "I need to talk to you."

She didn't like the sound of this.

"Thinking about last night . . ."

She'd rather not.

"The kiss," he said. "It seems to be a trigger for your panic attacks. Can you tell me why?"

She turned her face into his shoulder. Did they have to discuss this? But he'd asked a reasonable question. Perhaps he should know . . . some things.

He put a hand on her arm, stroked it lightly, and waited.

"At night . . ." She took a shallow breath. "When he kissed me hard and rough, I knew . . . I knew . . . it was going to be a bad time."

His hand on her arm paused and then began again.

Little dripping sounds came from the timbers, and the wind sent two crimson leaves skittering under the trestle. They glowed against the gravel like tiny embers.

In a choked voice, he said, "Any other triggers?"

She bent away from him. Why not pick up those leaves? Here was one more. Three pretty leaves—they'd make a bouquet.

She took her time, tucked them into the pocket of his shirt, and looked sideways at him. He stood there, waiting. Patient as always.

He drew her gently back to himself.

She couldn't bear for him to see what Brenn had done. How could she even tell him? But perhaps then he'd change his mind about her.

"Fire." Her breath came quickly, and she kept her eyes on the crimson leaves. "I am afraid of fire. Especially little bits of fire on little blue lighters."

He said nothing.

She glanced up and saw the pain in his eyes. She could trust him with this much. "It helps," she said, "to tell a nightmare."

But she had to lean back against him for support, had to speak reassuring words to herself: *This is Nathan. Breathe.*

"Bones," she said. "Bones and bone marrow—his specialty, you know. Ribs fascinated him. He liked to decorate . . . mine."

She put a hand on her ribs. "I have some scars. Burn scars, from where he . . ."

The memory loomed, and she hurried on. "After a while, it got so I'd faint when he took out his lighter."

She began to tremble, and great racking breaths tore through her.

Nathan groaned. He turned her to himself and wrapped both arms around her. She clung to him, pressing her face against his chest, and felt his heart thudding with hers.

He said he loved her, said it over and over again while she wept, rocked her until she stopped trembling. He prayed aloud, asking God to pour out His grace upon them and show His mighty power in her life.

Then he fell silent, stroking her hair, and at last she could lift her head.

She wiped her eyes. "I'm sorry about all these tears."

"Tears are good, Mollie. You're coming back to life."

"I know you're wondering why I let him do that."

She tried to fill her lungs with air but couldn't seem to get enough.

"He was strong, like you," she said. "Not as tall, but thick with muscles, except for his bad leg. I'm so small he could hold me down with one arm. I learned not to fight." She shuddered at the memory. "But I still feel like a coward."

"You're not. You amaze me." Nathan's voice was muffled by her hair. "He had a bad leg?"

"Something happened when he was young, to maim it. I wonder if I married him out of pity for his limp. He seemed such a fine person, so brave about his disability. I was a fool to trust him."

She half-turned, looking down at the muscled arm that held her. How was she to know that it would never pin her to a bed? Or this slender hand, that it would never cut off her scream?

Her voice wavered, and she hated her weakness, but she had to say one thing more. "I don't think I can ever trust another man, not in such a vulnerable relationship. I just can't risk it."

His hand closed warm on her arm, and he didn't answer.

She stole a look at him. His eyes were shut, the lines on his face more deeply etched than ever, and she winced. "I'm sorry, Nathan."

"It's true, I'm only a man," he murmured. "Even worse in your eyes, I'm a doctor." He paused, and then his voice grew stronger. "Perhaps you can't trust me, but you can trust the God who rules me. Try that, Mollie."

She drooped against him. Why couldn't he let her go? Such determination was exhausting.

He kept his arm around her. "Here's something I wanted to tell you. Ever since Timothy mentioned the book of Ephesians, I've been reading it over and over, trying to get it past my brain and into my heart. That's what I read after we talked, Wednesday night. You're reading it too, aren't you?"

She nodded. "I like that first chapter. And the second one. I'm camping on the third one right now."

"That'll help both of us. And Timothy's got an Isaiah verse he's going to preach about." He smiled. "He tends to practice his sermons on me. Perhaps we could learn it together."

He pulled out a piece of wrinkled paper.

Fear not, for I am with you;
be not dismayed, for I am your God;
I will strengthen you, I will help you,
I will uphold you with my righteous right hand.

The comfort in those words seeped through her, and after a minute she looked up at him. "Let's do it. I can hear Timothy saying, *You want to be strong, little lady? Hang onto this.*"

CHAPTER 26

I don't want to be vulnerable.
I don't want to need anyone.
He's so good to me . . . but
I must not let myself love him.
~Journal

The next morning at church, Timothy looked at the two of them with a smile as he quoted the verse—their verse. He'd been talking about the faithfulness of God.

"You'll notice," he said, "that God doesn't promise a life without pain or suffering."

The little man looked more stooped than usual, and more wrinkled, if that were possible, but his voice was as strong as ever.

"I've had a taste of pain," he said. "I know what it's like to be beaten and have bones broken. I was a new Christian, and I didn't understand why God could let that happen when I was trying to serve him."

He paused to cough. "I still don't understand God's reasons for allowing evil—that's His mystery. But it's not because He doesn't love me. Christ's cross proves that. Even though He let a bunch of thugs beat me up, I can trust Him."

Nathan slipped his hand over hers, as if he knew what she was thinking.

Timothy smiled, and coughed again. "Along with the hard things, God gives us His mercies. Sometimes it's a reminder of His love, like this verse. Or it's something beautiful He's made. Or a good friend. I call them the gifts of His grace. They keep me going."

Madeleine smiled to herself. Yes, that verse was a gift. Last night, she'd written it out and tucked it into her Bible. She took out the slip of paper.

Today more than ever, she needed it. Getting up this morning had been difficult. Even sitting here with Nathan on one side and Jude on the other, she had trouble concentrating. Why such lethargy? This was how she'd felt after a session with Brenn.

Yesterday, the rest of their hike had been uncomplicated and happy. They'd eaten their lunch beside the river, had talked and laughed all the way back.

Nathan hadn't asked any more difficult questions. At the door, he'd held her for a moment, his hand resting briefly on her ribs, and she knew he was thinking about the scars there. They'd said a restrained goodbye.

That evening, she couldn't eat much supper, so she'd listened to Logan's home-made CD, read through the whole book of Ephesians, and gone to bed early. Near dawn, her dreams became nightmares about Brenn. Because she'd told Nathan?

She unfolded the slip of paper, read the verse again, and prayed silently. Lord my Rock, write these words on my heart. I still have fears, and I'm afraid of them. Deliver me! Only Your power can do it.

She needed wisdom too. Jude had asked about her visit to Tara's, and he'd bristled at Tara's story. "Her dad gave that pendant to her mom? Impossible." He reminded her of the knots in the leather cord.

What should she do about this? Anything?

Nathan left her side to play the closing hymn, and she stood with the others to sing "Great is Thy Faithfulness." Never had the old song seemed more up-to-date.

She had given Jude and his grandmother a ride to church, and after the service, Gemma lingered, talking to friends.

Remi paused on his way out to ask whether he should come to work in the morning. "Please do," she said. "We can use your help." She lowered her voice. "I'd like to ask a favor of you."

"Mollie, I owe you, big time."

"Someone gave me a box to be delivered to Kent. I'd rather not do it myself."

"Sure," he said. "I'll give it to him."

"It's kind of peculiar. I have it down in the car." She glanced at the front of the room, where Gemma and Jude were standing. "Let's go get it."

Remi didn't comment when she showed him what was in the cracker box, but something in his face changed.

He repeated the message and took the box from her, saying, "I'll make sure he gets it this afternoon."

She ran back upstairs and found that Gemma and Jude were talking with Timothy, moving gradually toward the door.

Nathan appeared at her side. "You gave it to Remi?"

"Yes, and good riddance."

"And you're coming to lunch with me and Timothy, right?"

She smiled at him. "Right! I'm going to run Gemma and Jude home, and then I'll meet you. Tell me again— where?"

"Keeto's, just a little way out of town on Route 620."

A quiet lunch with the two of them. Something to enjoy. "I shouldn't be long."

In the car, Gemma arranged her cane, smiling. "I had a wonderful time at church, Mollie. Thank you."

From where he sat in the back, Jude said, "You got to talk to some of your old friends, didn't you, Gemma?"

"There's nothing like old friends." His grandmother turned to look at him. "I've been thinking about that yearbook, the one with your father in it. I'm sure I still have a copy. You might want to see it too, Mollie."

"He wasn't about to retire, was he?" she asked.

"No, it was a special Fifty-Year edition. They did a page featuring my son—Rhys—and a teacher who retired long ago, Hazel Marshon. She'd been his English teacher, and now he was teaching English too, in the same school district."

Gemma sighed, a remembering look on her face. "I knew Hazel. It was a terrible shame, what happened to her."

"What, Gemma?" Jude asked.

"Her house was robbed and set on fire. She died in the fire."

"Did they ever find out who did it?" Madeleine asked.

Gemma shook her head. "We heard a lot of rumors. Young punks, they said. I never did hear the official conclusion. "

She gazed out the window. "Rhys was upset, I can tell you. Hazel had been one of his favorite teachers. After they did the yearbook, he must have started thinking about it again, because he told me he was going to investigate. But then he died."

She waved a hand, as if to disperse the memory. "I've been meaning to ask, what's happening at the Manor these days? Any more discoveries?"

She told Gemma about the hats in the armoire, and their conversation veered to the Manor's future. Gemma suggested a nice little tea room with specialty cakes, and as they helped her walk up the driveway to the house, Jude teased her about it.

"Yes, specialize," he said. "We've got all these cranberries growing around here. Roasted cranberries. Boiled cranberries. Cranberries on toast. Pass the sugar."

"You are a rascal, young man," Gemma said with her fond smile.

Bria looked out the door. "Oh!" Jude said, "I almost forgot. Can you come see Bria's hooded merganser?"

Madeleine admired the distinctive white-crested decoy and greeted Paula, who smiled back without her usual vagueness.

"Kent has another idea for our decoys," Paula said. "He's going to western Canada to study trees, and he's taking a box-full to show some collectors."

So he'd decided it would be safer to sell phony antiques out West?

Her smile felt like a phony too. "Has Kent always been a friend of the family?"

Paula, sanding a headless duck, told how he'd been one of her husband's smartest students and had left for the West Coast after he graduated.

Paula turned the duck over to inspect it. "I knew his mother—poor Nancy. She often came to talk. She worried a lot about Kent. She had something wrong with her blood, and after her funeral, we didn't see him again." She smiled. "Until now."

Madeleine listened, thinking how sad it was to hear about the anxious mother from Paula, who trusted Kent so blindly. What had Rhys, the teacher, thought about him?

She felt a creeping weariness. Enough about Kent. "Thanks, Bria, for showing me your new creation. I'd better go now. See you later, Jude."

Keeto's was easy to find, thanks to its blazing neon sign and crowded parking lot. The two men must have been waiting for her in the Jeep because they joined her as she walked up to the door.

Inside was a long, narrow dining room with a well-stocked buffet dominated by two black tureens of soup. At a nearby table sat a blonde woman and Kent.

She ignored him as she headed for a table close to the windows, but she could feel the heat of his gaze. No! He wasn't going to spoil her lunch.

"It's not the fanciest," Timothy said, indicating the red plastic tablecloth, "but the ham is good." He asked a blessing on their meal, and a thin-faced woman hurried over to take their order and Nathan's credit card.

"Go ahead and help yourselves," she said. "Eat all you want. Drinks are on the buffet."

Madeleine filled a bowl with broccoli-cheese soup and chose a corn muffin. The men heaped their plates with sliced ham and vegetables that looked as if they'd been recently acquainted with a can.

Timothy ate a few bites and put down his fork. "Mollie, about Tara, I'm so glad you're staying connected with her. Don't give up. And I want to tell you about Remi." He coughed, the dry cough that seemed to be bothering him today. "Maybe I'll get some tea first."

"I'll get it," Nathan said.

"What's Remi been up to?" she asked. The soup was thick, with plenty of broccoli.

"He came to me last week." Timothy closed his eyes and coughed again. "He said all this preaching was starting to make him nervous."

Nathan set a cup of tea at his elbow, and he nodded his thanks. "We've talked, off and on. I've been sharing some Scriptures. I gave him a New Testament, and he looked as if he'd never seen one before. Just keep praying for him."

"Does he say much about his past?"

"Not yet, but he will."

She smiled. "As we all do, Timothy. You're so easy to talk to, and you manage to give advice without intruding."

Nathan smiled at her. "You're right."

Timothy said, "It was good to see Jude's grandmother again. She's looking quite perky."

"Gemma gave me a bit of historical detail," Madeleine said. "About her son, Rhys."

"A teacher, wasn't he?" Timothy said.

"He taught the Marrick boys. And Kent."

Nathan looked intrigued. "I'm going to ask Detective Birklund to do some checking out on the West Coast. But where?"

Madeleine spooned up the last of her soup. "He went to school at UCLA. And he mentioned something about living near San Francisco."

Kent's table was empty now, but it took an effort to talk about him. "He's leaving for Canada, Paula says. Taking some decoys with him."

"When?" Nathan's eyes had an icy glitter.

"The day after tomorrow."

Nathan looked at Timothy's plate and frowned. "You're not eating very much."

"Not hungry." Timothy coughed. "But this tea feels good on my throat."

Nathan pushed back his chair. "We're going to get you home."

"Oh, we are, are we?" Timothy said. "Put away the handcuffs—I'll come quietly."

Nathan smiled in answer, but he stood up and so did Madeleine. He helped her into her jacket, his hand lingering on her shoulder. "Wait just a minute before you leave," he said to her. "I want to tell you something."

After he unlocked his Jeep for Timothy, he crossed the parking lot to her car.

He picked up her hand and held it. "Here's what I want to say, among other things. I was hoping to see more of you today, but I'd better take Timothy home. And I need to stay around the clinic because we had a break-in last night. Someone set a little fire in my office. I've changed the locks, but you never know."

He turned her hand over and stroked the inside of her wrist. "Mondays are wild. Can we make a date for Tuesday lunch?"

Tuesday seemed a long way off. "Yes," she said.

He knew what she was thinking. "I miss you already. Let's both stay busy and maybe the time will fly. In the meantime, I wanted to give you this."

From inside his jacket he took out a white envelope. "For later."

Mac was waiting for her at the back door, as usual, and he prowled around the kitchen until she fed him. The house lay silent, as if it were hoarding its energy for another week of deconstruction.

Tomorrow they would work on the Blue Room, but the rest of the afternoon was hers. She changed into fleece pants and a warm sweat shirt, sat down on her bed, and browsed through *The Art of Eating*.

Talking to Aunt Lin about her course had left her feeling unsettled. Not that the pastry chef/bake shop idea was a foolish one. Timothy had agreed that it had potential, and when she told him that she wanted to get more training in New York, he hadn't tried to change her mind.

After the Manor work was finished, she would do that.

. . . After Nathan went back to Alaska.

So that was it. Like taking off your boot and discovering the stone that had tormented you during the whole long hike.

Not much employment for a pastry chef in Alaska, was there? Ideally, she should raise huskies. Or giant cabbages.

She put on a Bach CD, and "Jesu, Joy of Man's Desiring" brought the tears that had been threatening all day.

Coming back to life, Nathan had said.

This was life, this weary, broken feeling?

But God had given her so much—so many gifts of His grace: Aunt Lin, Timothy, Bria and Jude, Remi, Tara. She should be thankful.

And Nathan. What was she going to do about him? Never mind. What was in his envelope?

She curled up on the bed to open it and found a postcard showing the view from Apple Pie Hill. On the back, in small neat letters, he'd printed:

Denali . . .

Fearsome, formidable, wondrous.

We climb together.

I. LOVE. YOU.

N-----

He'd signed it with an illegible scrawl that made her smile. In the address portion he'd printed their verse. *Fear not, for I am with you . . .*

She leaned into the pillows, holding his card. How could he write this, after what he'd found out yesterday?

We will fight this together, he'd said. Still? And the verse? To remind her that they weren't fighting alone.

She closed her eyes and whispered, "Lord, thank You for Your promises. I love You, Lord my Rock, my Strength. Above all flesh and blood, I love You."

The phone was ringing. She reached for it, but slowly. Remi's voice. "Mollie, I can't come until around eleven. Is that okay?"

"Sure."

He said something about see you later, and she flopped back against the pillow. What time was it? Seven o'clock? In the morning?

She dragged into the shower, saying wake-up words to herself, and after a while, she could think. Must have slept that whole time. How are we today? Better, thank you. As if a virus had burned itself out.

Remi apologized again when he arrived. "Kent had a hurry-up research project, and I thought I should do that one last thing for him. He can't seem to find his way around a library."

"Did you . . .?"

"I gave him that box and the message. He took a look inside and pitched it into the trash. Not a word."

"He's going out of town?"

"Yeah. I quit working for him, so I'm staying put."

She followed him into the Blue Room. "Why did you quit?"

"Too much strange stuff going on with that guy. Besides, he had me typing a manuscript that's weird."

What did that mean?

Remi picked up his hammer and screwdriver and started banging at the fireplace shelves, so she went back to her lists.

Before long he had pulled off the rest of the shelves and taken down the heavy wooden mantel, leaving only the border of tiles.

"Look here." He slid the tip of his screwdriver behind one of the tiles. "They're mounted onto a piece of wood."

"What's underneath?"

"Hard to tell. I'll be careful."

He pried off more tiles, unscrewed the panel, and lifted it away.

"Marble!" He stared at the white-veined stone. "This is so cool."

He scratched at the blue paint on the hearth. "Marble here too, I bet." He stood up. "We need some paint stripper for stone. Okay if I go buy some?"

"By all means," Madeleine said. "Aunt Lin's going to love this."

While he was gone, Tara phoned. "I've got to tell you—that guy with the blond hair came over last night."

Her voice was high and shaky. "He smiled at first, but then Uncle Sid started yelling, and the guy drove off, and Uncle Sid told Dixie maybe we'd better move to Kentucky, and Dixie said she's not going to let any smooth-talking bimbo put us out of our home and she'd take care of him. I'm scared can you come see me?"

"Where's your aunt?"

"She's gone shopping, she's so mad. Don't worry about her. She was just jealous about the cookies. Uncle Sid will be sober. He promised. Besides, she smashed all his bottles. Please, can you come?"

"I'll come."

"Around three, okay?"

"Yes."

Madeleine poured herself a glass of juice and drank it in gulps. What had she agreed to? She didn't want to go out there alone. But how could she say to Tara: "I'm afraid. My God won't take care of me."

She refilled the glass with water and drank that too. Did He take care of His children when they did crazy things?

But loving someone like Tara meant taking risks, didn't it?

Her cell phone rang. Bria. She and Jude had been talking about that yearbook, she said, and she'd found something Madeleine might want to see. She could come around two o'clock.

Madeleine agreed. They'd have time to talk before she left to see Tara. Her mind spun with pictures: Uncle Sid swaying into the kitchen. Tara's anxious face. Dixie's cold eyes.

If only Nathan could go with her! But Mondays were impossible for him.

Jude? He had a meeting after school.

Remi? Too complicated. Besides, he had a job to do here.

She turned down the hall. Get back to work. Eat some lunch. She stopped in the doorway. What about Bria? Maybe she would come.

Bria looked worn out. They sat at the kitchen table with cans of root beer, and at first it seemed that she'd changed her mind about telling Madeleine anything. She studied the wall as if she were considering what color to paint it.

Madeleine popped her can open. "So," she said quietly, "you and Jude were talking about the yearbook."

"Gemma found her copy. We looked at it." She trailed a finger down the side of her soda can. "It's a good photo of Dad. So long since . . . since I've seen him. Mom won't have any pictures of him around."

Tears glistened in her eyes, and Madeleine waited, understanding.

"I know he didn't run off with some woman, like they keep saying." Her voice shook. "He loved her. He loved us."

She pulled at the tab of her can. "Jude asked if I remembered when they did the yearbook, and I did, because I was sixteen and so proud of him. I always wondered whether he was proud of me."

"Why was that?"

"Dad named me after some red-haired Celtic princess he admired. Brianna. It means *strong one.*"

Bria bent the tab back until it broke off. "I don't have red hair, and I'm not very brave. I knew I could never be the Brianna he wanted, but I kept trying."

She sent Madeleine a dark glance. "You lost your dad too. Was it hard to measure up to what he wanted?"

"Sometimes," Madeleine said. He'd taken her to a shooting range, and she could still hear the noise. "He tried teaching me to shoot a pistol. I hated the sound of it, hated to practice. I never could shoot straight."

The tense lines around Bria's mouth softened. "Like that," she said. "Anyway, last night I went into his study. I checked his favorite pair of bookends—they had a secret compartment—and I found some papers, mostly poetry and Celtic writings. And a couple of his old grade books. Skinny red ones, you know?"

"Yes," Madeleine said. She'd used them herself.

"I discovered that he wrote things about his students in the back of them. I looked for the year he had Kent in his class."

She handed a red booklet to Madeleine.

Rhys Castell wrote in spiky black letters that suggested confidence. Beside Kent's name, his cryptic note read:

Intelligent, but a smart aleck. Likes to write about fire. Set fire to V's braid. Hates me for taking away his matches. K's mother upset about SM's influence.

Madeleine flipped through the pages. He'd made notes on most of his students, insightful remarks. He'd pegged Sam Marrick as a delinquent in the making. She re-read the entry for Kent.

It was true, he liked to talk about fire. And his first book had been about fire. SM was probably Sam Marrick.

"I found something else." Bria handed her a small greeting card with *Thank you!* slanted across the front of it. Inside was a message written in green ink:

Dear Mr. Castell,

I appreciate your listening so patiently to a sick old woman. Last night I was sure it would help Kent if we tried to prove his innocence, but I have come across some information that suggests it might be wiser to leave things alone. I'll tell you about it if you wish.

Nancy Sanders

Bria was watching her with troubled eyes.

Madeleine fingered the small card. "From his mother. I don't know what to make of this—or the grade book. But you're right. They could be important."

She glanced at her watch. "Oh! I wanted to ask you a favor. I promised to go see Tara this afternoon, and I don't want to go alone. Do you have time?"

The girl shrugged. "I probably won't be much help."

Madeleine got to her feet. "I'd rather have you along than some princess," she said. "Let's pack a bag of cookies, and I'll tell you about it on the way."

As they drove, she described her visits to Tara's house and the encounters with Uncle Sid.

"I can see why you'd want company," Bria said. "Are you going to ask about the pendant?"

Jude's secret. How had she found out?

"It's okay," Bria said. "Any time Jude goes around with that mysterious look on his face, I suspect he's up to something. I made him tell me last night."

No wonder she hadn't slept.

Madeleine turned down the driveway. "Here we are," she said. The brown truck was gone. Good.

"Watch out for that iron thing by the porch," she said.

This time she didn't trip over it.

At the corner of the porch steps lay a pile of broken glass and the jagged neck of a bottle. To remind Sid of his promise?

CHAPTER 27

I don't want to talk to Sid Marrick,
drunk OR sober.
But I've got a feeling he knows
something about that pendant.
~Journal

Tara met them at the door and hugged them both.
"Two of you! Uncle Sid's got this cool project going in
the garage. He's building himself a '57 Chevy Bel Air.
Did you see the frame out front?"

Her glance swung to Madeleine. "He's fine today,
don't worry. C'mon into the kitchen."

She made tea, and Madeleine listened to the girls
talk, waiting for footsteps.

The back door closed and Uncle Sid strolled into the
kitchen.

He did look sober today. The red whiskers were
gone. A smile stretched across his gaunt features. Never
mind that it made him look wolfish. At least the man was
trying.

"May I, uh, join you ladies?"

"Sure," Tara said. "Have a cookie."

He helped himself to a can of beer from the fridge
and sat down.

An awkward silence fell. Tara was eyeing the beer
can, scrawled with black letters: MINE—KEEP YOUR
PAWS OFF. Bria was watching him as if he were a coiled
rattlesnake.

Madeleine waited for him to ask the inevitable question.

He gurgled down his beer, ate two cookies, and reached for a third. "So you gave it to him."

"As you told me to."

The man flushed. "No more hard stuff for me." He stared at the half-eaten cookie in his hand. "Questions, you said."

So he remembered. "Yes." She put down her cup. "I have questions about that pendant."

He looked puzzled, and she said, "That silver medallion on a cord."

He lurched to his feet, knocking his chair over backwards. "That bit of dirty metal? That ain't no silver medal. Just a piece of junk."

"Where did you get it?"

He sucked in his cheeks. "My brother found it."

"Sam?"

"Yeah. He's dead. Got what he deserved."

Tara quivered, and Madeleine put a hand on her arm. "Where'd he find it?"

"Just fell out."

"Out of what?"

"Glove box. Car."

"What car?"

"Confound it, woman, you sound like a plinkin' cop." He picked up the chair, reversed it, and sat down facing her. "We didn't do nothing wrong. I'll tell you the whole thing, just don't rush me."

She kept her eyes on his face. Please, Lord, let him tell the truth.

He spoke in spurts, as if the beer were firing his brain. "Me and Sam was out walking—nice day for a walk. We find this car in the bushes, kind of pushed away from the road. Windshield broke. Fender bashed in. Nobody around. So we take a couple things off."

He shrugged. "No point in letting good tail lights go to waste."

A pause.

"What about the silver medallion?" she asked.

"Yeah. Sam looks inside. There's something in the glove box. Binocular case. He gets all excited, but it's empty, except for that metal thing. So he puts it in his pocket, and then he takes out the radio. We've got as much as we can carry and we get out of there."

Regret passed over his face. "I went back the next day with my truck. Good tires on that car, but it was gone."

She frowned. "How could you go back and find a place like that? Do you expect me to believe this?"

He straightened, looking offended. "Listen here, I've walked these woods all my life. I swear, I know exactly how I done it. Let's see . . ."

He gave her a measuring glance. "Started at Quaker Bridge." His voice grew more certain. "Yeah, that's it. Walked up that road. Big white tree. There's some ruins. Past that, a little road goes off to the left."

"What's it called?"

He shrugged. "Went down it a good ways, along the river, sort of. Trees get thick and—don't rush me— somewhere along there . . ." He picked up the beer can and slowly crushed it into a handful of red and white. "Found that car. In the bushes, like I told you. Past a big old pine blocking the road."

He spun the fractured can across the table and leaned back, looking smug.

"But it was gone when you returned?"

"Somebody must've towed it away. Or dumped it in the bog."

"Who?"

The man chewed on his lip. "Dunno."

Bria leaned forward and Madeleine knew why, and she had to ask, "What kind of car was it?"

"Nothing special. One of them Ford Escorts. Black."

Bria made a tiny sound of distress, but Madeleine couldn't stop now. "So Sam took the metal thing?"

"Gave it to his wife. She fancied weird stuff like that. How come you have to know all this?" He smirked. "Sally and Dixie are always fighting over it. You want it too?"

He unfolded himself from the chair. "Got a lot of work to do. Buildin' me a car."

He was walking away, and she still didn't know enough. Quickly she asked, "When did all this happen?"

But he didn't hear or couldn't remember because he kept going, and a minute later the back door slammed shut.

Tara nudged the beer can into the center of the table. "You heard him. My dad found it."

Bria sat white-lipped and silent.

"It's more complicated than that," Madeleine said quietly. "We'll sort it out. Bria and I need to go back to the Manor now."

Tara looked downcast. "He always spoils our parties. Can you come back tomorrow? I don't have to go to school."

"Why not?"

"Sid says I gotta stay and help him with that car he's building. He's taking out the engine. You should see the pulley system he's rigged up. It's cool."

If she came back soon enough, maybe she could get a little more out of Sid.

"You're sure no one will mind?" Like Dixie.

"Nah. It'll be okay if we stay in the garage."

"Maybe just for a few minutes," Madeleine said, deliberately vague. "I'll have to see."

"Phone me tonight?"

The girl's persistence was heartwarming. Isn't this what she'd prayed for? "Yes, I'll phone you."

Bria didn't speak on the trip back. She looked out the window, her lips crimped as if she were struggling not to cry.

Her father's car must have been a black Escort.

But weren't there hundreds of cars like that? (With a pendant in the glove compartment?) If only they could be sure about the car. What had happened to it? Why had it disappeared?

At the Manor, Jude was helping Remi strip paint off the hearth. Remi grinned. "See this?" He pointed to the dirty white stone under the scum. "It's sure enough marble."

"Good for you," she said.

But Jude had read her face. "What's the matter?" He glanced from her to Bria, who was hunched in the doorway. His sister sent him a look, and he recoiled as if he'd been struck.

Madeleine ached for them both. Do something! "Do you know a place called Quaker Bridge?"

"Sure," Jude said.

"Can you tell me how to get there?"

He swallowed. "It's about the pendant, isn't it? About Dad?"

"Tara's uncle said something about finding the pendant. In a car in the woods. I don't know whether to believe him or not."

Did the man have enough imagination to make up all those details?

Jude wasn't asking questions. "Let's go. But it's all sand roads out there. You'd get stuck in a minute."

Remi stood up from the hearth. "I could drive my truck," he said. "It's a 4 x 4—we can go anywhere."

Bria straightened. "I want to come."

"Sure," Remi said. "It's got a crew cab."

Jude looked at Madeleine's sneakers. "You'd better wear your hiking boots. And bring a flashlight. It's going to get dark."

Hope pounded through her, but it had a sickening tinge of dread. She hoped Sid was telling the truth. She hoped there'd be a car. She hoped it wasn't the right one.

Surely Rhys Castell was still alive, somewhere.

It seemed a long way, and the sand roads were as confusing as ever, but finally Remi paused at a narrow metal bridge. "Now what?"

"He said he walked up the road," Madeleine said. "Mentioned a big white tree. And ruins."

The soft, furrowed sand had become hard-packed, but Remi drove slowly. They passed a clearing, and Jude pointed out a dead tree that was stripped of bark and pale enough to be white. He and Remi discussed whether white trees could refer to the Atlantic white cedars beside the river, but it seemed unlikely.

The farther they went, the less certain she felt. "Ruins," she said again. "And a little road that goes off to the left." She stared out the window into the trees.

From the back seat, Jude said quietly, "Not here, is it? I didn't think there were ruins around Quaker Bridge."

Bridge. Ruins. River. A warm hand holding hers, the shared happiness.

"Wait," she said. "There's some ruins farther up the river. Maybe not this river, even. At Hampton something."

"Hampton Furnace?" Jude said. "I've been there."

"It has a bridge too, not very big" she said. "With some ruins before you get to it."

"Yeah," Remi said, "from what I've seen, you can have ruins, sand roads, bridges, and rivers just about anywhere in these zillions of trees. It's a really cool place, but it makes me feel small."

Jude blew out an audible breath. "Keep going, Remi. This'll take us to Atsion." A minute later, he asked, "Mollie, how come you know about Hampton Furnace?"

"Nathan and I—Doc—did some exploring around there on Saturday. We were checking out a hike for the teens."

Beside her, Remi grinned, but he didn't say anything, and neither did the others.

Past Atsion they turned onto Hampton Road, which was as rough as she remembered, and much longer.

At last Jude said, "Here's the meadows."

"That big sycamore," she said slowly, "I remember it. Kind of white."

"There's furnace ruins in all that grass," Jude said.

Remi edged past a mud hole, just as Nathan had done, and peered at the road Nathan had wanted to come back to. "Think it's this one?"

Jude shrugged. "He said off to the left, didn't he? Whatever that's worth."

She nodded, and he spoke her thought aloud. "Still lying?"

Remi swung onto it. "Let's find out."

It was the narrowest road she'd seen yet, with trees crowding close on both sides, and it soon became a series of humps, but Remi sent his truck across them like a skier cresting moguls. To her right, she glimpsed the river.

"Lots of bushes here for hiding a car," Remi said. "When did you say this happened?"

"I didn't," Madeleine said. "He never got around to telling me, and I thought of it too late."

"Three years ago," Bria said in a stifled voice. "If it's Dad's car."

Remi didn't know all the details, and to his credit, he wasn't asking a bunch of questions.

Jude muttered, half to himself, "Might be all grown over."

"True." Remi crouched over the steering wheel, peering ahead. "Is that the tree?"

A huge pine sprawled from one side of the road to the other, an imposing barricade of wood and dead branches. Travelers had solved the problem by detouring around it through the underbrush, and Remi followed their tracks, accompanied by an ominous scratching sound.

"Huh," Jude said. "How many big old pine trees block the roads around here?"

"About five hundred," Remi said.

"Got to try it," Jude said. "Find a place to park."

Remi nosed his truck into the bushes. "This will have to do," he said, reaching for a flashlight.

After they'd pushed through the bushes, they came to a stretch of widely-spaced pines and Madeleine looked down the sandy aisles between the trees. "No car here. He said it might have been dumped in a bog. Where?"

"If he meant the river, it's on the other side of the road," Jude said. "Not nearly big enough to hide a car."

"Swamps anywhere?" Remi asked.

"Plenty. This used to be all cranberry bogs. Let's take a hike down here." He and Remi started at a trot toward a grove of cedars on the far side of the pines, and Madeleine and Bria followed more slowly.

The cedars gave way to another forest, thick with underbrush. "Wait here," Jude said. "We'll see how far this goes."

They disappeared into the trees and returned a few minutes later, breathing hard. "Swamp."

"You couldn't get a car through there," Remi said. "Not even three years ago."

Jude said, "Try up farther."

The four of them re-crossed the woods, patterned now with the long gray shadows of evening, and birds rustled in the branches, settling down for the night. Madeleine glanced at Bria's set face and tried to think of something hopeful to say.

They entered another dense growth of saplings and underbrush, and Jude kicked at a charred trunk. "Looks like a fire went through here," he said. "We'll probably run into that swamp again soon."

The air pressed cold and heavy against her face, and she knew Jude was right about the swamp. Should they turn back?

Remi paused. "What's that?" He peered through the gloom at a tangle of vines and branches that humped into a mound.

Jude ran to it and began pulling off handfuls of vine.

One part of her brain remarked that the vine was catbrier, and the other said they'd found what she'd been hoping wasn't there.

"A car, a black one," Jude gasped. He wiped a bleeding hand on his jeans. "But there's lots of abandoned cars in these woods."

He attacked the vines once more with Remi's help, and finally they stepped back.

The car must have been caught in the fire, because it was partially burned. The blackened skeleton of a tree lay across it, and the windshield was cracked. The fenders were bent and rusted, scabbed with blistered paint. The windows had disintegrated into fragments or disappeared altogether.

Bria stared at the ruin, her face carved in lines of grief. Jude stood motionless.

It was Remi who moved to the window on the driver's side. "Not too bad inside."

Jude darted forward, looked in, and struggled to open the door, but it was rusted shut.

"Hey, man," Remi said, "what're you after?"

"On the steering wheel."

"That silver inset?"

"Yeah." Jude pulled out a pocket knife and leaned through the window. "Give me a boost."

Bria crept closer. Jude pried a round object from the depression in the center of the steering wheel. He backed out, holding it in his hand.

It was a small black medal with a raised design of silver interlocking lines.

Remi bent to study it. "Isn't that what they call a Celtic knot?"

"Yeah. Celtic," Jude said, and he handed it to Bria. She closed her fingers around it and turned away.

They stumbled back to the road, following the beam of Remi's flashlight. The trees, muffled in black, seemed to close in around them with a hushed and weighty stillness.

It would be much too easy to lose your way out here, Madeleine thought. Already, Bria and Jude seemed lost in their own private world of grief.

No one spoke during the long trip back, but Madeleine knew the questions that burned in each mind. *Who?* and *Why?*

Remi dropped Bria and Jude off at the end of their driveway and turned toward the Manor. "I wonder if their dad had any enemies," he said. "Even a disgruntled student. I read once about a couple of kids who played a prank on their teacher, and the guy ended up dead."

"I don't know," Madeleine said. "He's been gone for such a long time."

"All those bogs around there," Remi said. "They'd never find his body."

Sorrow grew inside her. "Jude will think of that, after a while."

The headlights of Remi's truck lit up the driveway and then the porch. She tried to collect herself. "Thank you for coming. We couldn't have done it without you."

"Hey, no problem." He parked beside the porch. "I can't work tomorrow—I've got something to do for Timothy. Is that okay?"

"Sure," she said. "The Manor can wait."

Mac met her in the hall with welcoming noises, and she remembered that he hadn't been fed. She reached into a cupboard for the bag of cat food and stopped to think.

Had Rhys Castell been murdered? If so, this was no job for amateurs. More than once, her father had told her, "Don't try to play superman with criminals. If you're suspicious, talk to a policeman. He's a trained professional."

But who was the criminal? And how could he be found, three years later?

She set the bag on the counter and leaned her elbows against it. Who could she talk to?

Nathan was probably still working, but Timothy would be home. Maybe he'd be opening a can of stew for his supper. One of these days she'd have to invite him over.

She dialed his number, and it rang for a long time.

"Dr. Parnell."

"Nathan? Is something wrong?"

"Timothy's sick. I'm spending the night with him."

"His cough?"

"Getting worse. He might have a bad case of the flu," Nathan said.

She heard a phone ring and stop. His unhurried voice continued. "Did you have a question for Timothy?"

She told him about finding Rhys Castell's car, and the connection between it and Tara's uncle.

"I've been wondering how Kent and Sid fit together," he said. "If Birklund finds something useful, we can turn it over to the police. Even if he's gone, they'll catch up with him."

"Yes." Kent was leaving tomorrow. She should feel relieved, but failure gnawed at her. He was going to get away.

Nathan said, "I'll talk it over with Timothy when I can." He lowered his voice. "And pray for him, will you, please? He's a tough old guy, but he worries me."

In the background, Timothy was coughing, much too hard.

"I'm looking forward to our date." His voice softened. "Fear not, Mollie."

She smiled. "Fear not. See you tomorrow."

Her smile faded as she put down her phone.

She wandered from room to room in the old house, unmindful of the deepening night, and ended up on the window seat in the library. *"He worries me."*

Doctors didn't worry about little things like a sore throat or a cough. But the flu could be dangerous, and Timothy was old.

"Lord," she whispered, "Please. I ask you in Jesus' name to spare Timothy. We need him here. I need him."

She squirmed on the upholstered seat. "But if You want to take him away . . ."

Like He had taken Dad? What would she do? *Accept.*

She covered her face with her hands. "Be my Rock, my strong tower. I'm running to You as fast as I can. I bring You Timothy's sickness. And Kent's scam. And the horrible mystery of Rhys Castell. And Tara." Her eyes burned. "I can't even think straight anymore. Make me wise."

She sat for a minute, letting the stillness quiet her.

Whiskers brushed against her hands, and she lowered them from her face. Mac nibbled delicately on one of her fingers.

She pulled her hand back. "What's the matter with you?"

He gave her a mournful look.

"I never did feed you, did I?" Slowly she got to her feet. "Let's take care of that."

She fed him and took a bowl of chicken stew out of the freezer for her own supper. Before she could do anything with it, Aunt Lin phoned. "How's the work going?" she asked.

Madeleine told her about the marble fireplace, and her aunt exclaimed in delight. "And have you come up with any ideas for recycling the dear old place?"

"Someone suggested a tea room," Madeleine said. "With regional specialties, like cranberry-whatever's."

Aunt Lin laughed. "Now that's worth considering. We could call it Cranberry Manor. Maybe I'll see what Vance thinks."

Madeleine had to smile. The lunch with Vance must have gone well. "See you Wednesday," she said. That would be soon enough to tell her everything else.

She pried the top off the frozen stew, and the kitchen phone rang again.

A woman's soft voice said, "Hello? Hello? Is this Madeleine?"

"Cousin Willa? Is everything all right?"

"Oh, my dear." The voice faltered. "Vera was supposed to call and invite you. Last week. But she didn't, did she?"

"I don't think so."

"Maybe the phone lines were down out there or something. Such a wild place! Anyway, there's wonderful news. Your mother and Wayne."

Madeleine put the stew into the microwave and turned it on.

Cousin Willa sounded more cheerful. "She told you about him, surely. They just got married, and they're off to Bermuda for two weeks, and we are all so thrilled."

The bowl of stew revolved slowly, round and round and round.

She let Willa give her the details and said goodbye as sweetly as possible. So that was that. No need to feel guilty about deserting dear old Mom.

Dad, I miss you. Again, *again?* Yes. *You will hurt for the rest of . . .*

After she'd eaten, she tidied up her bedroom and searched for the paperweight once more. Was it in the closet? No, it definitely was gone.

She picked up her journal and sighed. Why did that little egg-shaped piece of glass seem so important to her? Because it was one of her last links with Dad?

Let it go. Get ready for bed, and then write about all the things that happened today.

She had almost finished when Tara called, sounding apologetic.

Eleven o'clock! She'd forgotten to phone her about tomorrow.

"Can you?" Tara said. "I waited as long as I could."

"I'm sorry. I'll come. Around ten in the morning, is that okay?"

"Thank you a million times, Mollie. You are my truehearted friend." She sounded like someone in a book.

Tara paused and let out a dramatic sigh. "Mollie?"

"Yes?"

"I have to tell you an awful truth. I must needs confess."

What *had* she been reading?

"I borrowed something from your room. I didn't think you'd mind. Really, truly, I wasn't going to keep it, but Mr. Kennedy made me leave, and so . . . and so I've still got it."

Madeleine sat up. "What?"

"Your forever stone, with the calico." Tara's voice hurried. "I just wanted to hold it for a while. I was going to creep in and put it back. And today, I was going to give it to you, but Uncle Sid would've caught me."

Her paperweight.

"Mollie? You'll forgive me all my sins, won't you, please? Lest I stay awake the whole night long with this burden on my heart?"

"I forgive you, Tara. Let's talk about it tomorrow."

Her paperweight wasn't lost. She'd get it back tomorrow—something to be thankful for.

Slowly she put away her journal, crossed the room, and opened the window. She leaned an elbow on the sill. For once the trees stood silent.

The calm night should be soothing, but it seemed that clouds were massing above her—storm clouds—shaped by the events of the day. Secret piled upon secret. Greed and hate and fear. How were they linked to Sid and Tara, to Bria and Jude? To Kent?

Cool air washed through the room, making her shiver, and she turned back to her bed. Mac was doing laundry again. After a while he'd stop, and perhaps she would sleep.

CHAPTER 28

I wonder why Tara keeps asking me to visit.
Maybe I'll get a chance to talk to her
about God's forgiveness.
She might be more receptive now.
~Journal

No bad dreams. No clouds in the sky this morning.
But last night's foreboding lingered.

She made herself an omelet for breakfast and dredged
up reassuring thoughts. She was going to take muffins for
Tara; they'd have a visit that might be long or short; she'd
talk to Sid, perhaps get some useful information; then
she'd come home.

As long as Aunt Dixie stayed away, all would be
well.

She repeated the litany to herself as she drove away
from the Manor, traveled one road after another, turned
down the highway, and then onto Salty Spung Road. She
ignored the sneaking little fears that dodged behind trees
whenever she tried to look them in the eye.

Be not dismayed, for I am your God.

Everything about the Marricks dismayed her.

I am your God. Think about this beautiful day He'd
given her, complete with a hazy blue sky.

She pulled off her jacket, tossed it into the back seat,
and opened her window to enjoy the sunlit breeze.

Here was the Marrick sign, with its flaking red letters.

Smoke?

She clutched the steering wheel, her hands gone cold. Long gray twisting threads of smoke rose from the Marrick's house.

The breath rasped in her throat. She couldn't handle fire, not anymore.

Keep going. Get the neighbors. *Danger-danger-stay-away*.

But Tara was there.

She gunned her car down the driveway, lurched to a stop, and called 911 as she ran for the house.

Wisps of smoke drifted from the kitchen window. It must have just started. Where was everyone?

She bounded up the porch steps.

"Madeleine!" Kent was leaning against a corner of the house. "Come help me." He looked panic-stricken.

His shirt had a patch of blood on the upper arm. "What happened?" More blood was seeping through his sleeve.

Had he been fighting? With who?

He groaned. "You've got to tie it up. Get something."

Her gaze fell on the knife at his belt. "This will work."

The knife cut like a laser as she slit open his sleeve and sliced off a strip. She wrapped his arm with care.

But the house! The fire must be spreading inside. Hurriedly she tied the last knot.

"I knew I could count on you." He took her by the wrist.

His hands were clammy with sweat, and she fought her distaste. What was the matter with him?

His voice dropped into pleading. "Come away with me, Madeleine. Tonight!" The blue eyes had a terrifying intensity. "I'm going to be rich. We can live in Canada, or France, wherever we want."

"Kent! The fire—"

"Don't think about that. Think about me."

She trembled deep within. Fire trucks were coming, but it would take a long time.

"Where's Tara? And Sid? Let me go."

He circled her wrist with his hand. "Such a tiny little thing. Such fine bones."

He looked at the smoking window and smiled. "Don't worry, there's no one inside. Come with me."

She started to shake her head, and he pulled her toward him. "I'll make you happy, Madeleine. I've always found married women more interesting. Experience counts, you know."

Nausea threatened, and she swallowed it away. Breathe. Breathe again.

He stared at her. "Is it that doctor? Him and his interfering talk. He's next on my list."

Kent tightened his hand until her wrist bones seemed to bend and crack.

She fought the panic, made herself stare up at him. What was this about Nathan?

Kent's face had turned red. "I saw you with him. Don't you dare waste yourself on that crusty old man."

"I don't understand you," she exclaimed. "The house is burning down. How can you—"

"I'm younger and smarter than he is." He spoke with tight-lipped confidence. "Ol' Doc's going to fry. Him and that clinic of his. Didn't do him any good to change the locks. Ever hear of plastic explosives?"

Her heart turned over. Not Nathan. *Not Nathan.*

Lord, help!

I will strengthen you.

To do what?

Delay.

"Madeleine! Are you listening?" Kent grabbed a fistful of her hair.

Determination settled into her bones. She smiled up at him and smacked at his hand. "Don't you do that again, or I might have to hate you."

He grinned, looking surprised, and let go of her hair. "Gutsy little woman, aren't you?" He waved at the smoking house. "Isn't that something? I did it. And it's going to get better."

His look was so haughty, so prideful, that she knew what to do.

She tilted her head and put on a teasing face. "I don't believe you did that. Lots of things can start a fire. And what's a writer know about explosives?"

He talked. He told her how he'd first learned to use explosives, fighting fires in California. How they were good for bringing down snags, and how a double line made a fire guard. How he'd taught himself to make different kinds of bombs.

She kept her eyes on his face and saw that he was watching the house with the avid look of a gambler who'd backed a winning throw.

He explained how his favorite bombs worked, how he'd used one to blow up a store in Tabernacle, just last week. It was quite exhilarating, he said, even better than fires.

An arsonist.

"Gives you a sense of power, doesn't it?" she said.

His eyes narrowed. "What are you implying, Madeleine? I don't need anything to make me feel powerful. I don't need anybody, either."

Shouldn't have said that.

He pulled her close. "Except possibly you."

In spite of her resolve, she took a step backwards. His arm went around her waist. "Don't do that, my pretty little elf. You know you want me."

Her breath came hard, snagged in her throat.

Fear not.

Tiny flames slithered from around the kitchen window. He stiffened, watching.

From the back of the house, thunder boomed. The house shuddered, its windows shook, and fire burst through the back roof. Flames licked out of a window and leaped onto the overhang above the back door.

He laughed, a growl deep in his chest. "Just a little one. Great stuff. Now we're off."

She had to stop him. She jerked free from his sweating hands, but he grabbed her arm, hauling her back. The knife. She snatched it up and aimed for his chest.

His hand closed over hers, incredibly strong, and wrenched at the knife.

A searing pain stung her, and she looked in surprise at the slash across her forearm.

He held up the knife with a triumphant laugh. "Silly girl. Look what you did to yourself."

Blood trickled down her arm, staining the back of her hand. The fire's breath struck her face, hot and threatening.

But this wasn't Brenn.

Fear not.

He bent close, and the rank odor of his sweat filled her nostrils. "Why did you come here, anyway? I warned you." He propelled her toward the driveway.

A gust of smoke blew across them and she began to cough, clinging to his arm, dragging at him, slowing his pace. "Where—?"

"My car, right handy in the trees." He stopped. The Bronco stood just ahead of them, but its tires had gone flat. His lips thinned to a cruel line. "Skulking redhead."

Tara! She was safe.

"We'll have to take your car. Give me the keys."

A car backfired—or was it a gunshot?—and Kent staggered.

Someone stood on the porch steps. Sid, with a gun.

Kent pulled her around in front of him. "You missed, Marrick. You're still a loser. Put down that gun."

But Sid was already falling to his knees, sliding down the porch steps.

The gun clattered ahead of him, and for the first time in her life, Madeleine wanted that cool, deadly weight in her hands.

A pine tree beside the garage exploded into flame and the porch roof began to smoke.

Kent laughed. He took her chin, turned her face toward him, and she didn't resist. "We're going to have fun together," he said.

Keep him talking. "How come Sid had a gun? Is it Dixie's pistol? Did you kill her?"

"Her own fault. Stupid woman, got into a wrestling match with me."

He glanced at the cut on her arm, oozing a little. "Just a scratch. Nothing like mine."

"You're still bleeding," she said. "Let me tie it up some more."

"Guess so." He looked pale. "Make it tight."

She ripped another strip off the dangling remnants of his sleeve, taking her time, but as soon as she finished the makeshift bandage, he said. "Give me the keys, okay?"

Stall him. Risk anything to keep him from Nathan.

"Someone's reported this fire," she said. "Why not forget the doctor?"

"You'd like that, wouldn't you? I'll teach you better. Let's go."

Not into that car, not with him—she wouldn't come out alive.

She tried again. "You're going to get caught. I don't see how you'll have time to set off your bomb at the clinic. People live around there."

"Won't take a minute." He pulled out a cigarette lighter and flicked it on. "That's all I need to do."

A rushing began in her ears, and she couldn't take her eyes off the lighter. Her vision darkened. The rushing grew louder. Not now! She had to convince him . . . but his face was swirling into gray.

Please, Lord, not now.

She was sagging against him, and she couldn't do anything about it.

"What's the matter with you?" He gave her a shake. "Not much use at all," he said. "Too bad."

He found the keys in her pocket and let go of her. She slid to the ground.

His feet went away. Her car door opened. It seemed to take him a long time to get in.

Now that he was gone, she could breathe.

Her car door slammed shut.

Breathe again. Think. He was going after Nathan . . . Get the gun.

He'd have to pull up and turn around. Hurry. Or he'd drive right across her.

The engine caught with a roar.

Move. Now!

She heaved herself onto her hands and knees. Something hurt. She crawled towards the porch. Towards the gun.

"Mollie! Over here." Tara took her by the shoulders and pulled her inside the iron frame.

She clutched Tara's arm. "I need that gun."

"Stay behind the wheel cutout." Tara darted off.

The car lurched forward, coming straight at her. Its tires bounced against the hump of iron and went no farther.

Tara pushed the gun into her hand.

He whipped the car into reverse and turned, the tires growling, spitting stones. Going after Nathan.

She crouched.

Steady. Dad's voice. *Hold it steady, Mollie girl. Breathe.*

She aimed for the back tires, squeezed the trigger, and winced at the recoil.

Again.

The car veered left and crashed into the trees with a tearing, splintering sound.

Another sound, a roaring, came from behind her—the porch roof was blazing high. A beam collapsed in showers of ash and sparks. Something stung her neck.

Tara was helping her uncle down the steps, pulling him to the center of the driveway. "Mollie! Get away!" she cried. "Get away from the house."

Another beam fell, and scorching heat lapped toward her. She pushed herself up off her knees and stumbled away from the heat and the noise and the smoke.

Check on Sid, lying in the sand. She bent to look at him, lost her balance, and fell.

She dragged herself back onto her knees. Phone.

In her pocket. All this blood—whose was it?

She pressed the buttons on her phone.

"Mollie, I was just thinking about you."

She could curl up into the warmth of that voice, curl up forever.

"Nathan." She closed her eyes.

His voice deepened. "Mollie? Talk to me."

Something important—she had to tell him. What?

"Your clinic," she mumbled. "There's a bomb."

"Okay, where are you?"

"Fire. At Tara's house." She took a wheezing breath. "I . . . I need you."

"Coming."

Tara was asking questions. Too tired to answer.

Tara was leaning her back to lie on the sand. Cold sand.

She shivered and bent her body so she couldn't see the fire.

All she wanted now . . .

She lost the strand of her thought and found it again. All she wanted now . . . was to look up into the face of that crusty old man.

CHAPTER 29

*I'm afraid to turn off the light because I'll see
flames licking across the roof
and the charred beams of the porch
. . . and Kent's face.*
~Journal

Nathan came. Right behind the fire trucks, with an ambulance and a police escort, he came. Her internal monitor must have clicked off as soon as she heard his voice because the next few hours went by in a haze.

His gentle touch on her face. His reassuring whisper. His hands, tucking her into a blanket. Someone bending over her, saying she was in shock.

After the ambulance left, he bundled her and Tara into his Jeep and drove them to his clinic. He kept a hand on her all the way and said little, but that might have been because Tara was talking non-stop about the fire and her uncle and the aunt she couldn't find.

At the clinic, someone took charge of Tara. Nathan gave quiet orders, and nurses came and went.

For a few minutes they were alone in a small room, and he held her until a nurse brought something for her to drink and ice for her wrist.

She couldn't remember much more, just that he stitched up her cut, and it didn't seem to hurt, and he murmured to her as he worked.

He drove them both to the Manor, had Tara help her change, and then had her sit at the kitchen table and drink orange juice.

His hand warmed her shoulder. "I gave you something for pain," he said, "and now I want you to take a good long nap."

She could taste the smoke. She rubbed at the grit on her face, saying, "I would like a shower."

For some reason, he smiled, but he said, "Maybe later. First, you nap."

Too sleepy to argue. He had her lie down on her bed and covered her with a blanket. He disappeared and returned with a warm washcloth. He bathed her face and found the stinging little burns on her neck. He spread something creamy on the burns, went away, and came back.

He knelt beside the bed and put his arms around her, cradling her. "Our mighty God! He protected you, Mollie."

She lifted a hand to his face, curving her palm against his cheek. "The Lord kept me . . . from being so afraid."

She frowned. "But then Kent pulled out that lighter. Why did God let me faint? I didn't want that."

The gray eyes glistened. "To keep you safe. To put the gun into your hand." He brushed back her hair. "Sleep now. My brave girl."

He stayed, smoothing her hair, and she drifted off. When she awoke, he was gone.

Tara stood at the kitchen window but she turned, looking dejected. "I thought you'd sleep all day."

Madeleine stretched. "Guess I'm hungry." And stiff. And hurting. And she wanted a shower. Where was Nathan?

"The doctor said for you to phone when you got up."

He answered with a smile in his voice. "We've got a date, remember? Do you feel like pizza?"

"Let's see," she said, "flattened, maybe a little crisp around the edges? Yes I do, now that you mention it."

He laughed. "You're doing better than I dared to hope. I'll be there soon."

While she waited, her energy seemed to fade, but it returned as soon as she saw him. Maybe she was just hungry. Keeto's takeout pizza tasted remarkably good, considering. She ate two pieces and began to yawn.

He stood up. "I'm off again. Back to bed for you."

She stood too, saw fire blazing across a roof, and had to grab for the edge of the table. But after a moment her head cleared and she asked him, "Please, sir, may I take a shower?"

His smile teased her. "One-handed?"

"Whatever."

"I don't want that arm to get wet." He sat her back down and covered the arm with plastic wrap secured by tape.

"How is Timothy?" she asked.

"He's responding well, and I'm keeping him quiet. I haven't told him about any of this, but he seems to have a sixth sense about you. He's been asking where you are. Bria is nursing him and running the store at the same time."

He took her hand, traced the bruises on her wrist. "You're dizzy?"

"Sometimes."

"When you think about the fire?"

"Worse then."

"That's it. You're processing." He smiled. "Be patient with yourself."

He began to pack up his bag. "Tara, stay close while she takes her shower, okay? And next time she gets up, make her a snack, something simple."

"Sure." Tara's face was as tired as her voice.

"Thank you," he said. "I think you're going to be a good nurse. Please excuse us for a minute? I need to tell Mollie something."

He drew her into his arms and whispered, "Sorry, not much of a date. I'll do better next time."

"Do you give such personal attention to all your patients?"

"Only the one I love."

She smiled into his neck. "Excellent varlet. Come back soon."

The next time she woke up, it was almost dark. She sat up slowly, and all she could think was: *Nathan*. Where was he? How was his work going? He'd taken so much time to care for her. Would he come back tonight? Tomorrow?

She eased out of bed, picked up her hair brush and sat down again.

He'd already spent hours with her. Couldn't she manage without him? She should get busy, get on with her life.

She began to brush her hair, taking long, weary strokes.

Remember the plan: he'd go back to Alaska, she'd go to New York and open her shop and . . . and . . . be miserable.

The brush wavered.

She didn't want to go to New York. She didn't want to go anywhere, except with him.

What about Strong-and-Independent?

The brush hit a snarl, and she yanked it through, hard enough to hurt.

Dependent? Perhaps.

Vulnerable? Yes.

Loving him? Yes.

She stopped brushing, frowned into the twilight.

She'd always thought of independence as a shining, glorious thing.

For someone else, it might be fine, even admirable. But in her case, it seemed to be tangled up with something more tawdry. Pride.

Kent's pride had kept him talking, and it cost him dearly. He would probably spend the rest of his life in prison.

Was she, in her self-absorption, any different?

She dropped the brush onto the bureau, folded her arms on the gleaming old wood, and put her head down.

Forgive me, Lord, for my pride. Thank you for the gifts of Your grace. For Nathan. Teach me how to love him well.

Tara was sitting in the kitchen with a book, but she jumped up right away. "I'll make our snack. The doctor phoned again. Asked how your shower went. Did we take off the plastic. Were you still sleeping. Where's the bread?"

Madeleine sat down and put a hand to her eyes. After a minute her brain caught up. "In the pantry."

"Found it," Tara said. "Looks good for toast. Never saw a doctor as nice as him. He likes you a lot, doesn't he? Do you want cocoa?"

Madeleine smiled. "Yes."

While they ate their scrambled eggs and toast, she learned what had happened before she arrived that morning.

Tara had been in the kitchen getting a drink when Kent drove up. A few minutes later, Dixie was screaming at him in the front room, and a gun went off.

Tara had run out the back door to warn Uncle Sid, but he'd already heard the shot. He was "bellerin' mad," as she put it. He stormed into the front room, yelling at Kent, and they started fighting, and she'd tried to phone the police, but the phone was dead.

He and Kent were still fighting when she grabbed a butcher knife and ran into the woods.

The next thing she knew, smoke was coming from a window and Madeleine had driven up.

While Madeleine was struggling with Kent, she'd taken the valve cores out of his tires and waited for a chance to throw something at him.

Tara stopped talking and stared out of the window.

Madeleine tried to arrange the sequence of events. None of it seemed real except the flames and the blood.

After a minute, Tara said, "You're a good shot."

"Not really."

"I saw it. You shot out the front tire so he'd crash into that tree."

"But that's just it." Madeleine hunched over her plate. "I was aiming for the back tires—to slow him down. I didn't know he'd crash."

"I hope he's dead," Tara said. "He killed Aunt Dixie. He almost killed Uncle Sid. I thought he was going to kill you."

"So did I," Madeleine said. Dizzy again. Too much thinking. "I hope your uncle's going to be okay."

"The doctor said he had some bad cuts and a bullet in his leg, but he's too ornery to die just yet. Do you have any rubber bands?"

"In that drawer."

Tara pulled her hair back into a ponytail and stared into space for another minute.

Finally she said, "Uncle Sid's going to be mad about the fire, especially his garage. And it spread into the woods."

Something in her voice warned of bad news. What now?

Tara shifted her gaze to the tabletop and began pushing breadcrumbs together with a finger.

"My hideout," she said slowly. "All my stuff is gone. I've seen those fires—like a furnace. Your stone. It's got to be melted."

Melted?

Tara swept the crumbs to the floor. "Guess it's a lucky thing you kept the pendant. Give it to Bria and Jude." Her shoulders drooped. "I don't know what I'm going to do."

Madeleine sat still. She should answer, should say something kind.

Tara was on her feet now, stacking up the plates. "Yeah, you're going to tell me that stuff about how God knows, and He's got a plan. I wish He'd let me in on the details for once. I'm going to take a shower."

She carried the dishes to the sink. "Can I borrow your shampoo? I'll sleep upstairs on that yellow sofa."

"Fine," Madeleine said. "I'll get you some pajamas. In a minute."

Her head was heavy, too heavy to hold up. She propped it in both hands and saw her paperweight, a shapeless lump in the midst of blackened rubble.

A hand flitted onto her shoulder and off again. "Mollie, you're my very best friend. I'm awful sorry about this. Specially your stone. I loved it too."

She pulled herself upright, but the girl had whisked away, and she didn't see her again until morning.

Aunt Lin phoned to say that the doctor had called and she'd drive back right away, but Madeleine told her that tomorrow would be fine.

Nathan phoned too, but he sounded worn out, so she made her voice cheerful, told him to get some sleep, and he said he'd see her tomorrow, around noon.

In the morning, every muscle still ached, but she managed to make breakfast. Her dazed feeling persisted, even after two cups of coffee, and she had to ask Tara what day of the week it was.

"Wednesday," Tara said. "I don't care if I miss the English test. I'm staying here."

That sunlit Tuesday morning seemed a long time ago.

Remi dropped by, saying he'd hang around and help if he could. He made arrangements to get her car towed, and he answered the phone and the door.

Official-looking men arrived, and the inquisition began.

When did you first notice the fire? Did you hear any explosions? How fast did it burn? Do you have a permit for that gun? Whose gun is it? How well did you know the deceased?

The deceased?

She'd killed him.

The questions still came, one after another, the same ones over and over. More questions, ranging further and further afield. She had to answer so many of them with "I don't know" or "I don't remember" that she began to wonder whether something was seriously wrong with her mind.

Nathan arrived at noon, spoke to the investigators in his doctor's-voice and convinced them that they'd asked enough questions for now. He sat her down at the kitchen table and checked her bandages.

"You're doing fine," he said.

"So why do I feel like my brain has turned to mush?"

"You're still processing." But he gazed at her with the same watchful look he'd had for Greta's baby. "In a few days you'll be your old sprightly self."

All she could do was mumble. "Sprightly?"

His face creased into one of those melting smiles. "You'll see," he said.

"C'mon, eat some lunch, you guys," Tara said. "I've made a bunch of sandwiches."

Remi grinned from where he stood in the doorway. "Us hungry guys thank you, heartily."

Madeleine nibbled on a sandwich and drank three cups of tea while the men ate and Tara chattered. When Tara paused for breath, Nathan said, "These are good tuna sandwiches, Tara. It's a shame Hey-You isn't here."

She looked uncertainly from him to Remi, who laughed.

"Take it as a compliment," Remi told her. "Hey-You is Timothy's dog, and he's a real connoisseur of tuna sandwiches."

His face grew serious. "Doc, did you find out anything about Kent's past? California, wasn't it?"

"A couple of things. He's been involved with forest fires for years. A volunteer at Yellowstone. He enrolled in the Firefighter Academy near King City but dropped out after almost killing a man with his knife. Oddly enough, he kept volunteering."

"Wasn't he a teacher?" Remi asked.

"Winters, he taught at one small school after another. About ten years ago he moved up the coast to Oregon. He taught school there and wrote a book."

He looked at Tara. "Your uncle, after claiming to know nothing at all, changed his mind. This morning he enlightened us about his relationship with Kent and an unsolved case from years ago."

"Hazel Marshon?" Madeleine said.

"Yes. He admitted that he and his brother and Kent robbed the old lady's house while she was off on a trip. A graduation prank, was the way he put it. But he claims that they left right afterwards."

Remi looked skeptical. "All of them?"

"Said he and his brother drove down to the casinos in Atlantic City for the night. They were plenty scared the next day to hear that her house had burned down, with her inside."

"Did they think it was Kent?" Remi asked.

"Apparently he liked to set fires," Nathan said.

"So did they get caught?"

"No one could ever prove anything, and Kent had already left town."

Madeleine felt her way through the haze in her brain. "Gemma told me that Rhys Castell was asking questions about the Marshon case."

"How come?" Remi asked.

"They did a yearbook page about him and Miss Marshon." She frowned. "And something else—a note Bria found. To Rhys, from Kent's mother. It sounded as if she'd asked him to prove Kent's innocence and then discovered something that changed her mind."

"She died about three years ago, didn't she?" Nathan said. "Did Kent come back for her funeral?"

"Yes," Madeleine said, "according to Paula."

He nodded, as if the pieces were coming together for him. "So Castell started his investigation. Maybe he talked to Kent after the funeral, and Kent thought he was trying to make trouble for him."

"Maybe," Remi said slowly, "Kent didn't know that old lady was in the house. He didn't mean to kill her. But he ran away, and the fear went with him."

He pushed back his chair. "Is there any relish?"

"I put some in already." Tara sounded miffed. "But there's more in the fridge."

Remi came back with a jar of Super-Hot relish. "This will make them even better." He spooned a mound onto his plate. "Doc?"

"No thanks," Nathan said. "Sid told me something else. One of his cousins worked in the police department, and he showed Sid the piece of evidence that made them think the Marshon fire was deliberately set—a tin can with half-burned matches inside."

Remi put down his sandwich, reached for his water glass, and drank it dry. "I can't believe this." He combed his fingers through his hair until it stood up in black spikes.

Tara folded her arms, smiling. "Too hot for you?"

He shook his head. "Not that. I've been typing a manuscript for Kent—his secret novel—and all this stuff is in it. Along with a lot of porn."

Tara eyed him. "What's it about?"

"An arsonist. And get this: the tin can thing. The guy used something like that to start his fires. He called it his signature. Sometimes it was destroyed in the fires he set, but most of the time he arranged things so it wasn't."

"How did it work?" Nathan asked.

"He'd fix up this empty can with matches wired together inside it. Attached them to about a yard of waxed cord. The guy laid the cord out so the end of it was stuck into dry leaves or whatever."

"How'd he start the fire?" Tara asked.

"One of those barbecue grill lighters—for the matches in the can. Then he dumped kerosene over the end of the cord in the leaves and got out of there."

Tara frowned. "So it took a couple of minutes for the fire to burn down the cord and get to the kerosene. But what was the can for?"

"To protect the matches until the fire got going," Remi said. "Maybe to keep his signature from being destroyed. From what I've heard, arsonists like people to know how clever they are."

"A fictional confession," Nathan said. "Did you read the whole thing?"

"As far as it went. He hadn't figured out the ending."

Madeleine looked at Remi. "So when Sid found that soup can in the fire, he recognized it. That's why he sent it to Kent."

Remi nodded. "I thought it might have something to do with Kent's story. Now it sounds like blackmail."

Tara got to her feet, took a bag of cookies out of the freezer and dropped it onto the table.

"Yes, help yourselves," Madeleine said. She gazed at Remi. Forest fire. Something that was burned.

"What about—" The room began to swirl. "Nathan?"

Remi's face had turned into flames that licked across the room, ash was falling, and she was falling with it.

Nathan's arm went around her, and she slumped against him.

His quiet voice said, "Here's some water."

She drank, and after a minute, the flames faded away.

"Want to lie down?" Nathan asked.

She shook her head, rested it against him. "Let me think a minute."

The burned car . . . Rhys Castell . . . that was it.

"Remi," she said. "Does the hero of that novel burn up cars?"

He stared at her. "Sure does," he said. "He has to stop this other guy from finding out that he killed the girl." He paused. "Bria and Jude's dad. It fits, doesn't it?"

She nodded. Kent must have set that Escort on fire to cover himself. She thought about Bria, and her grief at the sight of her father's car. Could this be the answer to *who* and *why?*

Nathan's voice was heavy with sadness. "The police need to see that manuscript."

"Why did he ever come back?" Remi muttered.

"Maybe he'd set one fire too many, out West," Nathan said. "He might have planned to disappear. In a place like this, it's quite possible."

Madeleine sat up, gazing at the bruises on her wrist. "He wanted me to go away with him. Said he'd be rich. Maybe he came back to get something he'd hidden."

"That's true," Remi said. "Sam and Rhys were gone." He glanced at Tara. "And he was going to get rid of your uncle."

"He sure tried," Tara said. "And now Uncle Sid's going to stay in the hospital forever, and I'll be an orphan."

"Not quite," Nathan said. "I made some phone calls last night."

Her eyes blazed. "Not a foster home. I'll kill myself first! I really will!"

"That might not be necessary." He opened the bag of cookies and took out a handful. "How would you like to meet that aunt you've been looking for?"

"Aunt Minna?" Tara's voice rose an octave. "She's not dead? Where'd she go?"

"She's living near Hampton Lakes, and she'd like very much for you to visit."

"Only visit?"

"I guess that depends. Would you like me to take you over there?"

"Now?"

"After I've had a few more of these excellent cookies."

"Oh wow! I've got to brush my hair." She jumped up and ran out of the kitchen.

Nathan put an arm across Madeleine's shoulders. "Nap time for you." He grinned at Remi. "I guess that leaves you with the dishes."

She slept for a while and was dozing with Mac beside her when Aunt Lin arrived with apologies, sympathy, and hugs.

Madeleine answered her questions as well as she could, and when she finished, her aunt said, "I was so blind about Kent. I should have seen this coming. Thank God, Mollie."

She got up from where she'd been sitting on Madeleine's bed. "Sleep all you can. I'm going to go see what Remi's up to. "

She and Remi seemed to get along well, because they talked for an hour. By the end of the afternoon, she had offered him steady employment at the Manor, with time off to help Timothy as needed.

After he'd gone for the day, her aunt said, "I get the impression that Remi is at loose ends right now."

"I guess so." If Remi was unsettled, what must Bria and Jude be feeling?

She had tried to phone them and couldn't get through. Bria would be at the store, and Jude must have gone back to school. Even at night, the line was busy. Maybe they'd taken the phone off the hook.

She didn't even know how to pray for them.

She must have sighed without realizing it because her aunt was gazing at her, looking worried. "Madeleine, I'm prescribing chamomile tea for you, and early to bed. Snuggle down with your kitty and stay there as long as you want."

She couldn't tell Aunt Lin that her sleep was haunted by Kent's voice, and his face, wreathed in flames.

At least she had Mac. She would awaken, whimpering, and find him nestled beside her. Each time, his rumbling purr slowed her pulse and lulled her back to sleep.

CHAPTER 30

I keep telling myself that
God has spared my life,
and I should be thankful.
But will the awfulness, the horror,
ever go away?
~Journal

The next morning after breakfast, Madeleine talked to herself about the baking course. Maybe she should watch a video.

Where was Nathan? What was he doing?

Mid-morning, he arrived with something bulky wrapped in newspaper. He checked Madeleine's stitches, and then he gestured to the parcel on the kitchen counter.

"Wild turkey," he said. "From one of my patients. I'm hoping you'll know what to do with it."

Aunt Lin, pouring coffee for him, answered, "Of course." She frowned. "Does it still have feathers on?"

"No feathers." He grinned. "It's been plucked and gutted, soaked and salted. All ready for the expert's attention."

He looked at Madeleine. "If you don't mind?"

"Of course not," her aunt said quickly. "And perhaps you could help us eat it tonight?"

He inclined his head. "Thank you, ma'am. I would like that very much."

Madeleine gazed at the mound of newspapers and pictured the huge bird inside it. Perhaps she should be alarmed, having never cooked a wild turkey, but she couldn't summon up the energy.

"That's settled, then." Her aunt put the coffee down in front of Nathan, poured a cup for herself and Madeleine, and joined them at the table.

Madeleine asked him the question she'd been wondering about. "How did Tara get along with her aunt?"

He gave her an apologetic glance. "I meant to call. They did fine, as far as I could tell. Aunt Minna seems to be a storybook aunt, the plump, motherly type, but from the look in her eyes, she'll tolerate no nonsense."

"That would be good for Tara," Madeleine said. But how likely was it that she'd see her again?

"The plan is that Tara will stay for two weeks, a trial run, I suppose. I left them chattering back and forth like a pair of chickadees."

Aunt Lin said, "I hope she'll have a better life now. This has been such a sad time." She poured milk into her coffee. "Especially for Paula Castell and those two children."

How Jude's eyes would flash to hear himself described as a child!

"I haven't seen either of them," her aunt said. "Are they doing okay?"

"They're busy," Nathan said. "Bria's nursing Timothy for me, and Jude helps around the store. He thinks you don't need him any more since you've hired Remi."

"But I do," she said. "He's a good worker. Will you be talking to them today?"

"Definitely."

"I wonder if they'd like to come to dinner too." She gave Madeleine a quick look. "Do you feel up to it?"

"It's a great idea." Madeleine ran a quick mental check on the contents of the freezer. "And how about Remi?"

"Perfect," her aunt said. "Too many ghosts in this old place. Let's liven it up."

That afternoon her aunt made a trip for groceries and afterwards showed Remi the upstairs rooms. They stayed there, talking, and Madeleine was thankful to have time in the kitchen with no interruptions.

When Remi left to go home and change, Aunt Lin bustled in. "How can I help the chef?" She dipped a spoon into the cooling cranberry sauce. "Mmm, this tastes wonderful."

Madeleine looked up from mincing an onion for the corn pudding. "Orange rind. None of that canned stuff at Cranberry Manor."

Her aunt took another lick at the spoon and put it down. "Remi has quite an unusual background."

"I've wondered about him," Madeleine said. "Want to chop things for the salad?"

"That might push the limits of my cooking prowess, but I'll do it." Her aunt took out the cutting board. "I never did think he looked like the product of an orphanage. And now I find out he's got this whole adopted family back in Seattle."

She scrubbed the celery and carrots. "I showed him my photos of kids, and he told me about his brothers and sisters and the dogs. Remarkable dogs. He left Seattle because he was worried about something—he never quite said what—and he wanted to see the East Coast, but I think he misses them."

Madeleine, wondering whether she'd added the salt, nodded.

Aunt Lin picked up a cucumber and began to slice it. "Mollie, are you doing okay? I haven't seen you smile since I got back."

"I guess so."

How could she explain what it felt like, to kill another human being? "Tired, probably," she muttered. "I'll catch up."

"I'm sure you will. Want me to check the turkey?"

"Please. This one doesn't have a pop-up timer. I braised it in chicken broth so it should be tender."

"What's for dessert? You had frozen cherries on the list."

"Just cherry pie. Streusel topping. It's done. Ice cream if they want it."

Her aunt's eyes glowed. "*Just* homemade cherry pie," she said. "I can't wait."

At supper, Bria was paler than usual and Jude was quiet, but Aunt Lin and Nathan kept the atmosphere light. Remi was the most entertaining, perhaps because of Bria, who sat across from him, and she finally began to smile at his jokes.

Over the cherry pie, they talked about hunting wild turkeys, which, Jude said, were both elusive and wily. Aunt Lin mentioned the local game pies, made of deer, or rabbit, or muskrat.

Nathan said, "Dan'l told me about muskrat. They're good eating."

Jude said he'd tasted one, and Remi looked envious. He begged for an invitation the next time anyone went hunting.

After the meal, no one suggested Monopoly, and Madeleine was grateful, remembering what her aunt had said about ghosts.

Much as she wanted to speak privately with Bria or Jude, she didn't have an opportunity. They were anxious about Paula, and Remi gave them a ride home, saying he had to go that direction anyway.

Aunt Lin looked at her and Nathan. "Would it be terribly rude if I leave you two with the cleanup? I've got some work waiting, and if I start now, I can finish tonight."

Nathan looked delighted. "Go ahead. Get lots done."

Such enthusiasm for washing dishes?

As soon as Aunt Lin's door closed, he put his arms around her. "Great meal," he said. "You did wonders with my turkey."

She looked up, and his smile dimmed. "What is it, Mollie?"

"I killed a man. The thought horrifies me."

He shook his head, and she said, "I'm the one who made the car crash against that tree. I didn't mean to. I just wanted to keep him from getting away. But I killed him just as surely as if I'd shot him."

He was still shaking his head. "You slowed him down, but you didn't kill him."

She waited, disbelieving, and he said, "Kent had two gunshot wounds—one from Dixie, and one from Sid. They weakened him. The collision with the tree broke his leg. He must have realized he couldn't get away."

He took her hand. "Kent used his knife to slit his arm, and by the time they got there, it was too late."

Blood. More blood. Her stomach twisted. "His knife was sharp," she said, "but it's not that easy. Not like in the movies."

"He was precise, and he severed the radial artery."

"Even if you get an artery, it seals itself up fast."

"I talked to the pathologist." His hand went to her shoulder, as if to steady her. "Kent knew the artery would stay open. He had a blood-clotting disorder."

"Oh." She remembered the panic on Kent's face.

"He kept bleeding," she said slowly. "I had to retie the bandage." She shuddered. "Nathan, he was psychotic. I saw it, at the end."

She closed her eyes. That nightmare gone.

"You were right about a bomb at the clinic," he said. "We found two of them, strategically placed."

"The Lord protected you too." Her voice broke with the fear of losing him.

He held her close, letting her compose herself.

Thank You, Lord, for keeping him safe.

For the first time, she put her arms around him, taking delight in his bones and flesh and the sinewy muscles of his back.

He nuzzled into her hair, lingering there, but that was all. He'd been so careful to keep that promise of his, *"not until you ask."*

Perhaps this was the day. It was up to her, he'd said, and they'd never win the war if she didn't fight. If she bumbled this skirmish, she would try again.

He said, "I have something for you."

"So have I."

"You first."

Quickly, before she lost her nerve, she said, "In the library. I'll show you."

He kept her hand in his while they climbed the stairs, and she was glad for the small gesture of support. This was no stranger. This was the Nathan she knew and loved.

Darkness had fallen, so she turned on the lamp beside the couch. A memory loomed in the shadows, a reminder of the last time they'd been here together. She turned her back on it.

He stood by the window. She gazed at him. The few steps between them seemed a vast expanse of ice, and at her feet lay a dangerous chasm.

What was it she'd been going to say?

He smiled. "You wanted to show me . . . ?"

"The view, it's quite pretty at night with the shadows on the trees and the trees rolling out like . . . like a carpet. That's it, a sort of carpet, all different colors of green, only you can't see the greens very well because of the dark, and the stars are nice too, when they come out."

"It's a lovely view." He didn't turn to look at it.

"Nathan."

Her hands began to shake. She held onto a corner of the bookshelf. Perhaps she should try this another time.

He gazed at her, his eyes shining.

She took a step and hesitated at the edge of the chasm. Cold. But all she had to do was say the words, and he'd do the rest.

Say it now.

She snatched a breath. "I would like you to kiss me."

The corners of his mouth turned up. "And I would like you to kiss me."

"You?"

He could have made some clever remark, but he didn't. He leaned forward. His tenderness swept through her fears and bridged the chasm.

She trembled, but she took one faltering step after another and crossed the ice. She locked her arms around his neck, still trembling. After a minute she could put her hands up to frame his face—dear, familiar territory.

He stood still, as if he dared not breathe. For his sake, too . . .

She brushed his lips with hers, endured a flutter of panic, and kissed him.

His response was gentle, soft as his lips.

She leaned back and gave him a shy glance. He grinned. "How does that go again?"

She lifted her face to his. "Show me."

After a while he drew away, rested his cheek against hers. "Dear heart." His breath warmed her skin. "You're better at this than you may realize."

She laughed for the sheer wild happiness of being loved by this man.

He kept his arms around her. "You're okay?"

"I've never been kissed like that."

"I'm glad, Mollie, so glad. Are you encouraged?"

Cold reason stirred. She hadn't panicked this time. But next time?

She leaned away, gripping his arm. "Nathan? Some days will be better than others."

"I understand," he said. "Think of it as a mountain. We'll climb it step by step."

He picked up a handful of her hair and let it drift from his fingers. "Think how we've neglected those dishes," he said.

"And whatever it was you brought me," she said. "I think it's a muskrat. You want it fried or stewed into a pot pie?"

"You'll see."

"Then let's hurry!" She smiled at him and led the way downstairs.

As they walked through the hall, he stopped beside his jacket to retrieve a package, and as soon as they reached the kitchen, he handed it to her.

A brown paper bag, small and rather heavy. Not a muskrat.

"Shut your eyes," he said. "You have to guess."

He took her hand and guided it into the bag. Her fingers closed around a cool, smooth oval.

She almost dropped it. "What!"

Laughing, she pulled it out and held it to her cheek. "I thought I'd never see this again."

He grinned. "So did Tara."

"She told you?"

"Every detail. Even her hideout."

"But how'd you find it? Why didn't it melt?"

"That black box of hers. She didn't know it was a fireproof safe."

"You went over there?"

He nodded. "I tramped through the woods by her house and found the old truck. And the safe."

She put an arm around his neck, still holding onto the paperweight. "In the ruins! How clever of you."

He touched his cheek to hers. "Tara said it was your forever stone."

"Dad's gift."

He took it from her. "Psalm 73:26 is written on the bottom. What's the verse?"

"My flesh and my heart may fail, but God is the strength of my heart and my portion forever."

She paused. "Dad's prayer—that it would be true for me."

He turned the paperweight over, and over again, looked up and met her gaze. "I think your father would be pleased, Mollie."

Joy rippled through her and became a song about the Mighty One, her Rock.

"God has given me so much," she said. "The gifts of His grace."

"Even Tara." He handed the paperweight back to her.

"Sent by God for his good reasons—Timothy said that."

"I suspect there'll be more to Tara's story." From his pocket, Nathan took a square of folded notebook paper. "She asked me to give you this."

Tara's exuberant script looped across the page.

*My dearest Mollie, I'm so glad about your
stone!!!!!!!! God must love you a LOT!*

Are you sure he loves me? Phone any time?????

~Your forever-friend ~ Tara

"Amazing," she said. "I can't wait to show Timothy."

The gray eyes shimmered, and Nathan said, "This afternoon Timothy remarked, 'God's been doing marvels again, I can see it in your face. How's our little lady?' "

She reached for Nathan's hand. "Let's go tell him."

Those Beautiful Barrens

One of Gloria Repp's favorite places in the world is the New Jersey Pine Barrens, and when she explored that fascinating wilderness, Madeleine Dumont's story came to life.

The Pine Barrens forests, crumbling ruins, and foaming, tea-colored rivers all played a vital part in Mollie's experiences, and they will continue to shape the lives of other Dumont women as well.

Looking Ahead

In the next book, photographer Lindsey Dumont, Mollie's aunt, takes a trip to Seattle with great hopes for her heart and her career, but she cannot forget her beloved Pine Barrens, and eventually she will return.

Furthermore

For photos and information about the Pine Barrens, please visit the Resources on Gloria's website:

http://www.gloriarepp.com

and also check out this helpful site:

http://www.njpinebarrens.com .

Books by Gloria Repp

For ages 2-8
Noodle Soup
A Question of Yams

Tales of Friendship Bog series:
*Pibbin the Small (*paperback and eBook)
The Story Shell (paperback and eBook)
Trapped (paperback and eBook)

For ages 9-12:
The Secret of the Golden Cowrie
Trouble at Silver Pines Inn
The Mystery of the Indian Carvings
        (paperback and eBook)

Adventures of an Arctic Missionary series:
Mik-Shrok
Charlie
77 Zebra

For ages 12 and up:
The Stolen Years
Night Flight

For adults:
Nothing Daunted: The story of Isobel Kuhn
        (paperback and eBook)
The Forever Stone (paperback and eBook)

Visit Gloria at http://www.gloriarepp.com

Made in the USA
Charleston, SC
09 January 2014